IN SEARCH OF LOVE, MONEY & REVENGE

Hilary Bailey was born near Bromley. She now lives in West London, not far from the Portobello Road. She is the author of about twenty short stories, and her first novel, *Polly Put the Kettle On*, was published in 1975. Her other novels include *Mrs Mulvaney*, *As Time Goes By*, and the best-selling *All the Days of My Life* and *A Stranger to Herself*. She has also written *Hannie Richards*, a thriller about a woman smuggler, and a short biography of *Vera Brittain*.

HILARY BAILEY

In Search of
Love, Money &
Revenge

PAN BOOKS
LONDON, SYDNEY AND AUCKLAND

First published 1990 by Macmillan London Limited

This edition published 1992 by Pan Books Ltd,
a division of Pan Macmillan Publishers Limited
Cavaye Place London SW10 9PG
and Basingstoke

Associated companies throughout the world

ISBN 0 330 32129 3

1 3 5 7 9 8 6 4 2

A CIP catalogue record for this book is available
from the British Library

Typeset by Macmillan Production Ltd

Printed and bound in Great Britain by BPC Paperbacks Ltd

Contents

1

In Mr Rothko's Surgery

'Is it hurting very much, Melanie?' asked Annie Vane in her light, well-modulated voice, the informed middle-class tone of a Radio 4 interviewer.

The girl sitting next to her said dully, 'It's not bad, really.' But her plump face was badly swollen on one side and it was obvious she was in pain. Must be, thought Annie, with a face like that.

Behind her white Formica counter the receptionist placed some papers in a grey filing cabinet and clanged the drawer shut. Turning round she swept the waiting room with a hostile look. She had already been cold to the three patients and a small child perched on plastic chairs, making it plain that those reduced to visiting the dentist on an emergency basis at this time of year must have been too feckless to have their teeth seen to at the proper time and were thus suffering the consequences of their own stupidity. It was that or they'd got themselves involved in some seasonal folly like a drunken fight or a car accident, or betting on how many walnuts they could crack without using the nutcrackers or had unwarily lost out in the traditional confrontation between a tooth and a sixpence in the Christmas pudding.

Annie felt she must have brought Melanie up by hand on a diet of Coca-Cola and Mars bars, which was far from the truth. As far as she was concerned, Melanie and her mouth were just about the last straw. This wasn't what she wanted or could cope with at the best of times. She sank down in her chair, glumly watching the young woman in the corner with a grizzling small boy sag visibly every time the receptionist looked at them. Giving her toddler a Smartie, the woman wheedled, 'Come on, Alec, love.

1

Be a good boy. Mummy'll soon see Mr Rothko and then we can go home.' The receptionist gave her a look like a dagger in the ribs.

The child appeared pale and sickly like his mother, Annie thought, although the woman had that very fair skin which never has any colour anyway. Still, if he lived on Smarties small wonder he was ill-looking. Colourless and unhealthy the woman might be, Annie thought sadly, but she presumably had a home and a husband. She hadn't been deserted. Tears of self-pity pricked Annie's eyeballs.

Pull yourself together, she told herself. He may come back.

She stared sternly at the picture on the wall above the receptionist's head, a gloomy watercolour depicting a range of broken rocks with a dark and turbulent stream below.

Three weeks ago she'd been decorating the tree, their fifth Christmas tree, the third they'd put up in the bay window of the knocked-through sitting room of the small house in a narrow street running off Foxwell High Street in South London. As she stood on the stepladder putting the silver star with its trailing metal fringe at the top of the tree, reflecting as usual about the way the tree clashed with the big abstract painting which ran along most of the wall towards the little patio outside, she heard the front door open. Making a final adjustment to the star Annie called out, 'Look – I've finished!'

Julian made no reply. Annie got off the ladder and gazed at her husband. Tall and very good-looking he seemed pale and his face bore a sad, nervy expression. And something else was different – when they left for the office that morning he had been wearing his new suit, a wide-trousered, baggy-jacketed number, in pale brown to match his near-blond hair. Now he was in jeans and a dark purple sweater Annie had never seen before. Had she just forgotten it, she wondered, or had there been an emergency? Had Julian been obliged to change his clothes during the day?

'Would you like a drink?' she asked. 'What's happened? You've changed your clothes. Vodka? Glass of wine?'

Still Julian said nothing. Annie went to the table at the far end of the room where a computer shared space with a telephone answering machine and a neat tray of drinks. It was a tidy room, containing only a brown leather sofa of modern design, a similar, cream-coloured chair and, opposite the drinks table, a black table on which stood a large green plant. Julian detested clutter. Although Annie always tried to avoid garish Christmas decorations, she knew Julian hated

2

the tree and couldn't wait to get it down on Twelfth Night.

Standing by the table, waiting for his order she looked across the room at the tree and remarked, 'I don't like you much. You're a boring, Victorian thing . . . Late Victorian,' she added.

Annie had got a first in history at Oxford and was the author of 'Threpp Street, 1888' to give her doctoral thesis its short title. 'Threpp Street 1888' was the close examination of one year in the lives of the inhabitants of a London street in the area close to Shaftesbury Avenue then known as Seven Dials, a district so notorious that policemen had to walk through it in pairs, then a sign of serious social disorder. Threpp Street had an infant mortality rate of forty per cent; only one child in five born there reached the age of five. Only half the male adults in Threpp Street were in regular employment; one woman in six was engaged in prostitution. Annie's research, involving drains, social mores, medical dispensary books, legislation, and parish, prison and hospital records was accurate and probing and considered a model of its kind. It was also written to reveal the breadth of her interests and in skilful prose – Annie's father was a well-known writer – and the thesis easily gained her a PhD, publication in a learned journal and the offer of a teaching appointment at her college, a rare distinction at a time of heavy government cuts in her field.

Annie's friends had thought her mad to refuse the offer of a university post in order to marry Julian Vane and spend the early years of their marriage helping him to set up his graphics firm. Almost the only people to support her decision were her parents, Howard and Juliet Browning, who both thought she might be broadened by contact with another sort of world, even if it was for a relatively short time.

Now Annie reflected mildly on the unhappy fate of one William Knipe, tenant at 20 Threpp Street, who on 22 December 1888 was stopped by a policeman at four in the morning pushing a handcart of small firs poached from a farm near Brighton. His idea had been to sell them on the streets of London to relieve the want and suffering of his wife and seven children. He'd got six months' hard labour. She looked at Julian a little guiltily, knowing she must have on her face the expression he described as 'dreams of Threpp Street' and asked again, 'Julian – do you want a drink?' He was still standing near the door.

'Whisky,' he said at last.

She poured it, though whisky was an unusual thing for him to drink, especially at this time of day. Julian reached out for the glass, as though he didn't want to get any closer to her, took a long swig and advanced into the middle of the room. Then he swung round and looked at her consideringly. She was tall with long black hair in a loose coil behind her head, wearing a dark green tank top and black trousers with pine needles adhering to them, and now stood framed against the bright colours of the abstract painting she didn't really like.

'You know your trouble,' he said. 'Annie? You don't live in the same world as everybody else. That family of yours pushed you out into the world without any sense of the way things really are.'

Shaken by his tone, she stared at him. It was a criticism he often made, generally jokingly. Now it seemed like a grudge. She examined the proposition, not for the first time. Her father and mother, both bone-thin, long-faced and mild-natured, like as brother and sister, though they were not related in any way, lived in the country, did their work – or rather, her mother did, her father, a novelist, hadn't written a book for ten years – looked after their garden and their chickens and goats, thought seriously about current events, listened to music, did no harm. Each time some criticism from Julian forced her to consider that her parents might have sent her out into the world, unworldly, academic, unable to cope with life, she instinctively rejected the idea. On the other hand, her academic training insisted that she, the subject of the criticism, was the last person able to come to an objective conclusion. Academically, she sought evidence.

Now she said, 'If I don't live in the same world as everybody else, as you say, which I take to mean that I don't share the common assumptions of our times, don't understand the conditions, and so forth, you can't really blame Howard and Juliet. You wouldn't claim that Jasmine's like that, would you? Yet she's just as much the product of Howard and Juliet's upbringing as I am.'

'Your sister,' Julian said, 'reacted against your family's vague ways, that's all. She couldn't wait to marry money, and start acquiring jewellery, giving parties, having fun and jet-setting round the world. And look what they think of her. Of course, they don't say anything – they're too tolerant, understanding and generally high-minded. But Jasmine knows perfectly well they think she's the black sheep of the family—'

'I don't think it's at all fair to go on as if Jas had married Nigel just because he was rich. She'd known him from childhood

4

and I'm sure she loves him. And I don't think Howard and Juliet are as condemnatory as you think – anyway, what's this all about? Have I made a mistake at the office? Is something wrong?'

Annie was patient about Julian's habit of not making his points in a clear and logical way. She put it down to his more creative nature. Her own training, she knew, was dull and academic.

'No,' he said in a flat, rather depressed voice, 'you've done nothing wrong, Annie.'

Puzzled, she moved towards him, only to see him flinch as if she were going to attack him. She stopped.

'What is it?' she asked.

'You've done nothing wrong, Annie,' he said again.

She sat down on the armchair and swung it to face him. She felt numb and faintly anxious. As he made no move and did not speak she swung the chair a little more and gazed into the imitation log fire under the abstract painting. They said you couldn't tell the difference between a real fire and the gas version, but you could. For one thing, the gas fire did not smell. At Froggett's, where her parents lived, the fire in the sitting room smelt, belched smoke, sometimes emitted sparks which landed on the carpet. She gazed round the clean white room with its clean-lined furniture and couldn't speak. A hostile and terrifying silence waited for her words, questions, statements. Julian wasn't going to say anything. Whatever bad news waited – and she was sure it was bad news – she would have to urge it from him.

The phone rang into the silence. Julian jumped slightly, turned and went quickly upstairs. He'd taken a lot of calls upstairs recently, she remembered. But this time he offered none of his usual explanations as he left the room – 'I'll take it upstairs – won't interrupt the music', 'I'll take it upstairs – there's a letter there I have to refer to', 'I'll take it upstairs—' This time, Annie crossed the room and picked up the phone, feeling furtive and ashamed of herself. She heard Julian saying, 'There's no question of me not telling her, Tamsin. Of course there isn't—' and then a woman's voice, interrupting: 'There's somebody on the line. I heard the phone being picked up. Someone's listening in—'

'It's me, Annie,' said Annie.

There was a silence. Then the woman's voice said coolly, 'Who else would it be? I'll put the phone down.' There was the noise of the connection being broken, then the purr of the empty line.

Annie, too, put the phone down and stood staring at the computer in front of her. Tamsin – Bell, was it? – worked as an account executive at the advertising agency, Churchill, Bromberry and Barlow. Vane Graphics occasionally did work for them. Tamsin had been on the account of Martha Kildare Kitchen Spices for whom Vane Graphics had designed new packaging though at the last moment after some presentations by Julian involving several meetings with Tamsin, Martha Kildare (in reality Gerald Robinson) had decided not to proceed. He was too attached to his grandfather's old packaging, reminder of the days when the product was called Robinson's Family Pickle and eaten all over the country at kitchen tables by men in collarless shirts and braces.

Stunned, Annie suddenly felt like a stranger in someone else's house and struggled to remember her first and only meeting with Tamsin Bell at a party at the advertising agency. Tamsin had worn a cream suit, for power, a silk shirt with a lot of buttons open, for sex, and had big white teeth and red lips for gobbling things up. In spite of Tamsin's grown-up appearance, Annie had immediately thought of hockey fields and seen Tamsin, with large red legs, pounding down the middle of the field, shovelling the ball along, then cracking it into the goal with a hefty swing. She wouldn't have been above striking a crafty blow at a contender's shin either, so long as it could be made to look accidental.

There were sounds overhead, as Julian moved about. Annie didn't know what to do. She heard the lavatory flush and feet on the stairs, then Julian came into the room, holding an airbag. He said, 'I suppose you've gathered what's going on?'

'You haven't had to tell me,' she remarked.

'Our relationship's been going on for about six months,' he said. 'It began at that conference in Paris you didn't come to. Anyway . . .' he paused, 'there it is. I think it's best if I move out. We can talk later. Will you be going down to Froggett's for a while?'

'Why – what's happening?' asked Annie. 'What are you doing?'

This seemed to irritate him. He had had time to think: she had had no warning. Julian said quietly, 'It's obvious, isn't it, Annie. Look – this thing hasn't been working out for some time, has it? We're not really that well suited, are we? It's been getting plainer and plainer, so now – well, I've met somebody else. I think it's best if I just go, for the meanwhile. We can discuss details later. So it might be better if you go down to Howard and Juliet's, put a bit of distance between us, get away from this house – you do see, don't you?'

Annie stood there with tears rolling down her cheeks.

He watched her. 'I'm sorry, love,' he said. 'There's no point in me staying.' He turned quickly and went into the hall, calling back, 'Ring Howard and Juliet, that's the best thing to do . . .'

Annie heard the front door open and close.

She did not ring her parents, or anyone else, and for the next three days and nights did not even leave the house. During that time she ignored the phone, left the post on the doormat, cried, and tried to work out what had gone wrong. She had had a happy childhood and an adolescence dominated by two passions: one for learning, the other for her cousin, Tom Pointon. A scholarship had taken her to Oxford, where she'd been happy for six years, had a couple of unimportant boyfriends and enjoyed acting. Then she had met and married Julian. Even when her cousin Tom had mysteriously disappeared to Paris without any explanation she hadn't mourned like this. She had trusted he'd be back. He had always been there and she had believed he always would be. In any case, almost immediately after Tom's disappearance, she'd gone off to Oxford and begun a new life. Nothing had really equipped her for this most commonplace of events – a happy marriage overturned, suddenly, because her husband had met and fallen in love with another woman.

During the three days of suffering a pain she thought would kill her, if she didn't kill herself first, Annie went over and over everything about herself, Julian, the time they had spent together, what the marriage had been like. Part of her wanted to escape the pain as she would have tried to evade a fierce dog. She could have gone to her parents, an old friend who lived in London (there had been few new ones, except those she shared with Julian) or just away, somewhere, by herself. But her instinct was to hide, to try and work out what had happened, and what was going to happen.

Thoughts swirled round her brain, memories surfaced and withdrew. What shocked her most was that Julian had been able to do what he'd done. She hadn't thought him capable of it, which meant, unless he'd gone mad and become a stranger to himself, she had never known him. She had not understood that he was a man capable of pretending to work late at the office, even at weekends, for six months, deceiving her all the time with someone she'd dismissed as superficial and not very bright. He'd been sleeping with them both too. She couldn't understand. How had he been able to do it?

7

Sometimes, as a long day turned into a long night, as morning came, and the sounds of traffic on the main road got louder, the milkman called, the postman left a few Christmas cards, she wondered how it was she had noticed nothing. Then she wished many things: that she'd never met Julian, that she'd had his baby, that he'd come back, at any moment, saying it had all been a mistake.

On the third night alone she awoke from nightmares of departing trains and the deaths of individuals she couldn't quite see, to a moment or two of perfect clarity in which she realised that for almost a month she had, on Julian's instructions, been winding up her own job at Vane Graphics. The contents of her address book, details of all her contacts, were on the computer now. She'd programmed in her system of checking mail and phone calls, records of action taken. She'd progress-chased the team, as Julian had suggested, and put on the computer all the details and deadlines she normally kept on a wall-chart backed by her own notes and what she remembered. All the systems she had devised for keeping things running smoothly and all the up-to-date information about Vane Graphics' current dealings were, for a successor, tidily to hand on the computer on her desk. Short of agreeing to clear her desk into a cardboard box and go in a month's time, she'd done everything a person leaving a job would have done. It looked as if Julian had not just unilaterally ended the marriage, but also her association with his firm. For some reason this recognition soothed her and she went back to sleep.

She awoke a few hours later, in the late dawn of a glum December day, and heard the sound of a key in the front door. Going downstairs, haggard, in a nightdress she had been wearing for two days, she found Julian in the sitting room, disconnecting the computer. At his feet was the video. He gazed at her, startled.

'My God!' he said. 'Annie – you look terrible. I just came for a few things – some clothes—'

She stared at him. It was seven-thirty in the morning. He was neatly dressed in a suit and fresh shirt. He wore a new tie, an expensive silk one, violet, with spots. His blond wavy hair was freshly cut, but there were dark shadows under his big blue eyes.

'Are you ill? I thought you'd gone to Froggett's.'

'Do you expect me to look well?' she asked. 'I still can't understand it. Why did you do it? And as for this . . .' she gestured at the computer, the video, 'it doesn't seem fair, coming and taking these things when you thought I was away.'

8

'Basically, I came for my clothes,' he said.

'You'd better take them.' She sank, shivering, into the armchair. She heard him moving about upstairs.

When he came down he asked, 'Can I take the picture? I think it'll go in the back of the car. You've never liked it.'

'All right.' She watched him quickly remove it. He carried it out to the car and came back for the cases he'd left in the hall. The door closed and his car started up. The video and the computer still sat on the floor. Annie went upstairs, slowly as an old woman, and ran a bath.

A few more days passed. Annie ate and slept a little more. Her mother rang up and this time she answered the telephone. Juliet told her she must come straight to Froggett's and not return to London at least until Christmas was over.

Annie looked at Melanie who, used to long waits, just shrugged. The pale young woman bent forward over her two-year-old and selected a tired-looking children's book from the pile of old magazines on the table in front of her.

Vanessa Doyle felt so tired. She had had to bring Alec with her because he'd screamed blue murder when she tried to leave him behind with her mother in the house in Leadham Common. The look her mother gave her meant she'd had no alternative, so she'd scooped him up and carried him to the bus stop. Now she wished she'd delayed and got his pushchair from the garage. Alec hadn't been prepared to walk from the bus to the dentist's surgery, and he wouldn't want to walk back either. He was nervy and woke at night. He knew something was wrong, poor little boy. She began to read to him, pointing at the pictures.

'So there's the goosey gander, and the duck and the owl, all looking at the dog,' she explained to the child. 'And the dog says, "Come and see the little pig" – and there's the pig.'

As for her, she'd had a terrible Christmas and this visit to the dentist felt like the last straw. Her sister Cherry had, of course, been there at their parents' over Christmas with her husband, the manager of a building society and their six-year-old boy twins. Although she said over and over again how sorry she was about her sister's predicament somehow Cherry made a point of continually mentioning her own family's mortgage, holidays plans and car. Too often she would straighten her husband's tie, arrange his hair with her hand and turn his face to give it little, proprietorial kisses. All too frequently she asked one of the twins to go and find Daddy, go and tell Daddy he loved him, request Daddy to come and help Mummy. This had depressed Vanessa, as she knew it was meant to, and had also disturbed her children, Alec and Joanne, who did not understand what was going on. But Vanessa knew there wasn't anything she could actually complain about, or have out with her sister – there never would be where Cherry was concerned. And if her mother had spotted what was going on she would pretend she hadn't, to keep the peace and because, Vanessa thought, she was on Cherry's side.

To Anita Davis there was nothing more shameful than losing your husband. Her father, Alan, had been kind, but the others had been horrible – her brother had been up in Scotland with Leigh Rangers for a Boxing Day match – and Vanessa had cried herself to sleep, quietly, so no one would know.

On Boxing Day, while the family was watching a TV film, Cherry's husband had offered her a chocolate. Biting down on it Vanessa had felt something hard in the centre – a nut, perhaps. Then, becoming suspicious, she spat the mouthful into her hand.

'Ooh, Nessa. What are you doing now?' Cherry had shuddered as if she'd spent all Christmas scratching her armpits and spitting on the floor.

Vanessa had looked in her hand while exploring her mouth with her tongue and there it lay, in her hand, covered in chocolate: half her top front tooth. She hadn't said anything, just gone to the bathroom and stared in the glass. She thought she looked like an old woman.

The next day had been hell. Cherry had taught her sons, who were only too glad to learn, to call her 'Auntie Gummie'. Her dad had seen her face and got in the car, going quietly to the cashpoint and coming back with £250, which he'd tucked in her hand when they were alone, muttering, 'Go to Harley Street if you have to, Ness. You want to get that seen to quickly.' She'd been grateful at the time but had decided to keep the money for bills and clothes for the children and see if Mr Rothko could do something on the National Health. Now here she sat, praying, just praying he could make it come right. Hours in the chilly surgery with Alec moaning and whining, and she didn't need that toffee-nosed bitch, with her long hair sliding out of the combs all over the place, to start stating her rights.

Vanessa decided that the dark-haired woman must be the podgy teenager's social worker. Nobody in a good coat like hers would allow their kid to wear worn-out trainers like those on the girl's feet, or that British Home Stores anorak. Vanessa sighed and glanced away. Well, there was someone who had it made – good job, wedding ring on her hand – some people had all the luck.

Alec tugged at her sleeve. She read, 'Goodness gracious me. Where's little piggy Edward gone? We must all go and look for him at once.'

On 22 December, not a good time for a family man to leave home and £100 from his back pocket on the kitchen table, Vanessa's husband, Geoff Doyle, had walked out. But Doyle was not a particularly good man. He had been one of those boys who from infancy know well the words 'little so-and-so' and 'little hooligan' almost always mean them. He'd grown up to become 'that sod' and 'that bastard Doyle', though to his mother he was always 'my Geoff'. From an Irish grandfather he had inherited his jet black hair, bright blue eyes and fine physique and from his English grandfather his habit of resolving problems without consulting the laws of reason, humanity or the land. Old Doyle had been a quiet God-fearing man, killed young in an accident on a building site. Old Robinson, his mother's father, had been a lifelong villain, starting life in the 1930s as a trainee in one of South London's razor-gangs, going on to desert from the British Army and take up black marketeering. He ended up as the manager of a run-down second-hand furniture shop with a strong line in stolen property in an upstairs room.

Geoff bullied his way through primary and secondary school, got a conviction for taking away and driving a car not belonging to him and, fearing prison, went at the age of nineteen into the building trade. Soon afterwards he met and married eighteen-year-old Vanessa Davis who gave up her job as a typist when Joanne was born. Her idea had been to return to work in order to save for a mortgage, but Geoff had said he didn't want his wife at work, too tired from the job and house and child to look after him properly. When the time came, he would supply the house. In the meantime they were all right as they were, in a small house rented from Kenton Council, on a low rent achieved by his accountant proving the family was almost on the breadline. Vanessa had half suspected Geoff wasn't always faithful to her, but now, ten years after the marriage everything had gone smash.

11

She'd known there was something wrong. Geoff was home late every night, once or twice at two or three in the morning – a game of cards, he'd said – and he looked at her as if she wasn't there while he was in the house. Then one morning in the supermarket she'd found herself and her loaded trolley of groceries, complete with Alec, sitting on the wire seat of the trolley, at the next checkout to Cindy Abbott, pretty, blonde and, according to Geoff, the mainstay of Doyle, Builders, South London Ltd. It was Cindy who kept the two sets of books, one in the files, the other in her head where the VATman and the Inland Revenue couldn't find the details.

In her wire basket Cindy had coffee, unsalted butter, croissants and a bag containing two bottles of champagne she had bought in the other part of the store. Vanessa immediately knew how things stood. Geoff had told her he was staying over at the electrician's that night, as it was closer to the building suppliers they'd have to visit next morning in order to make an early start on a job. Now here was Cindy in the supermarket with his favourite, his only, breakfast and two bottles of champagne sticking out of the top of a plastic bag. She needed no further evidence. She felt her loaded shopping trolley was growing from her arm like an extension to the limb while Cindy stood there in a cream mini-skirt, raspberry-coloured blouse and matching jacket casually holding a basket containing her, Vanessa's, husband's late-night champagne and – yes – breakfast, too. Taking her hand from the trolley she called, 'Excuse me. Would that be my husband's breakfast you've got in that basket, Cindy?'

The women behind Cindy gazed across at her. Cindy said loudly, 'I beg your pardon? Were you speaking to me?'

'Just asking if that's Geoff's drinkies and croissants you've got there,' said Vanessa clearly and steadily. 'Being his wife, I think I've got a right to know.'

'You're mad,' said Cindy. 'What are you talking about?' The woman at the checkout said to Cindy, 'Three pounds forty.' Cindy paid no attention as Vanessa continued, 'I'm talking about you and my husband, Cindy Abbott. You ought to be ashamed. Going with a married man with two children.'

'Thirty pounds, twenty-two pence,' said the woman at Vanessa's checkout.

Cindy, meanwhile, furious at being attacked, in the hearing of everyone in both queues, called out, 'Look here, whoever you are.

12

There's a law against saying things like that to people in public. You're mad, that's what you are!'

The tired checkout woman said, 'Please pay three pounds forty.'

Cindy took out her purse with dignity, saying loftily, 'All right. But I don't think you ought to be letting customers in here who are out of their minds.'

Vanessa quickly paid for her own things, pushed her trolley through the checkout and, at the other end, snatched up Cindy's butter, croissants and coffee and flung them on to her own pile of goods. She barred Cindy's way with her trolley, on which Alec was perched. 'That's my husband's money you're spending,' she said loudly, 'and I've got two kids to feed.'

Cindy stepped past Vanessa and the trolley and, still with the champagne, went a few paces towards the exit. There she turned, 'All right, Vanessa? You happy? You've got his breakfast – but will he be there to eat it? Have you looked at yourself recently? You look a mess. Take my advice and go and do something about yourself—' And she swung through the doors and went off.

Vanessa, her face blazing, had to pack all her goods, including the offending breakfast items, into four plastic bags in front of two queues of people who had heard every word, including Cindy's final, humiliating remarks. As they went through the checkouts the other women avoided looking at her. Alec, in the trolley, began to want to get out. Putting him in his buggy, she collected the bags together and walked back to 42 Rutherford Street. She was shaking and her face still felt flushed. Once in the house, she began to put the shopping away but the silence was terrible and she realised she couldn't let Cindy get away with her contemptuous remarks, or Geoff with his deceptions. She wanted, and needed, a confrontation, a crisis, some resolution. She phoned Geoff's office. Cindy answered, recognised Vanessa's voice, said, 'He's out,' and instantly hung up. Vanessa pushed Alec, still in his anorak and mittens, back in the buggy and half ran down Foxwell High Street, turned left into Carlisle Road, a long street of houses interspersed with small blocks of shops, through the shabby people on the pavements, down an alley to a group of three shops strung together, selling parts for cars and motorbikes. There was a yard behind the shops where a van marked Doyle stood, and items of building equipment were stacked. A tired-looking boy was sweeping up. She crossed the yard to the offices of Doyle, Builders, three Portakabins in a row. She could see Geoff through the window, standing up holding a phone. As she approached she saw a hand with painted fingernails extended, proffering a mug of tea or coffee.

She parked the buggy, in which Alec had fallen asleep, and ran up the wooden steps of the Portakabin.

'Geoff!' she shouted as she burst through the doorway. 'We've got to have this out.' He quickly concluded his telephone conversation. 'I think that's all at this moment, Mr Wainwright. If you get back to me when you've finally made your decision we can get down to the details.' Vanessa pointed at Cindy, sitting at the desk behind her, and said firmly, 'Cindy – out, if you don't mind.' Cindy didn't move.

'She works here,' Geoff Doyle said to his wife as he put the phone down.

'And that's not all she does,' Vanessa said indignantly. 'You're sleeping with her, Geoff – that's the reason for all this working late and staying round at Robbo's. You're round at her place.'

'So,' he said, looking down at her. 'What do you want?'

'I want it to stop.'

'That could be difficult,' he said evenly.

'Don't give me difficult – I'm your wife. Mother of your two kids. You're sleeping with her, aren't you? What are you going to do?'

'Nothing,' he said, looking her steadily in the eye. 'Nothing at all. Your best bet, Vanessa, and you know it, is to go home quietly and forget it all. Cindy and me are very close, now. There's nothing can change that.' He looked indulgently at Cindy. 'Go home like a good girl and forget you ever came here. You don't want things to get any worse, do you?'

The quiet, threatening tone stopped her for a moment. She began to cry. 'You're standing there and telling me I've got to put up with it – *her*, that common little dollop. How can you?'

He shook his head at her. 'Vanessa. It happens all the time.'

In one jump, Vanessa saw what he wanted, and what her life would be like if he got it. She'd provide clean shirts for when he went out with Cindy, get them back dirty. Dinners would dry up in the oven until it was obvious he wasn't coming in. She wouldn't be allowed to talk about it. There'd be explanations to make to the children about why Daddy wasn't going here and there with them – he's very busy earning money – and everybody would know she was being betrayed and tolerating it, for security, for a love that was being trampled on. She had no doubt that Geoff would want

14

to go on sleeping with her, having sex when he suddenly felt like it, telling Cindy he wasn't – while all the time Cindy would be scheming to get him to leave her and go for a divorce. She found herself saying, 'Perhaps it does happen. But not to me.'

'So you're different, are you?' he murmured with some menace in his voice. Then, realising he was angering her too much he said, firmly, because Cindy was listening, 'All right, Vanessa. We can't talk here in the office. We'll go home and discuss things.'

'What about me?' protested Cindy.

'You stop here,' Geoff told her, 'and keep the office open, love.'

'Oh – nice!' she exclaimed.

Doyle thumped his desk intimidatingly. 'Let's get this straight, shall we? Let's look at the facts of life. To live you need money and to get money you have to stay in business. That's why this office has got to stay open.' Then, in a more placatory way, 'Sorry, love, but there it is.'

In the car, with Alec and the buggy in the back, Vanessa said, 'Are you really so stuck on her?' She had to force the words out but felt she must know the truth.

'Save it,' he said, chasing a Mercedes up Foxwell High Street. 'Let's get home first.'

'I'm glad you still think it *is* your home,' Vanessa observed. At the word 'home' Geoff winced.

Ahead the Mercedes slowed down and Geoff had to stand on the brakes. 'Black driver,' he remarked with gloomy satisfaction. 'You can't trust a black driver in a Merc.'

Vanessa suddenly realised that Cindy would be nagging to move into one of the three smart new town houses, with their fitted kitchens, and integral garages, that Geoff's firm had just built. To Vanessa Geoff had said they all had to be sold to satisfy the bank and the Inland Revenue. With what was left, he would buy their council house, which would be useful as collateral as well as ensuring they owned their own home. A picture flashed into Vanessa's mind of Cindy stretched out on a recliner on the patio of her smart new house and herself still bringing up two children in a rented Victorian two-up, two-down.

In silence they went into the house. With Alec settled at one end of the room to play with his cars, Vanessa faced Geoff. 'Well – what's going to happen?'

'I told you, Cindy and I are close—'

Vanessa began to tremble. She was tempted for a moment to drop the subject, let him get on with it, wait for him to get fed up with Cindy and come back to her, or, if that was how it worked out, Cindy to snatch Geoff from her.

'You shouldn't be,' she managed to get out. 'You're a married man – I'm your wife. I thought you loved me.'

'I do love you—'

'Not enough to give her up.'

'That's something different.'

Vanessa stared wildly at the tinsel decorations looped along the picture rails, the gold and silver balls on the Christmas tree, on top, the angel made out of kitchen foil Joanne had brought home from school. 'It sounds all right for you. One for fun and games, the other for housework, cooking and kids. I'd like to know what she's thinking, in her heart of hearts.'

'Cindy doesn't want to be tied down. She's young. She wants a good time—'

Bitterly, Vanessa retorted, 'You've got it made, haven't you? Two women at your beck and call. And you really think she's something, don't you? She's a little tramp, that's all, going after somebody's husband—'

'And she gets them,' he said, relishing some memory. 'She certainly gets them.'

'So that means you're not the first?' sneered Vanessa. 'Well, I suppose not.'

'Don't start, Vanessa. Don't start,' Geoff warned. He was a big man and intimidating. But Vanessa was past caring.

'You admire her, don't you, with her tarty little skirt and not caring who's married and who isn't? That's what you really go for, isn't it, Geoff? She's got you, hasn't she? Never mind Vanessa. Forget Vanessa. I can take it or leave it as far as you're concerned, can't I? Well,' she said, a little fearful now, 'supposing I decide to leave it?'

Geoff Doyle would not be challenged by a woman. He stared at her, his face hard, 'Well, then, darling, that'd be your decision, wouldn't it?'

'You'd risk your kids for that?'

'You're risking me.'

'I still love you, Geoff.'

'Then don't do anything stupid.'

'Oh, no? While she tries and gets you more and more on her side? She's younger than me. She's got more time and money to

16

spend on herself. And,' she added shrewdly, 'her father's in the Planning Department, isn't he?'

He didn't like the last thrust. 'That's got nothing to do with it.'

'No – tell that to somebody else.'

Geoff was silent. Alec stopped playing with his toys and ran across the room. 'Mum,' he said. 'I'm hungry.'

Vanessa picked up the bags of shopping and carried them into the kitchen. She lit the grill, found a packet of fish fingers and put some under the grill.

'Ketchup,' said Alec.

Vanessa gulped, and said, 'Yes.' He had turned a dismal face to her, his voice was uncertain. She didn't want to cry in front of him. He was a quiet child but observant. He understood more than anyone gave him credit for. He was sensitive, already upset and doubtful. His father might leave at any moment. They'd have nothing to live on. Should she try to stick it out and win her husband back for the sake of the children? It would be like living in hell, she thought, though other women did it, God knew how. It seemed impossible Geoff was doing this to all of them, forcing these choices on her.

Then she heard the front door open. 'I've got to go,' called Geoff. 'There's a delivery in at one.' And he left, just as if this was a normal day. To him it was. He'd been running between her and Cindy for months. This particular day was nothing new to him.

Doggedly, she persuaded Alec to eat a few more bites, took him to the lavatory and tucked him in bed with his red fire engine for company. She went downstairs and, pushing a big red crêpe paper ball away with her foot, phoned her mother.

'Oh dear, oh dear,' wailed Anita Davis. 'Oh, Vanessa – what are you going to do?'

'I don't know, Mum.'

'He's been at it for years. I wonder you hadn't suspected long ago.'

'What?' asked Vanessa.

'Alan saw him coming out of the cinema with a girl ages ago . . . ' She did not add that Vanessa's brother had reported Geoff's arm was round the girl, or that Vanessa had been in hospital at the time. It had been just after Alec was born.

'I suppose it could have been innocent.'

'Oh, Vanessa,' her mother said impatiently. 'Word gets round, you know.'

'I suppose I thought he might have been unfaithful, once or twice, but I never thought – I never thought—'

'Keep calm. I'll come round now.'

But even before Vanessa's mother had left her own house Cindy Abbott rang. She began, 'Vanessa – he's not coming back to you. He's made up his mind and that's it. You might as well get used to it – it's me he loves, he's chosen me and we're going to live together.'

'I want to hear him tell me that himself.'

'He doesn't need to—'

'Put him on the phone, Cindy—'

'Wait, then,' commanded Cindy. Vanessa could hear voices, Cindy's and Geoff's, then Geoff into the phone, 'She's right, Van. You would make me choose. I'll send some money. But don't start mucking me about—'

'What do you mean?'

'No lawyers – no funny business.'

'Is this it?' Vanessa could hardly speak. Everything seemed unreal. How could he be ending things just like that?

'That's right. You'd better believe it. But I've got to tell you, if you start involving lawyers, there isn't any money, and there won't be. Have you got that straight?' He hung up.

'Three days before Christmas,' said Anita Davis, handing her daughter a little of the brandy she'd brought with her. She sat in a plum-coloured coat and large matching felt hat, holding her handbag. Vanessa in her jeans and jersey sat opposite. 'Oh dear. He might have waited.' She leaned forward. 'Quite frankly, Vanessa, I think it was a mistake to challenge him. You might have done better to have pretended you didn't know – hoping it would all blow over. These things often do.'

'You said yourself this probably isn't the first time,' replied Vanessa.

'Men!' exclaimed Anita, throwing up her eyes. 'Well, your dad'll be having a word with Mrs Doyle tomorrow but I don't know what good it'll do. To that woman her son can do no wrong.' She shook her head, 'I don't know, I'm sure. You're telling me he threatened you when you talked about a divorce?'

'I didn't mention it. I think that's what he was talking about—'

'That's the problem with self-employed men – they can use an accountant to creep out of anything. When the court looks at their books they've got nothing. The wife gets nothing. Even if she does, they can find a way of not paying. Just before Christmas too,' she repeated.

18

Later, Vanessa collected Joanne from school while her mother looked after Alec.

'Daddy's gone on a little holiday,' said her grandmother when they walked in.

'He'll be back for Christmas,' the little girl answered confidently. 'I've got his present – it's three red handkerchiefs and a blue comb.'

'You can go in now,' announced the receptionist.

The girl stood up. Annie Vane stood too. 'May I go in with her?' she asked.

'If you feel it's necessary.'

Annie followed Melanie into the surgery and closed the door.

The receptionist indicated her disapproval with a 'Tsk.' What was she doing babying such a big girl, thirteen or fourteen, in that way? Her glance at Vanessa said, Who does she think she is? She's not a regular like you. She doesn't know the rules. Vanessa's lifted eyebrows said in return, What do you expect? She thinks she's too good for us, thinks she can do as she likes.

2

George's Café

George's Café, busy, steamy and, frankly, a bit grubby, stands in a side street off Foxwell High Street. The area known as Foxwell Market is full of small shops and stalls selling everything from potatoes to boiling fowl, from watches to records and tapes. On the pavement outside George's, Mrs Patel sells underwear for men and women, T-shirts, sometimes in summer, cheap skirts and blouses. Next to her comes Roger Smith's fruit stall and, next to Roger, Roland Elliott, or some friend or relation of his, selling tapes, often reggae or rap. Roland is frequently shouted at by fellow stallholders or adjacent shopkeepers for making too much noise, whereupon he sometimes starts playing eighteenth-century music on his massive ghetto blaster.

Next to George's is a barber's, almost at the corner of the High Street. This broad Roman road leads directly south, to the coast, and north to the River Thames. On the opposite bank of the river lie the Houses of Parliament, the offices of Whitehall and other great buildings where laws are made and from which the affairs of a great nation are regulated.

On this cold January afternoon, George's customers were not thinking about any of this. No one – not the two market traders sitting at a plastic table, wearing their big pouched change belts over thick overcoats, or the six workmen having a post-dinner tea and smoke and a warm-up before getting back to work on a big cold building site, or Arnold, middle-aged and unemployed, stringing out a cup of tea before making his way to his afternoon appointment at the public library – no one in George's was dwelling on the wider issues or their part in them, though Mrs Patel, standing in a cutting wind at her underwear stall, did occasionally allow herself to think about the Home Office. She was waiting for a long-delayed official ruling as to whether two of her older children would be allowed to enter the country, DNA testing having proved what had first been denied: that she and her husband were their actual parents and not two tricksters trying to smuggle in children not their own.

At the middle table in the café Annie Vane and Melanie Pickering were sitting, pale with winter and the strain of a grim battle which had just taken place between them outside Kenton Town Hall, the large, ornate building which stood at the top of Foxwell High Street, a symbol of Victorian respect for civic government and the orderly, incorruptible management of local affairs. It had been on the steps of this building that Annie, wishing to regularise matters, had tried to drag a reluctant Melanie into the foyer. She wished to discover where to find the Social Services Department and enlist their help. Melanie, with more understanding of what such authorities are usually like imagined herself being packed on to the next train north and her family thereafter continually subjected to questions and intrusions they did not want. It would, she thought, either go like that or she would end up in a children's home. She was unable to explain to Annie which laws or regulations would lead to these undesirable events. She just knew from experience that something would go wrong once they found themselves sitting on the wrong side of a desk opposite a well-meaning young man or woman who would try to help and end up making things worse.

'They'll help you find your uncle,' Annie had claimed, as traffic passed and pedestrians steered round them.

'No, they won't – they'll end up finding my dad. I don't want that. Or they'll send me home – if not worse.'

Annie sighed. 'Melanie,' she said. 'Once you've told them the situation, they'll help.' Annie hoped to find in the Town Hall someone who spoke a language like her own and understood life as she did.

Melanie knew the system was against her. 'They'll send me to a children's home,' she said. 'Or something. I'm not going in there. I'll just get a job and manage for myself. I can find my uncle. I'll ask the Salvation Army—'

Annie looked at the obstinate face and realised there was nothing she could do to make Melanie go into the Town Hall. Inwardly, she groaned. 'You can't get a job,' she said. 'It's against the law. You're only thirteen.'

21

'There's plenty of jobs,' Melanie told her. 'No one'll ask.'

They ended up buying Melanie a new pair of trainers and dashing into George's to get warm and eat baked beans on toast.

'You'll have to ring your mother and say where you are,' Annie told the girl. 'She'll have reported you as missing to the police.'

'All right,' agreed Melanie. 'She'll be worried by now. Especially after our Ruth.'

'Who's Ruth?'

'Ruth's my sister. She ran away too. More than a year ago.'

'Where is she?'

'We don't know. They never found her.'

Annie looked in horror at Melanie. What had seemed so plain a fortnight ago was becoming more and more complicated. Now, it seemed, there was another missing Pickering girl. It was all beginning to sound like one of those long, complicated accounts given to the police by the residents of Threpp Street in 1888.

Annie had found Melanie asleep on her step on 29 December, when she returned to London after Christmas with her family in Hampshire. She had arrived late at Waterloo, then taken the notorious tube to Foxwell, amid drunks, families and depressed people of both sexes and all statuses. Everyone avoided looking at everyone else and there was a concerted effort in the carriage to render invisible a group of black youths in the middle of the carriage, playing loud music and occasionally glancing around, half enjoying and half resenting the way they were able to strike fear into nearly all the other passengers, just by being there and being black.

Annie walked up Foxwell High Street with her bag. There were people wandering about in groups and a police van parked on the other side of the road. She reached Rutherford Street, quiet and dimly lit, and started walking towards her house, worried at the thought of entering her home alone, and finding it empty. It was as she was about to cross the road that she saw the dark bundle huddled motionless on her own doorstep. She stopped, frightened. Somebody mad, or drunk, who would put out a hand and grab her, attack her, yell abuse or plead? Or might it be – horrible thought – a dead body? She supposed she could go back to the main road and ask the police to help but the van might be gone by now and if the person in her doorway needed help there was no way of knowing whether the police would behave well towards him, as they could, or turn him into another death-in-custody statistic. She knew no one in the street and the houses were nearly all darkened now. Even in houses where people hadn't yet gone to bed the residents might not answer the door at this time of night. She heard footsteps behind her, which made her even more uneasy. She turned. A tall figure stopped near, but not too near, her, under the streetlight. The tall black man in a cap said, 'That your house?'

'Yes,' she said. 'There's someone asleep there.'

'Looks like a kid,' he told her. Annie hesitated. 'You just step past him quickly, go in and shut the door and phone the police – they'll take him away to a children's home, or something.' She gazed at him. 'Well,' he said. 'You got to get in. What you going to do? Wake him up, give him a bath and a meal, take him to live with you? Do what I say – you'll be all right.'

She drew a deep breath, nodded. He moved past her and went on up the street with long, graceful steps.

Annie crossed the road, walked the few paces up her short path, leaned over the huddle in the doorway and put her key in the lock. As the door opened the sleeper fell across the threshold. Annie snapped on the light and saw a girl's face, a lot of brown hair spreading out from under the hood of a brown anorak. The voice said in a blurry northern accent, 'What's happening?' Then as the girl woke a little more and took in the situation, she mumbled, 'Oh – you were out. I thought you were asleep inside. Don't worry – I'm leaving.' She pushed some hair from her face with a grimy hand.

'What are you doing here?' asked Annie. 'Can't you get home? You shouldn't be sleeping in doorways.'

'Don't worry. I'm off,' said the girl, scrambling to her feet. Her jeans were very dirty.

'I don't want you to go off into the night,' Annie said. 'It's very late and the streets are full of drunks. Come in, we'll organise something.'

'Who else is in there?' asked the girl, glancing down the lighted hall.

'Only me,' responded Annie. 'Look – it's worse out there . . . ' Two young men, walking unsteadily along on the other side of the road, were stopped by a police car which had just eased up beside them.

'All right,' said the girl, coming inside. Annie shut the door.

'Would you like some tea? I'll see what there is to eat.' She put the heating on and opened a tin of soup.

Annie, conscious of Julian's absence, stirred the soup while the girl sat in silence. She asked, finally, 'Where are you going?'

'My uncle's. He lives in London.'

'You must have come from somewhere,' Annie stated. 'Come and drink this in the other room.'

Annie trod on a Christmas tree ornament as she walked into the sitting room. A pair of trousers and a sweater lay on the chair where she'd left them. Other ornaments lay on the carpet. The room looked neglected and felt cold. There was something else amiss. 'Oh, my God!' she exclaimed. Alarmed, the girl stared at her. 'The sofa's gone!'

'Have you been robbed?' The girl stared at the room.

Annie, noticing the absence of the computer and the video, which had been on the floor when she left for the country, rushed upstairs, saying, 'At least they left the TV.'

Julian's grandmother's walnut chest of drawers on the landing, had gone, leaving only a rectangle on the carpet. As far as she could see, nothing else had been moved. No drawers appeared to have been opened, nothing disarranged. She opened the airing cupboard and noted that two pairs of linen sheets, part of a wedding present from her parents, had been removed. She came heavily downstairs.

The girl was still standing in the same position, holding her mug of soup. 'Has anything else been taken?' she asked.

'It wasn't burglars,' said Annie. 'Just my ex-husband.'

The girl said, 'Bad luck. Are you going round there to make him give the stuff back.'

'He can have it,' Annie told her. 'Drink up.'

Annie sat on the remaining chair, the girl on a cushion on the floor. So – Julian had tried to take the computer when he thought she was away, been foiled, and come back when she really was. He and Tamsin must be asleep on her mother's sheets even now. She'd have to think about all this. In the meanwhile, there was the girl. She asked, 'Where does your uncle live?'

'Clapton,' she said, wincing as she bit into a piece of chocolate Annie had given her from a bar she'd found in her handbag.

'Toothache?' enquired Annie.

'Flared up on the train here,' the girl told her. 'My name's Melanie, by the way.'

'Annie Vane,' Annie said. 'You're a long way from Clapton.'

'I was stupid. I just took off. Dad was getting on to me again. I thought – I'll go. He'd threatened me with a bashing for something I'd done and I ran for it. I got a bus into town, took my savings out

24

of the Abbey National, the lot, and I got a train down here and then I was standing there in that big station, trying to make head or tail of the Underground map they have there and I was feeling frightened by then, what with being in London and what I'd done, so then a man came up—' She looked at Annie's face, which had fallen, and said, 'I know. Silly, wasn't I? So he said he and his mate had a cheap minicab service, and they couldn't go round the streets picking up passengers like a normal taxi, but they could offer to take me to where I was going. So – I said Clapton and he said well, he could do it for two pounds fifty. Anyway, we went outside the station and there was the car, one man in the back already, then the other fellow shows me in, fastens my seatbelt – that was when I started to feel worried. He kind of lingered over it. Know what I mean?'

Annie nodded. 'So after that he sets off at a lick and we go for miles. London's so big. I thought it was all right. They asked me questions, friendly, like why was I here and like a mug, I told them. Stupid, wasn't I? Then I began to ask when we'd get there – "Ten minutes," says the one in the back. Ten minutes went past so I asked again – "Soon enough," said the one driving and then he put his hand on my leg, right up there, and the other one laughed. So from that time my one idea was to get out of the car. I waited and waited and then we were somewhere, at the traffic lights. Fast as I could I unlocked the door and chucked it open and started calling out to people to help me, while the driver was trying to get his hand over my mouth and stop me from undoing the seatbelt at the same time. So I'm yelling, and the people going by are taking no notice. Finally I bit his hand and he yelled and took it away, just as I managed to undo the seatbelt. I threw myself sideways out of the car and landed on the pavement, and I got up and started running. When I turned back, the car had gone from the lights, and the traffic was moving on. I suppose they had to go on when the lights changed, but I just kept on running – I thought they'd drive round looking for me. So then I thought I'd go to a police station. I thought I'd rather face my dad than them. They were horrible . . .' She paused. 'But I couldn't see a policeman, or a police station, and it was so dark. I just turned into your doorway thinking I'd sit down for a minute – but, of course, I fell asleep . . .'

Annie was shocked. 'What an experience. Well – I don't know. You ought to phone home to say you're safe—'

'I only want to go to my uncle's,' Melanie said. 'I'll phone him, if you like . . .'

25

But Jim Allardyce of Clapton was not on the telephone, they discovered. Annie was tired. 'Look – I'm whacked,' she said. 'It's pretty late. Why don't you sleep in the spare room for tonight? We'll sort it all out in the morning. Have a couple of aspirin if your tooth's aching . . .'

Melanie, cautiously, agreed.

'You can lock your door,' said Annie.

As they went upstairs Melanie asked, 'Did your husband really take the settee?'

'Yes,' Annie said wearily. 'We're lucky he left the beds.'

As Annie turned back her counterpane she half-expected to find her sheets missing. But Julian had only taken the good ones. She lay down. It had been a long day, starting with her walk over the fields to visit her sister and say goodbye. She'd caught the train which stopped at every station, found a girl asleep on her step, found Julian had robbed the house.

It seemed a long time since she had rung her mother, saying, 'I'll come down for Christmas. Julian won't be with me – he's left. We're getting a divorce.' It was hard to bring out the words.

To her surprise her mother was instantly sympathetic and not disconcerted by the news. 'Come down at once, Annie. Have you got a good solicitor?'

'Not yet.'

'You'd better go to Mr Danby. I'll tell Howard. Come as soon as you can.'

As Annie put the phone down in Rutherford Street, she had the sense that the world she had thought so stable was changing quickly and would go on changing from that moment on.

Annie took the mainline train, then the small local train to Cottersley. She got out at the little station and, as the moon was full, walked quiet country roads for a mile and a half, stepped through the village of Belshaw and went on, in clear, cold air, with stars glittering overhead, until she reached the open gates of Froggett's, the big red brick house where her parents lived.

It had been built in the twenties by a prosperous farming family, who had pulled down the old farmhouse in favour of something modern and convenient. But war-time conditions led the ageing farmer to sell his land to his neighbour, Sir Henry Fellows. When Sir Henry would not meet his price for the house, Mr Froggett put it on the market and sold it, with an acre and a half of land, to young Howard Browning, a promising novelist and his first wife, a sculptor. Later the sculptor left, making way for Juliet Cunningham, a painter. Their daughters, Annie and her younger sister Jasmine, had been brought up in the house. The Brownings, unmarried on principle, had been happy together for thirty-five years. The sisters were used to Juliet's first husband, Howard's first wife and the children of their later marriages coming and staying for long periods – and their friends, children's friends, lovers. Annie's in-laws, the Vanes, and her sister Jasmine's in-laws, the Fellowses, called the set-up 'bohemian', and made it sound like a criticism.

Annie walked round the side of the house and into the vast kitchen-cum-living room. There was a small sitting room behind the kitchen, with a hard sofa, pictures the Brownings had acquired or been given over the years except for the ones they really liked, a lot of dark, flowered wallpaper and a piano. But the real life of the place happened in the kitchen, where an Aga and a selection of small electric fires kept areas of the room warm in winter, although you had to know where to sit. A long table took all the clutter of the house, and a big dresser at the back held plates, dried flowers, old, interesting bottles, Annie's mother's and grandmother's jewellery – in a biscuit tin – and other odds and ends. Juliet, who had been sitting beside Howard on a sofa at the far end of the room, watching a small television, stood up and came towards her. Her father looked up from his book. 'Annie!' he exclaimed. Annie sadly put down her small suitcase and a plastic bag containing Christmas presents bought in happier times.

When they were all round the table, Annie drinking soup and her parents some of Howard's powerful blackcurrant wine, her mother told her, 'Jas looked in earlier. She's invited us up to the castle for Boxing Day lunch. I couldn't really refuse. I hope you don't mind. I told her about Julian by the way. She's very upset. You needn't come to the lunch if you don't want to – Mary will understand. Jas is popping across tomorrow to say hallo.'

'How is she?' asked Annie. 'I haven't seen her for months. She sent me a postcard from the West Indies but I couldn't read her writing. I think she'd got something on the card – suntan oil, I expect.'

'She's still delighted with life,' Howard said. 'She and Mary are going round the village visiting the poor, though, of course, there aren't a lot of the poor left since Bernard sold off so many expired leases to his pals in the City. The real poor are all over on the council estate outside Cottersley.'

'Mary goes there, too,' Juliet told him. Her husband, even though his daughter Jasmine had married Nigel, son of Sir Bernard and Lady Mary Fellows, of Durham House, which stood half a mile over the fields from his house, was still in principle rigorously opposed to the Fellows family and all their doings. His wife, though, was a friend of Lady Mary.

'Isn't there usually a meet on Boxing Day?' Annie asked.

'Called off due to lack of foxes,' Howard reported with satisfaction.

'And the old MFH died last month,' added Juliet.

'Of a broken heart, I expect,' Howard said remorselessly.

'Your father's been canvassing the local farmers, with some success. They've been trapping the foxes on the sly too.'

'That's still not much fun for the foxes,' Annie said.

'Better than being hunted down by a pack of yobbos on big horses before being torn to pieces by dogs,' Howard told her. 'And at least people don't have to put up with their chickens being killed all the year round, and cats and everything else that moves. They might be in mourning for old Gilbert and the foxes at Durham House but people are pretty relieved they won't be out the day after Christmas knocking down their fences and galloping through their gardens.'

Howard looked thoroughly pleased with himself. Nearing seventy now he was still very strong and vigorous, hardened by his activities on the small area behind the house, where he grew vegetables, and fruit, and kept goats and chickens in the wooden hut he had built with his own hands so as to have a study away from the house while the children were growing up. Ironically, since they had, he had not written another of the novels which had made him fairly famous in the fifties and sixties, while Juliet, who had painted in the big kitchen during the period when her daughters were at home, putting down her brush to stir a stew on the Aga or find a missing kitten, was still at work, respected, though never very highly paid.

Annie sometimes wondered how her parents managed for money, even though they spent very little. Juliet referred to this obliquely when she warned Annie, 'There's a man staying at Durham House I'd like you to avoid if you go there. He's an academic called Dr Sam Anstruther and seems to be quite a friend of the family. An American. Ever since Jas casually mentioned we'd found an old suitcase upstairs with what looks like some stuff of Aunt Christian's in it he's been after us like a ferret down a rabbit hole. He works for

28

a large firm in New York which deals in old books and manuscripts. He wants to look over the contents and offer a price. Only we don't want to let him. Jas thought he was a medical doctor at first but it seems he's a doctor of literature.'

'Why don't you just tell him you can't be bothered?'

'I've tried, but he won't give up,' Howard said.

'What's in the case?' asked Annie.

'It looks like letters and manuscripts and a poem in Dorian Jefferson's handwriting,' Howard explained. 'We'd never have found it at all if I hadn't had to go through the attic to get at a leak in the roof. While I was scrabbling around up there I saw this small suitcase stuck behind a pipe. I think Dorian must have left it behind – he came down here to escape the bombing in 1942 after he'd been staying with Christian and her husband. He was drunk when he arrived and I think he must have been too drunk when he left to remember it.

'Christian and James had had a terrible time – he came down with two girls, one an art student and the other a WAAF who was overstaying her leave. They couldn't work out who was sleeping with who, they ate everything in the house and, obviously, food was very scarce at the time – they didn't even bring ration books. Then there was Dorian's drinking and vomiting all over the place, the WAAF declared she was pregnant, Christian was in despair – writing at the time, I suppose – and finally James, showing no courage or conscience at all, managed to persuade them to move off here. Dorian arrived without the girls and departed, if I recall, with my only two warm shirts. They were wool, and I missed them bitterly throughout the war years. I got some more towards the end but they were French and not as good as the others.' Howard never referred to his career in British Intelligence during the Second World War, nor to active service in France, before the invasion. Now he looked at his daughter and said, 'Annie. You're looking very thin. Juliet – cut her a sandwich. You're not eating enough.'

'I don't want a sandwich, really,' Annie said.

'Julian's left home, Howard,' his wife reminded him. 'I don't suppose she feels much like cooking. Have you forgotten what it's like when something like that happens?' She looked at Annie and said, 'I think he has. Extraordinary, considering how many times it's happened to him – well, I haven't forgotten. Is there another woman, Annie?'

'Yes. A client – Tamsin Bell.'

29

Juliet shook her head, 'Doesn't seem familiar.'

The room was very quiet. It was lit by a few lamps. On the walls Annie saw paintings and drawings by Juliet and others, on the big dresser, the collection of old ladles, from very small to huge, which she and Jasmine had played with when they were toddlers. The electric fire standing not far from them, on the flagstones, failed to warm and Annie was glad of her thermal vest and socks. Here in the silence she felt emptied and was not sure she welcomed the feeling.

When Juliet had wondered if she might have heard of Tamsin Bell she was not being unrealistic. In spite of thirty years of semi-rural life, the Brownings were still in touch with a larger world, though not, Annie reflected, Tamsin's or Julian's. Her parents had never got on with Julian. The Brownings had been astonished, on a visit to the Vanes, by the big house in Surrey, set in manicured grounds, with its own swimming pool. Howard had little in common with Julian's father, a well-off solicitor, and Juliet even less with Julian's mother. 'What does she do all day?' They had been surprised by Julian's job, producing artwork for large companies and advertising agencies, rejigging corporate images, even advising on the décor of offices. They had been amazed by the amount of profit in it, once the firm had got on its feet. Annie's claim, that the firm was only successful because Julian was so good at his job, had been received by them with astonishment. Annie had been furious with both of them as they expressed childlike interest and surprise which she knew to be masking distaste.

'Is this really a final break?' Howard was asking. 'People do come and go, after all.'

Along with the plain living and high thinking at Froggett's, Annie recalled, there had also been a lot of affairs, her parents' and everyone else's. When she was five a young woman had tried to hang herself in the orchard. Annie had found her dangling and choking and run in to tell her mother. They'd cut her down in time. 'She was in love with Howard,' Juliet had explained. It made no sense at the time. Now she frowned, uncertain whether the concept of coming and going, well understood at Froggett's, really applied to herself and Julian. She certainly thought Julian's departure had been final.

'Come and live here for a bit until you decide what to do,' Howard offered.

If Julian wanted to come back, thought Annie, he would never come to find her here, at Froggett's, where, he said, he was made to feel like a baby-eater or a Nazi. She said, 'Thanks – but I think I'd better start making a life for myself in London.'

She slept well in her cold room and woke with sun coming through the window. She'd needed to sleep but felt odd as she went downstairs, a jersey over her nightdress, as if her head were full of cold air and her legs full of lead. In the kitchen sat Jasmine, wearing make-up, in a smart tweed skirt, expensive country shoes and a cashmere twin set, her longish blonde hair held back with a barrette. Also at the table was a tall man in a tweed suit. His skin being more biscuit-coloured than red and his easy posture in his chair made Annie suspect he was the American book dealer.

Annie got some coffee from the stove, feeling embarrassed about her jersey and nightdress. Jasmine came over and kissed her cheek, whispering, 'Poor thing – we'll talk later.'

'You look like a picture in *Harper's*, Jas.'

'Have a roll,' Jasmine said, handing her one. 'Sorry – Home Baked, Day Three.'

How they'd longed for a sliced loaf from the baker's as children. How they'd hated Day Three bread, a unique combination of utter toughness and crumbliness. Annie succeeded in cutting it, tried to put butter on it. It crumbled.

Howard came through the back door, caught sight of the party, put down a bucket and left, saying he had to look at one of the goats.

'This is Sam Anstruther, Annie. He's a partner in Watney-Aspell in New York. They deal in old books and manuscripts. He's after some stuff in the attic they think belonged to Great-Aunt Christian. Sam – this is my sister, Annie Vane.'

'I'd love to take a look at the suitcase, Mrs Vane. Two American universities are already excited by the thought of some new writings by Christian Cunningham.'

'I couldn't work out what was in the case,' Annie said. 'I suppose somebody's looked?'

'They just opened and closed it,' Jasmine said. 'But they could see it wasn't the poet's socks – the luggage of the man who left it here in the first place—'

'*If* it was Dorian Jefferson who left it here,' Anstruther countered.

Anstruther seemed keen but cautious. The whole set-up – an old-fashioned house, the off-hand attitude of the residents to what,

31

in scholar's terms, was a crock of gold and which, if sold, would certainly pay for some central heating, perhaps a new house – could be some brilliant British con-trick. 'All I'd want to do initially is take a look, perhaps photocopy a page or two and consult my partners in New York.'

Jasmine seemed to support Anstruther in getting what he wanted, perhaps because he was her guest. Annie herself, although a professional trafficker in old documents like the records of Threpp Street Workhouse in the late nineteenth century, believed that if Howard and Juliet wanted to keep the suitcase, burn it in the garden or give it to the British Museum in their wills, it was entirely up to them. Nor did she see why Anstruther should come rolling into the kitchen without warning in the early morning, catching her unwashed in her nightclothes and making Howard hide in his shed with the goats.

Anstruther took his leave saying that Nigel had promised to show him a litter of hound puppies later on. After he had gone Annie asked, 'Did you have to bring him round at crack of dawn?'

'He's so keen on those old papers,' Jasmine said apologetically. 'And, after all, what does it matter? They'd probably realise a useful sum. Howard and Juliet could do with some extra money at their age.'

Annie was making more coffee as Juliet came in, saying, 'Has he gone?'

'It's like *The Aspern Papers*,' Annie said. Jasmine looked blank. Howard came in, followed by a goat, which he shooed out. 'Can I have a look at what's in the suitcase?' she said.

'If you really want to climb up to the attic.' Howard's tone was discouraging. 'I must say I wish I'd never found the thing.'

'You mean it's still up there?' Annie said, a trifle shocked.

'It's been perfectly all right up there for over forty years,' he said. 'The attic's as dry as a bone. I'm sure it really belongs to the literary executors, but I can't face them. One's that boring man from Oxford and the other's Juliet's nephew, Rupert.'

'He was an awful boy,' Jasmine remembered. 'He offered to drown Minnie's kittens in a bucket. I'd never met a boy who wanted to drown kittens before. Get some clothes on, Annie. Let's go for a walk.'

They went out into the garden, mostly lawn. At the bottom, on the right, was Howard's former study, in which a pregnant goat could be seen in a neat pen. Beyond the lawn the orchard began. Jasmine stopped under a tree.

'You look awful, Annie,' she said. 'You must have been having a rotten time. Why didn't you ring up? What have you been doing? Just sitting there?'

'More or less.'

Jasmine Fellows, her eyes very blue in her tanned face, looked at her sister and shook her head. 'Oh dear. What happened?'

As they walked on in bright sunshine, through the orchard and down the slope to the field below, Annie told her.

'Got you to put your job on the computer beforehand!' Jasmine exclaimed. 'What a bastard!'

'I'm still trying to believe it. How can a man who's behaving like a perfectly normal person be concealing so much?'

'Nature of the beast,' Jasmine replied. 'You've always been a bit naïve. I mean, you always had the brains, but not the guile. I got that, to make up for the shortage upstairs.' She tapped her golden head.

They had reached a stretch of pasture below the big house and were strolling across it. Almost a mile away, past the fields, gentle hills rose, green, scattered with clumps of bracken and gorse, glittering as the sun struck the moisture on grass and bushes.

'Coffee,' offered Jasmine, gesturing to the left, where the walls of the estate met the field. Annie nodded.

'Nigel wanted to buy Froggett's,' Jasmine observed. 'You know Bernard's father was annoyed when old Froggett sold the house to Dad instead of him. Nigel was thinking now Howard and Juliet were getting older they might like to move to somewhere more convenient, with proper heating. They refused, of course.'

'Was he annoyed?'

'He guessed they wouldn't accept.'

The two women went through a tall iron gate set in the high brick wall. Inside, they found themselves in a small wood, from which a winding path led them to the lake. Skirting it, they walked to the long lawn in front of Durham House which was L-shaped, built of whitish stone, with a terrace running the length of the longer part of the L. Old steps led up to the terrace and french windows through which they entered the house. Crossing the dining room where a long polished table stood empty, they went through the hall and into a small sitting room, in which a fire burned.

'Mary's re-covered the chairs,' observed Jasmine, sinking into a small chair, covered by fresh needlepoint.

'Hours of work,' Annie said, sitting down gingerly on the chair opposite. 'I feel I oughtn't to sit on this in such old trousers.'

A woman in an overall came in. 'Coffee, please, Mrs Bleasdale,' Jasmine requested.

Annie pulled a face. 'I can't get over all this grandeur.'

'It's got its disadvantages,' Jasmine told her, evidently sobered by some thought. Then she grinned. 'But I must say I enjoy it. Howard and Juliet can't understand – they must be the only people in Great Britain who can make out it's immoral to marry the man you love, who also happens to be very rich, and live in luxury. Of course, they earn their livings by being uncommercial so in fact being uncommercial is like a business for them – only they won't see it that way. And they can't see either that a lot of people don't want to live like they do—'

'Your side can't see why Howard and Juliet do what they do . . .' Annie said judiciously.

'No. They think they're sissies and cowards who won't face the world as it is.'

'I wish someone would tell me what this "world" people talk about is,' Annie said despondently. 'Where is it? What's it like? Everyone informs me I don't live in it – even Julian blamed me for that.'

'Well, he would, wouldn't he?' said Jasmine. 'He had to find some stick to beat you with. Still, I suppose he really is out there in it, the world where it's dog eat dog and so forth—'

Annie stared at her, thinking Jasmine must have learned this philosophy from Nigel. Then Jasmine broke off, asking, 'What's she like – Julian's woman?'

'She's the person he should have married in the first place,' Annie found herself saying.

Mrs Bleasdale chose this moment to bring in the coffee and some chocolate digestive biscuits. Jasmine poured the coffee and helped herself to a biscuit. She looked at Annie as she handed her a cup. 'What do you mean – should have married her?'

Annie was still startled by what she'd said. 'Well, I suppose she's more like him. Anyway, she's the kind who's always known as "terrific fun". You know, "Tamsin's coming – she's terrific fun", "Of course, Tamsin's a terrific hoot". They're all japes and anecdotes and telling everyone what fun it all is. I thought she was aggressive, but perhaps that's because when we met she was after my husband, although I didn't know.'

'You didn't put up much of a fight,' remarked Jasmine, eating

34

another biscuit. 'Oh dear, Annie, it's awful. What would you do if he suddenly came back?'

'I'd be delighted,' Annie said simply.

'It's not fair,' moaned Jasmine. 'I'd like to strangle him. I hope you're doing all the sensible things – got a solicitor and all that.'

'Sort of,' Annie said.

'Here—' Jasmine said, leaping up. 'Come and give me a hand with the flowers. I've got to check the dining room, drawing room and so forth to make sure all's in order for another bout of gracious hospitality. Nigel's driven the guests over to the Watkins's stud farm but they'll soon be back.'

'Who are the guests?' asked Annie, arranging laurel and chrysanthemums in an ornate vase.

'A couple of German businessmen, somebody from the National Theatre in search of some backing – and Sam Anstruther, of course. I'm counting on you for Boxing Day – there'll be more then.'

Annie eyed her flower arrangement now on a small side table in the dining room. Leaves and branches, and a few flowers lay on the floor beside her.

'What a mess,' said Jasmine. 'You're far worse at it than I am. I wish Mary was here. She's away visiting one of her sisters.'

'I'd better go,' Annie said. 'I don't want to bump into Sam Anstruther again today.'

She walked back to Froggett's across the peaceful fields.

After Christmas Annie knew it was time she went back to London to sort out her affairs, make plans, find a job. Perhaps, too, she thought, Julian would get in touch.

She packed and Howard drove her to the station past the static, frosty bushes and frozen stems of grass by the roadside. The fields were full of frozen pools of ice for the weather had turned much colder. Her father, in his leather coat and wellingtons, stood with her on the platform as the train came in. He looked older, and anxious.

'I'll come any time,' he told her. 'Do look after yourself, Annie.' She got into the train, leaned out to wave to him as it pulled away, and he waved back.

That was the night when she found Melanie Pickering in her doorway. Next day they had taken the long trip to Clapton, but found that Melanie's uncle and aunt had moved out, gone to Gravesend, said the new tenant, but without leaving an address.

35

'I expect we can track them down,' Annie had told Melanie encouragingly but now, two weeks later, after many phone calls and enquiries, they still had no clue about where Jim and Muriel Allardyce were living; everything seemed to be drifting and Annie was becoming despondent.

3

A Business Offer is Made

The lunchtime rush over, George's was now empty except for Arnold, finishing his tea and considering if it was time for the library, Annie and Melanie, wondering if a private detective would be able to help in the search for Melanie's Uncle Jim and a young woman who'd arrived late and now sat at a table in the cloudy window watching her toddler eating beans and some sausages, which she'd cut up in small pieces.

George Kypragoras, proprietor of the café, came out of the kitchen and shouted to the young woman, 'You're looking very happy today, Vanessa.'

'No wonder – I've just spent four hours at the DSS for nothing,' she called back, 'with a boy who hasn't had a bite since breakfast. Geoff been in?'

'No, Vanessa, he hasn't and if he had I wouldn't serve him.' Then he added, 'Hey – I need someone to keep an eye on things for a few hours while I go to see my solicitor. Business to discuss. You do it? There's a fiver in it.'

Vanessa looked up hopefully, then shook her head. 'I'll have to collect Joanne from school at four o'clock,' she said.

To Annie's surprise, Melanie spoke up. 'Excuse me – I can manage while you're gone.'

Head on one side, George Kypragoras considered. Then he said, 'No. Insurance.'

'All right,' said Melanie. 'I'll collect the girl for a quid. I've got two young brothers – you wouldn't have to worry.'

Annie was impressed by Melanie's speed and initiative and also by Vanessa's rapid, speculative glance.

37

'Or,' Melanie suggested, 'Annie and me can mind the café, while you go and get the girl. You can give us a quid or one of those big tins of beans you've got out there in the kitchen.'

'Sort it out between you,' George said, starting to take off his overall. He went into the kitchen and came back in a black overcoat.

'We don't need to be paid,' Annie said.

'Don't we?' countered Melanie. 'Pardon me but I think we do. Anyway it's something I fancy doing – serving teas and suchlike.' She went up to the counter and asked George for three more teas, daring him, as he took some money from the till and put it in his wallet, to ask for payment. But all he said was, 'I don't want my café left unattended,' and departed quickly saying he would be back by five.

Melanie took one of the teas over to Vanessa and said, 'Excuse me, but haven't I seen you in Rutherford Street?'

'Yes – I live at number forty-two,' said Vanessa. 'I think I've seen you.'

'I'm living temporarily with Mrs Vane at number twenty-seven. My name's Melanie. What's yours?'

'Vanessa,' she replied. 'You're from up north?' Everyone knew northerners were like this, a bit pushy. She nodded to Annie, 'That was you at the dentist's about a week ago, wasn't it?'

Melanie looked from one to the other. Two women who lived in the same small street and they barely recognised each other. It seemed incredible.

'That's right,' Annie agreed. 'Melanie had an abscess. Mr Rothko just about saved the tooth.'

'Half my front tooth fell out on Christmas Day. Nice, wasn't it? I could've screamed.' Vanessa looked from Annie to Melanie and back again. She couldn't understand what the set-up was. Melanie with her northern accent and cheap clothes didn't look as if she could have anything to do with Annie Vane. She recalled old Mrs Hodges next door telling her that on Christmas Eve she'd seen two men loading furniture from number twenty-seven into a small van. One of the men was the owner of the house – Annie's husband, that must be.

'And who're you?' Melanie asked Alec, who was sitting on his mother's knee. He looked at her cautiously. He was upset. His father didn't come home, his mother was unhappy, his sister was saying his dad had gone away and wasn't coming back, a girl

38

in her class at school had told her but he wasn't to tell Mum. But he'd forgotten not to say, so he'd told her and that hadn't made it better, but worse, because she'd cried. He'd almost forgotten it all now but he'd been feeling his mother's grief for weeks, like a big, dark cloud hanging over everything. And he missed his dad.

'He's Alec,' said Vanessa.

They both looked depressed, reflected Melanie, continuing, 'Quiet little chap, aren't you? Bet you've got a lovely smile, though, when you try? Eh? Why don't you show us?'

Vanessa began to feel tired of this extrovert thirteen-year-old who had volunteered for the small job George had offered her.

'Oh dear,' Melanie said to Alec. 'Never mind. Keep trying. It'll come out right in the end.'

Annie noted that for much of the time they'd been together Melanie must have been subduing a lively personality, as if she, Annie, were a teacher, a doctor, someone in authority.

Suddenly, Alec confided in Melanie, 'My dad's gone away.'

Vanessa rushed in. 'Kids,' she said, 'they'll say anything, won't they?'

Annie saw tears beginning in her eyes.

'Is it time to go and collect your little girl?' said Melanie.

'Not for half an hour,' Vanessa replied, getting up. She doubted if Annie had taken in the information Alec had imparted. The girl had at least shown a little tact in the situation. From behind the counter, Alec beside her but invisible, she said, 'I suppose I'm only here to guard the till, really. Still, I might as well wash out this display cabinet while I'm here.' She put Alec at a table in front of the counter and took some toy cars from her bag. 'Here, Alec, play with these for a bit and keep out of Mummy's way.'

'Where's Joanne?' he asked.

'I keep on telling you. She's had to go back to school. She'll be back in a little while,' replied Vanessa. It hadn't helped when Joanne had gone back at the end of the holidays. She was alone with Alec in the house now and sometimes she wasn't up to dealing with him. She was always telling him to keep quiet and sometimes her nerves were so stretched that she shouted at him. She regretted it later, but that didn't help. Her mother took him occasionally, but had told her Cherry couldn't help, being so occupied with her own home and family.

Melanie produced a comic from her pocket and began to read. Annie returned to her thoughts. The building society statement she'd phoned for had not yet arrived but the bank statement had turned up showing that Julian had withdrawn £1800 from the account before Christmas, leaving her with a little under £250. Imagining he might have made a swift transfer into the account of Vane Graphics, to cover an emergency – although, she thought, it was some time since the company had had to operate on that basis – she rang the bank and asked for a copy of the company account to be sent to her, to find that the manager had instructions that in future the company accounts were to be seen only by Mr Vane and that he understood she had resigned her directorship. If Julian had emptied the joint account, she'd better go to him and ask for the return of a £10,000 legacy she'd received two years before, and given him for computers for the firm. She felt numb. He hadn't been in touch since she'd returned and when she'd screwed herself up to ring the firm – she didn't know where he was living and didn't like to ask people who might know – she'd been told by the switchboard operator that he was at a meeting. 'I'm very sorry,' the woman had said, sounding as if she were sorry about more than Julian's temporary unavailability.

Annie was now struggling not to believe facts which were adding up to a conclusion she couldn't face – Julian had sacked her, taken nearly everything from the bank account and come round with a van to remove things from the house when he knew she was away. At the back of her mind she worried about the mortgage. What was left in the bank wouldn't meet the payments and the situation might be even worse than that. She'd have to find a job soon. She could borrow a few hundred pounds from her parents or from Jasmine, but her parents had little money, she knew, and Jasmine only her allowance from Nigel. What did people in her position do? Try the BBC, publishing, apply for an academic post? Such things would take time and she knew that vacancies were few. Times were hard and she had no experience. She supposed she might get a teaching qualification and work in a school, but, again, that would take time and, little as she was prepared to confront the fact that Julian had apparently asset-stripped her, she had a sense that her need for money in the short term meant she could not afford to delay, unless she could get her £10,000 back fairly quickly.

Vanessa, having swabbed out the display cabinet, started on the counter. Annie went to the pay phone by the counter, rang Vane Graphics, asked to speak to Julian and was told he was out. She sighed and went back to the table. Inertia hung over the café.

Arnold, silent until now, shouted from his corner to Vanessa, 'The place could do with a coat of paint, if you ask me.'

'You can say that again,' Vanessa observed.

Annie went on thinking. What could she do about Melanie? She'd have to go home. It could take months to locate the famous Uncle Jim, if they ever did. Melanie had sent a postcard to her mother saying she was all right, but that wouldn't console her much. Even now the police were probably trying to find her.

Melanie stood up. 'We ought to go now,' she said.

'That's right,' agreed Vanessa. 'Do you know the Celia Bracewell School, Tregear Road? Off Warrington Street, near the railway bridge?'

'I know Warrington Road,' Annie said and she and Melanie set off down the darkening streets of Foxwell to the school. Children screamed out. Melanie had no trouble in identifying Joanne, catching her outside the school door. 'You Joanne? Your mum's minding George's café and she wants us to get you down there.'

'Who're you?' asked the small girl, staring at them suspiciously. She wore a pink anorak. Her fair hair was untidy.

'I'm Annie Vane. I'm a neighbour of yours.'

'Not without asking my mum,' Joanne said firmly.

A teacher was found and a phone call made. 'Would you ask Mrs Doyle to come and see me,' said the teacher, a plump young man.

'You been getting into trouble?' enquired Melanie as they walked through the school gates.

'No,' said Joanne defiantly.

'What did you do, then?'

'I hit a girl – she hit me first. I always have an ice cream on the way home.'

'Not in this weather.'

'Crisps?' negotiated Joanne.

'All right,' Melanie agreed.

'D'you like Michael Jackson?'

'No. I'm more into heavy metal,' Melanie said firmly.

When they reached the café it was crowded with market traders who had knocked off for tea and a warm-up on this cold, dark afternoon. Vanessa gave Melanie a pound. 'Thanks,' she said.

'Any time,' responded Melanie, pocketing it.

Melanie and Annie walked home. 'I know you're going to tell me I've got to go back,' Melanie said as they stood at the traffic lights. She glanced at the Victorian town hall, looming over Foxwell High Street. 'Goodbye, bright lights,' she added.

Annie was relieved she'd mentioned it first. 'I can't see any other way. And your mother must be frantic.'

'I miss my brothers, too,' Melanie said. 'Nobody else would.'

When they got home Annie tried Julian again and was told he was in a meeting. 'I've left him your message, Mrs Vane,' said the switchboard operator, irritation creeping into her voice.

Annie put the phone down and muttered, 'I doubt if you'd have a job now without the efforts I put in when the firm began.'

Melanie said, 'I think you'd best go round there and have it out with him.'

The winter evening wore on slowly. Melanie, her dream of running away to a new life falling to pieces, was glum and went out for a Mars bar. Annie was trying not to believe that Julian, now he had put an end to the marriage, did not want to see or speak to her. Later, she lay in bed reading, while Melanie watched television alone downstairs. She heard people coming home from pubs, a row between a man and a woman in Rutherford Street, the slam of a car door, the woman crying 'Bastard!' as it drove away. Melanie was right, she decided. If Julian wouldn't see her, she'd have to make him.

Next morning Annie left Melanie sleeping and walked down the High Street already clogged with traffic and people hurrying to work. Fifteen minutes later she reached Vane Graphics. The offices occupied an early Victorian house with big arched windows, between the bus station and a large council estate.

She stood at the porticoed front door and pushed the bell. Inside, the receptionist pressed a buzzer and the door opened. Annie, who had calculated that at this hour, just before the staff arrived, the receptionist would assume she was just someone arriving for work, charged in. Pausing to say, 'Hallo, Jessica' she was met by an alarmed face under a mop of artfully tousled black hair and a voice saying warningly, 'Annie—'

'Sorry, Jessica,' she called, dashing past the desk and beginning to race up the elegant curved staircase to the floor upstairs, where Julian's office was. 'I've got to see him,' she called down as she went. 'He's left me in the lurch.' As she rounded the corner of the stairs and walked speedily along the carpeted hall to Julian's white-painted, brass-knobbed door, she thought the phrase she'd just used, in the heat of the moment, summed up the situation better than all her other thoughts, weeks of them, could have.

When she pushed open the door Julian stood up behind his mahogany desk – everything at Vane Graphics was in keeping, as far as possible, with the style of the building.

'Annie!' he said, startled and not pleased.

Annie sat down. 'I've got to talk to you, Julian. I don't think it's fair to avoid me as you seem to have been doing—'

'I think it's better if we use solicitors—' Julian began.

'No!' she exclaimed. 'It's not. We've been married for five years. I think we ought to be able to sort out ordinary things without solicitors. There are several simple issues, one being, why have you taken all the money from the joint account? What were you thinking of?'

'Setting up a new home is not cheap,' he told her. 'You'll get your half back, of course.'

He was wearing pale trousers and a cream shirt. His fashionable tie was slightly loosened and he looked the picture of the captain of the First Eleven in an old school story. Steel true Jack Hardacre, she thought, an hour to play and the match to win – yet he was beginning to be too old for his boyish look and his blue eyes were now a little hard. There were small lines developing round them too. Suddenly Annie felt slightly afraid.

The telephone rang and he answered it. 'I'm in a meeting at the moment, Brian. Can I ring you back?'

'I'm not a meeting, Julian,' she said. 'I'm your wife. When do you think you can let me have the money back? I can't cover the mortgage. I'll barely be able to cover the bills. I've been told I'm no longer a director.'

There was a pause. Then Julian said, 'Plainly, we couldn't go on working together in the circumstances. I imagine your family can give you some help in the short term. Jasmine's not exactly on her uppers. This situation's temporary. I have to keep going or, at the end of the day, there'll be nothing. You do see that, don't you?' he concluded, on the tough note he used when dealing with difficult business problems.

'I was hoping I wouldn't have to point out that we built up this firm together. We worked together—' Annie began to feel very tired. 'That's it, then, is it? You've left me, left the bills, cleaned out the bank account, taken the furniture – Julian – what do you think you're playing at?'

'Do we have to have a scene?' he asked.

She shook her head. 'This isn't a scene but it looks to me as if, thanks to you, I'll have to see a solicitor. In the meantime the firm owes me the ten thousand pounds Aunt Margaret left me, which I put in when we needed computers.'

'I assumed that was a gift,' he said too quickly.

'You've thought all this out, Julian,' she exclaimed. 'You don't plan to return that money, or any of it. You don't feel anything any more, so you've decided you can do as you like. For God's sake . . .'

She expected him to soften, to explain why he was behaving like this. Instead he looked at her firmly, almost pityingly, as though she'd made some ridiculous claim, bound to be refused.

She stood up. 'This is dreadful, Julian. It's dreadful,' was all she could say. She got up and walked unsteadily to his door, opened it and went out.

After she had gone Julian sat down behind his desk. His shoulders bowed. He stared into space for a moment, then, elbows on the desk, he put his head in his hands. 'Oh God,' he murmured. 'Oh, good God.' He heard the door slam behind Annie. The phone rang. He picked it up. Hardly able to speak he said, 'Yes. Let me call you back on that in half an hour.' He picked the phone up again and said, 'Jessica. Make some black coffee and bring it up.'

Back on the street, Annie walked rapidly, her long thin legs eating up the pavement as if she were trying to escape something. She wiped her eyes as she went into the house, not wanting Melanie to see her so upset. A note on the kitchen table informed her that Melanie had gone down to George's Café to ask for work. 'I need to get my fair to Gravsend,' it read. Annie stood in the middle of the room, sighing. Melanie must be made to go home and to school. The note proved she needed more education, not to be wandering about London, asking virtual strangers for work. She hadn't said much about the home she'd run away from but Annie had the impression of a bullying father and a mother managing on little money, too ground down to put up much resistance to him. Melanie was just the kind of girl who could be led astray, as it used to be termed in Threpp Street in the nineteenth century. With no idea of her own rights, how could she fight for them? Now, it seemed, she was going to try to get to Gravesend alone to search for her missing uncle, an unrealistic plan, if ever there was one. In fact, the whole situation was crazy for them both, Annie decided.

She determined to find Melanie at the café, bring her back, tell her she must ring her mother to say she was coming home. She, Annie, would have to go with her to make sure she arrived. She set off for the café and, as she walked, opened the letter which had been on the mat when she came in. It hardly surprised her now to discover that somehow Julian had managed, without her knowledge, to bump up the existing mortgage by another £20,000. The firm wasn't short of money, she knew, so either he was using the money for expansion or buying himself a house or flat. She pushed the letter into her bag and hurried along.

There were a few customers in the café but no one behind the counter. Then Melanie's indignant voice came from the kitchen. 'All right. All right. I've only got one pair of hands.'

'Only asking, love,' one of the customers said, turning round as Melanie came from the kitchen with two plates of sausages, beans, bacon and chips for the man and his friend. She put them down at their table.

Annie had had enough. Julian had pushed her away, there was a letter from the building society in her bag, she was cold, tired and her hair was falling down over the collar of her coat.

'Melanie!' she almost shouted. 'What do you think you're playing at?'

'Don't start a row in front of the customers,' she said calmly. 'I left you a note, didn't I?'

'I've been worried about you,' exclaimed Annie. 'And I can't imagine what the owner's thinking about. This is illegal. You're far too young—'

'I'm only trying to help,' Melanie explained. 'And there's no law against helping out . . .'

A woman with a bulging plastic bag came in and sat down wearily. Melanie, looking very capable in a white overall, served her with a cup of tea. Now she walked over to Annie and asked, 'You been crying?' Annie's shoulders bowed. She sighed.

Vanessa came into the café with Alec and was just in time to catch this exchange. Obviously Annie was in a bit of trouble and now the girl had done something stupid and put her in a panic.

'Sit down.' She took Annie's arm. 'You'd better fetch her a cup of tea,' she said to Melanie. She guided Annie, who now felt dizzy and sick, to an empty table. 'Are you all right?' she enquired. Annie nodded. Vanessa released Alec from the buggy and sat him down.

'Had a bit of a shock?' she asked.

Annie nodded again, reluctantly. She wasn't enjoying all this solicitude and she decided she hated George's Café, with its yellowing walls dripping with condensation, the hideous tiles with blue mermaids on them behind the counter, the permanent smell of frying. In a flash she recognised her own previous clear-headedness and confidence, and her present state of uncertainty. She was changing for the worse, she thought. The moment went and she was left on her plastic chair, looking at her cup of very brown tea, nervously brought by Melanie. It steamed in front of her. She felt sick again and an enormous pain seemed to fill her chest. The love she thought Julian had for her had been sucked from her atmosphere The vacuum had been filled with a thin gas, made up of betrayal and indifference, and trying to breathe it was making her weak.

'I'm all right really,' she told Vanessa.

'I'm sorry I gave you all that worry—' said Melanie, still hovering.

'Not your fault,' muttered Annie.

'What's the matter, love?' asked Vanessa.

Annie took a deep breath. 'I've just found out my husband increased the mortgage on the house without telling me. He won't pay and I can't. They'll expect me to sell the house now but I don't want to. Not now, anyway.'

Vanessa said practically, 'All you've got to do is go to them and explain, and get them to put everything on hold for a time, until you're straight. That's what you should do.'

'Are you sure?' Annie was dubious.

'A friend of mine did that,' Vanessa said. 'And maybe you should see a solicitor.'

'I haven't been able to believe it,' Annie said in a low voice. She didn't explain what she hadn't been able to believe, and didn't need to.

'I know,' Vanessa agreed grimly. 'It's like being suddenly murdered.'

'How are you managing?' Annie asked Vanessa.

Vanessa shrugged. 'Much as I expected. First the DSS have to check my husband's actually gone and this isn't some kind of a dodge to get money out of them. Then they have to check I haven't got money salted away in some secret bank account, I haven't got the Crown jewels hidden under the bed. I'm filling in form after form – it could take weeks, if not months – and when

I get it it's not going to be enough, naturally. In the meanwhile they tide me over with a miserable thirty quid payment which'll just about cover the food.'

Vanessa's voice rose. She didn't care who was listening. 'I ask you – I've got two kids, both needing shoes – I've sent the gas bill to my husband but I don't know if he's going to pay it. Then they tell me my husband should be supporting me and the children. Would I be here asking for money, I say, if he was? I'm supposed to take him to court, they say. He'll kill me, I tell them. Oh, you think he'll offer violence, says the woman behind the counter, getting interested now. I tell them I don't know – I don't want to find out. You'll have to see the legal aid and get an injunction if he's threatening you, she says. I tell her, look, I'm here because I haven't got any money for my children, that's all, the rest comes later. I say, I know you're paid to make it as hard as possible. Is there anyone in your family who can assist you, she asks me. I say, that's not the point. I'm entitled to this money – then she tells me to keep my voice down, she can't help me if I get emotional, i.e., they'll call the police.' Vanessa sagged.

'It's humiliating and I have to go through it because of the kids,' she said, looking at Alec, who now stood beside her, holding her skirt. 'I don't know,' she said. 'Sometimes I dream of killing him.'

A small round woman in her seventies came spryly into the café in black court shoes, a plum-coloured coat, with a big red and blue paisley shawl pinned over her shoulders. She wore a large royal blue felt hat. Her small lined face was heavily made up. She nodded briefly to the unemployed man and sat down. She asked for a coffee, which Melanie poured, and a Danish pastry from the plastic-fronted cabinet on the counter. Melanie served her the coffee and bun and came over to Annie and Vanessa. 'It's all very well,' she said, 'but I don't know how long you two are going to sit in this grotty caff crying in your tea. That can get to be a habit, you know. Look at that poor little boy you've got, he's going to start crying himself in a minute. My auntie used to say my mum was addicted to crying like a junkie – couldn't give it up now, whatever happened. That's my auntie Muriel, my uncle Jim's wife,' she added in explanation. She returned to the counter, followed by a sharp look from the woman in the plum-coloured coat.

Sighing, Vanessa said, 'She wouldn't understand. I feel like a bit of me's been torn away. And how can I help thinking about him and that woman – hallo, George,' she said on a different

47

note as the café owner came in. George merely nodded and went into the back of the café. From there he began to shout over the phone, in Greek, silencing with his passion all other conversations. The shouting stopped. Evidently he put down the phone. Seconds later he began to speak to someone else, also in Greek, in a more moderate tone. Then he began to get angry again.

'Spot of trouble there,' observed Arnold, the unemployed man in the overcoat, to the lady in the plum coat.

'So it seems,' she responded repressively in a clear voice which had traces of a middle-European accent.

George re-emerged from the kitchen, his arms raised in rage and despondency. 'Families!' he exclaimed. Talking to no one in particular he went on, 'When everything's OK you can't get rid of them. When you need them, everybody's got a train to catch.' Nobody was prepared to quarrel with this statement. To Arnold he said, 'Don't tell me I'm wrong.'

Arnold said, 'You're not wrong, George.'

The phone rang and George went back to the kitchen to answer it. He spoke again in Greek explaining, cajoling, protesting.

Vanessa threw her head back. 'I'd better make a move. I'm so tired, I feel as if I've been awake for weeks.' The two women looked at each other. Vanessa's pale skin had a greenish tinge, her blonde hair was scraped back over her skull and secured in a pony tail with a pink plastic slide on a piece of elastic. Annie, her long dark hair falling all over her collar, her long face sallow with big brown smudges under her brown eyes, hardly looked any better. They smiled at each other.

Annie called out, 'Melanie – I'm going back. Look – if you want to go to Gravesend we'll go together. I'll borrow my sister's car. Do you want to do that?'

Melanie looked doubtfully at Annie. There was a final burst of Greek in the kitchen and George came out into the café, an expression of determination on his face.

'Vanessa,' he said, 'I'd like to speak to you seriously. Excuse me,' he said to Annie. Annie stood up. George waved her down. 'No – no – listen. You can help me persuade her. Vanessa – this might seem a little bit of an unusual request but I'm taking my family back to Cyprus. It may be for a long time, or a short one. I don't know. Maybe I'd like to get my daughters out of this place, this town. I don't trust it any more, don't trust the people. Now it seems the family can't help me and I need to keep this place open

48

while I'm away. Might be for ever. Might not. Now, I know you need a job, feed the kids, all that. And I need an honest manager. What do you think?'

'Are you serious?' asked Vanessa.

'This is my business. I've had it thirty years. Course I'm serious.'

'I couldn't do this all on my own, George,' said Vanessa, appalled. 'I've got the kids to take care of. This is a full-time job. I can't get Alec in a nursery till Easter at the earliest. I've got so many problems—'

'That's what they all tell me,' George said disgustedly. 'I've got to keep this place open and who can do it? Who can I trust? The family won't help. Everybody tells me problems they've got. If I don't get to Cyprus pretty soon I don't know what's happening to my father's property. Round here, who is there to rely on? I look round and I see everybody's on the fiddle. Anybody reliable, they've got two jobs already to keep going. Commitments,' he said irritatedly. 'Everybody's got those suddenly. Commitments. Look, Vanessa – this is a nice little café. You can make a profit if you run it right. I've brought up a family on it with hard work. Temporary manager. You got to get a job, anyway. I know what's happening. Two of Geoff's workmen were here yesterday talking – you'll have to take the children to your mum's some of the time—'

'She won't do it, not regular.' Vanessa told him. 'Do you think I haven't asked? She says it's too much at her age—'

Melanie leaned over and said, 'I can help out.'

Annie was becoming accustomed to Melanie. She intervened quickly, 'You can't. For one thing, you're going to have to go home. Secondly, even if you didn't you'd have to go to school. Thirdly, you're planning to go to Gravesend.'

Vanessa was looking at Melanie speculatively. George chipped in, 'This girl can do anything, that's my opinion. Go to school, go to Gravesend, help Vanessa with the children, take over behind the counter from time to time—'

'There are *laws* governing what happens to thirteen-year-old girls,' declared Annie.

Vanessa and George, she noticed, were staring at her as if she were some rare animal. 'There are,' she repeated.

'Then,' George said encouragingly to Vanessa, 'get your mum to help from time to time—'

'Come on, George,' said Vanessa, 'you've given us an ear-bashing about your family – what makes you think mine's any different? Look,' she said, 'I'd like to help but—'

He spread his hands. 'Help, then,' he appealed. 'Three, four months.'

'I couldn't do it,' Vanessa said. 'There's the accounts—'

'You could learn—'

'No I couldn't, George. Don't tell me what I can do and what I can't do. I'm hopeless at money. Anything to do with figures is out of the question.'

'You're intelligent,' he said.

Annie had been listening and was intrigued. 'I'll help with the books,' she said.

Melanie, seeing Annie apparently trying to get a foothold in the café, chipped in competitively, 'You told me you only knew about history.'

'I ran a business,' said Annie mildly. 'When Julian started the firm there were only two of us and since he was the creative person I dealt with everything else. The firm's still there,' she paused, 'though I'm not.'

'You're honest,' George stated. 'Anyway my cousin does the VAT.'

'There you are then,' said Annie.

'All cash business here,' he said cautiously.

'So I would think,' Annie agreed coolly. They gave each other a long stare. Satisfied that she understood him, he turned to Vanessa. There was a long pause. In the middle of it the elderly woman in the plum coat got up and left.

Vanessa, Melanie and Annie all looked at each other.

'I could perhaps look at the books on Vanessa's behalf,' Annie suggested.

'Now – if you would help her generally . . .' hinted George.

'I might,' Annie agreed. 'If the business would stand it.'

'Then – what's the answer?' asked George.

Vanessa shrugged, 'OK, George – you're on.'

4

The Borough of Kenton with Particular Reference to Foxwell and Little Plastic Trees

Like all places, whether nation, geographical area, town or city, the London boroughs are not just labelled spots where people reside but over the years have accumulated round themselves a clutch of ideas, images and received ideas about themselves. If, for example, the name 'Bath' is mentioned, it evokes thoughts of Regency terraces, the Romans, a mineral spa. 'Bradford' may bring thoughts of wool, satanic mills, rows of terraced houses, the Industrial Revolution. 'The Cotswolds' and there is rolling English countryside, lovely villages, the sheep grazing peacefully (their wool destined to end up in 'Bradford'). These simple impressions may not be right, they will certainly mean little to people who actually live in these places when they think about their own homes, but they exist. So, it is with the London boroughs – Westminster stands for wealth and dignity, Camden for the loony left, Brent for the loonier, Hackney as the most deprived London borough, whether it is or not. Like these places Kenton is not just a London borough inhabited by a quarter of a million people but an image, a dream, part fact and part fiction. Publicly, Kenton competes with Camden for the title of the most loony, doctrinally dictated borough in London and with Hackney for its crime rate. Officially declared nuclear-free it also holds the record for the most prosecutions taken out against the police on the grounds of police brutality.

Kenton has two MPs, one Labour, in the southern constituency,

51

one Conservative representing the prosperous suburbs to the north. The borough has had a Labour council since World War II when men in shabby suits, remembering their bent-backed mothers toiling over stone sinks in terraced houses, hanging out laundry in freezing-cold yards, recalling overcrowded kitchens and baths in front of the kitchen fire, decided to clear the slums, so tore them down, filling the spaces formerly occupied by rows of cramped houses and the gaps left by bombs dropped during Word War II, with huge estates, which incorporated many high-rise buildings. When the estates had just been architects' models studied by councillors they were white and gleaming, with little green plastic trees and green plastic open spaces; paradise for the people. Everyone would have a modern kitchen, a bathroom, an airing cupboard and enough bedrooms. Later, of course, it turned out that they should have given the matter more thought, asked their wives for comments and checked the specifications more closely. Somehow the big estates, dream of the men who wanted to clear away the slums for ever, became something that another generation in turn wanted to clear away for ever themselves.

Kenton's problems as a local authority are numerous. They are rate-capped, so that they can't maintain services set up in more prosperous days; there are a quarter of a million people living there but in some areas a fifth of the working population is unemployed; the borough covers approximately fifteen square miles from the River Thames, running south. Central government hates it, punishes it whenever possible and would abolish it, if it could. The leader of the council is fifty-seven-year-old Joe Banks, one of the old guard. His deadly rival is thirty-six-year-old 'Red Les' Dowell. The Mayor of Kenton is Mrs Roxanne Fuller, who is black, a lay preacher, a mother of four and a primary school teacher.

The headquarters of Kenton Council is, of course, the ornate late-Victorian building standing at the top of Foxwell High Street, separating two streams of traffic which flow out to the borough's more prosperous suburban areas. Foxwell itself is a by-word, having suffered two riots where the nation watched television in horror, seeing fires, the police battling with the rioters in streets at night, seeing looting and stalled ambulances and fire engines trying to get through to help. After the first riot Foxwell police station was rebuilt as a fortress and after the second funds were produced to build a sports centre and plant trees in the streets which had been the focus of the riots.

Officially, Foxwell had been regenerated but, pore over the models as you like, no amount of little houses, sports centres and plastic trees can fill the civic coffers, produce money for repairing public housing or schools, produce jobs for the population and pay their bills. Only children playing with a model village on the living-room carpet are allowed to go on believing in that sort of dream.

5

Love, Money and Revenge

At eight o'clock one Monday morning in mid-January, as the market traders set up their stalls, tugging at struts, hauling canvas canopies, and as the survivors of the night before dragged themselves along the pavements heading for the nearest shop where they could pick up a bottle of cider, Annie swung the 'Closed' sign on George's Café round to read 'Open' and dashed back into the kitchen, where Vanessa was keeping an eye on a cargo of sausages under the grill and bacon sizzling in a huge frying pan.

The day before they'd cleaned the place from top to bottom, throwing out bucket after bucket of water stained with grease and tobacco smoke. Annie claimed George hadn't cleaned the café since he'd taken it over back in the fifties. Vanessa thought he gave it a good clean-up annually. What they were seeing now was normal wear and tear. 'I can remember when he decorated it,' she said nostalgically. 'I was in the fourth form – used to come in with my mates.' Nevertheless, when they had finished, the café still looked seedy.

'*We* know it's clean, that's the main thing,' consoled Vanessa. 'And the punters wouldn't thank us for turning it into the Café Royal. Still, if I'd known about the state of this oven before I wouldn't have drunk a glass of water in here, let alone had anything to eat.'

Annie, who was scrubbing the floor, bringing the lino tiles up to a magnificent blue, stood up, stretched and flopped down on one of the wooden chairs. She said vindictively, 'I wish Julian was on his hands and knees doing this.'

Their discussions with George had not assured either of them that

54

the café would cover their expenses, but if Vanessa could persuade the council to remit her rent until she could get rent support and Annie could persuade the building society to allow her some time on her payments, the café might at least provide both of them with enough to stagger along with and that, as they both agreed, would give them time to make better arrangements for themselves.

'It's not much, but it suits us and it's the best we can do,' Vanessa said, carrying a bucket of water out to the back yard and throwing it down the drain. She came back and put it under the tap in the sink. Across the noise of running water she added, 'Women are like the Third World, aren't they? Working like dogs, getting less pay, doing all the dirty jobs, got to keep in with the big boys, like America, and Britain – how much would bananas cost if you grew them in Surrey? About a quid each. Where they grow them they have to work for fifty pence a day and be grateful. Same with us. The men with the money walk out and here we are – tote that load and lift that bale.'

'It's not right,' Annie agreed.

'Ha, ha,' Vanessa said mirthlessly, pulling the bucket out of the sink and putting it on the floor by the stove. 'Well, Annie, in my opinion you can ask your husband for whatever you like but you won't get anything.'

Annie feared Vanessa was right. In a panelled office in Bloomsbury the solid and respectable Mr Danby, her parents' solicitor, had assured Annie it was possible to sue Julian for her part of what might morally have been considered a partnership but that, since Julian had not legally made her a partner, she must have been, from the outset, an employee. The directorship, he thought, was not a question worth pursuing. Even if she obtained a judgment upholding her claim that she had been a partner in Vane Graphics, and still was, the firm might not be able to cover any money she was awarded. 'In any case,' Danby went on, Annie sitting meekly in front of his big desk, hands clasped in her lap, 'I tend to advise clients in a position such as your own to be slow to act. All too often only a Pyrrhic victory can be achieved – the client may be awarded costs and damages, but they may never be paid.'

'At least there's my ten thousand pounds.'

'If you can establish that the sum was a contribution to the business operation and not merely a personal gift to your husband, for him to use as he wished. If he claimed the money had been a gift, then it was not an investment by you in the firm. And from what you tell me, he's not prepared to return the sum and may well use the argument that it was a gift such as a woman, receiving a legacy, might make to her husband.'

There was a silence. Gerald Danby, a large man in a dark suit, looked at Annie gravely. 'This must seem very discouraging. But from what you tell me, your means are small. To proceed against your husband in an attempt to prove you were a partner in the firm, or for the return of your ten thousand pounds would, if he put up a good defence, cost a great deal of money. Legal aid is difficult to obtain but if, by that or other means, you embarked on the case, and if you won it, then as I've said, your husband could declare the company had insufficient funds to pay you what the court ordered.'

They shook hands, Mr Danby murmuring sympathy. If she wished to see him again, having thought the matter over, he would be pleased to help. Annie was doubtful if this was really the case.

Now, a bucket at her feet in George's, Annie said to Vanessa, 'I don't think Mr Danby liked me, somehow. He was like something out of Dickins.'

'I told you you should have gone to Mrs Chatterjee,' retorted Vanessa.

'She didn't help you much,' Annie commented.

'Well, it came back to the same thing,' Vanessa admitted. 'Once a man's self-employed he can get an accountant to say he's broke, even if he isn't. And I couldn't tell her that from what I could see of Geoff's mood if I started a case against him he might get angry. That could mean he sends round a few of the gorillas he uses on the sites to wreck one of my dad's garages or pick a fight with my brother, who can't afford any injuries because of being a professional footballer. On top of that I've got kids and I don't want Geoff getting spiteful and trying to take Alec and Joanne away. Look here, Annie, the thing about law cases is they cost you thousands, take for ever and break your heart. They make you bitter and drive you mad. At the end of the day you're there in court and some crusty judge falls in love with your husband and you get nothing. Or if you do, probably he finds a way not to pay . . .'

She returned to the cooker while Annie finished the floor. Later Annie began taking down the white glass globes which covered the light bulbs, handing them carefully to Vanessa to wash at the sink.

'I suppose at a moment like this what you're supposed to do is say to yourself what you really want from now on,' called Vanessa. 'The trouble is, I still want Geoff to come back. After that, if he doesn't, I want him to fall under a bus while I'm watching. Crunch, crunch. Not nice, is it?' she said, coming back for the other globe. 'I was in the same class as a girl who's a top model now and when we were at school everybody reckoned I was the best looker – better than her, even. Now she's in Paris and Rome and New York. You see her picture in magazines while I'm a woman with no husband, no money, two kids and stretch marks. Ironical, isn't it? The same old story nobody wants to listen to.' She took the globe from Annie and went on, 'Carrying George Kypragoras's greasy lights off for cleaning – is this what I want?'

'I've been having awful dreams of being left behind at stations,' Annie said. 'Then,' she confessed, 'last night I dreamt I was pushing Julian out of his office window.'

Vanessa rinsed the globes and set them to dry. 'I suppose you want revenge now. So do I. Nasty, isn't it?'

Annie, scouring the scuffed table legs, looking up noticed the condition of the underside of a table. 'Oh, Vanessa,' she called. 'Look at this. Grease – chewing gum – ugh.'

Vanessa came over to look. 'We'll have to turn all the tables over and clean them. And go under that counter along the side – it's going to be just as bad. I thought we'd finished.'

They heaved the tables and chairs on their backs and began to rub and scrub. 'I hope this is going to be worthwhile,' Vanessa murmured. 'I can imagine what those blokes are doing now, on a Sunday morning in bed with their girls. I don't just need revenge. I need love and romance – I'm only a young woman, so are you. Whatever you feel like now, you'll need to marry again some time.'

'First, we both need money,' Annie remarked in a practical way. On her knees, she looked up and tasted the words – 'Love, money and revenge. Those should be our new goals.'

'Right, then,' Vanessa cried, levering a piece of chewing gum from the edge of a table with a bent knife. 'Love, money and revenge it is!'

Next day, they opened George's for the first time. Arnold hammered at the door at one minute to eight then banged on the glass and pointed at his watch. 'Cup of tea and two slices of toast,' he said, as Annie unbolted the door and let him in.

'On the house,' called Vanessa from the kitchen. 'You're the first customer under the new temporary management. Have what you like – sausage, bacon, tomatoes . . .'

'Don't even mention it – it'd turn my stomach. Still, this management is a lot prettier than the last one – you've cleaned the place up, too, not before time. Still do with a coat of paint, though,' he said, looking round.

'That'll have to wait,' said Annie, who had been up late going over the books and bills.

'You'll have to try and make it pay better, won't you,' responded Arnold, claiming his tea and toast from the counter. 'Hope you won't try putting up the prices – people won't stand for it.' He sat down by the window, adding encouragingly, 'Educated woman like you ought to be able to bring in more money. You could make something of this place if you wanted to. Course, you'll have to if you want to stay in business. Not enough here to keep both of you. And old George didn't leave for nothing, did he?'

Vanessa, who had been catching some of this while she thumped the old-fashioned chipper down on peeled potatoes, called out, 'What? What do you mean?'

'I don't want to worry you . . .' He paused.

Annie was bewildered. 'Is there something the matter?' she asked as Vanessa quickly came out of the kitchen, wiping her hands on her overall.

'Look, Arnold,' said Vanessa. 'If you know something, don't keep it to yourself.'

'They're saying up and down the market the company that owns it is going to raise the rents – nearly double them. The company which owned them sold out. It's a new company. They want more money, the idea is to drive out all the old shopkeepers and make it all go more upmarket. Yuppies and that. It's only a rumour,' he said. 'There'll be a protest, but what can anybody do?'

Annie and Vanessa looked aghast and Arnold added hastily, 'Like I say – it's just a rumour.'

'I hope so,' Annie said grimly. George's figures showed that the café made about £150 profit a week. Her own share would only cover her mortgage but if the building society agreed to defer her payments for six months at least she would have some money to live on. However little this was for her, it was even less for Vanessa, who had two children to keep. Annie knew that the profits would simply have to be pushed up over the ensuing months or, when they were both obliged to pay rent and mortgage payments again, there would be no way for either of them to manage. If the rent on the café doubled, it would be a fantastic, perhaps impossible struggle, to make the profits meet their needs. Realistically, the café would only provide a living for one of them.

'Looks as if he's left you with a few problems,' Arnold said, with gloomy satisfaction. 'Hallo – something's burning.'

Vanessa ran to the sausages. Annie, behind the counter, looked at Arnold with dislike. He sat there enjoying his tea and toast, tasting the effect of his bad news as well the sugar in his tea. No wonder in ancient times they'd killed such messengers, she thought. It might not have been the news, just the look on their faces. Was it for this man that they had scrubbed and cleaned and studied invoices and put in orders? But it was poor business to hate the customers, so she offered him another cup of tea.

Now the flow of market traders, cold and tired after setting up their stalls, began. The effort of keeping up with the orders – sausage egg and chips, sausage bacon and chips, sausage egg beans and chips, just chips, just toast, bacon sandwiches, ham sandwiches, cheese sandwiches, tea, coffee, Coke, Pepsi, Fanta, Mars bars for passing schoolchildren stocking up for the day – was exhausting. By ten that particular rush was over, the café empty but for a woman who had shopped early and needed a cup of tea. They began to clear up.

'I feel as if I've done a day's work already,' Vanessa said, adding hopefully, 'Maybe it gets easier as you get into the rhythm of it.'

Dinnertime was worse. Exhausted and greasy, Annie and Vanessa sent a boy to the off-licence for two cans of lager and they sat with their feet up, drinking from the cans to save washing up.

Melanie came in with Alec. 'He wants to see his mum,' she reported.

'Give him a Kit Kat,' Vanessa said weakly.

'You ought to think of his teeth,' Melanie told her.

'Shut up,' said Vanessa. 'What do you reckon we made, just from this morning?' she asked Annie.

'There's probably about seventy pounds in the till,' Annie said. 'We must have had seventy people in and out this morning, even if it was only for a Coke or a cup of tea. But it's not all profit, of course. I'll have to cost it properly. I should think we've earned ten pounds each, so far.'

'Not a lot,' Vanessa said.

'Ten pounds more than you had this morning,' Melanie chipped in. 'They'd go mad where I come from thinking you can drop into a job like this down here. You don't know what it's like up north. Let me take over for the afternoon. Bound to be quieter, isn't it, now the breakfasts and dinners are over.'

'You're only thirteen,' Annie reminded her.

Melanie bridled. 'So – I'm younger, aren't I? More resilient, like.'

'She's right,' Annie said. 'It won't be so busy this afternoon. Why don't you take Alec off and I'll keep going with Melanie? You've got to collect Joanne from school. We'll do it the opposite way tomorrow – and Sunday,' she told Melanie, 'we'll go to Gravesend.'

Vanessa agreed, and walked out on her stiletto heels, wincing.

'Sensible footwear, tomorrow,' Annie observed.

Vanessa turned round. 'Yes. And a less sensible face tomorrow, too.'

Earlier she'd nagged Annie, 'Look – half our point is being two good-lookers. That'll bring in trade. But not with your hair hanging round your face. Stick it in a nice plait down the back, put on a bit of make-up – it'll make all the difference. I'm not trying to be rude,' she explained. 'But we might as well use what we've got because that's all we *have* got.'

Some of the remarks they'd been making to each other on that first morning, especially when Vanessa dropped a fried egg on the floor, bent to wipe it up and Annie cannoned into her with a tray of dirty plates and cups, had been blunt, if not bordering on offensive. But Annie'd yielded on the question of make-up. Now Vanessa, even though she disliked the suggestion, yielded on footwear. As she went out of the door, holding Alec's hand, she called back, 'Love, money and revenge!'

'Some cry Liberty – we cry Love, Money, Revenge!' returned Annie.

Vanessa told her mother later that she didn't know how they'd got through that first week at the café. No bath or shower seemed to remove the smell of frying from their hair, no amount of washing could take the smell from their clothes. Their feet ached more and more each day. Chaos, in the form of spoiled food and discontented customers, was always in the offing, not always averted. Adults, teenagers, even children were constantly trying to filch food and money. They took the cutlery. Vanessa and Annie had been advised to watch the street. A gang was said to be roving the market, seeing what they could grab. Another gang, armed with iron bars, had entered some of the shops, threatened the staff, grabbed the contents of the till and got away.

That week, too, the weather had been bad and the small café was crowded with market traders in big coats and mittens and with frozen shoppers with bulky bags, all crammed together in the steamy atmosphere, desperate for hot food and boiling cups of tea. The floor was muddy from early morning on. Perhaps there were even more customers than would normally have sought George's during this hard time of year, when snow flurried in the streets and an east wind bit deep. They came to check out the new management or exchange a word or two with Vanessa, who appeared to have been at school with everybody in Foxwell. Meanwhile the regulars were snappy about delays and demanded better standards of tea and fried bread. The men took advantage of their confusion and made offensive remarks and suggestions to Vanessa and Annie and Vanessa had to bar a particularly obscene nineteen-year-old.

On Friday, just before closing time, Annie burst into tears and rushed into the back yard where dustbins overflowed and unpacked cartons of baked beans and soup lay despondently covered with a light veil of snow. She didn't know how she would be able to face the next day, which was bound to be busier still.

Vanessa came out and started shouting at her. 'Get back inside, you stupid bitch. There's two people waiting and then we've got to clean up. What's the matter with you? Can't handle it, can you?'

'Shut up and leave me alone,' sobbed Annie. 'This was a stupid idea. I'm worn out. It's no good. We're not even making any money. I'm sorry. I can't go on. I'm going home.' The thought of going through the café sobbing was terrible but she couldn't stand in the cold, untidy yard, either. She ran inside, and snatched her coat from the peg.

Vanessa shouted, 'That's it – that's typical – just cop out when you feel like it—' They scarcely noticed in the kitchen the elderly woman who had been there on the day when George made his offer to them.

'Look!' Annie cried. 'I just can't go on.'

'Oh, yeah,' sneered Vanessa. 'OK for you, isn't it, Miss Fancypants? Pack it in when you feel like it. Not so easy for me, old Vanessa from the council house with two kids. This is practically the only chance I've got of getting through the next three months, and here you go, copping out on me. But that wouldn't bother you, would it? People like you can always get out when it suits them.'

Annie sniffed tearfully. 'It's a disaster. We're dog tired. We're not earning enough and, all right, I can't manage. I'm admitting it – I can't. I'm just not good enough. On Sunday I'm supposed to go to Gravesend to find Melanie's uncle – I won't find him. I don't know what to do about that poor girl – every bone in my body aches – my feet are killing me – the smell in this place makes me sick – what can I do? If you need it, you do it. You can take all the money, that way you can probably survive . . .'

'Ah – what happened to all those plans?' Vanessa said contemptuously. 'The sandwich bar? The delivery service? That was all talk, wasn't it? You know damn well I can't manage alone. I couldn't manage the kids or the accounts. Face it – this partnership finished after a week because one of the partners couldn't hack it—'

Pale and shaking, Annie faced Vanessa. Vanessa's small figure was rigid with rage. Annie thought she might be going to hit her. She stared at Vanessa for a moment, then suddenly exclaimed, 'Oh my God, I think you're right!'

Vanessa, reared in a to-the-death-right-or-wrong tradition of argument, was startled to hear this admission. 'What?' she gulped.

Suddenly they both noticed the café was empty but for Arnold and the woman in the plum-coloured coat, composedly washing up a huge pile of plates on the draining board. Her rings, one a large diamond and the other an odd mix of sapphires and rubies with another, greenish stone, lay on the windowsill beside the sink. Vanessa peered at her. The woman said, 'I'm afraid after you both went out a young woman went straight to the till and tried to open it. I chased her out and closed the café.'

Annie sat down weakly. Now the woman put down the brush she was using to scrub the plates and dried her hands. Replacing her rings she said, 'I must leave you now – I'm only just back from Brighton. Arnold!' she called. 'They're shutting now. You must go.'

'Bit early,' he grumbled.

'Arnold,' she reproved him and he stood up. She straightened her hat and took up a suitcase she had left in a corner. 'Goodbye, Madame Katarina,' Vanessa said.

'I'm sorry, Vanessa,' said Annie, 'I just felt done in. I'm ready to go on, that's all I can say.'

'I don't know about "sorry" – it's not good enough, Annie. If you're going to keep on freaking out—'

'Oh, shut up,' Annie cried. 'Let's just get on with it, shall we? *We're closed,*' she shouted at two boys banging on the glass. They went on banging. 'Fuck off!' she yelled.

Vanessa burst out laughing. 'You're learning!'

An hour later, when they'd finished cleaning up and were walking back to Rutherford Street Annie asked, 'Who's Madame Katarina?'

'Haven't you seen her plate?' Vanessa was astonished. 'She's got the flat above the café and a brass plate by the door: "Madame Katarina, Clairvoyant". Haven't you seen her going in and out?'

Annie shook her head.

'Don't ever try to make a living as a detective,' Vanessa advised. 'I had a word with her the other day, before she went to Brighton. She's got another practice there – she commutes – spends most of the winter in London, only going to Brighton on and off, then in the summer she spends more time down there, doing consultations for holidaymakers. She does cards, palmistry, crystal ball and so forth. I asked her last week if she'd give me consultation. She was very polite but said best if she didn't, us being neighbours – she'd never given one to George till she finally took pity on him over the Cyprus business – she reckoned she'd seen in his cards he was going to be happy in Cyprus and wouldn't come back. What do you think of that?' They had reached Vanessa's gate.

Annie shook her head. 'I don't know. I suppose if you asked me I'd have to say I didn't believe in that sort of thing.'

'Well – I suppose you would say that,' Vanessa said tolerantly.

'What?' Melanie asked, coming out of the house.

'Annie doesn't believe in fortune telling,' Vanessa told her.

'She wouldn't, would she?' Melanie said. 'I asked that Madame Katarina if she'd give me a reading, about whether I'd find my uncle and that. She said I was too young. You have to be eighteen. Joanne's watching TV,' she added. 'So's Alec, but I think he's dropped off on the couch.'

Annie and Melanie went home. Annie glumly contemplated the sitting room, which seemed sparsely furnished since Julian's raid. Melanie's trainers lay on the floor and a heap of teen magazines on the table where the computer had once stood. Annie sprawled in the only remaining easy chair, her feet on a wooden one from the kitchen. Her head throbbed, her feet ached, she smelt only café grease and felt her hair sticking to her head. She was exhausted and confused – she recalled Minnie Knipe, of 20 Threpp Street, who had been observed leaving the Lion in Whitechapel at two one morning and staggering away the worse for drink, looking, she said, for a customer who would pay her sixpence, the rent being due next day. Described as previously a milliner and now a common prostitute, she had then disappeared and it was rumoured the customer she found had murdered her. She was only twenty years old.

Melanie came in with a tray on which she had nicely arranged a teapot, jug of milk and teacup. She presented this to Annie and sat herself down on a large floor cushion she had found upstairs, saying civilly, 'Would you like to watch telly, or shall I put a record on?'

Annie knew Melanie hated her music. 'Put on the TV, Melanie. I'm going to have a long, hot bath and go to bed in a little while. You'll be all right on your own?'

'Glad of the peace and quiet after those kids,' Melanie responded. 'That Joanne's a handful. She's violent. And poor little Alec – they can't cope with what's happening.'

'Nor can Vanessa,' Annie said, thinking, And neither can I.

They got through Saturday, somehow. At dinnertime the sink blocked. 'It's inclined to do that,' Arnold remarked at the counter.

'Where can we get a plumber on Saturday afternoon?' Vanessa demanded. 'We might have to close.'

'Tell you the truth,' Arnold stated, his elbows on the counter, 'I've done it before. All you've got there is a tight S bend. Wrongly installed – George has never spent the money to get it right.'

'Can you?' Vanessa enquired suspiciously.

'You'd be surprised what I can do when I get started,' he remarked flirtatiously.

'There's a drink in it for you if you can,' Vanessa said in a businesslike tone.

Arnold borrowed some tools from a friend and capably unblocked the sink.

'I can plumb, do electrics, the lot,' he said gloomily. 'Now I just do bits and pieces when it suits me. One day I woke up and thought, what am I doing out here on a building site, all hours, all weathers with no safety precautions, no tax or stamps paid? There was kids from the YTS messing about and getting half killed all the time, the contractors was all on the fiddle, shoddy work, done too fast. It was disgusting – you'd know.'

'Oh, I know all right,' agreed Vanessa.

'Worked for your old man once,' Arnold mentioned. 'Anyway,

what finished me was this bill from the income tax for four thousand pounds and the upshot was it took me a year and a half to pay it off – I'm anxious all the time and the wife ups and leaves me, taking the kids, and I develop a nervous breakdown. After that I think, thanks very much, but I can take this or leave it alone . . .'

He gave a final, determined twist with his spanner and stood up. 'There you go. You won't have any more trouble with that till the next time. Let me know if there's anything else you want doing. It all has to be' – he gestured with his hand. Vanessa nodded. 'All part of the black economy, isn't it?' he remarked as Vanessa gave him some money from the till then asked, 'Seen Andy Campbell yet?'

Vanessa was surprised. 'No. Who's he?'

'Don't worry – he'll tell you,' Arnold said. 'Ta ta, then. I'm off to watch Leigh Rangers. Hope your brother manages better this week than he did the last.'

'He scored a goal,' Vanessa said indignantly.

'One,' said Arnold. 'Wasn't quite enough, was it?'

'He can't do it all,' she said.

'He's going to have to, the way the rest of them are playing.'

The next morning Annie, tired from the previous week and having spent Saturday evening doing the accounts, hauled herself out of bed, roused Melanie and they set off for Gravesend.

'You've got to promise me something,' she said, once they were in the car she had persuasively conned from the housekeeper at her sister's small house in a Kensington mews the previous evening. 'You've got to promise me that if we can't find Uncle Jim or any sign of him at all this time, you'll ring your mother and father and have a serious talk about what's going to happen next.'

Melanie was enjoying the leather upholstery of the small but expensive car. 'They must have a bit of money, your sister and her husband. What does he do?'

'Melanie – don't change the subject,' Annie said.

'All right,' she said. 'I'll phone. But it'll only be my mum I speak to because my dad's gone off.'

Annie drove through Foxwell and entered the streets of Leadham Common, an area of small suburban houses, with neat front gardens. A long road of identical houses, under a leaden sky, lay ahead.

'Gone off?' she said. Over the past few weeks, Melanie had given her an impression of a sad household, facing many difficulties – shortage of work, shortage of money and a general despondency which made these things harder to bear. Annie wondered if it had been her sister Ruth's disappearance a year ago which had made Melanie's mother so worn out and hopeless, or the depressing atmosphere that had driven the girl from home in the first place. Now, here was Melanie's father, David Pickering, also gone. And, of course, Melanie herself.

Melanie explained, 'He went off to find work. There hadn't been any jobs since the summer.'

'How do you know?' Annie asked suspiciously.

'I rang Mo Patel at the corner shop,' Melanie explained. 'I paid for it myself,' she added. 'In a call box. Anyway, I told Mo to keep it a secret I'd rung – he told me Dad'd come south, he thought, looking for work.'

'What does he do?' asked Annie, impressed, as usual, by Melanie's initiative.

'Bricklayer,' Melanie replied shortly.

There was a silence. 'What drove Ruth away from home?' Annie suddenly asked.

Melanie did not reply. Annie recalled a girl at her school who had arrived at mid-term and had shared her room. At fifteen Annie had sensed that Celia, her pale, sleepless companion, who lay in bed at night surrounded by hosts of furry animals inappropriate to her age, who never thought of film and pop stars or, for that matter, escape from the school into that other world they all craved, had an affliction – a secret that, given encouragement, she might have wanted to discuss. But Annie had been afraid: without having any idea of Celia's trouble she flinched from the idea of finding out. She'd even been out to tea with Celia's family one half term, and had observed, with disquiet, the way Celia's father compulsively touched his daughter whenever he could – on the hand, as she passed him a plate, on the cheek, as they spoke, how he laid his arm across her shoulders at the table. She'd seen Celia freeze when this happened. It was with Celia's chalky, expressionless face in her mind's eye that she asked, 'What drove Ruth away?'

There was another silence which Annie broke by saying, 'I won't tell anybody—' and Melanie at the same time burst out, 'If you want to know my dad was too fond of Ruth – not me, she was the one he really loved. I don't know how bad it was but Mum knew, so did I and I expect the boys noticed something. He used to say, "Come over here, Ruth, and sit on my knee." This was when she was getting big, even when she was coming up fourteen, and she used to go but she didn't like it. He used to come in our room, too, and sit down on her bed and – and – well, I don't know but we both knew it wasn't right, me and Ruth. He had his hands everywhere. We all knew what was happening. It was embarrassing,' she said resentfully.

There was a silence. 'I had to ask,' Annie said eventually.

'I know,' Melanie replied. After a pause she said, 'I suppose it had to come to an end. At first, Ruth wouldn't come home from school till late. She started just coming back when Mum got back from work so she wasn't in the house without Mum, and Dad's saying, "Where's Ruth?" and that. We'd say, "She's hanging round with her mates", which was true, but it was because he'd be there – I think she asked Mum to make him stop but she couldn't explain it – I don't know—'

Melanie stopped, confused by having to describe what she could hardly understand and had put out of her mind as much as she was able. She went on, 'Then Ruth started not going to school at all. She'd start out pretending she was going but she'd turn off at the recreation ground, where the other kids playing hookey would go – and one day she didn't come home. I wish I'd told on her now. I wish I knew where she was. I wish I could see her again. Mostly, I wish I knew she was all right.'

Melanie's voice cracked. Annie had tears in her own eyes. She spotted a café sign and found a place to pull over. They sat down in a tea room full of stained and polished tables and shelves of blue china.

Across the table Annie looked at Melanie, drinking Coke from a glass with a straw. 'Did anybody tell the police?' she asked.

'Mum reported her missing and gave them a photo.' She paused, then added, 'There's hundreds, probably thousands, of kids go missing every year. They don't find half of them.'

The sky became darker as they drove and Annie yet again regretted the trip, which she thought would be futile anyway. They'd already checked the local telephone directory and, by means of a fraudulent call to the council offices, discovered no record of Melanie's uncle as a local poll-tax payer. Their aim now was to approach the local police in such a way that they would check their computer for Jim and Muriel Allardyce without their asking too many questions about Melanie's status. Melanie also suggested that, her uncle and aunt being strong Methodists, visits to the Methodist churches of the area and a word with the ministers concerned might reveal the Allardyces to be members of one of the congregations.

Annie turned up the heater in the smart little car. Sleet began to lash the windscreen. Four hours later they left the streets of Gravesend, which were silent, dark and swept over by crying gulls. The Methodists had been no help. The police, accepting Annie's story that she was a family friend who had driven Melanie to Gravesend to stay with her uncle and aunt, only to find on arrival that Melanie had left the letter giving the address behind, conducted a friendly search of the computer. Annie and Melanie sat in the police station waiting for the verdict feeling cold and depressed. Annie tried to prepare Melanie for disappointment. 'I'm not too sure they're going to find them,' she told her.

'I know,' Melanie had said. 'He's gone somewhere else, that's what I think. I'm sorry, Annie.'

A woman officer came back and said there was no record of the Allardyces – Annie and Melanie made their escape as fast as possible and headed for London. It had begun to snow. Melanie wanted to stop for a snack and Annie said they couldn't. They must keep going in case the snow got even heavier and finally trapped them. They were both irritable. Annie, pondering Melanie's account of her sister's disappearance, had to conclude that the plan for Melanie to return home wasn't as good as she'd previously assumed. Feeling stuck in a situation she didn't want, she drew a deep breath and said to the girl, 'If you stay here any length of time – if your mother will let you – you'll have to start going to school.'

Melanie protested. 'What's the point of that? I can be very useful to you while you get the snack-bar going, looking after the kids and lending a hand. What's the point of me being at some school? It's not worth it. Have you thought how you'd manage that café without me?'

'Yes, I have,' Annie said with resolution. 'I can't see any justification for keeping you away from school just because it's convenient. That's simply exploitation. Also it's illegal.'

'Did you have a car, before?' enquired Melanie.

Annie, who had spent her adult life among grown-ups, was wiser now to these diversionary tactics. She responded, 'Yes – but I shared it with Julian and he took it. Listen, Melanie. You'll never get anywhere if you don't go to school and get some qualifications. In any case, learning has some value – you should do it just for the sake of it.'

68

'Have you seen that school?' she asked. 'Jasper Rayburn Comprehensive? They're hooligans in there. Drug-pushers and everything. It's just not worth it. Look at it like this – Uncle Jim and Auntie Muriel are somewhere. I'm going to get the Sally Army on to it. They can always find people. So, in the meanwhile, if Mum says I can stop on, what's the point? I don't want to go there. I'll learn nothing. I can read and write and do sums. That's all I need.'

'I couldn't forgive myself,' Annie said.

'You don't understand, do you,' Melanie said desperately. 'I don't think you're accustomed to the kind of school I am. Those schools are places you have to go to to keep you out of harm's way while your mum's at work, while you're too young to go to work yourself. They teach you what you need in the primary school when you're little. After that, it's a waste of time. Education suits a few. Some take to it naturally. And it keeps teachers in work. But I'm not clever, never have been. I don't come from a clever family. Practically nobody bothers about school – pop stars and that. And footballers – do you think Vanessa's brother's got a hundred O levels? There's a man in our town plays for England . . .' she reminisced.

'But you're not going to play for England, Melanie.'

'No need to take up my words like that,' Melanie said reproachfully. 'You know what I mean. I'm not going to turn into some brain surgeon or – what are they? – cabinet minister no matter if I go to school for a thousand years—'

'Why not?' Annie said indignantly. 'Why can't you be a cabinet minister, tell me that?' She'd noticed that all her arguments with Melanie soon reached the level of a playground squabble.

'Because I'm a girl and I'm working class,' Melanie said, with finality.

'There've been women cabinet ministers, and working class ones, too,' Annie informed her.

'When was that? When dinosaurs roamed the earth? Anyway, I don't want to be a cabinet minister. I just want a job, good pay—'

'Well, it would help you do that if you got some schooling first.'

'So I can be a teacher on fifteen thousand a year, less tax,' retorted Melanie.

'Melanie,' appealed Annie. 'You say you're not clever, but you are—'

'How many O levels have you got, Annie? You went to

69

university, didn't you? What good has it done? You're running a snack bar.'

Annie didn't reply. Tired, hungry and infuriated, steering through thickening snow, she reverted to the playground again. 'You'll see. Just wait and see, that's all.'

Melanie sat stolidly strapped in her seat, exuding scepticism.

That evening Annie at last spoke to Mrs Pickering, Melanie's mother. She had a flat voice. She sounded tired, but she was sensible. She said, 'I can't ask Melanie's dad about her stopping on with you because he's gone away to work and hasn't got in touch yet, but if you're happy to have her, then I'm happy. I've spoken to her and she wants to stay. Only one thing . . .' she paused. 'I can't have her not going to school. I know she's useful to you. She's a sensible girl and I miss her. But you'll know there's not much of a chance for young people round here so I'm content to let her stay if she goes on with her education. I'm afraid if you can't see your way to putting her in a school, then she'll have to come home.'

Next day, even Vanessa, whom Melanie had counted on as an ally, joined in the process of forcing Melanie to take a trip to Rayburn Comprehensive. 'You get yourself up there straight away,' she said firmly, unstrapping Alec from his buggy. 'I know now a woman can't have too much education. Look at me – no CSEs, definitely not maths. So, I have to rely on Annie. If I'm lucky, when and if all this packs in, or if we can't get a living wage from it, I'm back at work five days a week, forty-eight weeks a year, Alec in a nursery all day long, or if I can't get him in, with some childminder who may be no good and keep him strapped in his chair all day long while she smokes fags and talks to the neighbours. What about your mum? In the packing department at the factory, you said? Working all day for eighty quid a week, I bet, not more, then home to the kids and the housework. Don't be a fool to yourself. Get an education and some proper training . . .'

'Annie's got a degree from a university and look—' Melanie said, pointing at Annie wiping down the counter.

'That's right,' Vanessa said. 'And she's doing all the paperwork.'

'You could, if you had the confidence – you could take a course . . .' Annie intervened.

'That's another thing an education gives you – confidence in yourself,' declared Vanessa. 'If I'd had anything behind me do you think I'd've let Geoff Doyle make a fool of me like he did? No way. Anyway, you've got no choice, Melanie. Your mum says you can't stay if you don't go to school. And so does the law. I don't want coppers round here asking questions.'

'I'll give it a go,' conceded Melanie.

It was still early as Annie and Melanie walked in silence down Foxwell High Street and along two back streets to the Jasper Rayburn Comprehensive School, Tredgarth Street. A few late pupils flew past them as they walked through the big metal gates and found themselves behind the wire in a big asphalt playground. They watched the backs of two large boys running for the entrance. To Annie Melanie suddenly looked very small. As if to herself, Melanie repeated, 'I'll give it a go.' Looking at the pupils cramming in ahead of them, she remarked to Annie, 'It looks like *West Side Story* here.'

The comprehensive resembled no school Annie had ever attended or approached. It was nothing like the village school in Belshaw she had attended as a child, nor the Quaker boarding school Howard Browning, in spite of his strong support of a state education system, had felt it compatible with his principles to allow his daughters to attend. That school had been founded in the late nineteenth century by two female relatives of his. The Jasper Rayburn Comprehensive was the kind of school that up to this point Annie had only seen from the windows of cars and trains or read about in newspapers.

As they walked through the front door, she thought of Hidge Lane Board School, which most of the Threpp Street children had attended in the year 1888 if not hiding from the truant officer or so unrecorded by any authority that no one had found them in order to compel them to attend any school at all.

'Love, money and revenge,' she said encouragingly to Melanie, who'd been told about the joke – or was it a joke? – she and Vanessa had produced between them.

'I'm going to need new jeans,' was Melanie's reply. 'These are disgusting.'

After a long wait outside the headmaster's office with four pupils, two of whom looked like escapees from Cell Block 11, one in heavy make-up and damp stilettos and one tiny red-eyed Asian boy, Annie and Melanie were ushered into the office of Mr Austin Framling, MA, a small man with a determined air. Melanie, with more haste than Annie expected, was enrolled at Jasper Rayburn Comprehensive and despatched to a classroom in the care of another pupil. She did not glance back at Annie as she left the headmaster's room. Annie had discovered there were 1300 pupils at Rayburn Comp. 'Fewer than at Eton,' Austin Framling remarked jovially. Now she said to him tentatively, 'She's an intelligent girl – her actual attainments might not show this at first.'

'We'll take care of her,' he told her. 'We'll be getting her records from her previous school, in due course.'

'Yes,' said Annie, wondering what she should ask next. There was to be no chance. Austin Framling stood up, extended his hand and said, 'Well, goodbye, Mrs Vane. Would you be kind enough to give your address and telephone number to my secretary on the way out. Don't worry, we'll look after her. If ever you want to contact me I'm here. I try to be as accessible as possible to parents. Of course, in these days of cuts and staff shortages I can't do as much as I'd like.'

Annie walked despondently back to George's Café, wondering how Melanie would manage. How much more could she take? The revelations about her father on the Gravesend trip had shaken Annie badly. Melanie's whole situation, including the new school, new demands to form friendships and avoid enmities, was entirely the fault of David Pickering, Annie knew. At that moment she could have killed him.

6

Lunch at Durham House

At Durham House, one Sunday in mid-February, Nigel Fellows and his wife were entertaining a small party for Sunday lunch. The guests included Charles and Matilda Head and their twelve-year-old daughter, Amanda, one Max Craig, Annie Vane, Vanessa Doyle and Melanie Pickering. Also present were the estate manager, Adam Cranley, and Dr Sam Anstruther. Charles Head and Max Craig were both, in their different ways, employees of Samco Ltd, the large group of companies owned or controlled by Sir Bernard Fellows. It was quite a small, dull group for Durham House, where it was not unknown for royalty to meet rock star, millionaire to meet famous musician, titled beauty to meet beast in the house or its grounds, lit with lanterns for a party.

Today, however, tall, fair, clear-complexioned Nigel Fellows presided over the big polished table in jersey and corduroys, his mother, Lady Mary, to his right, his pretty wife Jasmine on the left. Lady Mary, tall and thin, her fine skin etched with lines, said, as the housekeeper brought in a large joint of beef, 'I expect you'll carve, Nigel.' He stood up readily, picking up the carving knife and fork from the plate, starting to carve and asking each guest in turn what they would like. Jasmine fidgeted slightly. As she'd whispered to Annie earlier, 'I don't know why we have to go through all this at lunchtime on Sundays. Most people would prefer to help themselves – what a Victorian palaver.'

Some of the guests were subdued. Melanie Pickering was in shock – never in her life had she seen such a house, except on television, when she'd thought it was a fiction, less real than Southfork. She'd never believed there could be such a place and couldn't imagine, now, how anyone could live there. Vanessa was equally amazed, though enjoying it all and flirting with Sam Anstruther, next to her.

A portrait of Sir Bernard Fellows and his wife hung on the wall behind Nigel. In it Sir Bernard, thirty-five, and recently married to Lady Mary, stood beside his young wife whose loose dress barely concealed the bump made by their coming first son. The baronet appeared manly and at ease, in favourite grey trousers and sports jacket, his large hand lightly on Lady Mary's slender shoulder. Vanessa, glancing from the portrait to Lady Mary, sitting on her son's right, quietly making sure that vegetables, in rose-patterned tureens, were positioned properly on the table, that glasses were filled and plates reached the right recipients, thought that she had not changed greatly. She still had the same erect carriage, had gained no weight though her fine complexion was more lined. Her colouring, like her fair hair, had faded, but the kind of alterations Vanessa saw in women in Kenton – increasing weight, varicose veins and the counterbalancing change of hair colour to a brighter shade of black, blonde or red – were all lacking in Lady Mary.

Earlier Juliet had explained something about where they were going. 'Bernard Fellows is away – he often is – in the West Indies,' she'd told Vanessa. 'He's got property interests there. He leaves the day-to-day running of the Samco Corporation to his son Nigel. His wife, Lady Mary, is what they call "the real thing", meaning that her family have been noblemen and women since medieval times—'

'Robber barons,' interjected Howard.

'The Fellowses,' Juliet continued, ignoring him, 'began a lot later—'

'Got rich a lot later,' Howard again interrupted. 'All families began at the same time, I suppose.'

Juliet went on, 'They were farmers in Yorkshire until about the end of the eighteenth century when one of them went into shipping in Liverpool and made a fortune. The children mostly married into the aristocracy but they went on making a lot of money from ships and shipping up to fairly recent times. They diversified and, as shipping declined, the other interests turned into Samco, which is a vast group of companies—'

'My uncle worked at Prosser and Fellows shipyard till they closed down. Then he never had another job for fifteen years,' Melanie butted in.

'Anyway,' Juliet concluded, 'don't be nervous of Lady Mary.

She's very nice. Nigel's inclined to shout a bit but his heart's in the right place.'

'Don't let them intimidate you,' added Howard. 'If you feel worried by the silver knives and forks and the paintings on the wall, just remember both those families earned their money by taking away other people's. As soon as Melanie's uncle was no good to them, they dumped him on the scrapheap. That shipping company in the late eighteenth century,' he told Vanessa, 'was known as the Fellows Line. For many years they sent cannons and Bibles to Africa and brought in sugar and tobacco from the West Indies. The middle part of the voyage was the infamous middle passage—'

'Did that at school,' Vanessa said swiftly.

'I'm glad to hear someone did,' Howard said.

'Trade goods to Africa,' recited Vanessa. 'Slaves to the West Indies. Sugar, bananas, cotton back to England. A black kid beat me up for it,' she added. 'I told him it wasn't my fault but he wasn't listening. I suppose it was their fault, over there,' she said, nodding in the direction of Durham House. 'Pity they weren't there, so he had to pick on me.'

'That's the way it goes,' Howard pointed out.

'It was all a long time ago,' said Juliet. 'And I shouldn't mention it while you're there.' She added, 'Mary's a good friend of mine.' Then she left the long table where they were having breakfast at Froggett's and picked up a brush from the large dresser. Her palette was placed tidily beside it. She held it in her other hand, stepped back from her easel, which was at the back of the room, and contemplated the picture of two girls she was painting.

'It might be better to get some really decent heating in the studio,' Annie told her father. 'Then Mother wouldn't have to paint in the kitchen in the winter.'

'The wiring wouldn't stand it,' Howard Browning remarked comfortably. 'Anyway, she says she doesn't mind. It's less lonely in the kitchen.'

Annie shook her head.

'You'll get a good lunch tomorrow,' he went on. 'Nigel killed a bullock a few weeks ago – that's what you'll be eating.'

Now Melanie sat at the table at Durham House, stiff and still, hardly daring to take up a knife or fork until she saw Amanda Head do it first, and thinking about tall, handsome Nigel Fellows actually killing a cow. Did he do it with the same knife as he'd carved with? she wondered. Probably not. There was probably another, bigger one, or an axe. Or perhaps they gave it an injection while it wasn't looking, as with dogs and cats. She was about to mention this to her neighbour and glanced at her sideways, but Amanda, cutting up meat and forking it into her mouth, was hunched over her plate and didn't seem to want to talk. She had lovely fair hair but her dress was out of date, thought Melanie, and she'd have been pretty if it hadn't been for the sulky look on her face.

Further down the table Annie was surprised to feel Charles Head's hand on her thigh and sat still, imagining it to be an accident. Her gaze caught that of Matilda Head, Charles's wife, sitting opposite.

'We must take the girls out to see the vixen and her cubs after lunch,' Lady Mary said.

'That would be very nice,' Charles Head said. 'I'd enjoy coming myself but I think Nigel and I will have to shut ourselves up for an hour or so to discuss business.'

As he had not removed his hand from Annie's thigh she picked it up and dropped it. She was horrified that as she did so he managed to give her fingers a squeeze.

'Yes. I've got to drag him off,' Nigel said, carving the last slice for his own plate and sitting down, the joint having been promptly taken away by the waiting housekeeper and placed on a sideboard.

'Perhaps when you've finished your discussion?' said Lady Mary.

Charles shook his head and as he did so Annie felt the hand back on her thigh. 'We must start back to London fairly early,' he said. 'Got to be back by Amanda's bedtime – to be exact, in time for her French lesson, then bedtime—' His mouth opened slightly as Annie again removed his hand, and gave him a swift kick on the ankle. He drank from his wine glass and continued, 'Matilda's all for education, though she never had much herself.'

'I was too dim,' agreed Matilda Head, a glowing blonde in a purple twinset. 'But I'd love to see Amanda do well.'

Amanda hunched herself even further over the table. She carefully put her knife and fork together on the plate. Melanie quickly did the same.

'I was dim,' said Jasmine cheerfully from beside her husband. 'Annie wasn't, though. The teachers all used to threaten me with her and say I couldn't be trying. It was no fun.'

'Never mind, Jas,' Annie said. 'I'll write to the school magazine and tell them I'm running a snack bar in South London.'

'Are you enjoying it?' asked Nigel. 'Isn't there something better you could do?'

'I like it,' said Annie. 'And Vanessa and I have plans to expand – I think we can start delivering sandwiches and fruit to offices and workplaces generally, go in for healthier fillings, good home-made soups. We might get some trade from the sports centre and possibly other contracts.'

'You've no business training?' Charles glanced at her sideways. He had a large nose, no chin and a great deal of honey-coloured hair. His eyes were small, blue and unfriendly. He hadn't appreciated the kick on the ankle, Annie deduced.

'No. None at all. I've read about most of Britain's successful businessmen being totally untrained, though. I'm comforted by that. But I must admit it's nerve-racking.' Annie did not wish to challenge this man whose anger, she felt, was not very far below the surface. 'I expect you have business school training?'

'Harvard,' said Nigel. 'Thank goodness he has – I've no academic experience myself. Didn't even do very well at school.'

Further up the table Vanessa looked up at Sam Anstruther from her big, blue eyes. Enjoying the attention, Sam explained how temperature and humidity had to be carefully controlled to preserve valuable books and manuscripts. 'A city like New York has big variations in heat and humidity – more than over here, I guess,' he said.

'I've a cousin in New York,' volunteered Vanessa. 'He's a poet. Maybe you've got some of his books in your store. Dickie Barton, that's his name.'

'Richard Barton, would that be?' Sam opened his eyes wider. 'Sure – I've heard of him. Yeah, that's right. I'd heard he came from a poor background in London.'

'Dunno about the "poor",' Vanessa said. 'His family always had more than ours and we're not poor, as such. Well – maybe by your standards – but Dickie was the only one so he always got the best. They really worried about his education. Course, that wouldn't have helped me much. I was always dim at school.'

'The University of Life is one that most of us academic people could never get into, that's what I've always thought,' Sam said.

'Well, that's the only one I could get into,' Vanessa told him cheerfully.

'Nigel once had a most impressive school report,' commented Lady Mary. 'I could scarcely believe it when the Chaplain wrote

77

of the spiritual progress he appeared to have made that term, his intelligent work in the confirmation class and regular attendance at non-obligatory services in chapel—'

'I was keeping the Chaplain happy,' Nigel said. 'In fact I had a stray dog in the crypt. It was an elaborate system – early Communion, then round the back, through the little door at the side and down into the crypt – breakfast and early morning walk. During the day I'd nip in with my lunch in a hankie, another walk and a quick pray. Then Evensong – same story. I was hanging around the chapel all day long. Then they found the dog and religion went out of the window.'

'How old were you?' asked Annie.

'Nine or ten,' Nigel told her.

'And what happened to the dog?' asked Charles Head.

'I never found out,' said Nigel. 'I couldn't ask – they didn't know I was responsible. Pity – if I could have hung on a little longer I could have smuggled him back here in the holidays.'

'Tough luck,' said Charles Head. He turned to Annie again and asked, 'So – what's your ambition? To own a chain of South London snack bars?' His tone was not pleasant.

'Why not?' she said and had to put up with a nasty glare in return.

Charles beamed at his wife, 'There sits a woman,' he said, 'who has never in her life wanted to own a chain of snack bars. She'd spend the profits, though, gladly. That's to say if there are any,' he said returning his gaze to Annie. 'Tell me, honestly, would you advise me to invest Samco's money in the venture – make a bid for the company, perhaps? How about that, Nigel, a takeover bid for Annie's snack bar?'

Annie gave Charles a stony look. Her eye caught that of Max Craig, who sat next to Matilda Head. He was a pale and chubby late middle-aged man with brown eyes and a balding head. He had not accepted any beef, but had made his meal of the vegetables accompanying it. He was drinking only water and had not tried to talk to Matilda, on one side of him, or her daughter, on the other. His eyes were remote as if, Annie thought, he had some sorrow, perhaps known to the others, for they were making no attempt to talk to him. He looked back at her steadily.

Annie glanced past his shoulder and stared out over the terrace and down the lawn to the trees which marked the end of the garden, their trunks masked by light mist rising from the ground. In the distance Annie could see a motionless figure. She frowned, trying to remember something. She looked again; the figure seemed to be advancing. Whoever it was had been first by the lake beyond the trees and was now coming slowly up to the house.

Nigel, sensitive to what was happening on his land, caught Annie's gaze, and said loudly. 'Funny – who's that?' He called down the table, 'Adam – somebody's down by the lake. Any idea who it is? Should he be there?'

Adam peered across the table, past Max Craig. 'Hard to see. Doesn't look like one of ours. Shouldn't be anyone there anyway. I'll go and take a look.'

'Finish your lunch,' ordered Nigel. 'He seems to be coming up here anyway.'

'In that case I feel even more inclined to take a look,' said Adam Cranley.

Annie was aware that Lady Mary's face opposite her, which was perfectly composed, had an air of tension about it.

'I do think you should be allowed to finish your lunch,' said Lady Mary but Adam stood up, saying, 'Best to go now, I think.'

Jasmine covered the silence by saying, 'Adam's paranoid about these animal rights people. He's afraid they'll sneak in and release birds from coops, stretch wires across ditches, trail smelly fish about and so forth.'

Annie glanced at her. Jasmine had, so to speak, gone over to the other side since her marriage. In her youth she'd been happy to go about with their father, pushing holes in fences built by landowners across public rights of way and had bravely stood beside him as he told thirty angry huntsmen and women, surrounded by a pack of baying hounds, that they couldn't ride up the bank and through the orchard at Froggett's in pursuit of a fox. Now she was all for the rights of the landowner, particularly her husband, to hunt, shoot and fish as he liked on his own land or, in the case of hunting, on other people's land as well.

That, reflected Annie, wasn't the only Browning principle which had bitten the dust since Jasmine had married Nigel five years before. The Brownings believed in art, socialism, plain living and high thinking. Jasmine now didn't give a hoot for art unless it was connected with the saleroom or hung on her own walls. She wouldn't give even one cheer for democracy and socialism and, as for plain living and high thinking, at the Fellowses' many houses – Durham House itself, the big London house in Bedford Square, the Kensington mews house – plain thinking and high living were the order of the day and that was how Jasmine liked it. Even for a rich man Nigel Fellows lived high – he bought his wife the most expensive jewellery, even though there was much family jewellery available if she wanted to deck herself out: the yearly grocery bill alone would have kept the average family going for years; the couple took many holidays of the most luxurious kind.

Annie wasn't particularly surprised by this reversal in her sister, although her parents were. Even in her teens Jasmine had shown signs of being more luxury-loving than was considered appropriate at home. At sixteen she'd spent her summer holidays in the petfood factory at Cottersley working on a machine which stuck labels on cans. With the money she earned she had bought a white dressing table with a triple mirror, cheap gilded knobs and a slide-out make-up tray. She'd had this put in her room, where it didn't go well with the sprigged wallpaper, plain woven curtains and faded Turkey rug. No comment had been made about this by her parents but they all knew that Jasmine's dressing table was in the nature of a criticism of her home life. Annie thought she must be a throwback to some ancestress a hundred years ago who had liked a good hot dinner, plenty of gilt or pearl buttons on her dresses, a tune you could hum or whistle and a jolly good laugh. And that person, reflected Annie, had probably been thrown out of the family by earlier Brownings and Cunninghams wearing flowing Liberty dresses and loose cravats, ancestors who furnished their houses with glum furniture by William Morris and attended Fabian Society lectures. She herself had no opinion about Jasmine's life-style, although she thought there might be a bill to be paid later for all the fun and luxury. In fact Annie wondered if Jasmine hadn't hinted at the kind of bill she might be expecting as they'd crossed the fields towards Durham House earlier on. Walking along in her green wellingtons Jasmine had said rather gloomily, 'They're all looking to me to produce a son and heir. Five years and no result, that's beginning to be the message, though everyone's too polite to say so. I think they're wondering if I'm sterile – Nigel isn't suspected. That isn't the way it works. I don't really fancy a baby but I suppose I've got to do it. Of course, the joke is that Nige isn't the heir to the title or the land, most of it, anyway. If only Sim would turn up and get married I'd be off the hook.'

She referred to Simon Fellows, Nigel's elder brother. 'Haven't they tracked him down, yet?' asked Annie.

'No. They've got people looking for him in all the likely and unlikely countries of the world. Sometimes they get a rumour there's an Englishman mouldering in some gaol in Manaos or Macao or somewhere like that, but it's never Sim. That's why Lady Mary's so sad, of course, though she hides it. Never speaks about it but she's afraid all the time that he's dead. It's awful for everybody and I suppose I'll have to have the damn baby soon.' She paused, opening the gate to the grounds of Durham House with a practised hand, muttering, 'Could be easier said than done, though.' She then shepherded Vanessa and Melanie, who had been walking behind, through the gate and up the path to the house, so Annie had no chance to ask her what she meant by the last remark.

The invitation to lunch had been delivered by Lady Mary and Jasmine, who had ridden over to Froggett's before breakfast. This habit of theirs upset Howard, who got up early to feed the hens and goats and have the fresh morning to himself. Juliet also disliked it, being a late-night painter and, in the mornings, a determined bohemian slugabed. She did her best work at night, she claimed, and objected to Lady Mary's habit of dropping by in jodhpurs and a bowler hat while she was asleep or, at best, drinking tea in bed.

On this occasion Lady Mary and Jasmine had turned up while everyone but Howard was asleep. Only Melanie had got up promptly, intrigued by the pawing and huffing of the two large hunters which had been hitched to the tree under her window. She'd arrived sleepily in the kitchen in the T-shirt and knickers she always slept in and, peering from the kitchen window, seeing Howard in corduroys and wellingtons approaching the house with two strange women in riding clothes, had taken fright and run out. Annie, coming down, met her on the stairs and told her there was nothing to worry about. Melanie came back into the kitchen later, well brushed and polished, to hear the invitation to lunch that day being accepted by Annie.

Howard refused to come, saying that Juliet was working for an exhibition of her paintings in London and he had to help her repair some picture frames.

At Durham House apple pie and cream were being brought round. Amanda Head shook her head furiously. Her pin-thin mother caught the look and shook her head. 'The diet,' she said in an amused tone. 'Melanie will eat yours.'

Melanie shook her head also. 'I've got to lose a stone,' she said. 'I'm fed up with being laughed at at school.'

Amanda shot Melanie a sympathetic glance but Vanessa asked indignantly, 'Who's laughing at you?'

'They all are,' Melanie told her. 'They say I'm overweight through living on chip butties and I talk funny and wear funny clothes and I'm a Northern git.' She added, 'I knew they'd be like that when I went there. Half of them are black and I said I was more English than them, which is true, so they hit me and then they told Miss I'm a racist and she told me off and said I'd be in detention if I carried on like that.'

'Why didn't you tell me or Annie?' asked Vanessa.

'No point, is there?' Melanie said gloomily.

Amanda seemed more sympathetic. 'Which school do you go to?' she asked.

'Jasper Rayburn Comprehensive, in Kenton,' Melanie told her, adding rather grandly, 'It's only temporary.'

'I suppose that's a state school,' Amanda remarked. 'I'm at Hatley Hall. We have ponies there. I've got my own room.'

'Lucky you,' remarked Melanie ambiguously.

'It's in lovely surroundings,' Amanda told her.

At the head of the table Nigel Fellows had broken into a landlord's diatribe designed partly, Annie suspected, to make it plain that her sister had changed her views now she was his wife. Jasmine gazed at him as he told Annie loudly, 'I'm never, to be perfectly honest, absolutely sure exactly what stage these people would like to make the land revert to. Would it be the eighteenth century, with little ragged boys scaring crows from the corn at sixpence a day? Or a medieval system, with all the beasts destroyed each winter to cut down on winter fodder? Or are we supposed to let the land go back to thick forests, full of wolves? I'm curious. I'd like someone to tell me. I don't mind the attacks, the wrecked hunting, my fences being broken down by proles with out-of-date maps showing my land belongs to them. I don't even mind my pheasant chicks being let out to be eaten by foxes which, of course, we mustn't kill – I'd just like a clear explanation of what it's all about, where, according to these people, we're supposed to be going. Can you tell me, perhaps, Annie?' he asked, leaning forward.

'I haven't made a study of the subject,' she said.

'I doubt if you'd like people bursting into your snack bar and throwing away the South African fruit or the bread because it isn't macrobiotic or whatever notion they have at the moment.'

82

'We're going more health conscious,' announced Vanessa, trying to divert Nigel's attention.

'I'm pleased to hear it. But that wasn't the point I was making,' he said rudely.

'Nigel—' Lady Mary said in her clear voice.

'It's all very well,' he went on. 'But I'd like to see what a pig's ear these people would make of the land if they got their hands on it. Christ!' he broke off as Adam Cranley came in with a tall man in his thirties wearing navy blue corduroy trousers, an old brown jersey and what was evidently the jacket of a suit. He was thin, with a slight stoop, which seemed to indicate diffidence. A lock of black hair fell over his long face. Nigel smiled. 'Tom! Adam thought you were some damn fool animal righter, popped in to poison the lake – come and sit down.'

As he stood up to get a chair Jasmine said, 'Tom – where did you spring from? I thought you were in Turkey with that man—'

'Didn't work,' said Tom Pointon, Annie and Jasmine's first cousin and Annie's first lover. He sat down and turned to Lady Mary. 'Adam told me you thought I was a prowler. I should have phoned.' He was squeezed in between Jasmine and Nigel. He craned forward and said to Annie, 'Juliet said you were here. I thought I'd look in just in case I missed you. I was planning to hang about until after lunch but Adam spotted me.'

'What happened in Turkey?' Annie asked.

'I went out for a few months theoretically to be with a man who was writing a travel book. I didn't specially want to go by that time but it was a longstanding arrangement. To my surprise, as soon as we got to the less exploited area around the Black Sea he started buying up land for resorts and holiday developments. I was helping him, in a friendly way, but then I began to wonder if the people so eagerly selling up their family farms ought to have been doing so. I sabotaged one of his deals with an old couple I felt sorry for and obviously he wasn't very pleased . . .'

'I imagine they wanted to sell,' remarked Nigel.

'I thought they oughtn't to, that's all. Perhaps I shouldn't have interfered. Anyway, here I am.'

Nigel was about to comment when Lady Mary asked, 'Weren't your parents going to settle down in Italy? Have they gone yet?'

'Oh, yes. Last year,' Tom said. 'They're near Pisa – lovely weather, a very nice couple looking after them, my mother's got a garden going, Dad's peacefully going to seed . . . It's ideal.'

'I don't think anyone could persuade my father to go peacefully to seed in Italy, or anywhere else,' Nigel said.

'I don't suppose so,' Tom agreed. 'But Dad's never been an energetic man. Granny used to say even as a boy he used to sit about for months, limp as a lettuce leaf, with nothing going on in his head at all. She got a doctor to look at him once but he only said he had a slow metabolism, whatever that means. If anything. Your father's a different matter, Nigel.' He was rapidly eating apple pie. It occurred to Annie that Juliet must have told him Julian had left her.

At the bottom of the table Amanda hissed to Melanie, 'Dishy.' Her mother, who could not have heard, gave her a hard look. 'He is, though,' she whispered.

Melanie contemplated Tom Pointon covertly. 'Not bad,' she muttered, her head pointing at her plate. 'Scruffy. He must be poor.'

Lady Mary suggested visiting the stables to see the vixen and her cubs. Melanie and Amanda, delighted to leave the table, jumped up, and were joined by Annie. Tom also rose.

The vixen was in an empty stall. A piece of wiring was secured in front of her. As they crept up she looked at them, with sharp intelligent eyes, flattening her cubs behind her in the corner. The cubs gave little yaps and sniffles, one escaped and came up to the wire. Melanie knelt down. 'Don't put your fingers through,' warned Lady Mary. 'They can nip.'

Melanie gazed into the sharp points of the cub's eyes. Amanda said, in a deliberate way, 'Oh – I should love to have one.'

'They belong to their mother,' Lady Mary told her. 'She hurt her leg and when she was found she was expecting the cubs. She and the cubs would probably have died if she hadn't been rescued. But when the time comes she and they will have to be released.'

'Will you hunt her then, and the cubs?' enquired Melanie, who had taken in a lot of Howard's comments and was on his side.

'Perhaps,' said Lady Mary. 'But you may not have seen what foxes do to other creatures when they catch them. If you look in the far corner you can probably see what she and the cubs made of a freshly killed rabbit this morning.'

Against the wall of the stable Tom and Annie murmured in the dim light. 'Are you all right, Annie?' he asked. 'Juliet told me—'

'I thought she might. It's all right.' There was a pause. 'He met someone else,' she explained. 'Cleaned me out, too – and the living-room sofa. Just don't say, I told you so.'

Six years ago, when the news of her plan to marry Julian Vane came to him, Tom had arrived unexpectedly at the flat in King's Cross she had been sharing with a friend while researching at the British Library for her thesis.

She'd made him a cup of tea on a hot August afternoon – the wedding was booked for early September. 'Don't do it, Annie,' he'd said. 'You don't know what people like that are like.'

'I know what Julian's like. What are you talking about?'

'Bad faith, Annie – that's what they specialise in,' he'd said.

'I don't know what that means. And I can't accept that you're an expert. You were the person who disappeared to France without a word. For months I believed you were at the London College of Printing, on a course. I thought you'd get in touch when you felt like it. Finally, I rang Aunt Betty and she said you were in Paris – well, had been – by then you were in Grenoble. She didn't know the address. All you'd sent was a postcard. She was terribly embarrassed, too. Lectures on bad faith aren't very convincing, coming from your lips, Tom.'

'I was wrong to do that – I know,' he said. 'But, please, just think. Julian seems to be a very different sort of person from you. Howard and Juliet give the impression that they're worried . . .'

'Did they say that? Did they send you—?' she exclaimed angrily.

'No, of course not,' he said.

'Did they say they didn't like Julian?' she insisted.

He stared at her. 'Defensive, Annie?'

'Tom! This is intolerable – what are they playing at?'

'Sorry. They didn't criticise Julian in any way, Annie, I assure you.'

'You received an unspoken message, though. I know,' she said. 'The slight hesitancy – the look that suggests they suspect a dead mouse somewhere but don't want to mention it. They try to hide their feelings, but they're not very good at it. Julian noticed. And frankly, that wasn't the welcome I'd received at his parents' house.' She stood up and crossed the room, looking out on to the traffic in the main road below. 'I'm shocked at you, Tom. You disappear for years, then turn up to warn me about marrying a man you've never met.' Tom was silent.

'If you've got a sensible thing to say, then say it, Tom,' Annie went on. 'Otherwise, I'd like as a wedding present one of those woodcuts you did for that Christmas book by Sue Sloman. Have you still got the originals?'

'An American bought them,' he said uneasily. 'I'll do you one.' He fidgeted. 'Look – this man has a graphics firm. You're giving up an academic career to work there. Is this what you really want?'

'Yes,' she said.

'And all that involves?'

'What do you mean?'

'Oh, hell – you know what I mean . . .'

'I do not.'

'I think you do.'

'No,' she said, although she did.

'You love him?'

'Of course I do.'

Then there came a terrible traffic crash from the street. They both went quickly to the window to see, below them, at the crossing, a taxi rammed by a white car with a woman now slumped at the wheel. As they stared a speeding builder's van failed to pull up soon enough and rammed the white car from the back, jolting the sagging figure at the wheel of the car. Annie ran to the phone and called an ambulance and Tom hurried downstairs to see if he could help. The angry taxi-driver, self-exonerating van driver, unconscious woman and later the police and the ambulancemen ended their argument. As the ambulance drew away Tom said awkwardly to Annie, 'Sorry, Annie – perhaps I shouldn't have come.'

'I expect you meant well,' Annie had said, shrugging.

'Best of luck, darling,' he'd said, and walked off. She'd watched his tall, ungainly figure moving through the people on the hot pavement. She felt irritable and sad and knew he was feeling almost precisely the same. Before the wedding he sent her a woodcut he'd made. It showed two figures on a city pavement, leaning towards each other from the shoulders, but keeping a distance between them. A sun burned above them in a wooden sky. She left the woodcut in her room at Froggett's before the wedding.

Now, leaning against the barn wall, Tom said, 'It must be awful, Annie. What are you doing? Any plans?'

'I seem to be running a snack bar with Vanessa – assisted by young Melanie, there,' she said, nodding towards the preoccupied Melanie, who was snuffling at the cubs, all out from behind their mother and staring at her curiously. 'It's in Foxwell Market. It's temporary, probably. I'll have to get a proper job soon, to keep me.'

Melanie said, 'It doesn't seem right to save them and then hunt after them, after. Can't we take them away with us? Just one?'

Annie stepped forward. 'Not to Foxwell,' she said. 'You can't keep foxes like dogs, Melanie. They need their freedom. Here's the only place they can be.'

'They could live on scraps from the café. It wouldn't cost any money.'

'In a cage? Or they'd be run over.'

'Watch me,' Tom muttered to Melanie. 'Lady Mary,' he said. 'I've just installed myself in the cottage at the bottom of what used to be my parents' garden. They sold the house but they kept the cottage. I'm borrowing it and using the outbuilding for my work. I'm suffering from the loneliness of the old artisan in a primitive cottage on the edge of a wood. A pet,' he told her, with a smile which did not conceal his motive, to persuade and seduce, 'would be the answer.' He looked down at the cage.

'They don't stay with you as you perfectly well know, Tom,' Lady Mary said disapprovingly. 'And they are a pest . . .'

'Please,' he said.

'All right,' she said, smiling. 'Arrange it with Adam. But don't expect him to approve. Come on, girls,' she said. 'It's getting dark in here. Let's go and look at the pigs before teatime.' She turned to Tom. 'One of the sows farrowed. Can I write you down for a couple of piglets?'

Tom laughed. He looked at Melanie who was staring at him excitedly and he winked. He and Annie walked back to the house together and she told him more about the café. 'Are you sure this isn't the kind of crazy thing women do when there's a divorce?' he asked.

'I don't know,' Annie told him. 'I like it, though. What else can I do — train for merchant banking, teach or just sit in a chair and sigh all day?'

He put his arm round her shoulders and gave her a squeeze.

7

A Visit from David Pickering

It was Friday afternoon. The market was full of people, mostly women with plastic bags and wheeled shoppers, getting in the week-end shopping under a grey sky. In the steamy heat of George's Café Mrs Patel sat in a macintosh and red trousers, drinking tea. Two women were having Coke and cakes and a boy and a girl, who had probably left Rayburn Comprehensive after afternoon roll call, were drinking coffee with an eye on the pavement outside.

The café had now been under new management for a month. One half of the partnership, Annie, had devised new plans. The other half, Vanessa, was thinking them over as she slowly washed some cups. Starting on a huge pile of cutlery she changed gear, washing them in one sink, rinsing in the other, stacking them on a huge plate rack. A washing-up machine was a priority, Annie'd said, and she'd drink to that, in dirty washing-up water if need be. But, and it was a big but, it was all right for Annie to be smart, do figures and make plans. Vanessa had two children, she was hesitant about branching out, she needed security and was nervous about the extra workload. They couldn't afford more staff and she was finding it hard enough to manage already. Alec was at a child-minder's two days a week and in the café with her, if Melanie was at school, for the other three days. Vanessa was not keen on the minder. Nor was Alec. It was not easy. Then there was the housework, washing, iron-ing and sometimes she was so tired, so numbly hurt that she snapped at the children and upset Alec more. At Joanne, too, who was show-ing her upset by getting aggressive at school and being naughty. There was probably nothing wrong with Annie's plans, thought

Vanessa, except that they would mean more work, more thinking and more risk.

She thought bitterly of Geoff, who had seen his children twice since Christmas. He'd taken them out for two hours one Sunday afternoon, and brought them back sooner than he'd said because, she thought, it was raining and he didn't want their muddy feet climbing in and out of his new car. He'd whisked them off to the cinema another day. It was likely Cindy wasn't too keen on his seeing his children. It might be better if he didn't anyway, she considered, for afterwards on both occasions, Joanne, white and pent up, had actually attacked her, Vanessa, kicking and screaming about some trifle, while Alec had simply withdrawn into blankness, staring at her as if she weren't there, seeming to lose most of his power of speech, saying only, 'Drink' or 'toilet' like a much younger child. Next day she'd still had to drag him to the minder, although she knew she ought to spend the day with him. There was no one to help her now – not Geoff, of course, nor her sister, busy with her own life and afraid of Vanessa somehow as if she thought divorce was catching, not her mother, enjoying a life free of the commitments she'd always resented, Vanessa now realised. Anita used to complain about the restrictions imposed on mothers of children, the noise, the mess, the housework, as if Vanessa and Cherry had been foisted on her by a bureaucratic government and she must bring them up or go to gaol. And if Cherry thought divorce was catching, or hereditary, and so wanted to distance herself as much as possible from her sister, then her mother thought it was caused by something a wife did or didn't do and the wife was therefore to blame for it. 'There must have been *something*,' she'd insisted. 'Didn't you notice *anything*, Ness? I can't believe it came as a bombshell, like you say. Women always *know*, really, when the marriage is going wrong.'

One day, after Vanessa had been obliged to take a day off to look after Alec, who had a bad cold, she'd said to Annie, 'It's no good asking Mum. She won't help. She's quite annoyed with me because of all this. On the surface it's all, "Oh, poor Vanessa. Geoff's a villain. Fancy doing a thing like that", but underneath it's like I'm a leper and I've let the family down.' She added gloomily, 'I think she'd stand by my brother more if he'd done a real crime, like robbing a bank, and got arrested. She'd be able to find excuses, like his wife was nagging him for money, or he'd been led into it by a friend – it'd be somebody else's fault. He's the son, the only boy and the sun shines out of his backside. Girls are there to get married and have the lovely grandchildren, a nice house and all that. That's the way she is, Mum. There's no point trying to get her to help.'

Annie tried not to show how much she disapproved of Vanessa's mother but Vanessa noticed and said defensively, 'Well, when it comes down to it, where's your mum? We could do with an extra pair of hands, couldn't we?'

'She's getting her exhibition together—'

'Same difference,' Vanessa claimed. 'That's the point, isn't it? In a situation like we're in the family's supposed to roll up its sleeves and help you out. But nine cases out of ten they don't. You look round and there they are – gone. Families like winners – people who do what they should do and make a go of it. Your family doesn't think much of you running a snack bar – mine thinks I should have managed to keep my husband – so we're not getting the support. I bet if I told them tomorrow I was getting married to a wealthy man they'd be all over me, congratulations, invitations, the lot. They'd rush off for new outfits, get their hair done, tell the neighbours who he was and what car he drove – that's what they're like.'

Vanessa yawned as she dried the ladles, the big knives, the sieves. She dropped the cloth into the laundry bag behind the back door and yawned again. There it was – she'd got it all straightened out. They could look the public health officer in the eye again if he happened to turn up. But Annie wasn't satisfied. She wanted to go further and, in fact, she was right to want to expand the business, because it wasn't producing enough income for them to live on. She would not have been able to pay her gas bill if Geoff hadn't given her £70 the last time he came round.

Vanessa fantasised about a wealthy and handsome lover, a man who would give her, Alec and Joanne a nice home in a nice area – a garden, a modern kitchen, two bathrooms. The end of the day had come and it was time to close the café. She put on her coat, picked up her bag and stepped out into Foxwell Market, emptier now, and full of paper blowing about. Cabbage leaves and old cardboard boxes lay on the pavements.

It was quite dark. She started as a man came out of a doorway opposite, laughing a high-pitched laugh, then made his way with a stumbling gait into the High Street. She sighed and had taken only two paces away from the café, after locking the door, when a thickset man in a donkey jacket put his hand on her arm. He had come up quietly behind her without her noticing.

'I want to talk to you,' he said. 'Let's go inside.'

'In the café? No way. And let go of my arm,' she said vigorously.

'You open that door for us,' he said. 'Or I'll have you arrested.'

He had a northern accent. Vanessa pulled free and started to move away from him quickly, towards the lights of the High Street. 'Come back here,' he called.

'What's happening?' said Annie coming into the market from the High Street. She flew towards Vanessa. Vanessa grabbed her arm and pulled her away from the market towards the High Street.

'You've got my daughter. I want her back,' shouted the man in the donkey jacket. 'Aye. That's right. Melanie Pickering,' he went on as the women turned round. 'Now will you come back here and open up? Unless you want the whole world to know you're keeping her and exploiting her.'

'Better do it,' muttered Vanessa.

They returned to the café. Vanessa unlocked the door and they went in. The man was broad, fairly tall and had large blue eyes, from which he now stared fiercely at Annie and Vanessa. 'So,' he said. 'I understand from my wife that you've got Melanie. Which one of you is Mrs Vane.'

'I am,' said Annie.

'Well, I want her back home where she should be. I've told my wife she's coming. Where is she now?'

'At my house,' Annie said. 'She's been at school all day.'

'School?' he said, his voice rising. 'School? What right have you to send her to school? She's got a school, at home, where she should be. What's the name of the school? I'll soon go there and tell them what's what.'

'Melanie's mother knows all about it,' Annie said. 'She thinks it a good idea for Melanie to stay—'

'Thinks – thinks,' Pickering said threateningly. 'Mrs Pickering is my wife. I'm the child's father. I say where she's to go and not go. It's not for a pack of women to decide between them what happens.'

'She has a right to say—' began Annie.

'She's no right,' he contradicted.

'Melanie herself wants to stay,' Annie said.

'She's told you a pack of lies, no doubt,' David Pickering said. 'She'll have got round you like she does at home. You ought to know better than to believe what a child of thirteen tells you. Now, I'm telling you two, you'd better let her go. I want my daughter back.'

Vanessa went behind the counter. She withdrew some of the day's takings from a canvas bag she had concealed in her shopping bag. Pickering watched her. 'Mr Pickering,' she said, 'Melanie's very useful to us while we're just starting the business. I'm wondering if she could stay on a little longer with us?' She held up some banknotes. 'Could you see your way . . . ?'

'I might,' he said, regarding the notes closely. Vanessa added two more.

'All right,' he said. 'I suppose working for you is a form of training – could come in useful when she leaves school and wants to go to work.'

'That's what I think,' Vanessa came slowly round the counter, holding the money in front of her. Annie stood paralysed. 'After all,' Vanessa went on, 'she's in good hands, she's going to school so . . .' David Pickering's hand came up to meet hers '. . . you've nothing to worry about.'

Pickering carefully put the notes in an inside pocket and turned as if to leave. 'Well, ladies,' he said, 'I can't see any harm in her stopping on for a little while. Plainly she's being looked after . . .'

Vanessa nodded, held open the door and watched as he strode across the street.

'That's that, then,' she said, turning back to Annie. 'I'm glad you came down, though. I wouldn't have fancied facing him all on my own.'

'I only came to see if you wanted a hand,' Annie said in a stunned voice. 'But I still don't believe it. How did you know he'd take money.'

'I've seen it all before,' Vanessa said. 'It's an instinct.'

Annie was shaken. 'He took money for his daughter! How much – fifty pounds was it?'

'Seventy,' Vanessa said, adding grimly, 'And he'll be back.'

They turned into Foxwell High Street. Vanessa gestured at the people, the traffic, the borough in general. 'What makes you think all this is different from Dickens's time – a few cars, shops with videos and fridges, different styles – but where's the real change? It's the same underneath. You've still got rich and poor, people desperate enough or rotten enough to do anything for a bob or two. D'you know what I mean, Annie? It's all still here – women going on the game, or stripping for the rent, people doing dodgy things for money. Still here, the lot of it. Just the same.' She was

92

walking rapidly, talking quickly. She glanced at Annie. 'I'll tell you, though,' Vanessa continued, her voice still fast and nervous. 'I've decided we ought to go ahead and try for the lunchtime contracts and the more health-conscious food. Looking at that man taking money for his daughter made me realise what we're up against. It's dog eat dog and we're going to have to be that little bit better to survive and not get eaten. I can't afford to mess about. I've got my kids to think of. I don't want them fetching up like Melanie. It's love, money and revenge, like we said, from now on. I'm serious.'

'Thanks, Vanessa,' Annie said. They walked along for a little while. 'Do you think he'll come back for more money?' she asked.

'I expect so. It's too attractive, isn't it? Getting money from women for a young girl. Next time we'd better be ready for him,' said Vanessa.

As Annie, Vanessa, Melanie, the children, Tom Pointon and Lady Mary walked back from the pigsties a great red sun was setting to their left over the trees and hills in the direction of Froggett's.

The Heads left and then there was tea in the drawing room, where a log fire burned. Vanessa sipped her tea politely, staring at the paintings on the walls, the huge Renaissance picture of a biblical subject, the Romney painting of an ancestress which Lady Mary had brought with her when she married Sir Bernard. Sam Anstruther had cornered Annie on the sofa. 'Do you imagine,' he was almost pleading, 'there's any chance at all of my persuading your parents to let me just take a peek at the contents of the suitcase? Even if your mother doesn't wish to offer her aunt's papers for sale, or, it may be, is prevented by the terms of the will, I'd really like to ascertain what there is. It would be of enormous interest to scholars of Christian Cunningham's work—'

'I can ask,' Annie replied wearily, 'but I don't think it'll make any difference. They just don't want the disturbance. I don't think, you see, that my mother really believes, deep down, that the case is hers, anyway. It was left behind by accident . . .'

'I do understand,' he assured her. 'Your parents are busy people with a right to their privacy. I understand that. But quite frankly, I'm a little afraid that the case is vulnerable to an accident – fire, flood, something like that, however minor, could irreparably damage the contents. There's the insurance, too – that ought to be considered . . .'

93

'I suppose so,' Annie said, her eye caught by the sight of Nigel flirting with Vanessa. 'I don't suppose you get out much, because of the children,' he was suggesting.

'Oh – I went out to a disco last night,' Vanessa said. 'Didn't enjoy it much, though.'

'Why not?' he asked.

'I went with the wrong man, didn't I?' she said, looking at him from under her eyelashes.

After tea they walked back across the fields to Froggett's. 'I wouldn't trust that Nigel very far,' exclaimed Vanessa. 'He's a real flirt.'

'He even propositioned me at their wedding!' Annie said.

'Never!'

'I don't think he really meant it,' Annie said. 'I think he loves Jasmine very much.'

'I think you're right,' Vanessa said. She thought of the rotten evening she'd had at the disco with a friend of her brother's who'd asked her out. She'd felt old, every woman there was younger than her. The friend had taken her home, expected to come in and make love to her and been angry when she'd sent him away. She was hoping this wasn't the best she could expect in future. She said, 'Guess who that bald man is?'

Annie said, 'I know. Max Craig. The company astrologer. Apparently it's not uncommon these days for firms to have them. They're supposed to predict snags, advise on what the market's going to do next. It does seem strange, doesn't it?'

'Thought that stuff was for women – you know, am I going to get married, who to, will my first child be a girl or a boy?'

When Annie and Vanessa got back Tom and Melanie were already in the kitchen, talking about the foxes. 'I've put the kettle on,' Tom said. 'I'll make some tea. Or would you rather have a drink? Nothing's changed,' he added, looking round the room. 'I haven't been here for seven years.'

'Where are Howard and Juliet?' asked Annie.

'They went out to see friends in the village,' he said. 'They'll only be gone an hour. Howard put some baked potatoes in the oven for the children. There are sausages in the fridge. Shall I cook some for their tea?' He put the frying pan on the Aga. Vanessa, her head on one side, watched his long, gangling figure going about his business with ease. Digging in, she thought.

Annie poured some wine. 'I don't think Lady Mary's really all that comfortable with the house now it's been done up. I think she preferred it before Sir Bernard and Nigel made it more like a film set.'

Tom was capably sorting out the children's supper, cutting up a tomato, splitting the baked potatoes and turning the sausages in the pan. He said, 'Well, she was trained to deal with what was handed her. She probably feels a bit strange with the house full of businessmen and astrologers and so forth – foreign bankers – but she doesn't let it show.'

Annie was leaning against the big dresser, framed by a cascade of strung-together sea horses on one side, and half a Roman pot Howard had found in the garden. Tom, at the table, was getting Alec and Joanne to sit down. The trouble was, Vanessa reflected, that the tension between Annie and Tom was enough to make you twitch. It was obvious that he'd left Durham House a few minutes after them and driven rapidly to Froggett's by road. Now he was in charge of the Aga, doing an imitation of an old friend of the family which wouldn't have deceived a child. Annie was staring at him as if he was doing magic tricks. It was, Vanessa thought, pathetic to see two grown-up people, both with hundreds of degrees, going on like that. She said, 'Why don't you two hop off for a quick walk while Alec and Joanne have their supper?'

Tom and Annie went out and without thinking about it turned towards the orchard, where they'd always gone after supper when they were lovers.

'Well?' he said as they walked down the orchard path. It was piercingly cold. They both had their hands in their pockets.

'Well?' responded Annie.

'I love you, Annie,' he said. 'I'm glad you're free.'

She pulled his hand from his pocket and held it.

'It was a shock. Julian going like that – I'm not . . .'

'You are,' he said. It was without surprise that Vanessa, spying on them from the kitchen window, saw them kissing as they later made their way back to the house.

8

A Picnic in Savernake Park

'Thanks a lot,' cried Melanie indignantly. It was only 1 March, but the temperature had soared into the 70°s and so they were having a Sunday picnic lunch on the grass in the beautiful setting of Savernake Park. Once the estate of the Rodwell family, Barons Savernake, owners of many ships carrying wool out of the country in the seventeenth century and tea, sugar and cotton back in the eighteenth (the usual slaves on the middle passage) to the left of the park now lay a council estate built on the site of the original house. The view down to the river where the Savernakes must have enjoyed watching ships go by was unfortunately now broken by a couple of high commercial buildings, but you could just glimpse the water between the buildings down a long stretch of rolling grass, interrupted only by some swings, hanging tyres and a dilapidated slide. Two traffic-laden roads circuited the acres of parkland and flats, turning the area more or less into a triangle with Foxwell at the top, as the broad end, and the River Thames as its apex.

The picnic party consisted of Annie, Melanie, Vanessa, Joanne and Alec who sat on a rug under a chestnut tree. Annie had only just revealed to Melanie that her father, for the second time now, had paid a visit to the café. Melanie was furious.

'Thanks a lot! Thanks for telling me. *And* you gave him money!' she was saying angrily. 'That was the last thing to do. Now he'll think he's on to a good thing, and keep on coming back.' She paused to think. 'I wonder if Mum knows where he is. Honestly,' she said, 'you two are daft. I had a right to know he'd come round, you know. I had a right to be told.'

Joanne asked, 'Can't we start on the sandwiches, Vanessa?' To

Vanessa's irritation, now Geoff had left Joanne had taken to calling her mother by her Christian name. Vanessa felt as though she had lost authority but complaining about it made no difference.

It was pleasant in the park, but in spite of the gleam of the Thames at the foot of the grassy incline, and the sunshine, the party was tense. Alec and Joanne were upset, Vanessa anxious about them. Annie wasn't sure what to do about Melanie, and Tom hadn't been in touch since they'd met over a fortnight before.

So no one answered Joanne.

'If he goes to the police,' Vanessa said, 'he could accuse us of being kidnappers.'

'Don't be stupid – I've not been kidnapped. My mum knows where I am.'

Joanne, who was furtively picking at a packet of sandwiches, stared at the word kidnappers. She looked round, as if one might be lurking in a bush. Alec, wanting a sandwich, began to cry.

'Give him one, Joanne,' Vanessa instructed absently.

Annie said, 'I hope she feels all right, with two of you gone.'

'Two?' demanded Vanessa. 'What's this?'

'My sister Ruth ran away,' Melanie told her flatly. 'Nobody knows where she is.'

'Oh, my God,' Vanessa said. She looked at Annie, who shook her head, meaning the story Melanie told was sad and serious. But Vanessa saw complications and imagined herself in the dock giving evidence. She looked desperately at Joanne and Alec and said, 'Oh dear.'

'I suppose all this means I've got to go home,' Melanie said bravely.

Vanessa leaned over, moved Alec's prying hand from the box of food, handed him a sandwich and said, 'Eat this up first, then you can see what else we've got.'

'My sandwich, Vanessa,' Joanne said loudly and rudely. 'You deaf, or what?'

'Jaffa cakes,' Alec said.

'Don't be rude, Joanne,' Vanessa responded mechanically. To Annie she went on, 'Look – Melanie's mum says she can stay, that's got a lot to do with it. Right, Melanie? Otherwise, David Pickering's just trying it on. He can't do anything.'

'Mum'll have to go along with what Dad says,' observed Melanie, 'for the money. If he's sending any,' she added.

'You'd better ring her again,' advised Vanessa. 'She must be worried, with your dad gone, two boys to look after. I'd go mad, in her shoes. Especially with your sister – do you mean nobody knows where she is?'

Melanie changed the subject. 'This picnic's great!' she said, helping herself to a sausage roll.

The tall buildings of the Savernake Estate were slightly cracked due to the use of shoddy materials and poor workmanship by the contractors in the sixties. The tenants, in and out of work, self-employed in legal or illegal ways, or sometimes a bit of both, old, young, married, pregnant, happy, sad, were all tucked away behind balconies and curtains – tidy nets looped up to let the people see the pot plant and the plant see the light, flat dwellers' orange and brown curtains, Venetian blinds, neat or collapsing. Their cars were at the back in the big courtyard. Now on this sunny spring afternoon, the tall towers gleamed magically on the other side of the park, like a vision, perhaps the same vision seen by the original planners in the fifties, as they stood in their suits in a municipal building dreaming municipal dreams.

Annie gave Vanessa some coffee from a Thermos. 'Don't look so bad from here, does it?' Vanessa said staring across at the flats. Two young men, in T-shirts and jeans, each with a straining pit bull terrier half suffocating itself at the end of its lead, walked past, eyeing the group on the grass unamiably.

'When we've finished our picnic we ought to go back and ring your mother,' Annie said to Melanie.

'Sooner the better,' Vanessa said.

Later, in Annie's house, a dispute arose about who should ring Mrs Pickering to check that Melanie could stay in London. Vanessa maintained Annie should do it as she had a posh accent, Annie that Vanessa should do it because a posh accent implying authority might put Mrs Pickering off. Melanie claimed she herself should do it because Jenny Pickering was her mother. Finally Vanessa picked up the phone and dialled. Mrs Pickering's phone had been disconnected. 'So he isn't sending her any money,' Melanie said. 'That's the last thing she saves money on – the phone. I'll try Mo Patel.' She dialled the corner shop of the street where she lived and left a message for her mother to ring London. Then they sat down to wait for her call and watch television. Two hours later they were still waiting.

'I'll have to take Alec back soon, to go to bed,' said Vanessa after they had all consumed a Chinese take-away. Then the phone rang.

'I'm all right, still at Annie's,' Melanie's response was a mixture of pleasure at hearing her mother's voice and anxiety lest she could not placate her. 'I'm working in the café. Yes. I'm going to school. No. It's not very nice. Why's the phone off, Mum? Haven't you got any money? Well, he's here. Aye, Dad's here.'

Melanie's mother spoke at length.

Melanie said, 'I don't know, Mum.'

There was more from the other end of the line.

'Well, I'm sorry, Mum. I haven't seen him. Annie and Vanessa saw him. He's been round to the café asking them for money—'

Mrs Pickering's demands for explanations were now so audible that Vanessa took the phone, saying loudly, 'Now, Mrs Pickering, don't upset yourself. As long as you don't mind Melanie being here, we can cope with your husband. I expect he was desperate at the time. Well, you can be, can't you? Do you want to come down here and see what's going on? Or shall Melanie come and see you in the school holidays? You what? Oh—' she laughed. 'No – I don't know where he's to be found – I know. I know – I know. You don't have to tell me. I'll try, if I see him, but I don't suppose he'll say. If you want my opinion you'd better try FIS, the DSS, try for a rebate off the council – see if you can get a single-parent increase on the family allowances. I know – I know – I know. So if Mr Pickering comes round again, I'm just to tell him you'd like to hear from him. Yes, I know, believe me, I know . . . And I'm to tell him you're perfectly satisfied with Melanie stopping here. Good. Well, talk to you soon. All right,' she said, putting down the phone. 'That's it. She says I didn't have to shout, they've got ears north of Watford Gap! She can't afford the fares down for her and the boys at the moment, the place she works is cutting the hours back, but she's sending you your bus fare one way, Mels, you're to keep it and use it if you want – don't spend it, it's hard to come by. And if anybody spots your father she'd like to know where he is, what he's doing, and some money for the boys. You've got to keep on going to school religiously. Nice woman, she sounds, but she's had enough to put up with, so she doesn't need any more problems, so you behave yourself, Melanie Pickering.'

'What a relief,' said Melanie. 'Fancy Dad not telling her he'd found me.'

Annie felt bewildered. Practical Vanessa had no trouble in comprehending the Pickering family relationships or the other issues involved. She recalled, vaguely, Jessie Knipe of 20 Threpp Street, first floor back, who ran off with an itinerant accordionist and came back ten months later with a baby girl. There had been an argument with the workhouse authorities about a Scottish wedding certificate, she remembered. She shook her head to clear it. These thoughts had nothing to do with the present day.

Vanessa turned off the television and said to her children, 'Up, you two. Alec, do you want to go to the toilet?' She departed, tired but strong, saying, 'See you tomorrow, Annie.'

Annie made Melanie get on with her homework while she settled down to do the VAT.

The contract sandwich business had taken off fast, almost too fast for the weary proprietors of George's. Local firms had been keen to take up the offer of sandwich and fruit lunches for their employees, who complained of the lack, locally, of acceptable cafés and restaurants. And the recent acquisition of a contract with the sports centre was a triumph financially, but an even greater strain on an already taxed organisation. Melanie acted as a delivery person, claiming she was pleased to have a lunchless lunch break cycling round Foxwell. It would help her lose weight. The small sum they paid her she saved for clothes and presents for her brothers. She was growing, getting thinner and, at school anyway, had abandoned her northern accent. She'd taken on both the dreaded Godwin twins who intimidated and extorted from both boys and girls in their class, and although she'd come home hardly able to walk for bruises, she'd achieved much credit not by winning, but by going berserk enough to terrify the watchers, as well as slightly alarming the twins. 'They're soft down here,' she'd muttered, through gritted teeth, leaning on the bathroom door while Annie ran a hot bath for her. Annie had been in favour of seeing the headmaster. Vanessa rejected the idea, but got her brother Malcolm who played for Leigh Rangers to go to collect Melanie from school next day in case the Godwin twins had roped in their big brothers to avenge the fight. Melanie's reputation sky-rocketed.

Meanwhile, Annie and Vanessa were strained, anxious, short of cash. They were always running: to George's, to the cash and carry, to do a last-minute sandwich delivery, back and forth to the primary school and the child-minder's. They couldn't have managed without Melanie. And the rumour that Geoff Doyle was up for a big contract, and almost bound to get it, and a friend's phone call to Annie telling her Julian planned to set up in a smart West End office, did nothing to soothe their feelings.

100

Annie, juggling figures on the table while Melanie lay on the floor, sucking her teeth and chewing her pen over an essay she was supposed to be writing, 'A Local Scene and what it means', for Miss Godber, NUT, SWP, English teacher at Rayburn Comprehensive, was surprised to hear the front door bang and jerked her head round to see Julian in the doorway. He looked thinner, tanned and was well dressed in a dark suit and a black Mafia-style overcoat and hat, so much like a parody of the originals that Annie's first thought was that he looked as if in his hand he should have carried a violin case. She was astonished to find that the distress which had turned her first into a sobbing insomniac, then into a numb and frozen shadow, appeared to have transmuted into another emotion – anger.

Julian looked round the room, observing its neglect and, of course, Melanie, in her T-shirt and jeans, watching Esther Rantzen and scribbling on an A4 pad in her big, unformed handwriting.

'Hallo, Annie,' he said pleasantly. 'How's things? I wanted to take you out to dinner.'

'I've eaten, thanks,' she said. She wanted to hit him, but then had a little shifting thought, that perhaps, against the odds, he was coming back.

'Shall we go out for a drink, then?' he asked.

In the pub she was forced to realise that he was not only not in love with her, not even friendly, but that he did not really want to be with her. At a small table in a corner of the crowded Duke of Westminster he said, 'The house doesn't seem to be on the market, yet. I'm rather worried . . .' Behind him the juke box played: 'I could be so happy, happy, happy . . .'

'I haven't had time,' responded Annie, still bewildered by his stiff, wary attitude. 'I don't want to do it, anyway . . .'

'You agreed,' he told her.

She thought, Did I? Surely I didn't.

'Well, it has to happen.' Julian could barely conceal his impatience. 'Neither of us can afford to keep it. I need the capital. You can't, presumably, pay the mortgage. I imagine you've obtained six months' grace from the building society but why wait till the last moment . . .' He paused, then said quickly, 'Perhaps Howard and Juliet are paying?'

'Julian,' Annie said resignedly, 'I'm too busy to do all this. Sell up, find somewhere to live—'

'I don't want you letting, either,' he said quickly. 'The building society takes a dim view—'

'I'm not planning to.' Annie was surprised. She spotted that Julian had given away an idea about how to continue to pay the mortgage and keep the house and he was annoyed with himself.

'And how's your own life?' Annie asked more cheerfully. She still hoped that somehow they could be friendly.

'Well, it's busy, obviously.' Julian gave the impression he was fatigued, but then, rallying, added, 'That's why I'm here. Frankly, I need the house to be sold fairly soon. I want to expand. There's a lot of business in design on a bigger scale. There's just enormous scope. With a team – architects, interior designers and so forth – there's the chance to see a whole project through, start to finish. This is why I want to realise as much capital as possible. There's a guy – he'll match me pound for pound, and a bit more, I suspect, but I have to – well, you can see why I want the house sold. Fast. You see that, don't you?'

His enthusiasm for this new opportunity, and the way, suddenly, he was addressing her as the wife, friend, workmate and well-wisher she had once been, startled Annie again. For a moment she almost responded as she might have done, by agreeing to his proposal, making suggestions, discussing possibilities. Then she realised Julian's plan had nothing to do with her. In fact, she now needed the house so as to live near the café, which was possibly going to start producing a modest living wage for herself and Vanessa. She tried to explain the situation to him.

'A snack bar?' he exclaimed.

She couldn't help boasting. 'We'd be quite pleased to lay on a reasonable lunch for your staff . . .'

'My new offices,' he pointed out, 'will be in Sackville Street.'

Annie stared at this handsome man, with his cold eyes, who wanted her out of the house they'd shared, cared nothing for how she felt, or how she was to keep herself in future. No longer a husband, he was not a friend, not even a friendly stranger. He only saw that she was standing in his way, and must be made to do what he wanted. 'I could be so happy, happy, happy . . .' went the music. Panic swept her as she noticed he was looking at her speculatively, wondering what he could do to get his way. She stood up, picked up her bag. 'I've got a lot to do,' she muttered.

Julian grasped her arm. 'We've got things to talk about.'

'Julian.' She looked down at him, 'You can divorce me. I won't oppose you.'

Pushing her way out of the pub she half ran to Vanessa's

house and rang the doorbell. There was no response and she rang it again. Annie was sure Vanessa must be in – unless there'd been an emergency and she'd gone out leaving a nervous babysitter behind with instructions not to open the door. She could hear angry voices and then the sound of something breaking inside the house. On the other side of the street she caught sight of a blue van with Doyle, Builders, painted on the side. She turned back and leant her head against the front door. Alec was crying. Annie's first instinct was to leave, since if Vanessa and Geoff Doyle were having a row an intrusive third party would not be welcome. But then she remembered how, on many occasions, Vanessa had expressed fear of Geoff's size and his readiness to use violence. She hesitated, then pressed the bell again, wondering what she could do if no one answered. To her relief, Mrs Hodges from next door came out on to her step, accompanied by an elderly dog. 'You her friend?' asked the old lady, nodding towards the house.

'Yes,' Annie said. 'I can't get anyone to answer the door.'

'Kid's screaming in there,' Mrs Hodges reported. 'And no wonder. There's a hell of a row going on. It's her husband. You can hear it right over the telly.'

'I don't know whether I ought to . . .'

'Up to you,' said Mrs Hodges unhelpfully, taking in the dog and closing her front door.

Annie felt at a loss. But how could she leave Vanessa alone with Geoff Doyle? She'd have to risk the consequences, from embarrassment to a punch on the nose. She put her thumb on the doorbell and left it there.

The door crashed open and Geoff Doyle filled the doorframe, saying aggressively, 'What?'

'What's happening?' Annie said weakly. Vanessa staggered into the hall, half doubled up. She'd been crying. Her hair was all over the place. 'Vanessa?'

Doyle jutted his head forward. 'Fuck off!' he said, and closed the door with a bang.

Annie stood there, listening, hearing nothing. For all she knew, this scene might be a prelude to a reconciliation. Violence, followed by sex, that wasn't uncommon, she speculated. She and Vanessa had never really talked much about sex and if there was that element in her relationship with Geoff, she might not confide it readily, Annie thought. She hoped Mrs Hodges' door would open again, but it stayed tight shut. She pressed the bell again. Feet ran to the door. It was wrenched open. Vanessa faced her. Geoff Doyle, behind, caught up with her, and grasped his wife's shoulder.

'I told you to fuck off, so fuck off!' Doyle said angrily in one breath. He tried to pull Vanessa back.

'Get the police,' sobbed Vanessa as Doyle pulled her in backwards and shut the door with his foot, but not before Annie had glimpsed Alec at the foot of the stairs in his pyjama suit, white and silent, staring. Annie ran straight home and called the police.

'They'll never come out for that,' predicted Melanie. But they did, perhaps persuaded by Annie's diction, although by the time they arrived Geoff had gone.

Anita Davis shook her head at her daughter, lying on the sofa with ice cubes wrapped in a tea-towel pressed to her cheek. 'You shouldn't have let him in, Vanessa,' she said.

'I know that now, Mum,' Vanessa replied patiently. 'He said he'd come to see the kids.'

'Well, you know better now.'

Annie stared at Melanie, who raised her eyebrows.

'What started it, anyway?' asked Anita.

'He wants me to agree to a divorce and ask the council for a transfer so I'm not around – says Cindy's upset because I'm so close, with the kids. She's been trying for a baby and the specialist says it might be because she's upset I'm near by, and Alec and Joanne.'

'What did you say?' asked her mother.

'I told him to get stuffed,' Vanessa said.

'In so many words?' Vanessa nodded. Anita shook her head. 'Why did you do that?'

'Well – what did he expect me to do? Go down and live at Dungeness? What chance do I stand if I leave here? I was born here. The snack bar's here.'

'Forget the snack bar – if you got a divorce he'd have to support you,' her mother told her.

'How could I make him? Out of sight'd be out of mind.'

'The law could force him . . . '

'He's self-employed, Mum. You know what that means—'

Annie could bear no more. 'Whose side are you on, Mrs Davis?' she demanded angrily.

'What exactly do you mean?' Anita Davis asked hotly. 'I don't know what makes you think you can speak like that to me—'

'I don't suppose I should,' Annie said, 'but I must say so far you've made me believe you think it's Vanessa's fault that her husband came round to beat her up.'

'I think I've heard enough,' Anita said tartly. 'I raced round here at your request, to help Vanessa, now I'm forced to sit here listening to insults – well, if you really want to know what I think, I think Vanessa's played her cards wrong. If she'd made it plain to Geoff she wanted him back he'd come running soon enough. She's got the kids. All this nonsense about the snack bar is ridiculous. What she needs to do is go round, get upset and make a bit of a fuss of him. At the moment she's made it look as if she didn't care whether he came or went. Now, a man doesn't like that – why should he? A woman's got to compromise a bit in this world. I'll be honest. I think you're at the back of it, egging her on—'

'We were broke, Mum,' Vanessa said. 'I had to do something.'

'Yes – gone to him, that's what he wanted. Anyway,' she continued, 'I'd be just as happy if you, Annie, kept your nose out of our business. You're a different kind of person and what works for you doesn't work for us. And Geoff and Vanessa have got children, something you wouldn't be in a position to understand.'

'I understand that you're condoning your son-in-law beating up your daughter,' Annie returned.

'I won't stay to bandy words with you,' the older woman said, picking up her handbag. 'I deserve an apology. I come here to be with my daughter in a crisis and this is the treatment I get – thank you very much, Vanessa.' Angrily she said from the doorway, 'I expect you'll want to explain this to me tomorrow, Vanessa.'

After the door had closed Annie said, 'I'm sorry. So sorry. I just got so angry. It's so unjust.'

'She's always been like that. Everything for my brother – us girls came last. That's how Cherry's bringing up her boys, too.'

'I'll have to apologise. I won't mean it. How are you?'

'In pain,' Vanessa said. 'And three words have been running through my brain, all this time – love, money and revenge.' She sat up and the improvised ice-bag fell on to the carpet. 'I've been dragging my heels about all these improvements, I know, Annie. But I've been pushed around by Geoff Doyle in front of my kids because he wants a divorce and I've had enough. You know the barber next door is giving up his lease because of the rent rises? I'm wondering if we should take it. My dad might back me. We could expand.' She paused and said doubtfully, 'Am I barmy, Annie? Is it the shock?'

Annie, thinking, shook her head.

Melanie, excited, said, 'Go for it. Go on, Annie.'

Vanessa, speaking stiffly through a bruised lip, managed to catch her father having a nightcap with the landlord of his local. He said, slowly, 'Get your friend to work out some figures, go to a bank. Take advice. If the bank thinks it can help, I'll consider it. Not a word to your mum, though. Take care, Van. Don't let him in again, love, because next time it'll have to be the law.'

That evening the Arcadia restaurant, Foxwell Market, was born.

9

The Birth of the Arcadia

'I'm working for yuppies,' said the gloomy Arnold from his usual corner. 'That's what it is.' It was a hot afternoon in June. The door of the snack bar was open.

Madame Katarina, sitting at his table drinking a cup of tea and eating a pastry, said severely, 'You're working – that's the main thing.'

From next door to George's came the sound of hammering, as the old barber's shop became the Arcadia restaurant. Some deplored the elderly barber's retirement; others, especially local black men, were glad to see the back of the old reactionary who'd say offensively of their hair, 'Sorry, you can't expect me to cut that,' if they happened to stray in.

'Say what you like,' Arnold confided to Madame Katarina, 'he was one of the old school.'

Making one of her very rare personal observations, Madame Katarina replied, 'Yes. I remember that old school – from before the war. Without the old school, I wouldn't be here.'

'There's the builder's van, Arnold,' said Annie, who was standing at the door. 'It's probably brought that wood you ordered.'

Arnold got up and went into the street.

'So you're calling the restaurant the Arcadia?'

'We ought to name it P. J. Shaw's,' Annie smiled ruefully. 'That's who it belongs to – the bank manager.'

Madame Katarina smiled back. 'It should be successful.'

'Is that your professional opinion?'

'I never give that.'

'I'm tempted to ask for a consultation,' Annie told her. The

107

opening of the restaurant had been postponed for two weeks. It still wasn't ready. The cook, a young woman called Abigail Green, who was assisted by her cousin Annabelle, was protesting about Annie's and Vanessa's resistance to the *nouvelle cuisine* approach. By now they would almost have been glad if she'd left, but with the overdraft for the renovations running at £200 a week and the rent for the space at £100 a week being paid out of the café profits, both Annie and Vanessa needed the security of knowing the cook was in place, even if she was on a retainer she hadn't yet earned.

'Don't worry,' said Madame Katarina.

Annie sighed.

Madame Katarina said, 'I'll tell you this – when you need to worry, I'll warn you.'

'Thanks,' Annie said in a discouraged voice.

Melanie came in with two friends, and sat down. 'Can we have a Coke, Annie,' she said. 'That Arnold told us to clear out. Only Justin's there. It's not fair. He always makes us girls go away when he's there. And we're just as good as Justin. Better – we even sweep up.'

Annie felt very tired. Excited into rage by Geoff Doyle's attack on Vanessa, and her own disillusionment with Julian, the idea of scooping up the barber's shop next door to the café had greatly appealed. But three months, a bank loan and plumbers, electricians and carpenters later, she and Vanessa were tired and very nervous.

Annie handed out the Cokes and looked up from the counter to see Jasmine walk in with Tom.

'Hallo, Annie,' called Jasmine from the door. Annie didn't often meet her sister in London. Jasmine was wearing kid shoes, a dress of very fine cotton and a string of pearls. As usual she was tanned. 'We came to see the restaurant. Thought you were open. Grotty round here, isn't it? Do you think anyone's going to want to come here?'

'You picked up a lot of upper class rudeness when you got married, Jas,' said the tired Annie.

'That's what I keep on telling her,' Tom said. 'Can I help, Annie? What can I do?'

'Get a drinks licence from the council, fix the air-conditioning, try and get the cook to stop acting like a débutante who's helping a friend cook luncheons for City chaps. Oh – and bring down the base rate on bank loans—'

'I'll try the air-conditioning.' Tom turned as if to leave the café. 'OK if I sleep on the sofa tonight? I haven't got anywhere to stay.'

Jasmine gave Annie a long look.

'Where's he been?' Annie asked when Tom was safely next door.

'He's been starting up his workshop in the country, apparently. He rang up to get your address. I was coming up anyway, so I offered him a lift.'

Jasmine looked round the café suspiciously. 'Cup of tea?' offered Annie. A big man in workman's overalls came in and went to the counter. 'Tea, sausage, egg and chips,' he said.

'Right,' said Annie. 'I can't stop, Jasmine, I'm afraid. Where are you staying?' She ducked into the kitchen.

'The mews, of course,' called Jasmine.

'Not Bedford Square?'

'No – we prefer our own home.'

'Pardon me,' Annie said.

'I know you think this is all a joke,' said Jasmine making no attempt to lower her voice, 'but it's not. Do you know why I'm here? To see the specialist about why I can't have a baby. Mary had a tactful word with me. I had to come. To see a Harley Street gynaecologist.'

The workman, sitting to one side of the café, looked surprised.

Annie, turning sausages, called back, 'Don't shout, Jas. People are trying to eat in here.'

Mrs Patel, who had caught the exchange coming in, turned from the counter and said to Jasmine, 'Don't worry. You're very young. My sister waited ten years for her baby son. Then she had five more, in six years.'

'Oh,' said Jasmine nonplussed. 'Is there something you want? I'll get it.'

'I will have two teas, with sugar, to take away,' Mrs Patel said. Jasmine went behind the counter and got the containers. As she poured tea from the giant teapot Annie emerged from the kitchen and said, 'Don't do that, Jasmine. You're not insured.' She carried the loaded plate over to her customer and took his order for a cup of tea.

Arnold came in, hammer in hand. 'I've sent that Justin down to casualty,' he reported. 'He dropped a big piece of four by two on his foot. I've got to say he's useless.'

'I told you,' Melanie looked up from her conversation. 'We all did. You're sexist.'

'Good,' Arnold said viciously. 'That's just how I like it.' He went out again. Annie pushed past Jasmine to get Mrs Patel her teas.

'You're ratty,' Jasmine said.

'So would you be.'

'I suggest,' Madame Katarina said to Jasmine across the café, 'a consultation. I can use my crystal ball, or read your palm, or the cards.'

'Here?' asked Jasmine, startled.

'Madame Katarina's a clairvoyant,' explained Annie. 'And very successful. She works upstairs.'

'I'm on,' said Jasmine and followed Madame Katarina out of the café.

The phone rang with a sandwich order which Annie recorded. With her fingers crossed she then took a reservation for the new restaurant for the following week. She asked Melanie to go down to Mr Punjani's and ask if he could come to the café with a telephone answering machine. Tom came in for the phone number of the man who'd fixed the air-conditioning. He needed a spare part, and thought the other man might have one. She thought of cleaning the kitchen cupboards and sat down at a table. The phone rang again. Annie got up and answered it. It was Geoff Doyle, asking for Vanessa. He'd phoned her several times over the last fortnight, ostensibly to discuss the divorce, but Vanessa thought it was to find out about the Arcadia. 'Now, if you need any help with the builders, Annie . . .' he offered cordially, as if their last meeting had been a friendly one. Annie thanked him, though more afraid of his insincere goodwill than his open enmity.

Twenty minutes later Jasmine came in beaming. 'She told me some amazing things about myself. And she wouldn't take a penny for it. She told me things I've never told anybody. And she says I'll have two boys and a girl, the girl next year. She can see twins somewhere, too, but she's not sure they'd be mine. They might belong to someone close. That could be you, Annie, so watch out.' She looked round. 'I'll have a cup of tea. Is it all right not to be insured if it's for me?' She sat down with the tea. 'I popped next door just now. It's going to look very nice. Tom says he's got a couple of blue and white vases you could put on shelves in that alcove. He can do the shelves himself. He says don't worry – it won't look like a cosy tea-room. Nice of him, isn't it, when he's so busy? He's got no money at all. He couldn't afford the workshop but he got a – what is it? – government . . . ?'

'Enterprise allowance.'

'That's right. It's wonderful of them, isn't it, to give this help to people setting up their own businesses? Did you get one?'

'It's only forty pounds a week,' Annie said.

'Oh,' Jasmine seemed shocked. 'My goodness, that's not much.' She looked round. 'Juliet's wondering why you don't go and get another sort of job. She gave me this, by the way.' Jasmine opened her bag and gave Annie an invitation to a private view of their mother's paintings in three months' time, at a West End gallery. 'This place is a bit off the beaten track, isn't it?' Jasmine went on. 'Do you think it's going to work?'

'I don't know,' said Annie. 'If it doesn't, we'll be really in the cart. We'll probably go bankrupt. Vanessa'll go back to copy-typing and I don't know what I'll do.'

Jasmine looked at her anxiously. Annie looked anxiously back, asking, 'Are you really worried about not having a baby?'

Jasmine replied stoutly, 'No. I'm not. Well, only when they worry. I'm only twenty-six.'

'What are you bothered about, then?' asked Annie. 'There's something on your mind, I can tell.'

'I don't know what it is. I wake up nearly every morning feeling – I don't know – as if this was the day when I had to take an exam or face something horrible that had happened, like when Granny died. You know what I mean, don't you? But there isn't anything. I told Juliet and Howard and they said I ought to get something to do, become a brain surgeon or paint a picture, I suppose. But you know me, I'm a birdbrain, and in any case I'm Nigel's wife. What I have to do is different – entertaining, and going with him to places, that sort of thing. I found that difficult at first, but now I'm OK. Of course, when I told Mary she was very nice, but that was when she thought of my coming to the specialist, to see about having a baby. But is a baby the answer? I know it's spoilt . . .' she said, her voice trailing off as she glanced round the café and at two black teenagers who were peering through the doorway.

'Came to ask if there was any work going next door,' one said.

'I don't think so. Let's go and see,' Annie said. 'Coming, Jas? Melanie, can you keep an eye on things?'

In the Arcadia Arnold was screwing panels into the wall. A man looked up from the floor and said with emphasis, 'Lady – if anyone walks on these tiles I have to start again for the second time. I'll be here for a week at this rate. Normally the tiling's got to come last, not during.'

There was a whirring noise and cold air began to flood the room. 'Got it!' cried Tom.

'I don't like the noise,' said Annie.

'Get an orchestra,' he told her, nettled.

'Arnold!' called Annie. 'Any jobs going round here?'

Arnold turned round and looked angrily at the young men. 'There isn't room in here to swing a cat. See for yourself.' It was true that with the stacked planking, Arnold on his ladder, the tiles on the floor and Tom in the kitchen at the back, the Arcadia already looked overcrowded. It was only sixteen feet long and twelve feet wide in the first place with a step making a platform area at the kitchen end to give the appearance of more size.

The young men looked cynically at Arnold, then Annie, and left.

A delivery man in a blue uniform appeared round the door. 'This the Arcadia? Tables and chairs outside.'

'I said Thursday,' Annie said. 'Not today. You'll have to take them back.'

'Can't do that.'

'You'll have to,' Annie told him. 'You can see for yourself there's no room in here.'

'Well, we can't take them back. Sorry, lady—'

'Take them back,' interrupted Jasmine. 'This is your mistake, not this lady's. She is not accepting the delivery and she will not sign the receipt.' Something in Jasmine's tone spoke of country houses, influential menfolk and solicitors' letters.

The delivery man retreated.

'Insolent man,' remarked Jasmine as the van started up.

'Hand it to you, Jas,' Tom said, 'you've acquired the voice of those who can genuinely get a chap transported to Australia for the rest of his life. Why don't we all go off for a drink?'

'Arnold, can you close up here?' Annie asked. 'See you tomorrow,' she said to the tiler. She opened the door at George's. 'Can you shut the café, Melanie?' she asked.

At the Duke of Westminster they were playing 'Walk on By', sung by Dionne Warwick. It changed to 'My Way' as they sat down. Tom got some drinks.

'God, you look tired, Annie,' Jasmine remarked. 'Where's Vanessa?'

'She collapsed. I made her go and see the bank manager on the grounds that she had to learn what money was about. I told her if I got run over by a bus she wouldn't be able to understand what was going on. So when the day came for another chat with Mr Shaw, explaining further delay over the opening of the Arcadia, I said that this time I'd do the sandwich orders and she could stop acting like a child bride. So she departed, dressed for a wedding, and eventually had the bank manager eating out of her hand, as they say. He pressed money on her, and she came back to the café in tight shoes, and began to scream and shout about the chip fryer not being properly clean and we had a tearing row in front of the customers. So she took the day off. Unfortunately she's gone to see her mother, with the children, and that always upsets her—'

She broke off, looked at Tom's calm face, Jasmine's concerned expression. 'All right,' she said. 'It's chaos. I'm doing the wrong thing—'

'No, Annie,' protested Jasmine. 'If it's what you want . . .'

Annie sighed. 'I'm not sure – not at all. But I suppose we're enjoying ourselves in a peculiar way.'

Jasmine was laughing. 'It's so unlike you, Annie.' She quickly swallowed the remains of her white wine. 'I must go – I've got to meet Nigel and catch the eight forty-five.' She stood up. 'If you want any help, ask me. Do you want me to ask Nigel if he'll put some money in?'

Annie shook her head. 'Too dicey. You'd get the blame if we failed.'

'Will they ring me a taxi? I don't fancy this area,' Jasmine said.

'Get a bus, Jasmine. It's broad daylight,' advised Tom. Jasmine went out in her high heels.

'She looks the most obvious candidate for mugging in broad daylight I've seen for a long time,' Annie remarked disconcertedly.

'She's planning an affair,' Tom told her.

'Oh, God – who with?'

'Nobody special. I was a candidate—' Annie's mouth opened. 'Don't think badly of her. You might say it wasn't personal,' he explained. 'She's been nowhere near that gynaecologist. You see, she's pretty sure she's not infertile. She got pregnant when she was fifteen and had an abortion. But she snooped around and found out

113

that in the course of Nigel's vivid life before he married her there was never a baby, or the hint of one. So to cut out the complications and save face for him, because she feels he'd hate to be the infertile one of the pair – Nigel hates a low score on anything – cricket, income, sperm, you name it – Jas evidently thinks it's best to take the law into her own hands. Thus the search for a healthy white male donor. She thought of me first on the grounds that she knows me and trusts me not to blab, and as we're cousins, any baby she had, even if it didn't resemble Nigel a lot, for obvious reasons, would be more likely to resemble her, or some authenticated member of our family. No unexplained bright red hair or hereditary webbed feet. She's thought it through.'

Annie was stunned. 'Why didn't she tell me? I didn't know about this abortion.' A horrible thought struck her. 'It wasn't you, was it? You weren't the father?'

Tom grinned. 'No – some local boy. You were at university at the time. Don't forget Jas has always been a bit in awe of you. She thinks of you as a remote, strange brain, not like everybody else.'

Annie was hurt. 'Juliet and Howard could have told me, so I wouldn't be tactless, upset her feelings . . .'

'She didn't have any,' Tom assured her.

'Why do you know all this?' Annie challenged.

'I was in the house at the time. I was working near Cottersley with old Bert Weatherall, learning woodcutting – the artistic kind, not sawing planks – Juliet and Howard put me up for three months because I was too much in debt, after France, to get a place of my own. That was when the storm over Jas broke. They were very upset, Juliet and Howard, of course. Jas was more angry than anything else. I believe it toughened her up. Mind you, be careful, the Fellowses don't know anything about her early mistake.'

There was a silence. Annie asked, 'Why didn't you get in touch while you were in France? You've never told me. Why not? How long were you there?'

He had expected the question. He did not meet her eyes. 'Nine months. Annie – don't ask me.'

'Oh, Tom,' Annie groaned. 'What happened?'

'I'll explain, one day,' he said. 'I expect.'

Annie said despondently, 'I don't understand.' She gazed at him. She had loved that long, sallow face, his pale, gangling body, long boy's back, tender shoulders. He'd hurt her badly by his disappearance, yet, even now, she couldn't guess why he'd done it. He'd

114

loved her. He'd never lost affection for her. She felt now he still did love her, in some ways. He got up and brought her another beer.

She drew a deep breath. 'So,' she asked, 'what did you say when Jas turned up and put her unusual proposal to you?'

'I told her I thought it was bloody stupid and dangerous. I said even if I found her irresistible I'd throw myself in a duckpond to keep her off me. I began to explain the principles of DNA testing to her, but it turned out she knew all about it. She's not dim. She just said it was very unlikely the Fellowses would run a test on the baby. They'd be only too glad to have it.'

Annie considered. 'It's very stupid. They could adopt a baby, I suppose. It's not as if Nigel's the heir, anyway. Presumably it's a son she wants. Supposing the baby's a girl? Is she going to do it again? Supposing Nigel really knows it's his fault they aren't having a baby? Or finds out later? He might divorce her – she'd hate that.'

'Jas says she imagines it isn't the first time in four hundred unbroken years of the Fellows family that some woman hasn't kept the line going on her own initiative.'

'I don't think she really wants a baby so much.' Annie said.

'Nor do I. Not really. She wants an heir. For Nigel. For his pride, and for the family in case Sim doesn't turn up. The crux of it is that they're all beginning to wonder if Sim is dead. Sir Bernard won't hear of it. Sim turned up in Barbados, he says, with a black girl in tow a bit less than a year ago. They spent a few nights at his house there, then pushed off again. But though Lady Mary and Nigel aren't saying so, Sim's never been out of touch for so long. He's never been around much, but he's sent the odd letter or postcard and he's drawn on his bank account in London, not a lot, but from time to time. He hasn't got much, just a few thousand left by an aunt. But since Sir Bernard saw him last he hasn't taken a penny out of the bank. That's why they're so worried. Myself – I just think he might have taken a job.'

The jukebox was playing 'Leader of the Pack'. Tom took her hand across the table. 'Annie,' he said, 'I'm sorry I haven't been here to help during these last weeks.'

'I knew you'd come eventually,' she said.

He nodded. 'Let's go back to your house. Is the kid there – Melanie?'

'Did you get the fox? She talks about it constantly.'

'A brother and sister. It doesn't go down well with the farmer next door.'

As they walked up Foxwell High Street Tom grinned at Annie and said, 'Admit it, you never really got over me, did you?' He added, 'It's going to be difficult with that girl eating chip butties in front of the TV.'

Annie didn't argue about his assumption but replied, 'She's gone to a film with her friends.'

'I'm glad to hear it,' said Tom, taking her hand. He prevented any possible embarrassment for them when they got back to the house by taking all his clothes off as soon as they got in.

Annie, staring with surprise at his bare behind, asked, as he took his socks off in the hall, 'Haven't you got a girlfriend?' She recalled that Julian had always been careful to remove his socks and shoes before undressing, knowing a naked man in socks and shoes looks ridiculous. Tom didn't know, or care.

'I haven't got a girlfriend,' he replied firmly. She led him past the living room and upstairs.

'Well, I love you, Annie,' he said, kissing her and pulling up her T-shirt at the back, 'even if you do smell faintly of cooking fat.'

'I love you, Tom,' she said.

'I was that embarrassed,' Melanie said next morning, 'when I came in with Chris and Viv and there were those horrible Y-fronts on the mat. I didn't know where to put myself. We didn't hardly dare come in, in case there was a naked man in the room. Viv screamed. I don't know. I thought you had so much class, and now look. Who is it? Where is he? Upstairs?'

Annie was standing up in her dressing-gown drinking a cup of tea and drying her hair. Melanie had obviously abandoned a Saturday-morning lie-in when she heard water running in the bathroom and had sprung up to find out what was going on.

'Tom, upstairs,' Annie said awkwardly.

'Him with the fox?' asked Melanie.

'Two, a brother and sister. It's silly, really. They'll have cubs when they're older, then what?'

Melanie hesitated. 'I suppose we could go and stay with him.'

'Yes,' Annie said. She opened the drier and pulled out clean trousers and a T-shirt. 'Well,' she said, 'I'm sorry about your friends having a shock.'

'It'll be all over the school. It's really embarrassing.'

Annie didn't really think the news of Tom's discarded clothes

116

would create a major scandal among the resilient pupils at the Jasper Rayburn Comp.

'I'll tell them you're engaged,' Melanie decided.

Annie said, 'Please yourself. When he wakes up can you tell him I'm at the café?'

'Do I have to stay here, with him?' Melanie said with alarm.

'He won't be here long. He's coming down to do some painting in the Arcadia. Go to Vanessa's if you like.'

She heard the television go on as she left the house and walked quickly down the road and into the High Street, uncertain of her feelings. She realised she'd thought that as long as there was no one else in her life her marriage wasn't really over. She felt sad when she realised yet another point on the road to its real ending had been passed, yet knew she felt joyful, the sun was shining, and the bad dream of six months without Julian was nearly over. It had been an effort to leave the sleeping Tom to go and open up the café, and she was still tempted to turn round and go back.

Arnold was outside, waiting crossly with two stallholders from the market all dying for a cup of tea. Annie brushed off their complaints.

Vanessa came in at ten, pale, with circles under her eyes after a bad encounter with her mother and sister. Cherry had come over to their parents' house in Leadham Common with the twins the previous afternoon. As the children played in the Davises' well-tended big garden, Cherry had expressed grave doubts about the restaurant, Annie, Vanessa's sudden conception of herself as a restaurant-owner and Geoff Doyle's attitude to all this. 'I was relieved when my dad came in,' Vanessa told Annie. 'They stopped. And all the time my mum was pointing out how wonderful the twins were. It was as if Alec and Joanne didn't count. It's not fair, you know. Then Cherry's husband turned up to collect her and had a few little jokes about the restaurant. Who needs it?'

At the end of a busy day as the council trucks were already coming down the market sweeping and cleaning, three large West Indian men in suits entered the café.

Vanessa spied them from the hatch and made a warning sound to Annie, who was at the counter.

'We're just closing,' Annie said cheerfully. 'What can I do for you?'

117

'It's business really,' said the biggest man in the middle of the group. 'I hear you're the owners of a new restaurant starting next door.'

Vanessa, to Annie's surprise, left the kitchen and stood in the doorway.

'That's right,' said Annie. 'Do you want to make a booking?' She got the diary from a shelf behind her.

'Not really,' said the big man.

Vanessa moved behind the counter, beside Annie now, and asked, 'Then what's it about?'

The other men moved back, blocking the doorway. The man in the middle continued, 'This is not a nice neighbourhood. Full of bad people, as you know. Most people round here like a little protection from getting broken into, having their windows broken, held up for the profits – all kinds of bad guys harassing them, that kind of thing . . .' He paused to let his words sink in.

Annie could feel Vanessa trembling. But she answered steadily, 'I know what you mean. We've been talking about that, haven't we, Annie? We don't want our clients disturbed by undesirable people hanging around while they're eating, all that. You can understand that.'

'Certainly do,' he said.

Annie looked at his two henchmen in the doorway. They looked back at her. Vanessa was still talking very quickly. 'So if there's any way you could find us somebody to keep the situation under control, stand at the door and so forth, looking respectable but tough, you know the kind of thing, generally protecting the premises, keeping an eye on things, and that, well, we'd be very happy.'

'There'd have to be a financial arrangement—'

'Of course,' Vanessa said. 'Mr Campbell, isn't it?'

He nodded. 'We're talking about round-the-clock protection,' he said.

Annie could feel Vanessa shaking harder. She didn't dare move past her towards the phone. She saw to her relief a van stop outside. Tom with Alec and Joanne. He looked into the café through the van window, Joanne just visible beside him. But he didn't get out. He started up the van and drove past a rubbish-collecting truck. Annie was surprised, but Vanessa, who had also seen the van, was still talking. 'Round-the-clock protection, sure, Mr Campbell. But we still need a guy on the door.'

He nodded, 'We can arrange that for you.'

118

'But somebody a bit civilised-looking. Nothing threatening. We don't want to give the customers the impression they're coming into a shebeen – I'm sure you understand me.'

Campbell nodded again. Vanessa swallowed. Her mouth must be dry, Annie thought. She took a deep breath and said, 'Your fee will have to appear on our books.' Vanessa tried to kick her and missed, but she felt the movement. She went on as calmly as she could, 'We'd be able to pay you direct and rely on you to pay your . . .' She didn't know how to describe this situation. Sensing her difficulty Campbell said, 'For the services of my associate you pay me three hundred pounds a week. He guards your premises. That way, you can be quite sure of peace of mind. You can run your business with no worries.'

'That's precisely what we want to do,' said Annie, thinking three hundred pounds a week on top of everything would put strain on, if not actually ruin, the business. But by this stage she was so intimidated by the man in front of her that she wasn't prepared to argue. She just wanted them to go away. 'Well,' she said, her voice coming out strangely, 'then, good—'

'I can't see we have any problems, then,' Vanessa said recovering. 'We open next week, mid-week.'

'All right,' said one of the other men. 'We're in business. Evening, ladies.'

In the doorway the big man turned. 'Ladies, I wish you all luck in your enterprise. Nice to see people raising standards in the area.'

'Thank you,' Vanessa replied.

The two women stood behind the counter, side by side, until they were sure the men were really gone. Annie's knees were like jelly. 'My God,' she gasped, leaning on the counter, 'I thought they were going to attack us. I've never been so frightened.'

Vanessa put an arm round her and helped her to a chair, which she took down from the top of a table.

'Protection money,' Annie groaned. She looked up at Vanessa. 'Oh, God. Perhaps everyone's right. We're making a big mistake. Oh, Vanessa. What now?'

'Well, we pay,' said Vanessa. 'Come on, Annie. It's not such a big deal. I don't like it. I almost fainted when Tom drew up, with Alec and Joanne.'

'Yes,' Annie replied with indignation. 'Why didn't he come in?'

Vanessa stared at her, 'Because he's got more bleeding sense than you have, I should think. That's what frightened me.'

Tom came in carrying Alec and leading Joanne. His concerned eyes took in Annie, slumped on her chair, white as paper. He said to Vanessa, 'What was that about?'

'Just the local Mafia coming round for a donation to charity,' responded Vanessa. Annie got up and went to the phone. 'What are you doing?' asked Vanessa.

'No, Annie. No,' said Tom.

'I'm ringing the police,' Annie said shakily. 'They ought to be told this is going on.'

'I expect they know already, Annie,' Tom told her gently.

'Know? They'll be round for their cut, shouldn't be surprised,' Vanessa added.

'The police tolerate blackmail?' Annie demanded. No one replied. 'What is it – a jungle?'

There was another silence, broken by Vanessa who shook her head as she said, 'It's like anything else, Annie. You've got to know the rules. I thought someone might turn up. When Arnold mentioned Andy Campbell, I guessed. A lot of the pubs round here pay him to stay away. Look – on the good side we're getting a doorman. We may not like him, but he could be handy.'

'A criminal on the premises,' Annie pointed out. 'And do you know how many more meals we'll have to serve to pay that three hundred a week? Thirty or forty. How many tables have we got, even if we can fill them? Twelve, seating for forty. It's a day's profits washed out to pay those hooligans. What are we supposed to do? Open on Sundays or pass the blackmail costs on to the customer? There's nothing on a tax form allowing for relief on protection money.'

'Extra staff,' Vanessa told her. 'That's what you call it. I'm sorry, Annie, but there isn't anything else we can do at the moment.'

'Do I understand we're to submit to extortion and intimidation?' Annie asked.

'Yes, Annie,' said Tom. 'If you want to open on Thursday. The natural life of man is nasty, brutish and short. Come on, you need a drink. Let's go to the Duke of Westminster. I'll drop the children at Rutherford Street and meet you there.'

'He's not bad,' Vanessa said consideringly of Tom as they watched him drive off with the children to leave them in Melanie's care.

Annie, still shaking, muttered, 'I wish I knew why he'd gone off the first time.'

10

Opening Night

It had been a hot day, but a late shower and the coming of darkness had cooled the market down. Abigail and Annabelle had been in the kitchen at the Arcadia all day, chopping, cutting, whipping, mixing and stirring food while Annie, Vanessa and Melanie popped in from George's to stand entranced in the kitchen doorway.

They were excited at the elegance of the restaurant. Two big plate-glass windows balanced a smart wooden door. In a frenzy of creativity, Tom had made and attached to the door a big wooden oval on which he'd carved a scene showing trees, a fountain, some sheep, a lamb, a shepherd and a shepherdess embraced. Tucked behind a bush, Pan peeped out, a wicked smile on his face. A flock of birds flew overhead in their wooden sky, full of wooden clouds. He'd been carving in Annie's small garden for days, after driving down to his workshop for his tools.

He'd been congratulated by everyone from Annie's mother, in London to talk to the gallery owner who was mounting her exhibition, to Edward, the bouncer, a huge, young black man, with biceps like grapefruit who commented, 'A work of art, man. Work of art.'

Tom was pleased. But earlier Vanessa had spotted Juliet, looking uncomfortable in a suit, giving Tom an odd look on the pavement; and heard Tom say impatiently, 'For Christ's sake, Juliet . . .' Vanessa thought the exchange was about something serious. Would it harm Annie, who, Vanessa thought, was falling in love with Tom, or perhaps had never fallen out of love with him?

Just beyond the coathooks inside the restaurant door was the till, mostly behind stout bullet-proof glass, the result of a suggestion from

121

their extortionist Andy Campbell. As Vanessa said, he didn't want strangers coming along to rob them – he wanted them all to himself. Along the wall beside the till were two banquettes, capable of seating six, with backs ensuring privacy. Further down the restaurant were six tables. On the raised part of the restaurant, up a small wooden step, were more tables, seating two people each. Two more were in alcoves where couples who didn't want to see, or possibly be seen, could sit. The restaurant was panelled in dark wood, tables and chairs were in lighter wood. The tablecloths were white and red, and had small vases of roses on them. Everything gleamed.

At seven they unbolted the doors. Abigail and her helper could be heard having words in the kitchen. Vanessa, in a new rust-coloured top embroidered with gilt flowers sat down at the till. Annie and Melanie, in dark dresses, stood by with their pads, ready to take orders. At eight-thirty, a couple came in, looked startled and left immediately. Shortly after that three boys asked the way to the tube station. By nine Abigail was whispering doubtfully to her fellow cook, who was glancing at her watch.

Annie stood beside Vanessa at the till. Vanessa was praying, 'Oh, God. Oh, God. Please send us a customer,' under her breath. 'Any customer. Send two. Please, God, just two customers.' Annie was adding up the cost of the advertisements in her head. At nine-fifteen Madame Katarina came in with a well-dressed, heavily made-up, rather worn-looking woman in dark glasses. Madame Katarina pretended she didn't know the management and made favourable comments on the décor.

The worn woman ordered champagne. She insisted Madame Katarina had oysters. Madame Katarina agreed and Annie breathed out, for there is not much you can safely do next day with a large amount of yesterday's uneaten oysters. At the same time, the excitement of having Madame Katarina and her customer in the corner, discussing the woman's part in a coming West End play, soon wore off and it was plain to see the woman's elated mood collapsing as she ate an expensive meal in an empty restaurant with her clairvoyant. At ten Edward had to tell two drunk businessmen and three young men in T-shirts, jeans and large boots they were not welcome at the Arcadia. A little later an older man in a suit and a young woman in a blue work-suit came in and sat in a booth, drinking the house wine, murmuring to each other, and eating only one course. 'Not just an adulterer but a cheapskate,' Annie said to Vanessa in a low voice.

'You stop caring what people are up to, don't you?' Vanessa murmured. 'As long as they spend money.'

They closed the restaurant sourly, having outnumbered the customers all evening. It wasn't just the money – they felt as if they'd given a party no one had come to. 'I've had more people round to mend the washing machine,' moaned Vanessa.

'We've got ten days before the bank manager starts threatening,' Annie said.

Vanessa closed her eyes, 'To think we've got to open the snack bar at eight tomorrow morning.'

'Melanie's doing it,' Annie said.

'I don't know how you're going to keep your love life going on this basis,' yawned Vanessa. 'As for mine – it's never going to start.'

'When this restaurant becomes successful you'll meet someone,' said Annie.

'That doesn't sound too promising!'

Abigail and her friend had straightened up the kitchen and went past them, saying a hollow goodnight. Annie and Vanessa got wordlessly into Tom's van and went home.

The next night was no better and on Saturday night, when they thought business might pick up, they served only one meal, to a lonely man in a suit, who ate three courses, left a large tip and departed praising the food and the atmosphere. 'Good suit and a well-fed face,' Vanessa said. 'Perhaps he'll recommend us to his friends.'

'He'd better,' said Annie.

On Sunday, their free day, Tom and Annie were sitting in her small paved garden. It was a sunny afternoon and they were eating smoked salmon, a cold chicken and raspberry mousse. Annie looked at her roses. 'You eat well when you run an unsuccessful restaurant,' she said. 'My God. This is a mess. In a fortnight, I'll have to put the house up for sale, hoping someone buys it. Vanessa'll struggle on until she can get Alec in a nursery and then get a secretarial job and I'll have to find a flat and some kind of teaching post.'

'You won't think like this if business picks up next week,' said Tom in a practical voice.

They were both seized by the melancholy of parting, though neither said so. Tom stood up, 'Better go, I've only got a fortnight to complete the screenprinting order. I don't think I can get back then.' His long face looked dismal.

123

Annie, too, felt unhappy, although her unhappiness was mixed with a certain relief. She had the idea she'd rather face the collapse on her own, without Tom's sympathy. She also wondered where, if anywhere, the relationship, if you could call it that, was going. She didn't know if she wanted it to continue, or if Tom did. She certainly felt happier when Tom was with her, but uneasy, too, and she didn't know precisely the source of the unease. Perhaps it was still some pointless and unavailing commitment to her husband. She shook her head. 'I'll miss you.'

They kissed and he left through the house. She sat down sadly, feeling confused. She said to herself, 'I don't know what he wants. I don't know what I want.'

She heard his van start up outside and realised she was already beginning to miss him.

A Meeting at Bedford Square

Jasmine sat neatly on a chair by the marble fireplace in the long first-floor drawing room of the Fellows house in Bedford Square, her feet, in expensive shoes, together, pointing forward to the grate. A matching handbag lay in her lap. She was very still. Behind her, standing round the table at the other end of the room, from which the plane trees of a London square could be seen through long windows, three men spoke softly. She could barely hear them and was not trying to listen. Her smooth face revealed none of her thoughts. She and Nigel had been in London since the day before, staying at their mews house in Kensington. Nigel had had meetings since they arrived and Jasmine had taken advantage of his absence to phone Timothy Ray, the thirty-year-old bob-sleighist, hang-glider, water-skier, good shot, man about town and lady killer. She'd asked him to give her lunch, during which, by a certain amount of knee-nudging, hand touching and eye contact, she'd conveyed to him her desire. After a long lunch, they'd gone back to his flat, a short walk from the restaurant, Timothy quite delighted by his conquest of the unapproachable Jasmine Fellows, Jasmine less delighted but bent on an affair which would end on the day her pregnancy test proved positive.

Tanned and naked he had bent over her – she recalled the scene, as the three men by the window bent over the model on the table, showing a park, with plastic trees, low buildings on two sides, on a third a taller red-brick arcade, with arches and domes, and all cunningly arranged round a fountain. The whole charming complex looked down over an open area of landscaped garden, in greens and blues, towards a blue-painted river.

'We could have put flats over the shopping arcade,' explained Nigel Fellows to his father, a tall, heavy, tanned man, with a head of thick, pale brown hair, streaked with silver. 'We decided, on balance, to increase the facilities with two restaurants, and a cinema, even if the profits come in more slowly – I think that was wise.'

'It's a very intelligent plan, Nigel,' said Sir Bernard, 'and brilliantly executed. George – I must congratulate you.'

Jasmine, staring blankly at an arrangement of lilies and roses in front of the empty grate, sat motionless. What a waste of time! As Timothy Ray, all blue eyes in a tanned face and about as much going on inside his head as a large bass drum on an empty bandstand, had leaned over her on the satin sheets, he'd murmured, 'Don't feel anxious. I've had a little snip – no more babies for Timmy.' Phew, thought Jasmine, what a waste! She hoped he hadn't noticed her reduced enthusiasm when she'd heard the unwelcome news. On the other hand, who'd want to have his baby anyway? Another few notches down from Timothy Ray on the IQ scale and you could be faced with real problems at school. Perhaps his vasectomy was a blessing in disguise. Not that it was a crime to be thick in Fellows circles, a welcome change, she always thought, from her own family, the Brownings, Cunninghams, Seymours and Knights, authors, university dons and civil service mandarins for four or five generations. Nevertheless, there were limits. She prevented herself from sighing. With half the world vasectomised and the other half nervously using condoms what was a poor woman to do? At fifteen she'd been horrified to find herself pregnant. Now she wanted to be, nothing happened. At the other end of the room the men's voices were still murmuring.

'A small nursery school here,' George Kelly, head of the architectural team, said, pointing. 'Only enough room for ten or fifteen children over a year old, but a boon to mothers and nannies stuck in London for some reason. They share that building with the gymnasium and pool, slightly separated from the houses and flats, since there's a noise factor in both cases. Ladies in the gym, baby in the nursery. We have to consider the ladies these days,' he explained to Sir Bernard, who nodded. 'That's why we've left extra space in the car park – a school bus can collect and deliver. The area isn't well served with suitable schools, but with a private bus the problem dissolves. Our aim's been to take care of the needs of all our potential residents.'

'Security?' questioned Sir Bernard.

'Absolutely,' agreed Nigel. 'Perimeter fences, basically, all in nice wrought iron. Bringing in a design firm from stage one has been an excellent idea, saves time and money. Vane's designed the fencing and the lighting in consultation with the electrical firm etc. There'll be three gates, a man on each twenty-four hours a day, no one but residents gets through without a phone check. It's all pleasant and discreet, of course. Not your Johannesburg white enclave effect – barking dogs, heavy lighting effects. That's intimidating, not what we're after at all.'

Sir Bernard nodded.

'Privacy, a civilised atmosphere – everything you might want, or need, to hand.'

'Except a brothel,' said Sir Bernard. The men laughed.

'Got to think of the ladies,' said George Kelly. 'There's a red light district up the road in the badlands, in Foxwell, if anyone wants to try it. Here's a plan of the whole area . . . I must say, this chap Vane's been a godsend. Very talented man.'

'I hear we're getting enquiries already,' said Nigel. 'But we're going to have to give priority to people who look as if they're going to live there at least part of the time. We don't want to turn round and find the whole place sold to Japs and small oriental businessmen from Honkers.'

'Or arms dealers and drug barons,' added his father.

Jasmine wasn't listening. She was wondering if she could still blackmail Tom into becoming the father of her child. She could threaten to tell Annie what had really happened that spring, before he went away. She was sure he still didn't want her to know. Small wonder, she thought, if he wanted her to commit herself.

'Well, as to that, no problem,' Nigel was continuing, 'they badly need seven million and we'll be happy to supply it. We're prepared for a protest, of course. We're planning a three-month campaign to deal with it so it doesn't cut into the time when we'll actually be starting work, around September, we hope. Stir it up and win that fight early, I thought, get it over with. Councillor Banks is with us every step of the way on that. Very co-operative chap. Then we start. Given a mild winter and a workforce going night and day, we'll be open by next spring – of course, we'll be selling earlier to keep the finances even. Not that that's too much of a worry at present. I'm fairly sure the Jap banker is coming in.'

Sir Bernard nodded. 'Very good. Very good all round. I'll take it all away to brood over, but I think it's an excellent project. Well handled. Whatever happens, I'll speak to you in a few days' time. I'd like to get back to Barbados next week, if all seems well. Come on, let's get some lunch – Jasmine,' he called, 'you've been waiting so patiently. At last we're off to lunch.'

Jasmine stood up. 'You're a beautiful woman,' Sir Bernard said. 'Every time I see you, I think Nigel's a lucky chap to have you.'

Jasmine smiled, 'You're very kind.' She decided she couldn't face blackmailing Tom and smiled at Nigel. It would be worth it, whatever it took to get pregnant, but there wasn't much time before they went to Portugal on holiday.

12

Mr Abbott Makes an Offer

By July, a month after the opening of the Arcadia, business had picked up at least to the point where profits almost covered the interest on the loan, which had encouraged the bank manager to extend credit, on a fortnight by fortnight basis, in the hopes of better times. Nevertheless, to Annie, living with the Arcadia felt like having some wasting disease, which didn't kill you but left you a little weaker every day. With business still comparatively slack there'd been no reason for Vanessa to refuse her parents' offer of a much-needed fortnight in a villa in Portugal. Joanne's school was about to break up, and Alec would benefit from a fortnight on a beach with his mother and grandparents. Melanie was now perfectly capable of running the snack bar alone from time to time, and in recognition of this Annie gave her and her friend Viv £30 a week each, although she was sure she was breaking the law by employing two thirteen-year-olds eight hours a day. Viv's parents, who both worked, were pleased, saying it was better for her than hanging about the house alone in the holidays.

While Vanessa was away a small plump man, with greying hair and a small black moustache, had come into the restaurant and sat alone, eating Abigail's steak and kidney pie, drinking a glass of red wine and staring round mistrustfully. Melanie, who had popped in to see what was happening, said, 'Looks like a typical DSS snoop to me.' A few days later, with a booking for two in the name of Abbott, the same man came into the Arcadia, accompanied, to Annie's horror, by Geoff Doyle. He nodded, giving her a hard stare and saying, 'Nice place. But you've had a leak up there, I see.'

'The old man upstairs let his bath overflow,' Annie told him.

'Unfortunate. You don't need too much of that in a place like this.'

There was menace in his tone, she thought. She couldn't imagine why he and Abbott, who she assumed must be connected with Doyle's girlfriend, Cindy Abbott, had chosen to come to the Arcadia. Were they just spying? Or was Doyle planning to cause trouble? She got Melanie to go outside and warn Edward there might be trouble. She suggested a side table.

'No,' Geoff said, 'we'll sit in the middle and look about us.' They sat down quietly. She gave them menus and got Abigail's assistant to take their orders. Geoff, obviously paying, ordered generously – avocados, peppered steak, two bottles of wine. Annie, busy with seven other customers, took as little notice of them as possible. The two men, for their part, were friendly, but engrossed in discussing a topic of importance to them in low voices. Annie overheard the name of the Mayor, Mrs Roxanne Fuller. She studied them from the kitchen door as they sat, heads bent towards each other, talking. Geoff Doyle, with his mop of dark hair, bright blue eyes, wide shoulders in a well-made jacket, was the original handsome brute of a romance novel. With the emphasis very much on the brute, Annie thought, remembering his pushing Vanessa back from her front door and the blow he'd struck her. Abbott wore an anxious, fussy expression, giving the impression of being a small businessman or a minor executive somewhere. Annie looked away quickly as she felt Geoff beginning to sense her gaze. Two of the other customers, she suspected, had been sent along by Jasmine. They seemed somewhat appalled to find themselves in Foxwell and anxious about the welfare of the Porsche they had arrived in. They were unlikely to return, she considered, although they were plainly enjoying the food. The Arcadia was now making a straight loss of £50 a day, a situation which could not be allowed to go on for more than one more month, until August; Annie knew, even if the bank would go on carrying them, that the deficit would be too terrifying. The restaurant would have to be sold, and her house, too, in order to cover the loan. Vanessa's father would lose the money he'd put in. At least the snack bar was making money, but the snack bar, of course, didn't belong to them. It still belonged to George Kypragoras.

They closed early. Annie went home, heavy-hearted.

At four the next afternoon Annie arrived at the Arcadia to let in some deliveries and found that someone had sprayed 'This is NOT a yuppie-free zone' across one of the plate-glass windows. She bought some white spirit and started to rub and scrape it off, pushed by the shoppers trying to get at the stalls in the street. The man in front, selling from his fruit stall, was sympathetic, but she'd been aware for some time that the restaurant was not popular locally. She'd defaced, but not obliterated the message an hour later, interrupted by the deliveries, when Abbott came up beside her. 'Could we go inside?' he asked. 'I'd like to talk to you.'

Annie offered him tea or coffee, then realised he expected better entertainment than that. He agreed to a whisky. She put ice in it. He moved to a booth where they were out of sight of the street. 'I'll come to the point,' he said. 'I've got some money to invest. I'm planning to open a restaurant, rather like this one, something a little better than you find round here, and it crossed my mind that since neither of us need competition, and I've looked at this place – well, have you ever considered selling it? I'm talking about a fair price.'

She stared at him, feeling uneasy, a little sick, almost as if he were trying to bully her. And yet here was an answer to the problem of debt that was plaguing her. She and Vanessa could get out of a worrying situation, might even make a small profit, if Abbott took over the Arcadia. No more debt, no more exhaustion, no more having to accept, each day, that their activities were being reported back by Edward to the terrifying Andy Campbell . . .

'I like the restaurant,' said Abbott, looking round. 'It has character, atmosphere.'

A thought struck her. She remembered something Vanessa had said. 'You work with the council planning department?'

He nodded. 'That's right. Of course, this has nothing to do with my council activities. I've some money coming to me from a legacy and I'm keen to start a business against the time I retire. I'm aware your partner might be prejudiced against me, for personal reasons, but I'm hoping you'll be able to point out to her that Mr Doyle's relationship with my daughter has nothing to do with me. And Mr Doyle will have no interest in the restaurant, I tell you that quite candidly. To be even more candid,' he said, leaning forward, 'and strictly between you and me, I don't like the situation. He's a man with two children and I think people should take their family responsibilities seriously. It's old-fashioned these days, I know that, but it happens to be what I believe. I've no objection to Mr Doyle personally, but I don't like what he's doing. That's by the way. What I'm here to say really is, I'll take the lease, all the

131

fixtures, goodwill, etc. lock, stock and barrel for £100,000. You go on running the snack bar, of course. We'll be good neighbours. My wife'll be running the restaurant for the time being.'

Annie bit her lip. The offer seemed fair. But was it? And did she want to sell? Would Vanessa? As if he read some of her thoughts he said, 'You might think because of my offer you could go elsewhere and get more, but I've thought it over. It's a fair price. I doubt very much if you could do any better – no agent's fees.'

'I'll certainly think about it,' Annie said straightforwardly. 'Vanessa's away on holiday. I'll have to talk it over with her. Can you give us a week or two to think?'

'Agreed. But not too much longer than that.'

'Another drink?' Annie hoped he wouldn't say yes.

'No,' he said, standing up. 'I've got to get back. There's two hours' work sitting waiting for me on my desk. I'll be hoping to hear from you within two weeks, then, or earlier, perhaps.'

Annie went back, mechanically, to getting the slogan off the restaurant window. She wasn't sure what she thought about Abbott's offer, or what Vanessa might think, faced with selling out to the father of the woman who was living with her husband. She went into George's for a cup of tea. The café was crowded, the only seat free was opposite Madame Katarina, whose corner table at George's seemed to belong to her as if by right. Even strangers to the café hesitated, then apologised sincerely when they needed to sit with her. Annie greeted her, then fell silent. Madame Katarina's presence was undemanding; she felt as if she were sitting in a very quiet spot, like a field or on a river bank. The sounds of washing up, the distant sound of Melanie's radio cassette player in the kitchen, the chat of the other customers seemed to dwindle. The silence lasted for about five minutes, while Annie thought about Abbott's offer and wondered if she should make the effort to contact Vanessa in Portugal to tell her about it.

Then Madame Katarina bent forward. She said in her slightly accented English, 'My dear. I told you one day I'd warn you when I felt you needed my help. Sometimes I have feelings I can't deny about people and situations. I have them now.' She observed Annie's doubtful look. 'You are an educated woman. You will know the ancient world was full of signs, portents and omens. Men and women greater than us believed in them absolutely.' She paused. 'Like you, my brother was a student of history,' she said.

'Where is he now?' asked Annie, although she had an idea what the reply might be. Madame Katarina must be seventy. Everything about her spoke of exile, from Germany, or perhaps Austria, in the thirties.

Madame Katarina said merely, 'He died young. Will you come and talk to me upstairs, in my flat? I could make you some coffee – better coffee than you sell here,' she added reprovingly.

'I agree the coffee could be better,' Annie said. 'It's the cost.'

'Of course.'

Abigail came in, followed by Annabelle whom she was bullying more and more. Annie gave Abigail the keys to the restaurant so that they could start preparing for dinner. Then she followed Madame Katarina out of the café, through her front door and up the narrow stairs. She had never yet visited the flat, had not been invited, although Melanie was in and out all the time, it seemed, except, of course, when Madame Katarina was engaged with clients. So from Melanie Annie had heard accounts of the piano, on which Madame Katarina could be persuaded to play tunes from *West Side Story* and other pieces of old music, and the generally gloomy, but not spooky, as Melanie put it, atmosphere.

There were two rooms off a narrow passageway which was papered with light, embossed wallpaper. Madame Katarina opened a door to one of the rooms, the other, Annie supposed, being the bedroom, and led her into a sitting room overlooking the market, where dark wallpaper, with large silver and black flowers, gave a shadowy atmosphere. The windows were masked by cotton net curtains with floral patterns. The curtains were old, made of blue-green tapestry. There was a heavy sideboard covered with ornaments – paperweights, porcelain figures, a pair of brass vases; a heavily carved black table covered with a cloth embroidered in gold, dark blues, reds and greens, stood in the middle of the room. At the back was a sofa upholstered in sombre, ornate material. Madame Katarina sat down in a chair by the blocked-in fireplace, in front of which stood an electric fire. She put a brass kettle on a gas ring beside it and asked Annie to sit down opposite her. She said, 'I've been getting feelings of crisis. Is there anything wrong?'

'The restaurant's doing badly. I've just had an offer from a man who wants to buy it,' Annie told her. 'I don't think—'

'No, no,' Madame Katarina said. 'I don't think it's that. It's something in your own family.'

'I'm having an affair with my cousin,' Annie said, seeing no

133

reason not to be candid. And these walls, she suspected, had heard more startling confessions than that.

'Good.' Madame Katarina's face was expressionless. 'That will be good for you – eventually.' She took a canister of coffee and a curiously shaped pottery coffee pot from a cupboard beside her chair. She continued, in a practical voice, 'Persist in spite of difficulties. Love is rare. But what I sense is more serious than that. I seem to see children, and some large buildings. And a death, not one of someone close to you – but someone important to you. Perhaps you could go into the kitchen and get milk and some cups for us.' Which Annie did, at the end of the passageway in a small, neat, old-fashioned kitchen. When she returned, Madame Katarina had made coffee. It dripped through the pot slowly, each drip sounding very distinct. Annie could hear voices in the market below, even a clang as a saucepan fell on the floor of the snack bar, but the sounds seemed remote. Madame Katarina continued, 'There's a church also. Some kind of church. It's important,' she warned. 'You must be very careful what you do from now on. Very careful.'

'How?' asked Annie. 'It's all very well – this – but frankly, Madame Katarina, it's rather obscure – children, a death, buildings, a church – these things are common.'

'Not a Christian church. There's a woman with a star on her head, carrying a baby – who can that be, I wonder?'

'A goddess?' Annie suggested.

'Possibly. She's holding a horn of plenty, a cornucopia, in her other hand.'

'I have had an offer for the Arcadia,' Annie repeated.

Madame Katarina shook her head. 'Don't do anything. These events are very close. Wait and see.'

On the terrace outside the drawing room at Durham House, Lady Mary Fellows handed a drink to her companion, a short, bald man in a white, polo-necked jumper, and stared down the sweep of lawn, to the glitter of the lake just visible through the trees. The sun was going down, the lawn now half in shadow. Max Craig felt awkward. Summoned to Durham House by Nigel Fellows to give a consultation to Samco, by whom he was retained, the astrologer had arrived at eleven to find a message for him from Nigel that he'd been held up in town. Craig had lunched alone with Lady Mary – Jasmine was also in London. Another message from Nigel that he was further delayed meant tea and a walk with Lady Mary. The vixen, now released, gambolled up to them across a field, flashed away again through a hedge.

By six Nigel and Jasmine had still not turned up. Yet another message arrived – this time Nigel and Jasmine had broken down on the road. They would be at Durham House in time for dinner at eight. Lady Mary had held up dinner for half an hour and in the end she and Craig, alone at the big dining table, had again eaten another meal together. Now it was nine-thirty, and Craig was detained, at this stage, more by Lady Mary's well-disguised but detectable anxiety than by the prospect of Nigel's arrival. At any rate the long day's waiting had let them know each other better.

Max Craig was a famous clairvoyant. Prominent clients, film stars, rock stars, notables of all kinds, as well as commercial clients such as Samco trusted him to guide them. Privy to so many famous secrets, believed to be in touch with mysterious forces, he was not unaware that even the most sceptical and least superstitious people regarded him with some awe, much as they might attempt to conceal it. As people will eventually reveal their health worries to a doctor they meet socially, talk to an architect about their building problems, or mention the state of their mouths to a dentist, so, Craig knew, after a day of chatting, discussing the siting of a tree, looking at the pictures in the house, that Lady Mary, reassured by his calm and sensitivity, was beginning to wonder if he could help her, although she was too polite to ask directly. Craig, who had cast the company horoscope the day before and seen in it some extraordinary features, said gently, 'Forgive me, Lady Mary, if I'm being too blunt, but your son – Simon – in my opinion, he's alive.'

Lady Mary looked at him and did not respond.

'I don't expect you believe in my mumbo-jumbo,' he said. 'But, of course, I do. Simon isn't dead, I'm convinced.'

'I can't believe it,' said Lady Mary. 'I feel sure I'd know.'

Craig nodded. He refrained from telling Lady Mary what else he knew, or thought he knew.

Foxwell Market, under a July sun, looked, if anything, slightly worse than it did at other times, the bright sunlight remorselessly revealing littered streets and the tawdry state of the stalls, with their heavy load of vegetables, cheap shoes, underwear, tablecloths and clothing as the dim autumnal or winter light did not. The market certainly smelt worse in summer. The odours of fish from the fish stall, meat from the butcher's shop in the arcade, the smells of frying, curry-cooking and traffic fumes mingled and blended, causing small children to make faces when led by their mothers from the High Street into the market. In contrast, behind the counter at George's, Vanessa Doyle, back from Portugal, glowed, her skin gold, her hair frizzing out, bleached by the sun.

Arnold said sourly from his seat in a corner, 'Your holiday's done you good, Vanessa. You in love or something?' He sipped his tea.

'Yes,' declared Vanessa. 'My heart's singing. Congratulate me.'

'I'll wait and see for a month or two before I do that,' he told her. 'Holiday romance, was it?'

'You could say that,' Vanessa replied. 'And what can I get you, gentlemen,' she added, as two workmen came up to the counter. 'Oh,' she said, recognising one of the figures in jeans and T-shirt and heavy boots, 'Mr Pickering. What a surprise!' She gave him a cheeky smile.

'I thought it might be,' he said, intending to convey menace.

Vanessa was unimpressed. 'Hear you're working for Mr Doyle these days. Don't worry – we haven't given you away to Mrs Pickering. I hear she's managing to get by, luckily, no thanks to anybody here. I wonder if Mr Doyle actually employs anybody who supports their wife and family? I suppose not, really. Perhaps it's a condition he makes before he gives out the jobs. What do you think?'

'I think you'd better be careful what you say,' said Pickering steadily. 'I don't think Mr Doyle would like to hear you talking like that.'

'I don't think I'm bothered about what Mr Doyle thinks,' Vanessa said recklessly.

'I'll tell him that,' Pickering said threateningly.

'Thank you,' replied Vanessa. 'Now – what's it to be? Teas, coffees, sandwiches? I'm ready to go. Just say the word.'

'The word is, what about my Melanie? I hear she's working all hours in this café. She's only thirteen, you know.'

'Fourteen, Mr Pickering. She had her birthday a fortnight ago. You must have forgotten. You never sent a card, anyway.'

'It's not good enough,' he continued. 'You're exploiting her and that's all there is to be said about it.'

'Holiday job,' said Vanessa. 'She's happy. Her mother's happy. Now just what are you suggesting?'

'This man's a witness to the fact that you've got my under-age teenage daughter here, you're exploiting her labour. And maybe worse. I want her returned to her mother's protection forthwith. Is that clear enough? I've got a solicitor.'

At this point Melanie came into the café with her friend Viv. She rapidly took in her father's presence, grabbed Viv by the arm and turned her round when, following Vanessa's eyes, Pickering spotted her.

'Melanie!' he shouted. 'You stop here!' Melanie halted.

'What are you doing here, Dad?' she asked meekly.

'Looking to your welfare, that's what I'm doing,' Pickering said in an aggressive tone.

'Well, I'm all right, so you needn't worry,' Melanie said in the same placatory tone.

'You,' he said, pointing at her, 'had better get back up north where you belong. And you,' he said, turning on Vanessa, 'had best get my daughter on a train pretty soon, or you'll regret it.'

Melanie beckoned her friend into a corner, where she sat down, watching her father fearfully.

'I can't see why you want this, Mr Pickering,' said Vanessa.

'Maybe I could be persuaded,' Pickering suggested.

'Oh, don't give me any of that,' Vanessa said. 'Just get out of here.' She appealed to the other man, 'There's a man who'd literally sell his own daughter. What do you think of that? Nice, isn't it?'

Pickering said nastily, 'You'll keep a decent tongue in your head, young lady.'

'I'm sorry,' responded Vanessa. 'You may be very good at intimidating your family, but you can't do it to me. Now, talk to your daughter if you want to in a reasonable way. That is, if you know how. But don't come in here threatening and blustering, because I think I know what kind of a man you are, Mr Pickering. I don't know what kind of a story he'd told you,' she said to Pickering's companion, 'but I doubt if it's all true. You can see for yourself this girl is all right. There's nothing wrong with her at all. She goes to school every day. Her schoolwork's improving. She just works here in the holidays and she gets paid for what she does. Her mother knows all about it and she's perfectly satisfied. If I was you, I wouldn't get involved.'

Baffled and embarrassed, the other man did not reply. Pickering said with dignity, 'You'll be hearing from my lawyer, Mrs Doyle.'

He stopped near where Melanie was sitting, head bowed, hands in her lap, gave her a hard stare and said, 'As for you, madam. As for you—' and left without completing the threat. His companion, still standing at the counter, followed him after a pause.

'Brute,' Vanessa said after him. 'He's a brute – that's what he is.' Turning to Melanie, she said, 'Don't you worry, darling, it's just a try-on. He can't do nothing.'

'He does seem to be her father,' Arnold said repressively from the corner.

'It's not always who you are, it's what you are,' retorted Vanessa. 'You could be my father, technically, for all I know.'

'I should hope not,' said Arnold.

A tall fair man in a grey suit and trainers came round the door somewhat awkwardly with a bunch of flowers. Vanessa glowed. 'Ben!' she called out.

He marched across, smiling, watched by the workmen, Arnold, Melanie and Viv, and gave her the flowers.

Vanessa was grinning. 'Is that her boyfriend?' asked Viv in an undertone.

'This is Ben Gathercole,' Vanessa announced to Melanie.

'How do,' Melanie said dourly.

'I've heard about you,' he said. He sat down next to her.

Melanie didn't like this. She shifted in her seat and responded, 'Pleased to meet you,' in a discouraging voice.

'Can you take over, Mels, while we go for a pub lunch?' Vanessa asked quickly. 'Half an hour. Then can you pick up Alec and Joanne and take them to the park?'

'We'll take them down the War Museum,' said Viv. 'My brother wants to go.'

'All right,' Vanessa said. She picked up her bag, gave them some money and went off with Ben Gathercole.

Viv went behind the counter, pulling a face at Melanie. She made a noise. 'Wehay – well, he's not bad, anyway. A bit old. Got a suit on.' Melanie said nothing.

Two middle-aged women came in, one a fruit stall holder. 'Two teas, one egg and cress sandwich, one Danish pastry,' she said.

'I'll bring it over,' Melanie said.

'Something happened?' the woman asked.

'What d'you mean?'

'Well, that reporter—'

'What – him? With Vanessa?' Viv said quickly.

'That's right.'

'Nothing's happened I know of,' Melanie said. 'Here's your teas.'

'What's-his-name, Ben Gathercole,' Viv went on. 'He's a reporter?'

'He come down here a few months ago interviewing people when they put the rents up round the market. Brought a photographer.'

'What? A reporter like the *Sun*, or the *Guardian*?'

'Local paper. *Kenton Post*,' said the woman.

'Nothing the matter with that,' Viv said.

But Melanie's life in London depended on there being a place for her, and no changes. She was worried. 'You think they're going to send you back, don't you, if they get boyfriends?' Viv deduced. 'That's why you don't like that Tom. Look – they need you. They can't manage without you. Men are no good with caffs, or kids.' But Melanie, upset by her father's visit and this new development, still looked disconsolate.

In the pub Vanessa and Ben held hands. They were both very fair, Ben's burnt nose was still peeling from his holiday. Vanessa was on the verge of asking him to move into Rutherford Street with her. They'd spent last night there together, after they got back from the package tour to Portugal, and she'd felt very happy with Ben in the house, safe, for once, from the invisible presence of Geoff Doyle. Apart from anything else, as a reporter, Ben was on reasonable terms with the local police, which might be a help if she had any more trouble with Geoff. But she was holding off her invitation. Once burnt, she was twice shy and didn't want to make a foolish move. She wasn't sure Ben might not think she was jumping the gun. Perhaps he didn't want to live with her. He'd just split up with his wife, leaving her in the house they owned, with their toddler, a boy called Martin. And now she was disconcerted by what she heard from Ben.

'Frances seemed to know I'd met somebody,' he was saying. 'She rang me at work, said she'd been trying to get hold of me all the weekend. Normally, she never rings me. I ring her, to go and see the boy. Then half the time she says it's not convenient. But she says I can come this evening. She suggested it. You don't mind, do you?'

'No, of course not,' Vanessa lied.

'I don't want you to get upset. It's only that I want to see Martin. I told you what it was like – after what I went through with her I don't want to see her any more.' Ben had told Vanessa in Portugal how his wife Frances had rejected him, for reasons he could never get her to explain or understand himself. Now he returned to the subject. 'She just turned away from me after she had the baby. She went right off me, finally she told me to leave. I pleaded with her – I suggested marriage guidance – it was no good. I had to go, get a room, tried to get on with life, sort of hoping she'd have me back. Believe it or not, I ended up in the pub, telling my father about it and I broke down, suddenly, I couldn't help myself. Imagine that, you're in a pub in Leadham Common full of men on a Sunday lunchtime, sobbing your eyes out. They all looked away, pretended I wasn't there. Some of them were my dad's friends . . .'

They had found a corner in the saloon bar at the Duke of Westminster, Frank Sinatra singing 'New York, New York'. 'I daresay most of them had cried, one time or another,' Vanessa told him consolingly.

'Not in a public bar at Sunday lunchtime,' Ben said. 'With blokes trying to have a pint and playing a quick game of darts before they went home for their dinners.'

Now she said tentatively, 'You'd never – go back to her.'

He shook his head. Vanessa didn't know whether to believe him or not.

'There's Martin . . .' she suggested, feeling she must know her chances.

'No,' he said glumly, and changed the subject. 'I don't suppose you've got any contact with Kenton planning department, have you?' Suddenly he became the reporter again.

'Are you joking?' Vanessa asked indignantly. 'After what I told you about my husband and Cindy Abbott?'

'Sorry,' he said, 'I'm just asking around. There's a plan to widen Savernake Road up from the river to Foxwell High Street and it doesn't make a lot of sense. It must be the only road in London which doesn't need widening. But I can't get an answer from my contact in the planning department. She thinks there's something funny going on. The plans are in a locked filing cabinet they used to have access to. And something's up with the computers. A bit they can't get into – a missing code. Now, Sam Abbott's the second in command there—'

'I'm the last person to ask,' Vanessa protested. She was getting depressed now, as she thought about the Abbotts and Geoff Doyle and Ben's wife wanting to see him. She felt weakened. Had her

140

affair with Ben been only a holiday romance? The Arcadia, on which she'd pinned so many hopes, was going wrong. Suddenly it seemed to her nothing was ever going to be quite right again. Her good days were over.

Ben sensed her mood, and patted her arm. 'Cheer up,' he said. 'I've fixed that write-up about the restaurant in the paper. Can I come round late, after I've seen Frances?'

Vanessa smiled, happier again.

That evening, while Vanessa was bathing Alec, Annie dropped in on her way to the restaurant. 'Something important came up while you were away . . . ' And having warned Vanessa she wasn't going to like the news, she told her about Sam Abbott's offer to buy the Arcadia.

She was surprised by Vanessa's reaction. Hauling Alec from the bath and wrapping him in a towel, Vanessa frowned. 'Funny, that's the second time Abbott's name's cropped up today.' She told Annie about the widening of Savernake Road. 'You can see it doesn't make sense,' she added. 'Savernake Road's just a normal grotty little street. Ben can't understand why they want to widen it.'

'Who *is* Ben, by the way?' asked Annie irrelevantly. 'Melanie's very depressed. She seems to think he's a threat to her.'

'Silly girl,' exclaimed Vanessa.

'That's what I told her,' Annie stated, waiting.

'I met him in Portugal, Annie. I really like him,' Vanessa said. She was putting Alec into pyjamas. 'But he's still married to his wife, separated, you know, but not divorced.'

'Oh,' Annie said flatly.

'It's not like that,' Vanessa protested.

'No,' Annie said. 'Well – here's hoping.'

'I can't make up my mind about the Arcadia, Annie,' said Vanessa, returning to their joint preoccupation as she persuaded Alec into his sleeping suit. 'What do you think?'

'I don't know,' Annie said. 'We know if it operated as it's supposed to we'd both have a living, but at the moment it's not. At the moment it's not a living, it's an incipient disaster.'

'Your house is backing it. You've got the most to lose so you should have the biggest say in the decision.'

Annie pointed at Alec, now staring from face to face as they spoke. 'My house, your children – and your father's guarantee – we've both got a lot to lose.' They stared at each other. Alec looked grave.

141

'I feel sick,' claimed Vanessa.

'I do, too,' Annie said.

Only seven customers ate in the Arcadia that night. Melanie, who had been to the cinema, put her head round the door and grimaced. Annie went over to talk to her outside.

'Not many in,' said Melanie, eating a hamburger.

Edward stood well away, in case a passing group of friends thought he had anything to do with her.

'You don't have to tell me!' Annie said.

'I think a bigger bar would go down better round here.'

'You've mentioned that before,' Annie said. 'You might be right, but I wish you wouldn't keep on saying it.'

'A really good club would be great,' Edward butted in. 'Good music—'

'Go home, Melanie,' Annie ordered. 'Edward, you might as well push off, too. Maybe you could just see Melanie up the High Street, to the corner of Rutherford Street.'

'I don't need a minder,' protested Melanie.

'Please,' Annie said dispiritedly. Edward, whose bosses came in every week and collected a large sum from the Arcadia's overdraft, might as well do something more useful than waiting outside the Arcadia, on a quiet night, frightening no one but his own employers when they thought of his connection with the intimidating Andy Campbell.

But as it turned out, sending Edward away was a mistake. Half an hour later three of the kind of shaved-head young men who used to hang about outside when the shop belonged to the old barber with his fascist views, tried to get in. When Annie refused them, they pushed her aside, shoved in, sat down and began to abuse two middle-aged women customers. Annie phoned the police, but by the time they came the young men had gone, though threatening to return. Departing, one spat on the floor by the till. Annie was shaken.

'I wouldn't have thought you'd get the trade for this type of restaurant in this sort of area,' observed the police sergeant.

Annie looked at him despairingly.

'I must bring my wife along some evening,' he said kindly. 'She's all for gourmet food.' But Annie, frightened by having to have Andy Campbell's Edward to keep off other marauders, was thinking about Sam Abbott's offer.

13

Public and Private Developments

That same night, in the discreet restaurant of a central London hotel, two men who might have been assumed to have nothing in common, indeed, to be natural enemies, met over dinner.

Sir Bernard Fellows, chairman of Samco, a great billion-pound pyramid of companies from supermarket chains to helicopter manufacturers, poured more wine for his guest, Joe Banks, leader of the Labour majority on Kenton Council. Joe, now sixty, son of a dockworker more in than out of work during the Depression, had been born in an upstairs flat in Savernake Street and brought up, he said, on bread and dripping. He'd done well at school, gone to a teacher training college, married another Labour Party activist and been elected to Kenton Council at the age of twenty-five. He'd been there ever since, fighting the left of his own party as hard as the few Conservatives on the council. Fighting and, on the whole, winning. He was a short, thickset man with a reddish complexion and broad shoulders. To a superficial observer, such as one of the restaurant's underpaid Mediterranean waiters, he might have appeared not dissimilar to his host, though Sir Bernard was slightly taller and more tanned and his suit was considerably more expensive. Both men looked overweight and uneasy. Both, if the truth were told, had unsatisfactory family lives. They were also earnest, practical, and after a result.

Seven million pounds was their subject. They had settled that this would be the sum the Samco Corporation would pay Kenton Council for a hundred-year lease on the eight acres of Savernake Park and vacant possession of the 104 flats and houses of the Savernake Estate. Savernake House and Rodwell House, each fifteen storeys high, housed sixty families; Grenfell and Raleigh Houses, both low blocks, each contained twenty-four flats, and there were twenty small houses. All in all, the sale would involve around five hundred Savernake Estate residents, men, women and children, tenants and owners, from bank clerks to traffic wardens, many of them discontented with the estate's sweating and cracked walls, flats in poor repair, lifts out of action, dirty stairs and balconies, and their lives made unhappy by the high level of sickness in children, caused by damp, isolation in tower blocks, the noise of the estate's disaffected teenagers, the barking of large dogs kept to deter break-ins, next door's record players and television heard through thin walls – and fear, especially in women and the old, of going out at night. Savernake was not a bad estate, just not a good one. The question for Sir Bernard and Joe Banks was how many people, happy or discontented, would, in the event, be prepared to leave the estate without a fuss.

'So,' said Sir Bernard. 'Can you guess at all how many of the tenants and owners will be prepared to leave at stage one?'

'Owners – offer a decent price and you should pick up a third to a half of them, possibly more. Tenants – well, we'll be making it plain we're moving against those in arrears – that's a good half of them. That way they'll be keen to take an offer – we offer them a lump sum, as agreed, no more said about the arrears and a clean start in alternative accommodation. That could leave about a hundred not wanting to sell, and half the tenants not prepared to go. What they'll do, I don't know. You just can't predict these things. It also depends on how strongly they can organise, who's organising, if they get outside help and support and who from. These are imponderables. I'd be mad to predict, but one thing I'm sure of – we'll win.'

'How long?' enquired Sir Bernard.

'Three months at best, nine at worst. The more people we can clear out at stage one the better – the construction work will get the rest out, noise, dirt, etc.'

'And will members of your own council put up serious opposition to the sale?' Sir Bernard asked.

Joe Banks looked uncomfortable for just a second, then responded, 'I'd be a liar if I told you that might not happen.'

'And the vote?' The vote by the tenants about whether they wanted the sale at all was the most important issue, as they both knew.

'In August,' Banks said. They stared at each other.

Sir Bernard nodded. 'According to the regulations, those residents who do not vote are counted as having voted yes to the sale of a council estate?' he suggested.

Banks nodded. 'Correct.'

'Excellent,' said Sir Bernard. 'I believe you know I have the ear of a senior person at the Department of the Environment?'

'Gerald Rafferty,' Banks said in a low voice. Sir Bernard's glance confirmed this. 'I hope we won't need . . .'

'I, also,' agreed Sir Bernard. 'But it never hurts to have a friend at court.'

Their waiter solicitously enquired if they required dessert. Sir Bernard ordered profiteroles for Joe Banks and chose bread and butter pudding for himself. 'My wife would disapprove,' he said. Banks sympathised.

'Not much red meat seen at home in the past few years,' he said. 'It's well meant, I suppose. They're trying to keep us on our feet. What's the difference between a wife and a terrorist?' he asked Sir Bernard.

'You can negotiate with a terrorist,' Sir Bernard replied promptly.

'Right,' said Joe. The men smiled as the waiter brought their puddings.

'So,' said Sir Bernard. 'If everything's in place I take it you'll reveal details of the scheme as soon as you can.'

'Neither of us wants delay,' said Banks. 'One of our information officers, sworn to secrecy of course, is liaising with your – Samco's – PR firm and they expect to finalise the relevant material in a few days – that's leaflets for all households affected, giving details of the offer, a press campaign in various stages over several months and the like. The posters are already printed – followed by a leaflet to all the tenants and owners on the estate. Of course, there'll be a letter making an offer to each household first. Then posters – simultaneously, of course, a press conference to selected members of the press. We know there might be public opposition to all this. We'll need to be very careful to put this in a favourable light. Your PR firm is seconding an executive to Kenton information department for up to five months, depending on the public reactions.'

'We'll do it,' declared Sir Bernard.

Banks nodded. 'There are only about four hundred adults on that estate – we can't be sure of the exact numbers. The poll tax returns ought to show us, but of course, they don't. They can't be allowed to stand in the way of the benefits the Samco money will bring to the borough.'

'Quite agree. We've got to move quickly now. Leaks would be fatal. But so far we're ahead of the leaks and I believe we can strike first. What will you do with the money?' asked Sir Bernard.

'A new old folk's home, modernisation of a couple of others. A crèche, a repair fund for existing properties, sports facilities.'

'Very nice,' said Sir Bernard. 'Brandy?'

'I'll take an Armagnac, thank you kindly.'

Banks conjured up in his mind a running track, Astroturf, a gym, showers, the Joe Banks Stadium, the Joe Banks Retirement Home, company directorships, a knighthood. The face of Mrs Roxanne Fuller, Mayor of Kenton, loomed up in front of him, large, black, righteous and angry. He pushed the face back. Outside the restaurant he saw his host into a taxi, shook hands through the window and heard Sir Bernard tell the driver, 'Colindale, sixty-three Hall Avenue.' Banks took himself to the tube station.

Foxwell High Street was crowded that Saturday morning. It was hot, the traffic fumes seemed worse than usual. George's was crammed. Vanessa and Melanie stood behind the counter, while Annie, near them in the corner, served ices and cold drinks from the new fridge she had installed. Though the till clanged merrily open and shut it was small comfort when Annie and Vanessa thought of the static, empty Arcadia next door, swept and garnished, expensively appointed, waiting to do another slow, expensive night's business, its till a funeral march to the café's fandango.

Ben Gathercole charged in, accompanied by a slight, fair woman with cropped hair who, Vanessa knew, was not Frances Gathercole. Vanessa had seen Ben's wife in a photograph and she was a tall, dark woman, with a big nose, not as pretty, she noticed happily, as Vanessa herself. She summed up Ben's companion quickly as a radical activist, from her large canvas shoulder-bag to her small feet in round-toed black shoes. Ben, meanwhile, had grabbed the only free seat in the café by the window, having managed to glare a woman finishing her cup of tea out of her chair, which he had plonked himself down in. On the other side of the table Madame Katarina made room for his long legs and big feet by politely moving the suitcase she was about to take down to Brighton for a week of consultations at her south coast practice. Ignoring her, Ben

146

said to the slight woman who squeezed in next to the clairvoyant, 'So what's it all about, Sue?'

'Most of it's in the print-outs. Look – I'll shove them to you under the table. I don't want to be conspicuous. They're all labelled "Secret" – nice, isn't it, in the so-called Socialist Republic of Kenton?'

'OK, just push them to me casually. Thanks, by the way.'

'Don't thank me, just do something. In the end, I don't care if I lose the job. I've had it up to here with Kenton Council anyway – I don't care if I sell my flat and go back to Leeds. I want to nail that bastard Joe Banks. Socialist? He's about as red as your laundry when it goes pink in the washing machine. What you've got there, no doubt about it, is the plan to sell off Savernake Park and the Savernake Estate to a property firm, Savernake Developments. And, of course, before that they've got to get the tenants out fast, so they can go ahead. Can you get that on the front page of the *Kenton Post*?'

Madame Katarina, who had made no effort to pretend she wasn't listening, and whose face had slowly taken on a look of satisfaction, stared at Ben.

'Unless they start digging up a garden in Rutherford Street and find Dennis Neilson's been at work again,' Ben told her, 'that story will go in.' He felt movement under the table and grasped the large envelope she was pushing towards him. 'I'll have to read this and ring my editor. He'll probably have to contact the managing editor. Will you be around over the weekend?'

'Stick a message on the answering machine if I'm out,' she said. 'Or you can leave any message with my flatmate. She knows all about it. I've got to go. See you, Ben.'

'See you, Sue,' he murmured, watching as she disappeared into the crowd on the pavement outside. Madame Katarina, catching his eye, smiled at him. He was startled. Then he turned and looked across at Vanessa, and smiled.

'What are you doing here?' she mouthed.

Ben got up and went over to her. 'I'll ring you tonight,' he said.

'I thought you were going to—'

'I'll have to cancel it. Something's come up. A big story, biggest of my career, possibly. Will you be in?'

She nodded, 'Yes. I'm a sucker. Sorry, love, no Coke at this counter. Ask the lady over there.'

147

'Can I have a glass?'

As Vanessa turned to reach for a glass she heard Ben shout across the café, 'How far is Savernake Road from here?' He was already in the doorway.

'Straight down the High Street, past two sets of lights, then right, left, right again and that's it,' said a man near by. And Ben was gone.

In bed that night Ben went methodically through the dealings of Kenton Council with Savernake Developments for Vanessa's benefit. 'Two months of secret deals between planning department officers and the company involved,' he concluded. 'And only some of the department privy to the deal. My informant works there and found out by going in on Saturday morning and hacking into a computer while pretending to do something else. She guessed at the key word. Got it second guess. "Savernake" – not very bright, eh? The road-widening scheme went through that department on push and pull and I don't know if the roads people knew why they were passing it. The whole plan was designed, of course, to assist traffic flow for the new development no one had heard about. Two months of secrecy, in a council pledged to open government. You can bet your socks most of the councillors don't know. It's a major scandal.'

At the start of the story, Vanessa had committed herself to lying there dreamily, looking sometimes through the bedroom window at a patch of dark sky, and sometimes at her lover as he spoke. She felt pleasure as he told her the story, because he was telling her, because he was there, and not with his wife. However, the words planning department brought her back to reality with a start. Horrible memories of the row in the supermarket with Cindy Abbott, the equally nasty scene in Geoff's office, the whole awful business began to flood in. She began to pay attention. 'I'll check Companies House tomorrow,' Ben was saying, 'and find out who's in charge at the so-called Savernake Developments,' when Vanessa said, 'Cindy's father, Mr Abbott's in it. He must be. That must be why he wants to buy the Arcadia.'

'He what?' Ben said, startled. 'You didn't tell me.'

'He rang again yesterday,' she said. 'Annie spoke to him. She's worried. "Time's nearly up," he said. We've got to make up our minds. We've more or less decided to go ahead and sell it. We've only got till mid-week, and nothing's improved. He said

148

it was for his retirement. But do you think this has got anything to do with it?'

'He must think the plan's going to go through,' Ben told her, 'bringing people with a lot of money into the area, making an up-market restaurant a better proposition.'

'Oh, wow,' Vanessa said. 'I must tell Annie. What are we going to do?'

'He must be pretty sure Savernake Developments will have their way with Kenton Council,' said Ben.

'It's a shame to think of the park going,' Vanessa said. 'There's hardly anywhere else near by you can take children. We've always moaned about the dogshit and the dossers and muggers, but that's better than not having it at all. And what are they going to do with all the people on the estate? It makes you feel insecure. If the council can do that to them they can do it to me, tomorrow. All they need to do is decide they want to turn the bit of Rutherford Street they own into a multistorey car park and then what happens to my home? It's like the wicked landlord. I mean, it's not just those people who're going to worry – it's all the tenants in Kenton.'

'Good point. Still, they're not going to do anything here. Anyway, to do them justice, they're offering terms—'

'I can imagine,' Vanessa said. 'Alternative accommodation on the worst estates—'

'Savernake's not much to write home about—'

'It's their homes,' Vanessa said fiercely. 'You can't go taking away people's homes.'

'Well, that's exactly what they're planning to do,' Ben said.

'I think I'd better phone Annie straight away,' Vanessa said, getting out of bed.

To Nigel Fellows's annoyance Jasmine arrived late in their box at Covent Garden. Her husband might have been surprised at the reason for her unpunctuality: the demand of handsome Gerald Rafferty, Nigel's old schoolfriend, now at the Department of the Environment, for one last act of intercourse in his Tufnell Park maisonette. Jasmine saw it as helping herself to another card in the game of life to which she was committed.

She smiled apologetically, assuring herself of her husband's forgiveness for her childish lateness, and slipped into the empty chair on Nigel's right. Jasmine knew she looked beautiful in a shimmering dark blue dress, golden hair piled up on her head, a double row of pearls round her throat. On Nigel's left sat Mr Katario and Mrs Sumi Ikeda and just behind them the glamorous Tamsin Bell, in purple shot silk, with Julian Vane. Right at the back of the box, half in shadow, Max Craig, the company astrologer, like Nigel, pursued his own thoughts. The much-delayed consultation at Durham House had, to Nigel's way of thinking, been unsatisfactory, and a further meeting was planned for later that evening in Kensington.

'I see a death,' Max had said. 'And I see a project which may be hard to bring to fulfilment. The reasons are obscure. The strands involve love, and money, and vengeance, and something which is almost, but not quite, supernatural. It's a very cloudy picture, and my strong advice is to do as little as possible at the moment. If you wait, all may yet be well—'

'Waiting's not my strong suit, Max,' Nigel had said, with some impatience in his voice. They were sitting in the library at Durham House late at night. Nigel's long day and car breakdown had made him tense. The news he was receiving was not what he wanted to hear. 'With all due respect, Max, I'm an impatient fellow, active – and sometimes circumstances are such that one just cannot wait.'

'I know. But my advice is to put as much as possible on hold.'

Nigel had the idea the clairvoyant was trying to punish him for having made him wait about all day. He sensed malice in the less-than-good prognostications. He also wanted to hear something about a coming child, but was reluctant to expose his need, in all its depth. He'd thrust his hot hand at Craig and said, 'Here – take another look at the entrails.' But Max Craig was standing and trying to excuse himself.

'I've done the chart, for you and for the company you asked about, and I'm tired. And that means, quite frankly, I can't start on palmistry.'

'Oh, do your stuff, Max,' Nigel said irritably.

Then, seeing Craig's face and suddenly recognising that if he gave way to any more impatience he might lose a perfectly good forecaster, he paused. He recalled what had happened to Sammy Tideman at Grosvenor Mutual when Craig had walked out on him just before he went ahead with the takeover against Craig's advice. A nice combination of the Monopolies Commission and the Fraud Squad had put old Sammy firmly into retirement in the Canaries. Of course, Sammy had rejected a lot of other advice and warnings over eighteen months, not all of it from Craig and his crystal ball, so the collapse wasn't such a surprise. But there were other examples of the dangers of ignoring Craig's predictions – of a coup over-throwing a government here, a dawn raid there. Those who retained him, when you discovered who they were – the managing editor of ten newspapers, a royal prince and an African dictator – seldom did anything but praise him. To be on the safe side, Nigel reflected, he'd be well advised to keep Craig sweet. He had apologised and blamed the long day followed by a difficult journey for his bad temper. An owl hooted. Craig, about to reply, paused. Another hoot came. Craig smiled. 'Let's meet again, shortly. I'll work on it all, see if I can give you a more exact picture.'

Nigel masked his boredom and impatience as *Turandot* went on its noisy way. As the tenor belted out 'None shall sleep', he noticed Jasmine's head droop and her eyes close. Giving her a little friendly jab in the ribs, he thought how very, very fond of her he was. She was lively, affectionate, pretty and good-humoured. But he wanted, needed, a child. Aside from his natural desire, there were practical reasons. At their father's death, Sim, his elder brother, would become a baronet and inherit half his father's majority shareholding in Samco, Nigel receiving the other half. Durham House was en-tailed to the eldest male heir – Sim, Sim's son, his grandson would inherit it. Their sister, Claudia, would get a lump sum, a few Samco shares and little else, since it was assumed, by custom, that she would marry and that her husband would be responsible for her. If she needed other help, Sim would be expected to supply it. But now things were changed – if Sim was dead everything which would have been his would go to Nigel and then to his son, if he had one. Embassies had been contacted, foreign governments appealed to, detectives employed, but all the searches had not produced Simon Fellows. The family were terrified now that he would never turn up.

Nigel tried not to slump in his seat. The thought that he might never again see clever, peculiar Sim drained him. But there it was, and already his father was making provision for him to receive everything if Sim never reappeared, or was found to be dead. It had to be done. He waited impatiently for the end of the last act. At least they had all had dinner earlier, so once the opera was over they could part. His guest, Mr Ikeda, had more or less assured him that afternoon that his bank, given all the necessary guarantees, would front up ten million for the Savernake development, a bit less than half the full sum required. Samco would produce the other half. The interest payments on Ikeda's loan would be heavy, but on balance that method of financing the scheme would be better than digging too heavily into Samco's pockets. In fact, Nigel wasn't sure that if he went to the Samco board and asked them to finance the Savernake development in full they would be all that happy to do so. Harry Paine, a senior director, had hinted as much to him a month or so before, warning him obliquely not to ask.

Meanwhile, the thought of Sim's death, perhaps in a foreign gaol, or bowing out in a shabby hotel room in a small town in Thailand or Peru, produced a heavy lump in Nigel's chest. On the other hand, if Sim was alive, he'd just like to get his hands on the bastard. Their mother was growing ever more papery and silent, and if Sim were capable of getting in touch and wasn't doing it, then it was cruel beyond belief. But it was hardly possible that Sim would behave like that. He must be dead, or in bad trouble somewhere. Max Craig was as useless as the Foreign Office and the private investigators, except that Craig had apparently declared to Lady Mary that Sim wasn't dead. Thin comfort, thought Nigel, and he'd believe it when he saw Sim with his own eyes, and not before.

Jasmine was managing to nod off again, the finale in full flow. Nigel nudged her once more. It was understandable that she hadn't wanted to have dinner with the Ikedas, Julian Vane and Tamsin Bell, since Vane had dumped her sister for the Bell woman. For his part, he could see why. In her light, shiny number, all out at the front and in at the waist, with flashing eyes and teeth and tossing hair, Tamsin Bell looked like a hotter number than Annie, nice as his sister-in-law was. Annie was no doubt a lot more civilised in a cardigans-and-hard-library-books sort of way but she lacked glamour. She was the wife you went into the jungle with, as was Jasmine in her way, but who wanted to go into the jungle?

Nigel had had to explain that Jasmine had another date and couldn't be with them for dinner. Julian had left his wife high and dry, without any warning, and had apparently refused to consider repaying the legacy she'd trustingly put in his hands while he was building up his firm. It was a bad business and Nigel was angered by the sneaky, victorious little look the couple exchanged when they guessed the real reason for Jasmine's absence from the dinner. It was a snub to him, as Annie's brother-in-law. Stupid to be caught out in a silly thing like that, Nigel thought, especially in a matter concerning someone's family, an area always about as safe as picking primroses on the Irish border. He had to deal with Julian because

Julian's services were extremely useful, in many ways unique. He'd heard Julian had expanded the firm quickly on the strength of his new woman's rich family – yet another of Julian Vane's enterprises funded with the help of money produced by the woman he was living with. Obviously, some men were like that. He, Nigel, was quite pleased he wasn't one. Nevertheless, when they stood up to applaud and get ready to leave, Nigel observed Julian greet Jasmine cordially, as if there was nothing wrong.

'And it's such a wonderful opera,' Tamsin said enthusiastically. 'Don't you think so, Mrs Fellows?'

Nigel had to introduce his wife to her sister's supplanter and wasn't surprised when Jasmine ignored the introduction, turning immediately to Mrs Ikeda, saying, 'My goodness. That is a lovely dress. And so cool in this weather,' and to Nigel, 'Nigel, shall we start to leave, before the crowd gets too thick? It's terribly hot.' And again, to Mrs Ikeda, 'We're just not used to such heat in this country.' Without forcing the pace, she led the way out of the crowded box and into the corridor. Julian would have to listen to some protests from his snubbed woman on the drive home, Nigel reflected, but she might have expected something like that. In the circumstances it would have been more tactful to have stayed at home.

Nigel took Tamsin's arm as they walked out, saying to Julian, who came behind, 'I know the quickest way out. If we move, we may be able to avoid the crush.'

'But I love that moment when the whole audience is outside Covent Garden on a fine night,' Tamsin said, meaning, Nigel presumed, that she wasn't averse to being seen in select company, if that's what you could call it these days.

Julian's response was, 'Well, not if it means queueing up for the car, darling.'

Tamsin hadn't given up. 'Julian was telling me about your beautiful house in the country. I'd so love to see it.'

'So would I, at the moment,' Nigel said. 'I'm afraid we're all going to be stuck in London for a little while, until we've got things moving.'

'It must be wonderful to be able to go to such a lovely place, after London,' Tamsin persisted.

Jasmine, further along with the Ikedas, called, 'Hurry, Nigel. We're getting separated.'

'Yessir,' called Nigel, thinking, She's a lovely girl, Jasmine. I do love her.

Joe Banks was in the Arcadia with Councillor Leslie Dowell, unofficial leader of what was termed the Kenton Cadre, a group of five very socialist councillors from five very poor wards of the borough. Banks had known all along they would spearhead the attack on the plan to sell the Savernake Estate and Savernake Park. Looking round the restaurant, empty but for four salesmen celebrating the birthday of one of them, Banks said, 'It's a nice little place, good food. I can't understand why more people don't come here.'

'I should think the prices put it out of the range of the average Kenton resident,' Les Dowell said glumly. He was a tall, lantern-jawed man of forty in a white open-necked shirt and black trousers.

'I know you'd rather have a pie and a pint, Les,' Banks said, 'but, as I've explained, I'm having to be careful about my stomach. I'm getting on, and I'm taking tablets for ulcers. The doctor tells me it's not unusual where people had a poor diet in childhood. Four of us on a docker's wages – when he was in work, which wasn't always—'

'Yes, Joe,' Les Dowell said. 'I've heard that song before. Let's get down to business. What am I here for?'

'You're going to have to hear me out on this one,' warned Banks. He put it to himself that he hated Les Dowell and his side-kick, the angry red-head Betsey Jones. He firmly believed they were covert members of the Workers' Revolutionary Party. They'd challenged him two years running for leadership of the Labour group on the council; he'd beaten them off fairly easily so far, but he knew they were always at his heels. He feared that one day, for some reason, they'd win, and start working to make the Socialist Republic of Kenton not a joke, but a reality. They'd declare war on central government, which would come down on them like a ton of bricks. The residents of Kenton would wake up and find they'd become cannon fodder in a civil war between Kenton and Westminster. The Government would starve and batter Kenton into submission, the cadre would have scored a moral victory, Kenton residents would find yet another old people's home shut and a large feeder road for the Channel Tunnel traffic going right through their homes.

He glared at Dowell, who stared back. A cloud of rage and

154

disgust hung over their table. And he was a vegetarian, Banks thought, giving orders to the young waitress in a black dress.

'How old are you?' Les Dowell asked Melanie, looking her up and down.

'Oh my God,' groaned Banks under his breath.

'What do you want to know for?' demanded Melanie who still left a lot to be desired as a waitress.

'You're from up north, aren't you?' said Les.

Melanie's nerve failed her. She went back into the kitchen and returned with a grim-faced Annie. 'I'd prefer it if you would let my waitress get on with her job,' she said.

Dowell looked up. 'I'm concerned about her conditions of employment, that's all.'

'So am I,' Annie said. 'And I don't want her harassed by the male customers.'

Les drew himself up in his seat. 'I am Councillor Leslie Dowell. I represent McCorquodale ward on Kenton Council. I perceive that girl to be an under-age northerner—'

'Well, Councillor Dowell,' Annie said firmly, 'she's here with her mother's permission, helping out. I appreciate your concern, but there's nothing wrong with her situation. She lives with me, she goes to school in term-time, she's invaluable to my business. She's paid for what she does.' She paused. 'I'm afraid I misinterpreted your motives in speaking to her.'

'Understood,' said Les Dowell. 'I hope I didn't frighten her.'

'Well, you did,' Annie said. And, having taken their order, returned to the kitchen.

'Well, now you've done your bit for the youngsters the system's exploiting, Les,' Joe said, 'can we get down to business?' He had not had very much hope of turning Les Dowell in the first place, but Les now had to know what was going on and he had to get a rough idea, if possible, about what Les and the comrades would do to obstruct the project.

In the kitchen Annie hissed, 'Keep listening, Melanie. If you hear the word Savernake, tell me what they say.'

Melanie served pâté to Joe Banks, produced the half grapefruit asked for by Les Dowell and heard Banks's opening gambit.

'What I'm going to tell you, Les, concerns a new project in Kenton which could net us seven million, and jobs for upwards of two hundred people, some permanent. Try to think about that as I go along.'

There was no expression on Les Dowell's lean face. He removed the cherry from his grapefruit and put it on the side of his plate.

Banks continued, 'We've agreed some plans for a building project, the Savernake Village project. A small area, filled with homes and other facilities, all bringing work and prosperity to Kenton.'

Les Dowell stared expressionlessly. 'A yuppie compound,' he said. 'Where are we, whoever *we* may be, putting it?'

'It'll involve Savernake Park.' Banks paused.

'You want to sell off Savernake Park,' Dowell stated flatly. 'The only green space for miles around. And, ah,' he said, 'you'll have to get rid of the estate.'

'That's about the size of it,' Banks said steadily.

'Got the plans, Joe?'

'I can let you have them.' There was a pause.

'I'm thinking,' said Dowell, 'this plan isn't just a gleam in your eye. How far has it gone?'

'There's to be an announcement next week.'

'Who's making it?'

'The company concerned and Kenton Council.'

Dowell let rip. His voice rose. 'This is a scandal, Joe Banks. You've been working on all this for, what, three months, four, since Christmas? Of course you have. In secrecy. Without informing councillors, departments—'

'Les,' Banks said, trying to quieten him down. 'You know the position. The borough's crumbling round our ears. We can't even touch the money on sales of housing for repairs on housing stock. We've got the second highest rate of unemployment in London. People are living like pigs in Kenton. Walls sweat, roofs leak, kids get ill, lighting on the estates is broken, Telecom's given us a quota of phone boxes they're prepared to repair. We've had to put all the old people in Golightly House into bed and breakfast. The social services are cracking – we haven't even got enough people to inspect, let alone maintain services. The kids at the Fairweather children's home would be better off in prison, as I understand it – don't give me your socialist principles. In this climate, all it spells is human misery. It's getting as bad as the Depression round here, you know it. Sitting on your bum talking about how bad it is isn't going to do anything. What we need is money and jobs. This project will give us cash in hand, no big constraints on how we use it. It'll produce jobs in the short and long term, and bring trade to the area.'

'I take all those points, Joe,' Dowell said, 'but you're going to sell off what was paid for by Kenton and belongs to Kenton, including their homes, without any kind of consultation with the people's elected representatives.' He shook his head. 'No, Joe. Not without a fight. I want to know who's in charge of this project.'

'We are. Stop shouting, Les. You're not making a speech here.'

'Where's the seven million coming from?' demanded Dowell. 'Is that a secret too?'

'The company's called Savernake Developments,' Banks said.

'That tells me precisely nothing. Are you going to give me details, or do you want me to convene a special council meeting? Well, don't answer that question, I'm going to do it anyway. Thanks for the grapefruit, Joe.' Dowell stood up, pulled a pound out of his pocket and slammed it down on the table before walking out of the restaurant.

Banks gazed after him, then looked down, drank from his wineglass, spread a little pâté on his toast. He sighed. This was very much what he'd expected. But he was ready and they weren't. The letters to tenants would go round in a few days, the whole plan would be public next week, the bulldozers would probably start on the park in September, while the remaining, unyielding Savernake Estate tenants slowly crumbled. He'd go home shortly and await the furious call from Mrs Roxanne Fuller, Mayor of Kenton.

A complete silence, imposed by Annie, reigned in the kitchen. Les Dowell had not spoken quietly. They had heard everything. Even the celebrating salesmen had intermittently fallen silent at his angry speech, delivered in a voice accustomed to hitting the back of the hall, and piercing confusion at council meetings. Now one of them shouted, 'We asked for more bread half an hour ago. And this man wants seconds of duck, greedy pig. You dead in there?'

'If the kiss of life's what's needed . . .' said another. They laughed.

'I'll see to them, Melanie,' Annie said. 'You go and ask the other man what he'd like to follow.' She pasted on a smile and went over to the table where the four men sat, 'Bit of a row over there,' said one. 'What was all that about?'

'You can't hear anything from the kitchen,' Annie said blandly.

'You're telling me, darling,' said one. 'So now you're here, one more duck, and simultaneously, we'll take a look at the sweet trolley.'

'D'you do flambés?' asked another.

'Not at the moment, unfortunately,' Annie lied. 'The equipment's under repair. We can do it in the kitchen and bring it to you, flaming.'

'Good. I like hot stuff,' he said.

Annie smiled, and went away. She made a face at Abigail.

'He wants salmon, and a phone,' Melanie reported of Joe Banks.

'Well, just this once,' Annie said. 'Take him the handset from the portable, and we'll see if we can hear anything.'

'A Mrs Fuller. He's going round to see her. It sounds as if she's angry,' Melanie reported a little later.

Now the salesmen, as boys will, all wanted a go with the phone. The restaurant resounded with laughter.

14

The Savernake War Begins

The following Sunday, Vanessa, Alec, Joanne and Melanie and her friend Viv and Annie all went for a picnic in Savernake Park. The temperature was in the 90°s and the grass was covered with little groups of people, some lying getting suntans, playing the radio, or tapes. There were children eating ices, playing on the swings further down, people walking dogs, losing control of dogs, all in bright sunshine.

'There must be hundreds here,' Vanessa said. 'Oh – get away!' Alec was crying because an Alsatian was trying to eat his ice-cream. Vanessa looked round for the owner. No one seemed to be in charge. 'Oh, God, look at that!' she appealed as the dog stopped four feet away, squatted and trotted on, leaving a pile of steaming excrement.

A small girl in a baseball cap and party frock sat down beside her. 'Disgusting, isn't it?' she said.

A boy swinging a big ghetto blaster walked past calling, 'Charlie!' above the music. A boy and two girls in shorts and T-shirts shouted back from the plaid rug on which they were reclining. Annie lay on her back, looking at a bird flying overhead.

'I like it a little bit better at Froggett's,' Joanne said to her. 'You can't get ice-creams, but the animals are nicer and it's more quieter. It's sometimes nice when it's really quiet and you can only hear birds.'

'This isn't bad, for the middle of a city,' Annie said. She turned her head, glimpsing the two white towers of the Savernake Estate to her right, across the huge sweep of grass covered with people. When the great house of the Rodwells had been torn down in the fifties it

159

had been derelict, one corner sheared off by a war-time bomb. No one at that time had questioned the decision to pull down a stately home in order to build the Savernake Estate on the site. Now, the house would be preserved. In the fifties, Annie imagined, people were accustomed to the idea of bombed buildings; reconstruction was a priority, the whole city must have been full of sites ripe for redevelopment.

Ben Gathercole was putting a print of the old Savernake House in the *Kenton Post*. It had been a long, low, eighteenth-century building with big windows all along the ground floor, a porticoed entrance and a semi-circle of stone in front for the carriages. It had been built broadside on to the river and Annie wondered why they'd placed it deliberately to avoid facing the water. The Thames wouldn't have been banked by then. Was it to discourage people who might see the lighted windows and come ashore to rob them, to avoid direct blasts of the smell from the sewage-filled river in summer, or fear of facing that disease-carrying miasma said to come from such rivers?

It must have been nice in summer, Annie thought. Not so jolly in winter, with fog coming thickly from the water, and wet, dank fields all round. Today you could hardly see the river for vast office blocks. Now, she reflected, the council was trying to sell off the park. Having passed from the wealthy Rodwells to the people of Kenton, it seemed the park was to change hands again, back into the hands of the wealthy, to Nigel Fellows and his shareholders.

Annie was recalled to the present by Joanne's shrill voice, 'Can we have our picnic now, or can me and Viv go over to the kiosk for some crisps? Viv didn't have any breakfast, and we're thirsty. Alec's thirsty.'

'I'm thirsty,' Alec said, getting to his feet.

Vanessa, hunched over, stared at the rug they were sitting on. 'Are you all right?' Annie asked.

'I'm tired,' Vanessa said.

'You're always saying that,' remarked Joanne.

'I wonder why,' remarked Vanessa.

Annie opened the picnic basket. Their neighbours cast covert looks at the professional-looking boxes of salad, salmon, pâté, the slices of duck and the French bread. The children, fed up with an expensive diet, weren't pleased. Joanne found it nearly impossible to discover anything she liked, but settled for smoked salmon made into sandwiches. 'Why can't we have normal food sometimes?' Her eye followed her mother's, observing Ben's form weaving through people on the grass.

'Him again,' remarked Joanne, not pleased, knowing her mother's attention would now go to the intruder.

'Wow,' said Ben, arriving and looking admiringly at the feast. He sat down and helped himself. 'The Mayor's furious,' he said. 'I've just been to see her. Nice woman – came over here from Jamaica in 1957, with small children; her husband died almost immediately so she got a job in a launderette with a flat above. Now she owns several and her four daughters are all teachers . . . '

'Yes – well . . .' said Vanessa. 'What's she got in mind?'

'She can't do much. It's up to the council. It isn't even on the agenda yet. Joe Banks just contacted her, wanting it put on as any other business, an obvious attempt so slip it through before anyone noticed. But Les Dowell had already phoned her. She was furious. Banks has been working on it for ages, that's obvious. The phones must be ringing hot all over Kenton. She's dead against the scheme. When I left she was ringing Willie Carlyle, the local MP.'

'Old Sam Abbott must think it's going to go through,' Vanessa said. 'He phoned again this morning, to see if we wanted to sell the Arcadia. He's pushing us, now. Cup of tea?'

'Nothing I like better than a smoked salmon sandwich and a cup of tea,' Ben said comfortably.

'I don't know what we're going to do,' Vanessa continued. 'We're still losing money. But, of course, once this yuppie paradise goes up, the Arcadia could be flavour of the month. I think we'll have to sell, though.'

'Let's hang on,' Annie said. 'It's nerve-racking, but let's just give it a little longer. He's agreed we can wait until next week. We'll decide then.'

'Pretty good, though,' Ben said. 'As a plot. Abbott fixes the plans – I'm sure he has – then offers to buy the restaurant. I wonder what else he's getting out of it?' He jumped up. 'I'd better run. I'm going to see Les Dowell and Betsey Jones, to get an update. Les is talking about a riot—Hallo,' he said in surprise, 'what's this?'

An old lady with a letter in her hand was advancing across the grass propelled by a big man in a stretched T-shirt who led her up to Annie's and Vanessa's group. 'Are you the reporter from the local paper?' he asked Ben. 'Thought I spotted you. This lady's had a letter from a company and she's upset.'

The woman was about seventy, small and bent, wearing an old

161

black skirt and a well-ironed flowered blouse. She said, 'I've had this letter pushed through my door. Can you explain it? What's happening?'

Ben scanned it and looked up. 'They're moving fast,' he said, startled.

'What's it all about?' asked the woman. 'It's Sunday afternoon. I was so shocked when I got it I just came straight out to talk to the caretaker – what are they going to do?'

'Do you know what's going on?' demanded the big man. 'This is Mrs Walters, by the way. I'm the caretaker at Rodwell House. Harold Smith. You did a story on our insect plague. Can you explain what's happening?'

The letter, headed Savernake Developments, said that, subject to council approval, the Savernake Estate was to be sold. Offers would be made to home owners on the estate. Tenants would be offered alternative accommodation by the council. Their rent arrears, if any, were subject to negotiation with the council and might be waived. In addition, Savernake Developments was prepared to pay home owners and tenants willing to move the sum of £2000 per household to cover expenses.

'I've never been behind with my rent in my life,' protested Mrs Walters. 'They're selling the flats, aren't they? They can't do that, can they?'

'The council's got to agree to a vote,' Annie told her. 'Haven't you got a tenants' association?'

Mrs Walters ignored Annie. 'I don't know what my daughter's going to say about this. It isn't right, being shoved about from pillar to post like this at my age. What's this about a vote?'

'If the council agrees to allow it, there has to be a vote by all the tenants to see if they want the estate sold off. She needs to sit down,' Annie said to Vanessa.

The caretaker said, 'Why don't you all go back to this lady's flat? Then this gentleman,' he looked at Mrs Walters, 'can talk to you. He's from the paper, people should know about this.'

'You go,' Annie said to Vanessa. 'We'll stay and have our picnic.'

Ben, Vanessa, Margaret Walters and the caretaker began to walk towards the estate through the people on the grass. The two towers of the Savernake Estate flats came closer. Through the gaps in the buildings a courtyard could be seen in which cars were parked. Facing inwards, on the right and left of the courtyard, were low blocks of flats separated from the cars by a strip of green. Beyond the big archway between Rodwell House and Savernake House stood a row of small houses, with little front gardens. Behind, out of sight, was Savernake Road.

'You make her a cup of tea,' the caretaker advised Vanessa. 'I've got to get back and sort out the hot water.'

'Any chance of seeing you later?' asked Ben.

He shook his head. 'Not me, mate.'

'Worried about the job?'

'What would you think? I've got to keep my head down till we see what's happening. Sorry,' he added. 'As a matter of fact, I think it's disgusting. Don't quote me.' He ducked away.

The courtyard was littered, the lower parts of the building ragged with graffiti: the names of football clubs and the slogans 'NF' and 'Troops Out'. Several brand-new cars were parked in the centre and in one a large, thirsty Rottweiler barked.

'I'm on the first floor,' said Mrs Walters as the group reached Rodwell House. 'We can try for the lift but I expect it's stuck on one of the floors. If it's not broken there's someone on the eighth floor who wedges the doors open for their own convenience. I don't dare ask who it is. Well,' she said, when they'd climbed the unclean stairs, 'here we are . . .' She opened a door on the balcony corridor overlooking the park and led her visitors through a narrow hall and into a neatly furnished sitting room with a three-piece suite, a large television and family photographs on a big table covered with a cloth.

Ben took out his notebook while Vanessa was making a cup of tea in the kitchen. 'I'm sixty-seven,' Mrs Walters said. 'I've had three children all brought up in this flat. My husband's been dead fifteen years.' She had a job cleaning two of the shops in Savernake Road. 'I'm slow but I'm thorough,' she said. 'I've done my best all my life – and now look.' She was recovering her nerve.

Mrs Walters beckoned them to the window and pointed across the courtyard. 'A lot of them over there have bought the houses. Some of the flats have been sold, too. See – new front doors, taking care of the garden. Do you think they'll be trying to get rid of them?'

'They'll have to try to buy them out, if they're going to rebuild,' Ben said.

'That black woman with all the kids has had one of these letters, too, look – she's going next door to see if the neighbours had one. I've been here since the flats were built – brought the kids up here.

I've seen what they offer you in exchange – rubbish. I'd never get the rooms – if they didn't look at my age and push me in an old folk's home. I've got friends here. And a job. It isn't fair. Is it fair?'

The doorbell interrupted her. After an agitated conversation in the hall Mrs Walters ushered in a plump, middle-aged woman whom she introduced as Mrs Wainwright.

'This gentleman's from the *Kenton Post*,' she explained.

'I'm shattered,' said the newcomer. 'I just don't know what to do. Ted's up north working. I can't get hold of him. What are we going to do? Move? It's disgusting. Mrs Walters says you're from the paper – I hope you'll quote me,' she addressed Ben. 'It's disgusting – we ought to fight it. Who's our MP?'

'Is there a tenants' association?' asked Ben.

Mrs Wainwright looked at Mrs Walters doubtfully. 'There's a woman who pushes things through the letterbox. Or is that the Social Services?'

'I've got one about dogs fouling the courtyard,' said Mrs Walters. 'Did I throw it away – no, here it is.' She showed Ben a photocopied circular letter headed Savernake Estate Tenants' Association.

Vanessa came in carrying a tray with a teapot and cups on it. Mrs Walters drank some tea and sighed. 'Who'd have believed it?'

'Them down there in the houses'll sell and make a killing,' Mrs Wainwright said. 'They're laughing. Half of them are having trouble with the mortgage.'

'You can't sell until you've owned the place for three years,' Ben told her.

'Is that a fact?' said Mrs Wainwright. 'That won't please them.'

'They'll get round it somehow,' Mrs Walters said. 'What do you think?'

There was a silence.

'I think it's been cleverly done,' Ben observed, looking out of the window at the silent estate in the sunshine. A man came out with a transistor radio and a bucket, to clean his car. The music came faintly up to the windows. A girl with blue hair opened a window and flapped a duster out.

'Oh, come on,' said Vanessa. 'Who says they can get away with it? Who? Haven't you got any right to stay in your home if you want to? Get organised, get the MP on your side and lobby the councillors. Ben – you can get it in a paper, can't you?'

'The meeting's on Wednesday, too soon to do much,' said Ben.

'Nevertheless,' Mrs Walters declared, 'she's right! We're not beaten yet.'

On another estate a mile away Betsey Jones interrupted herself to ask her daughter to make coffee.

'Well, Les,' she resumed, 'that's agreed. We refuse a vote on Wednesday and ask for an inquiry.'

'Joe Banks'll force a vote,' said Les.

'We'll ask for a vote on the vote. We've got a probable nine on our side and the same on theirs. Then there's the undecideds and do you know what I'm going to do? Ring Emily Littlejohn, Hugh Patterson and Jim Lloyd. I'm going to try and recruit them.'

The only three Conservative councillors on Kenton Council were hardly the natural allies of the extreme left-wing faction headed by Les Dowell and Betsey Jones.

'You never know with these Tories,' continued Betsey, transfixed over a cigarette she was rolling, her red hair pointing down at the carpet. 'OK, Jim Lloyd'll be all for the project. He's a surveyor. His brother's an estate agent. They'll be licking their lips. But the other two are turning against this ruthless capitalism.'

'I'll ring Emily,' Les said.

'No. She'll trust you less than me,' declared Betsey, and seized the phone from him.

Not long after this it was established that, unusually, two of the Conservative councillors would be voting with the loony left against a vote on the Savernake Village project and in favour of a motion demanding an inquiry about how it had reached such an advanced stage without the knowledge of the council.

'That's stopped Joe Banks in the short term,' said Les with satisfaction. 'Now I'd better ring this woman who runs the Savernake Tenants' Association. Time to get some grassroots activity organised. Where's Susie with that coffee?'

In Bedford Square, tea was being taken. The maid wheeled in a trolley. Jasmine poured. Sun came in through the windows on to green and gold walls. Jasmine said discontentedly, 'I wish we could be in Portugal.'

'I'm sorry, darling. Not until this Savernake business is a bit more resolved,' Nigel told her. To his father he said, 'It's all going pretty much as Joe Banks predicted. Or so he tells me. The opposition's started to mobilise. The MP seems to have taken the point that half the new residents at Savernake will be voting in other constituencies, in the country, or not voting in this country at all. So he's gone for the consultancy we'll luckily be able to offer him. He's got no choice really – Joe Banks has got a lot of pull on the Labour Party selection committee. So our sitting member for Kenton South isn't going to create too many problems, and Kenton North's hardly involved.'

'It all looks all right,' declared Sir Bernard. 'God willing.'

Nigel nodded but felt less than happy. After the opera he'd endured a bad hour with Max Craig. Jasmine had gone to bed and he and Craig had settled in the study at the Kensington mews house. Craig had told him bluntly he was paying his fee for nothing, that if a man went to his doctor and was told he had a certain condition, returning to the doctor next week and hoping for a change in the diagnosis wasn't likely to be productive. Perhaps Nigel wanted a second opinion, he suggested, and offered to give him names. Nigel's annoyance at being ticked off by Samco's astrologer was mingled with some awe. In the dimly lit study it was very quiet and Craig's brown eyes regarding him so steadily made Nigel ill at ease.

'Well, Max, all right, but you told me you'd come up with some details, so, have a drink and how about it?'

Max told him, 'This building project is going to be more trouble than it's worth. The outcome's unclear but what's certain is that there'll be many problems on the way. There'll be a death, and a birth in your family, and both, to some extent, shocking and in some way connected with business matters.' He stared at Nigel. 'All this is very serious, Nigel.'

But suddenly Nigel was too excited to pay proper attention. He believed Max was telling him Jasmine would bear his child. The pleasure he felt outweighed the rest of Craig's message. Craig continued remorselessly, 'The immediate future gives indications not just of financial problems on quite a large scale, but also of a scandal, legal proceedings and some further, rather odd, problems – arcane, mysterious, not evil, though. It's a complicated pattern, but my conclusion is that you'd do very well to put everything you're doing on hold. Weather out the storms. You cannot make progress at present. And,' he added, 'there are several women gunning for you.'

This warning Nigel completely ignored. He considered the news of a child more important. As far as business went, it was unlikely women could have any damaging effect. They were seldom involved, so how could they make any trouble?

He was canny enough, however, to ask the crucial question, 'The child, will it be mine?'

'I'm not sure,' replied Craig. 'It might be.'

This was a true answer. It wasn't very clear to Craig himself. As a man of experience and intuition he'd sensed from the moment Jasmine Fellows had come into the box at the opera that she'd come from someone's bed. The secret of his success, Craig considered, was partly that he heard rumours early but also that he had an ability to observe, even scent people as animals do. Now, and without much difficulty, he could tell that Nigel was in a state of obstinate irritability, verging on anger. His head was down, he was about to charge. The thought that he might be about to become a father, head of a family, was only reinforcing his aggression. Craig knew it would be wiser to leave before a scene took place. He said coldly, 'Is there anything else?'

'Times?' asked Nigel.

'It's going on now,' Craig said. 'There's one thing – it'll be all over by Christmas. And I must tell you, when you think you've won, you will not have. My advice is to do nothing.' He stared at Nigel. 'Nothing,' he repeated emphatically. 'And I must also say that if you ignore my advice I'd prefer it if you didn't call me in when things start going wrong.'

Nigel felt annoyed. How could he have a child by Christmas? It was July already. He wanted to ask about this, but didn't want Craig to know how desperate he was to have an heir, or, even if the child were a girl, at least to confirm that he and Jasmine could eventually produce one.

Craig guessed this much, but did not wish to pursue the subject. He rose. 'Good luck,' he said. 'Please remember – your best course at present is to block dangerous loopholes and take as little action as possible. Defence, not attack, for the next few months at least.' They shook hands.

Nigel went gloomily up the pretty staircase of the mews house. Jasmine was already asleep and Nigel's lonely thoughts, accompanied by the thin sound of late-night traffic in the hot July streets, kept him awake until the early hours of the morning.

15

Rivals

The Savernake Tenants' Association had been unable to get the community centre attached to the church next door unlocked, so they held the meeting in the courtyard. The residents leaned against cars or sat on kitchen chairs and stools from adjacent houses for a lively, argumentative, muddled and sometimes ferocious protest meeting. Les Dowell's contact on the estate had rung him about the impromptu assembly and Dowell had been there, checking strengths and weaknesses, assessing the revolutionary potential of the audience, but as yet no one knew what attitude Kenton Council would take to the proposed sale nor who Savernake Developments actually were. Meanwhile home-owners on the estate who had the chance to sell were attacked by tenants who had not. Some tenants wanted more information about the terms of the deal before they made up their minds. Some felt they had no choice but to accept the offer, whether they wanted to or not, because if they didn't accept the Council could somehow punish them. Some swore they'd never move, not even when the builders came in.

The group broke up just before eleven, to let the children in the flats get to sleep. Les Dowell, emerging late from the crowd, made a speech saying he would fight for the council to reject the sale, and suggesting a further tenants' meeting a day after the emergency meeting of the council, called by him, had taken place. His remarks, made standing on a car bonnet, were energetic and cliché-ridden and he conveyed the air of a man all too keen to lead a peasants' revolt anywhere, anytime, on virtually any grounds. He went down badly with all but experienced trade unionists, who were used to that sort of thing. 'He's an agitator,' said Kathy Slater, chairman of the Tenants' Association to Ben Gathercole in the pub afterwards. 'I don't like them – but at least he turned up, which is more than you can say for the others. I'll invite them all along on Thursday, but I don't envy Joe Banks if he comes. Whatever anybody thinks, for or against, everybody knows he's been high-handed. The old people are worried to death. They're afraid they're going to find their few sticks out on the pavement. That's the sort of thing they can remember from the old days. This could kill some of them, that's what I think. It's no way to run things.'

'Joe Banks had better come,' her husband said grimly.

'So you'll be lobbying the council on Wednesday?' asked Ben.

'Bloody right we will,' he said.

'Get in touch with Thames TV,' Ben advised. 'They might send cameras.'

'Yes,' said Kathy Slater. 'We'll do just that.'

On Monday Vanessa and Ben Gathercole were having an early breakfast at Rutherford Street before Alec and Joanne got up. Both were tired, Vanessa because she always was, Ben, because after the tenants meeting he had spent the rest of the night first with Les Dowell and Betsey Jones chewing his ear off, then, on the telephone, to Joe Banks, listening to his justifications of his position.

'Well,' Ben now said, as Vanessa passed him his breakfast of sausages and tomatoes, 'by the end of today I should have an idea who's behind all this. This could be a major story. I'll ring the papers, and *South East News*, see if I can get some mileage out of it myself.'

'Those tenants haven't got a chance, no matter what they do,' Vanessa said.

'Why do you think that?'

'Because Abbott wouldn't be trying to buy our restaurant if he thought they were going to fail. And,' she added, 'because people like that get what they want.'

'Not if the council refuses to allow a vote. And even if the Department of the Environment overrules them, the tenants can go to court and challenge the decision.'

'And who's the court, and who's the judge?' asked Vanessa. 'The same people who want that estate sold off. This is the sort of thing the Government wants. Even if they say it's illegal today, they'll make it legal tomorrow. Are you sitting there telling me that isn't what's going to happen? Ben . . .' she appealed, 'you weren't born yesterday. These people can do as they like.'

'If there's enough fuss they won't.'

Putting Alec's and Joanne's breakfast in the oven to keep warm, she said diplomatically, 'Perhaps.'

Ben put down his knife and fork. 'I've got to go and see Frances tonight,' he said abruptly. 'She'd left two messages on my answering machine when I checked it. Martin is asking for me. Also she wants to talk about schools.'

Vanessa looked at her plate. 'Yes,' she said. 'Will you be back tonight?'

'Of course, love,' he said. He came round the table and kissed her. 'What she wants,' he told her, 'is money for school fees to send Martin to a small fee-paying school round the corner.'

Vanessa looked up at him pleadingly. 'Don't be too late.'

He said, 'I won't.'

But Ben was – very late. For two days, forty-eight hours of nightmare for Vanessa, she heard nothing from him. Her concentration failed her and her temper became short. She snapped at Annie's suggestion that she ring Ben at the paper to find out what was going on. Melanie muttered to Annie, 'He might be in hospital, or lying in bed with flu. Anyway, look at the state of her . . .' She nodded towards Vanessa, drooping over the till. 'It's pathetic. And there's not even anything to do.' Melanie gestured round the near-empty restaurant.

'She should find herself another man,' was Edward's opinion. 'No point in sitting and pining away.' He looked at Vanessa speculatively.

At that moment a hot-looking Sam Abbott came into the restaurant wearing a dark suit. 'I haven't come here to eat,' he said as Annie advanced with a menu in her hand. He added sarcastically, 'Place full, as usual, I see. Have you got an answer for me?'

'I'm discussing it at the bank tomorrow,' Annie said inventively.

Abbott looked around him, an aggressive expression on his unimpressive face. 'The facts are staring you in the face, Mrs Vane. I've come to tell you my offer's only open to the end of the week.'

Annie decided to flush him out. 'Your offer's connected with this Savernake development, isn't it? That's why you want the restaurant.'

Abbott was annoyed. 'That's part of it,' he said curtly. He was not going to reveal more. To create a diversion, he walked over to

Vanessa. 'Message from your husband. He doesn't like what he hears about you and that reporter from the local paper. He's married, I hear.'

Vanessa didn't reply.

'So's Vanessa's husband, they tell me,' Melanie piped up to Annie so that Abbott could hear.

'Not when his divorce goes through,' Sam Abbott said, and left the restaurant. Edward followed him closely, lending a hint of menace. Vanessa blew her nose.

'Take no notice, he's a nasty little man,' said Annie. 'Why don't you go home?'

'My mother's there, looking after the kids.'

'That's unusual,' said Annie.

'Dad's gone to Bristol,' Vanessa said flatly. 'She doesn't like being on her own.'

But in the end Vanessa did go home. Her mother was watching television. Vanessa made some tea. Anita Davis enquired about Ben Gathercole. Vanessa didn't tell her she feared Ben had gone back to his wife. 'It seems all right,' said her mother. 'These journalists can be well paid. Maybe he can get on TV. Once his divorce is over you can pack in that restaurant and settle down.'

Vanessa didn't reply. The phone rang and she picked it up eagerly. It was a wrong number. Her mother, instincts aroused and chin up, demanded, 'He's gone back to his wife, hasn't he? You'd better do something.'

'I'm going to bed, Mum,' Vanessa said.

'Ring him, meet him, get round him. Do you want to live alone, running a snack bar to the end of your days?'

Vanessa walked out of the room. Her mother followed. 'I'm talking to you, Vanessa. Don't walk out of the room when I'm talking to you.'

'He has gone back to his wife, Mum, if that's what you want to know. There's nothing more to say, is there?'

'You're a fool, Vanessa. How many men are you going to let walk out on you? And do nothing about it? Look – I'll stop over tonight and tomorrow you can go into town, get your hair done, buy a dress. Ring up, say you want to meet him. If this is important to you, you've got to fight.'

'Like Cindy Abbott fought,' Vanessa told her, 'to get my husband off me. Thanks, but no thanks.'

'That was different,' her mother told her.

When her mother had left Vanessa took herself to bed and cried for most of the night.

It was a dreadful week. Strangely, the Arcadia was fuller on more evenings than it had been since the opening. The weather was hot and humid. Somehow Vanessa and Annie, together with Abigail and her partner, managed the extra work. But they were increasingly tired, going home each night with swollen feet and smelling of food. Melanie and her friend Viv, now on holiday from school, did most of the work in the snack bar, even ordering supplies and pretending to be Mrs Vane.

On Saturday night Annie reported, 'We'd have broken even this week, if it hadn't been for Andy Campbell's pals' usual visit.' The improvement in trade made it even harder to decide whether or not to accept Sam Abbott's offer. Time was running out.

'Let's go down and see Tom tomorrow,' Annie said to Melanie. 'You still haven't seen the foxes. It'll be fresher in the country and it's a good way of dodging Abbott's phone call if he rings to ask us for a decision. Vanessa needs to get out, too.'

The *Kenton Post*, which had come out the day before, had a full front page covering the Savernake Estate story, by-line, Ben Gathercole. There were pictures of the Savernake residents picketing the council on the day of their emergency meeting. Local teachers had mobilised their pupils – 'Save our Park' read the banners. 'Playspace must be saved' read a banner, upside down, in the hands of a small child in a balloon-festooned buggy. In the event, chiefly because of Betsey Jones's recruitment of the Conservative councillors, Kenton Council had voted not to allow a vote on the project by tenants until there was more information and the residents had met to make their views known. Annie glanced at the story, but threw the paper away and didn't mention it to Vanessa as it would have made her think about Ben Gathercole.

Of course they should have rung before they went down to Charters House, in the grounds of which Tom's cottage stood, but they all piled cheerfully into the van they'd borrowed from Vanessa's father, planning to give Tom a surprise. Even if he wasn't in, they could drive on the fifteen miles to Froggett's and surprise Annie's parents instead.

But as she headed down the overgrown path in the grounds of the empty and shuttered Charters House, where Tom's cottage

stood, Annie felt a qualm. Was it really such a good idea for
five of them, she, Vanessa, Melanie and the two children, to
arrive without notice? They'd set out excitedly, but would Tom
be annoyed by this unexpected arrival? As they went on, thick
trees began to overhang the path darkly. It was very quiet and
still. They proceeded in Indian file, Annie in front, Vanessa and
the children next, Melanie to the rear. The cottage was silent. They
knocked on the door in vain. Annie pushed open the door of Tom's
workshop, a large shed a little distance from the cottage in which he
had installed big windows. It was very tidy. At the back stood his
small printing press and the screenprinting equipment. On benches
which ran down both sides of the shed lay piles of paper, a shelf of
type, tidily arranged, pieces of wood, stacked. Tom's wood-cutting
tools hung neatly ranged on one wall. A half-completed woodcut
six inches square, showing a field full of sheep, lay on the bench
near the door.

They stood and pondered outside the shed. 'Well, that's that,'
said Annie, in some ways relieved, for her feeling they should not
have come was getting stronger and stronger. 'I'll just try the back
door, for luck.'

It opened. Followed by one of the foxes, which, to the children's
delight, ran in from the wood to stare at them when they arrived, she
went into the old kitchen, observing unwashed but tidily arranged
dishes on the wooden draining board, a saucepan and a casserole
soaking in the sink. She ignored a sinking of the heart. She went
into the passageway, calling, 'Tom! Tom!', and went up the wood-
en stairs, the fox still in attendance. Perhaps Tom had worked all
night and was sleeping heavily enough now not to have heard their
knocking. The fox's claws clattered on the stairs behind her.

Annie opened the bedroom door. Tom sat up holding the bedclothes over his naked chest, an expression of fear on his face.
There was another figure in the bed, burrowed down under a sheet
and a quilt. Annie in the doorway was stricken. She cried out, 'Oh
Tom, who is it?'

'Oh, God, what are you doing here?' Tom shouted. 'Why did
you come?'

She muttered, 'I suppose you never told me you'd be faithful.'
And, not knowing what else to do, turned to go. Then the fox
jumped on to the bed and flooded the quilt with a stream of
urine.

'This is a farce,' declared an infuriated voice. The figure sat

173

upright, and energetically cast off the bedclothes, knocking the fox to the floor. Annie stared at the bright gold hair, defiant stubbled face and bare chest of Tom's best friend at school, John Woodford.

'Oh,' she moaned, and turned quickly, flying out of the room, bolting down the stairs, pushing past Melanie standing in the kitchen, and out up the path, away from Vanessa and the children in the garden, crying, 'Come on! Come on!' She had the engine of the van running when the others arrived slowly, baffled, at the road.

'Get in the back, Mels,' said Vanessa calmly. 'Joanne, jump in.' She slammed the door on them and carried Alec to the front. Barely had she got in herself when Annie roared off.

'What's happening? I wanted to play with the fox,' said Joanne from the back. Melanie kept quiet. After a few minutes, as, far too fast, Annie took the road towards Froggett's, Vanessa said quietly, 'Slow down, Annie, love. No point in all of us getting killed.'

Annie slowed down. Minutes later, out of the strained silence, she said, 'You were right. We should have stopped en route and phoned.' Later, on the leafy back road to Froggett's she muttered, 'They knew. They knew all along.'

'Who knew?' asked Vanessa.

'My parents,' Annie said.

Her father told her, 'We knew, of course. That was why he ran away, all those years ago. We thought it better not to tell you, Annie.' Annie, her parents and Vanessa sat in the warm sunshine after lunch at Froggett's.

Vanessa was still very shocked. She'd realised Annie had found Tom in bed with someone, but had assumed it was another woman. That would have been bad enough. It was more horrifying that the lover was a man. She was amazed that Tom had carried about him no clue that he was homosexual. Her shock was increased by the Brownings' acceptance of Tom's behaviour. Even Annie, upset as she was by the betrayal, seemed to take Tom's taste more for granted than she could. In the bright open air, with a view of the valley and the rolling countryside beyond the lawn, Vanessa could hardly believe what had happened only three hours ago.

Melanie, Joanne and Alec had been sent off to Durham House, to ask Lady Mary if they could swim in the lake. Melanie, discreet as ever, had not this time protested about being treated like an eldest child, put in charge of the younger ones, but had left the adults like a lamb. She was not too concerned that something had obviously happened at the cottage to put Annie off Tom but she was afraid of any changes which might result in her being put on a bus bound for the north with a suitcase. What Melanie really wanted was to get her mother and two brothers down to London, where life had more variety and far more possibilities. Getting her family south, finding her sister Ruth and having a chance encounter with her favourite rock star, leading to romance, were the dreams she kept firmly in mind. Annie's relationship with Tom did not promise to bring these dreams any closer. Though sorry for Annie, and wondering what had happened at the cottage, she set off for Durham House, holding hands with Joanne and Alec, not feeling too unhappy.

Juliet refilled everyone's glass and said, 'How could we tell you, Annie? The relationship began at school. Tom's parents knew all about it. They thought it was over when they both left school. Then John arrived, years later, and he and Tom just took off for Paris. Tom was going to study, John write. The Pointons couldn't do anything. So – Tom *did* study, John didn't write—'

'Rich parents, no talent,' interpolated Howard Browning. 'We watched you pining, but it would have been too cruel to explain. Or perhaps,' he said, 'it would have been better, but we knew you were going off to Oxford and exciting things would happen for you there. Then came Jasmine's event, the abortion, which I gather Tom's told you about, and you were at Oxford, enjoying the life – the moment to explain passed. I think the affair between Tom and John wore itself out on Tom's side in Paris. When he came back a year later, he seemed sobered. That was when he apprenticed himself locally to the old craftsman and stayed with us. He had no money. He did seasonal work for the local farmers when he could, saved the little he earned, gave us what he could, asked for nothing at all. He'd seen a bit of a friend of mine, a writer, Arthur Leclerc, also a homosexual, in France. Arthur said John had got him into a fairly hectic scene there, young people from rich families, geared to going round the world, staying with their wealthy friends and relatives – there were drugs, as you'd expect, and finally a scandal, where some Tunisians set up two of the girls to carry drugs into France. The girls were caught and put in prison. Tom was out of his depth, financially and morally. And, of course, he's an artist. He was trying to keep a footing in a world which didn't suit him, for John's sake, I imagine.'

'We thought,' continued Annie's mother, 'that he was shocked when the girls went to prison. He'd seen suddenly that that sort of life didn't work for him.'

'Though Arthur's opinion was that he and John were through, even before it happened,' added Howard.

'Oh, God!' said Annie. 'I've been nicely taken in. Whenever I asked him anything about Paris he told me he'd tell me one day. I had no idea how much there was to tell.'

'I think he loves you,' Juliet said mildly.

'Hah!' Annie said in a weak voice.

'You can't be too narrow about these things,' Howard told her.

Vanessa stared at him. They were mad, these Brownings, she decided. The telephone had been ringing in the house since they'd started lunch, but no one was even thinking about answering it. It was probably Tom, who'd guessed Annie might come here, but no one was mentioning that either.

Later they all strolled downhill and through the back gate in the wall to Durham House. They watched Melanie, Joanne and Alec swimming, then had tea on the terrace with Lady Mary.

'I don't believe you're a boy,' Lady Mary said laughingly to Alec. 'I believe you're a fish. I think I'll have to give you flies for tea, instead of cake.' But Annie thought she looked thinner and more worn than ever, and detected that her mother was very sorry for Lady Mary.

There were geraniums in the huge pots on the terrace, the lawn spread below them and the lake glittered in the distance. On the way back Annie remarked to her mother, 'Lady Mary doesn't look at all well.'

Her mother said, 'Bernard's in England, but he's scarcely been down. He's in London with Nigel and Jasmine. None of them have been near the place for a fortnight. I've told her to go and stay with one of her many sisters, but whether she knows it herself or not, I believe she's hanging on in the house as if Sim were a kidnapped child and she was waiting for news. It's quite awful.'

'What about Nigel's sister?'

'Still in New York, running an ad agency,' Howard joined in.

'Everything's so lovely here,' said Vanessa. 'You'd never believe there'd be any trouble but really it's like everywhere else.'

'Like everywhere else, only with money,' pointed out Howard, a Marxist in his Cambridge youth.

* * *

They left early and drove silently back to London. The children slept, Melanie listened to a tape through her headphones. It was getting dark when they got to the outskirts of London. Stalled in the traffic, Annie said bitterly, 'We're not doing too well, are we? There's the restaurant, Ben's gone missing and—'

'I'm very sorry, Annie,' Vanessa said gently.

'Not much of a day in the country for you,' returned Annie.

'Never mind,' Vanessa said.

'Love, money and revenge isn't going too well,' Annie groaned.

Even then a long day wasn't over. Since Annie had suppressed the news of Ben Gathercole's feature in the *Kenton Post* for Vanessa's sake and not even read the article properly herself, it was late on Sunday evening when Melanie rang excitedly from her friend Viv's house to tell Annie about Ben's story in the paper. 'Listen, it says here,' she said, 'that Savernake Developments is a subsidiary of the Samco Company, and the managing director is Nigel Fellows, and the chairman is Nigel Fellows's father, Sir Bernard Fellows. I was telling Viv what we did today and her dad recognised their name and got out the paper. Viv's auntie lives on the Savernake Estate and now she's having a nervous breakdown. It's tipped her right over the edge, she's that worried and upset. She's going to hospital on Tuesday.'

She left Annie speechless, holding the phone.

16

A Sudden Death

For the council's second meeting on the Savernake Village project, a week after the first, there was a bigger crowd. Several hundred people assembled with banners and home-made placards outside Kenton Town Hall. Most of the demonstrators were tenants from the Savernake Estate and other estates, but here and there were groups of young political activists, and an older crowd, Les Dowell's friends. There were also reporters, *South East News* cameras and a heavier police presence than would ordinarily have been needed to keep order in a crowd of a few hundred men, women and children. But word had gone out from the Home Office that Savernake Developments' prospective take-over of council property might trigger feelings among local residents, a comment the detective-superintendent in charge of Foxwell police station rightly interpreted as a suggestion that, with the continuing hot weather, a riot might be expected, the last thing needed by Kenton, the Government, and the country at large. Kenton had had two riots. One more with yet more pictures on television of people running through the night, shops in flames, ambulances and fire engines trying to get through, would damage the reputation and prospects of the area irreparably.

Inside the hot, airless council chamber, built with much use of wood to impart a dignified and semi-Parliamentary atmosphere, Les Dowell, reluctant to alienate his two invaluable Conservative supporters, had spoken with less than his usual ferocity against the sell-off of the estate. With a certain satisfaction, Joe Banks had referred to the Department of the Environment's refusal to mount a public inquiry into the affair. Betsey Jones had insisted that this decision meant strings were being pulled somewhere.

Though the left-wingers were being subdued, there were still mutters of 'Bastard!' at Joe Banks, and anger even from the moderates when he tried to make out a case for supporting the project. There was annoyance that Savernake Developments had declined to send a representative to the meeting. 'Let's have these faceless men in here,' cried one man, to a chorus of agreement.

A motion that no decision on the sale should be taken until the matter had been investigated by a sub-committee and their report studied by the whole council went through easily on the strength of the two Tory votes rallied by Betsey Jones, some further unexpected support and several abstentions.

The unlikely alliance of Les Dowell, Betsey Jones from the far left, and Emily Littlejohn and Hugh Patterson, the Conservatives, met after the meeting to congratulate itself at the Duke of Westminster, round the corner from the Town Hall. Mutual congratulation was short, however. 'Someone came to see me the other day,' Emily Littlejohn, a retired headmistress, said in her clear voice, 'and said they were delighted about the opportunity to sell their flat at a good price. And the rumour is they'll be allowed to sell earlier than the regulations permit. It's likely to set the owner-occupiers on the estate against the tenants. Divide and rule.'

'There's a meeting on the estate tonight,' Betsey Jones said. 'Will you be coming?'

'I think I will,' Emily Littlejohn agreed. 'I take it I'll be asked to speak?'

'We're on the same side,' said Les Dowell, with an effort. 'Hugh?'

'I'll come for an hour,' the other Conservative answered. 'Can I pick anyone up?'

When they had discussed transport arrangements, Emily Littlejohn took up the subject of the development once more. 'All in all, I'm afraid these people, the developers, have the ear of the Department of the Environment.'

Les Dowell said, 'We can go to court.'

Betsey Jones said, 'Much good would that do.'

They were interrupted by the arrival of Ben Gathercole. 'Thought I'd find you here. Any comments?' He opened his notebook.

'You can collect Mrs Littlejohn here in your car for the meeting tonight,' Betsey Jones said firmly. 'Then you can get your comments.'

Ben Gathercole got into his hot car and drove out of his way, to Rutherford Street, in the hope of catching a glimpse of Vanessa or the children. But the street was deserted, there was no sign of life around her house and Ben felt despair. His wife had persuaded him his child needed a father, as indeed he did. But each morning Ben went into his own bathroom and looked at it as if he were staying in a hotel. His ironed shirts on their hangers in the wardrobe did not seem to belong to him, his wife, taking off her make-up in the bedroom at night looked like a stranger. Only his boy, the sound of his small feet running up the hall, both his small hands grasping his breakfast orange juice at the table in the morning, the body he soaped in the bath at night, had any reality for him and he thought, how long can I go on? Heavy-hearted and not knowing what else to do, he drove to the *Kenton Post*.

At a humid meeting later that evening at the Savernake community centre, Councillor Joe Banks was shouted down angrily by a crowd of two hundred of the estate's residents. Many were standing, due to a shortage of chairs, and there was a feeling of tension. Councillor Littlejohn, nominated chairman, had a job keeping any order at all. Joe Banks had noticed the hostility emanating from the meeting when he stood up, but continued unwisely to speak against the shouts of protest. In the end Emily Littlejohn had to rise and whisper in the shouting Joe Banks's ear, 'Sit down, Joe, it's hopeless. As soon as I close the meeting, get out to your car as fast as possible.'

Joe Banks sat down and observed the rest of the proceedings with a face as black as the thunder accumulating overhead. His hope that the Savernake meeting would be mostly attended by residents keen to sell their homes had been disappointed. To begin with the home owners were outnumbered by the tenants, and worse, from his point of view, half the owners were apparently just as furious about the prospective sell-off of the estate and park as those with less to gain. His chief ally, Councillor Arlene Phipps, sat beside him, glumly reflecting that Joe had predicted that opposition split into property owners and non-property owners on an estate never notable for its energy or cohesiveness would crumble fast. For once he'd been wrong. The audience, men and women of all ages, children, black people and white, some Asian was tough, vociferous and against him. Mrs Walters stood up and remembered her house being destroyed in the Blitz, her husband and herself living, with their first child, with her parents, their relief and pleasure when her flat was allocated to them. She had brought up her children there, she said. She didn't want to move.

Mohammed Nasruddin, described on Joe Banks's list of residents as a newsagent, asked detailed questions about the legality of the sale in the first place. He asked what guarantees tenants would have about their future accommodation, if they agreed to rehousing. He attacked the whole concept of building an expensive housing project in that area, speaking fluently and logically and getting, when he concluded, a rousing cheer.

A large, overweight woman who did not identify herself stood up and said loudly, 'This is our home. Mr Banks has told us what he'll do with the money to help Kenton, but that won't help us. We live here too. We don't want it sold off to a lot of rich people who'll bring nothing to Kenton. I was born here, my parents were born here. My children were born on this estate. We belong here. We don't want the place sold off to yuppies. We want to stay.' She sat down to applause.

Les Dowell sat stony-faced in his seat, in some ways almost as appalled as Joe Banks by this clear manifestation of the public will, entirely unmanipulated by himself on revolutionary principles. Joe Banks had thought the residents would be torn by differing interests, private feuds, and racial tensions, Les Dowell, totalitarian at heart, had a private belief in the Mob, unwashed, illiterate, benumbed and easily swayed, destined to be introduced to revolution by people like himself. Now here they were, these latter-day peasants and workers, acting on their own initiative. In different ways the meeting was a shock to both wings of the Kenton Council Left.

Meanwhile, Ben Gathercole, who'd got what he wanted for the *Kenton Post* and could no longer bear to sit in the sweltering heat found himself writing 'Vanessa' on his pad. Restless and unable to face going home, he slipped out, drove to a bar in Leicester Square, got a bit drunk and then went on to a party in Kensington. Angry when he didn't turn up, Frances hid her feelings when he at last came home, his face so unhappy that she realised dully she was losing him.

At nine that night, just as Mohammed Nasruddin was depressing Joe Banks by suggesting that even if the Department of the Environment was prepared to let the sale go ahead, the law courts might overturn the decision, Sir Bernard Fellows, at his son's mews house in Kensington was talking on the phone to the spy Joe Banks had planted at the meeting. From Nigel's little office, more like a cupboard than a room, he could hear the noise of a party in full swing. Jasmine and Nigel were entertaining.

He finished his conversation, hung up, then pushed through the crowd, found Nigel and explained he was tired and must go home. Nigel saw him off.

The house was full of people, the small patio lit with spotlights discreetly placed in the trailing foliage. Jasmine, having heard about Annie's discovery at the cottage, had rung her sister and persuaded her to come. 'Come and enjoy yourself. I promise you Julian and that nasty Tamsin won't be there. Apart from anything else, Nigel can't stand them. He has to put up with them. It's business.'

'Julian's business,' Annie had said nastily, 'was built up on ten thousand pounds left to me by Aunt Margaret.'

'But come to the party,' insisted Jasmine.

'I will,' agreed Annie.

'Sorry about Tom, and everything,' Jasmine said.

Annie had been more upset than she would have imagined by Tom's treachery but, unused to confused feelings, felt she couldn't discuss it with Jasmine, so she changed the subject.

'What's happening about the suitcase?' she asked Jasmine.

'Anstruther's back at Durham House on a visit and he's still trying to get Howard and Juliet to let him go through it and they keep on fobbing him off. One day when he came round they actually locked the door and hid, pretending to be out. But he's been getting at Rupert and the other executor, that man from Oxford, and now they're trying to persuade them to yield up the case. They'll have to give in, I suppose. I don't see why they don't just sell it to Anstruther—'

'Neither do I,' Annie said. She knew Jasmine still wanted to talk about Tom. 'It's peculiar, isn't it?'

'So you're coming – definitely?' Jasmine pressed.

'Yes. Thanks, Jasmine. It'll make a change,' said Annie obediently, and hung up quickly. Jasmine wanted to raise issues she didn't want to think about. There'd been little time after the shock of Julian's walking out before she had rather suddenly found Tom back in her life, and in her bed. She'd not had a chance to work out Tom's impact on her. She'd been avoiding emotion, like someone who's been beaten up and is avoiding any situation where it could happen again. Vanessa, she thought, wasn't like that. She had been happy once with her husband, had wanted to find the same kind of happiness again. Still, they had both been shockingly let down and at the moment she did not feel like going to a party.

Nevertheless, she slowly got dressed, watched sourly by Melanie who'd hoped the invitation might have been extended to include her.

'Are you wearing that for a party?' she exclaimed incredulously, when Annie put on a beaded brown top above a long plain linen skirt.

'It belonged to my grandmother,' Annie told her. Melanie shook her head pityingly.

When she arrived, late, at Jasmine's small, perfect house in a mews off a quiet, paved street in Kensington there were several people outside with drinks while inside, the little house was bursting at the seams. She couldn't see Jasmine, as she pushed in, took a glass from the waiter's tray, looked for someone she knew. The long room leading out on to the patio was crowded with well-dressed men and women in shiny dresses, smoothly made up.

'Who're you?' asked a jacketless man in black evening trousers and a ruffled white shirt, leaning into her slightly.

'Jas's sister,' responded Annie. 'Who're you?'

'Captain Armitage – you're the sister who when the angel handed out looks, you thought she said hard books, so you asked her for ever such a lot – the history professor – am I right?'

'Annie's my name,' Annie said sourly, hating Jasmine's friends, wishing Jasmine wouldn't always tell people about her brainy sister. A woman in a large pearl necklace collided with her and gave her a hostile stare, as if she, Annie, had barged into her.

By the time five minutes had passed, Annie, fresh from Kenton, found this assembly of rich, or rich-seeming people more familiar. She remembered that at such gatherings scents clash, voices are very loud and from time to time boredom and brutality surface. There was no sign of Nigel or Jasmine and she knew no one else. She was staring at a framed photograph of Nigel and his brother and sister, Sim with a bat, in cricket trousers, and their sister Claudia, sulking in shorts beside them, and wondering whether to leave, when she was bumped into from the back and almost pushed into the white marble fireplace.

'I came to say hallo,' said Ben Gathercole in a rather drunk voice. 'You might not like me much, but you're the only person I know in the room.'

'How did you get here?' asked Annie not bothering to be polite to the man who was making her friend Vanessa so unhappy.

'I might ask you the same,' he responded. 'I've been at the Savernake Estate. Now I'm here as part of a scheme to seduce and influence the press, I suppose. I've had a frank and friendly chat with the Honourable Nigel. He told me how wonderful the Savernake Project was going to be. Likeable chap, the Honourable Nige. Then he introduced me to a friend of his, the editor of the *Daily Mirror*, or something. I got an invitation from a PRO – I thought it was a press party. Nigel was explaining it all to me – he said he just wanted me to hear the other side.' His speech was blurred, his manner belligerent. Annie planned to get away soon.

Meanwhile, she asked, 'What did you think?'

'I know the other side. I present it. My job,' he explained.

'Good, then,' Annie said, trying to move away.

But she was trapped by the fireplace and Ben Gathercole leaned towards her. 'I miss her,' he said earnestly. 'You don't know how I miss her. You probably think I'm just a rotten sod who took advantage—'

'Oh, God, Ben, I don't care,' she said. 'You did it, didn't you? Spare me your maudlin explanations—'

'Don't call me maudlin,' he began in a maudlin tone.

'Annie!' said a voice behind her.

'Hallo, Veronica,' Annie said, without much enthusiasm. 'How are you?'

'I'm trying to tell you,' Ben went on, 'that I can't stand it, not seeing her.'

'Tell *her*, Ben,' pleaded Annie. 'Not me. I've got my own problems to solve.'

Veronica Stern, a schoolfriend of Annie's, looked at Ben's drunken face with distaste. 'Oh,' she said. 'I must tell you, Annie, about Jane. Jane North.'

Annie said, 'I've got to go for a pee, Veronica,' and pushed through the crowd. Upstairs she had to wait outside the lavatory until a man in a white suit speaking on a cellphone came out. Then she went in, locked the door and sat on the seat for a bit. She heard two people outside. 'No,' said a woman, 'Alexander is Harry Buchanan's, not Malley's. He was born after Malley, during Buchanan.'

'Well, she told me he was Malley's,' said a man. 'Malley'd married Dora by then, but that wasn't the point.'

'Never was with Dora, was it?' the woman said.

Annie pushed the door open and came out. 'Sorry,' said the man who'd been outside. Annie spotted Nigel leaning against a picture, talking to someone, and greeted him. He introduced her to a German couple who plainly didn't want to know her. Annie turned away, deciding she'd take the spiral stairs which led from a corner of the landing down to the small kitchen area Jasmine had created. She remembered a back door and decided to use it to escape this party she was disliking so much. Half-way down the stairs, she looked into the kitchen and saw Tom, his sister Miranda, and the golden hair and very blue eyes she had last seen in a stubbly face peering over Tom's sheets – John Woodford. She paused for a second, studying the handsome trio, Tom and his sister, tall, long-boned and dark, with identical bright brown eyes and dark hair, and John, with his curly gold hair and broad, classical, Greek-god face. Then, turning, she ran quietly back up the spiral staircase, cursing Jasmine for not bothering to tell her they were coming.

As she went along the landing Sam Anstruther waylaid her. She pushed past him, muttering an excuse, and was half-way down the front staircase, easing her way past two politicians laughing, one clinging to the banisters, and the wife of a merchant banker, famous for her own parties, grimly forging her way up towards the bathroom, when a voice above her cried clearly over the party hubbub, 'Annie! Please come here.' She turned to see Jasmine on the landing. Annie, knowing her sister's expressions and stance by heart, saw that, though she appeared calm, Jasmine was violently upset. Once more she turned and went upstairs, keeping her sister in view all the time. 'What is it?' Annie asked urgently.

'Upstairs,' Jasmine said in a low voice, turning and heading the way rapidly up another flight. In Jasmine and Nigel's bedroom there was a smell of scent and cigars. Nigel, his back turned, was leaning against a carved chest which served Jasmine as a dressing table. There was a leather briefcase with a combination lock lying on a red silk dress on the carpet. Jasmine closed the door and leaned against it limply. 'Oh, Annie,' she said.

'What on earth's the matter?' asked Annie, very alarmed. Nigel put his arm over his eyes and she heard him sob. Jasmine ran to him and embraced him. Annie swiftly locked the door. There'd been very bad news, she saw. Had they heard, in the middle of the party, that Sim was dead? Jasmine, one arm round her husband, turned, with tears in her eyes, 'It's Bernard,' she said. 'He's dead.'

'Oh, God, Nigel – I'm so sorry,' Annie said. 'What can I do?'

'We've got to ring Mary,' Jasmine appealed, partly to Nigel, who was obviously so shocked by the news that he hadn't yet been able to ring his mother. Jasmine led Nigel to the bed, where he sat down burying his head in his hands. 'Shall I go and explain to everybody?' she asked.

'No, no,' Nigel said.

'Nigel. We must send them home' Jasmine told him.

'Why don't you two go to Bedford Square?' Annie suggested. 'You must ring Nigel's mother from there. You'll have to go sooner or later. Pack some things, Jas. Go out through the back door. I can hold on here and wind the party down. I'll lock up and put the keys through the letterbox.'

As Annie spoke, she was thinking that it would be better in the long run for Nigel to go to the house, see his father's body and sort out from his father's desk all the complications which would follow the death. It was only after she had ushered Nigel and Jasmine down the stairs and through the front door, fending off puzzled enquiries from guests startled by the departure of the host and hostess, and flagged down an empty taxi, that she heard Nigel say to Jasmine, in a stunned voice, 'But what was he doing in Colindale?'

'I don't know, darling,' Jasmine said as he climbed into the taxi. 'I'll ring you,' she said to Annie.

The taxi went off leaving Annie pondering Nigel's question. If Sir Bernard had died in Colindale, what indeed was he doing in that rather bland northern suburb of London? She went back into the house to speed the guests, most of whom left fairly quickly, though some saw it as an excuse to stay longer, to celebrate life and speculate on death.

'Did you foresee this one, Max?' asked one of the guests with apparent scepticism, masking, as Craig knew, adult curiosity and childish superstition.

The astrologer did not reply, but searched out Annie. He told her quietly, 'I believe Sir Bernard and Nigel were arranging the transfer of his assets to Nigel, Sim having been gone so long. But I don't think they'd completed matters. You might think it inappropriate to raise the subject now, but I have to warn you there'll be a muddle.'

'Yes,' said Annie perfunctorily. 'I expect so. Thanks.'

'I like Nigel and Jasmine,' he announced, 'quite apart from the handsome retainer I get from Samco. And I'm pretty disinterested, so if you need advice, feel free to call me.' He handed her his card and shook her hand saying, in an undertone as if to stress the gravity of the coming situation, 'There'll be complications. A scandal.'

17

August

In early August the report of the council committee on the sale of the Savernake Estate and Savernake Park was issued. To the annoyance if not the surprise of Joe Banks, the report concluded that the sale of Savernake was a bad idea. No vote by residents on the question should be permitted. On balance, the report said, the advantages of the seven million pounds to the borough were outweighed by the permanent loss to Kenton of the Savernake area. It severely censured the semi-secret operation preceding the plan.

The report was a nuisance to Joe Banks and his supporters, many of whom had plans for themselves or their families to get something out of the development. But it had been anticipated by Banks and Savernake Developments, who had allowed for the possible rejection of their plans by the council. There would follow an already-organised overruling of the council decision by the Department of the Environment, followed by a stepping up of bribes, threats and promises for the estate residents, an intensification of the PR campaign and finally a vote by residents in favour of the sale. However, with what looked like a fight ahead, the last thing Banks and his friends and supporters needed was the unexpected death of Sir Bernard Fellows.

'Well, I can only say I'm shocked,' Joe Banks said uneasily to Geoff Doyle, who, through Cindy's father, the complicitous planning department chief Sam Abbott, had secured a nice contract for building parts of the expensive village-to-be on the Savernake site. Joe Banks had been cornered by Doyle after four days of phone calls, and had agreed to give up part of Sunday afternoon to visit the couple in their town house on Foxwell Hill. Now Banks sat on a cream leather sofa in the long lounge-diner. Double doors gave out on to a patio, and trim green gardens. Cindy, in a tight top and skirt, shook up a cocktail at the drinks bar, poured it out and handed it to him. 'It's a tragedy,' Joe added. He was unhappily aware of Doyle's physical advantages: he himself was short, overweight and sixty, Doyle was a big muscular, sun-tanned six-foot-two piece of public nuisance, with a dreamy satisfied-looking bimbo and a slightly menacing air. 'It's a tragedy,' Banks said again, 'and I've got to say it creates problems.'

'That's the point,' Doyle said. 'I've been turning away work for the autumn, I've taken on extra men and what I'd like is a firm date for the go-ahead.'

'It was always dependent on certain factors,' Banks said. 'All I could ever tell you was October – there were always going to be problems.'

Cindy handed Geoff his drink and sat down on the edge of a leather armchair with her own. She stood up and held out a plate of snacks to Joe. 'Do try one of these, Councillor Banks – Japanese,' she said.

'No thanks, Cindy,' Banks said gloomily.

Geoff imperceptibly nodded her back to her chair. She sighed. They were supposed to be going to Portugal in September, which would be all right if the big contract started in October, as Joe Banks had said. But before he'd arrived Geoff had told her if he didn't get some answers from Banks they could kiss Portugal goodbye. 'You're looking forward to a week in Clacton if I get the wrong answers,' he'd said. She'd tried to point out that a cheap package holiday in Greece would cost them hardly any more than Clacton, but he'd interrupted her, 'Look, darling, give me a rest about holidays. I know you've bought your outfits, you've been sunbathing for weeks in the back garden, but if the money's not coming, it's not coming. I'm doing my best.'

She'd pouted, and said she was sad, and got him to promise they could go to Portugal anyway, but in the end she didn't believe the promise. If this contract her father was involved in fell through, Cindy thought vengefully, she'd tell her mother what she thought and Mum would give her dad a hard time, and serve him right. He was late – where was he, anyway? The fact was she needed a holiday. Everything was getting on her nerves. It was time Geoff got round to making Vanessa give him a divorce, so they could get married, but he kept on saying he was too busy. Her mother was already planning the wedding; her cousin's mother was selecting materials for the bridesmaids' dresses, but where was the divorce?

She got up to answer the door to her father. He should have commented on her tan and her new top, but he didn't. 'How's it going in there?' he asked in a low voice.

'Don't ask me,' Cindy said, nettled.

Sam Abbott said, 'All right, Cindy. What have I done wrong?'

'You could've spoken to me, first, before you started asking questions about business.'

'Sorry, love. You look very nice,' Sam told her. 'But I'm late. I'd better go in.'

Cindy shrugged, twisted her head to make her hair swing out and followed him into the lounge-diner. Her eye swept the room. She took away Joe Banks's ashtray, even as he smoked a cigar, and replaced it with a clean one.

'Cigar, Sam?' offered Banks.

'Thank you, Joe. Very kind.' Sam Abbott took the proffered cigar.

'I was just explaining to Geoff about these hold-ups on Savernake,' Banks said. 'To sum up, the tenants are in revolt, the council report's against us and the one unanticipated factor, the death of the Samco chairman, is also a bit of a problem. I'm just telling him there's no cast-iron guarantees in this kind of business, but the odds were all right when we began and they still are. Bernard Fellows's death does constitute a hitch. A very sad business. I knew him well, a brilliant businessman and a very pleasant man personally. But there we are. As far as Savernake goes it's not the end of the world. Not to worry – and don't tell me you're going bust, Geoff,' he said, looking round the room, 'because I'm not going to believe you. Not sitting in this lovely home of yours—'

'I've got to put it like this,' Geoff began. 'I don't like this death. It's bad news. If I can't have a firm starting date soon, I'm going to have to make my own arrangements.'

'That's your choice,' said Banks firmly. He had plenty to do without coming here to pat Geoff Doyle's hand. He thought irritably that if Geoff had stuck with his wife instead of taking up with Abbott's expensive daughter, he might have been better able to see the financial wood for the trees. Here was a contract worth approximately a quarter of a million to him, and he was nagging and fretting, instead of thinking and planning. That was what a wants-it-all little baggage like that could do to a man. He said, 'All right, these are the details. The position is, Sir Bernard Fellows will have given his eldest son a major share of the business. Savernake's a subsidiary, so Savernake's involved. And they can't find the eldest son. He's been missing for months. He could be dead. It makes probating the will difficult and that holds up business. Basically they have to find this son, or prove he's dead. They're making every effort to resolve the situation and obviously they will. A team of lawyers is on it at the moment. The truth is, it doesn't matter so far. At Kenton we're not in a position to sell the property yet, and hopefully they'll have the situation ironed out when we are.'

At this point Sam Abbott decided privately he didn't like the sound of all this. For the time being he'd stop pressing Vanessa and Annie to sell the Arcadia to him, and he'd reduce his offer drastically if they rang to say they wanted him to buy it.

Geoff Doyle felt edgy. The chance to take on much of the building of the Savernake Village, which had come his way through Cindy's father who knew what figures the other builders were tendering for the job, had seemed like a real opening, a chance to get into the big time. Now he had to decide whether to start taking on other jobs, or hang on hoping the Savernake project would get off the ground as and when planned.

Joe Banks stood up. 'There we are, gentlemen. I hope I've explained the situation to your satisfaction.' He shook hands all round and left.

'I don't know what to make of all that,' said Abbott despondently when Banks had gone. He poured himself a whisky at the bar, raised an eyebrow at Geoff, who signalled yes, and poured one for his daughter's future husband.

Cindy said, 'I've got a roast in the oven. I hope you two aren't going to sit there drinking all evening.'

'Shut up, Cindy,' said Geoff, in a neutral tone of voice.

'Tsk,' said Cindy, raising her eyebrows to the ceiling, and sat back in the cream leather armchair.

Geoff said, 'It doesn't make sense, all this hanging on one bloke's death. It may be a story they're telling Banks to slow things down.'

'I don't think so,' Abbott said. 'I saw this in the paper. Samco's a vast corporation, quite a few of the companies were still controlled by Sir Bernard and that's where there's a problem. It's not just Savernake – a whole group of provincial newspapers are on hold while it's sorted out, a pharmaceutical company, a chain of pizza parlours – you name it. Millions involved. It's just one of those stupid things that happen. But like Banks says, probably it's only a hold-up, not a disaster.'

'Let's hope they find this son, or his dead body, soonest,' Geoff said uncomfortably. 'And the silly buggers at the council pull their fingers out.' He glanced sideways at Cindy who was pouting, and knew she was seeing Portuguese beaches receding. They'd have to go, he decided. At least she'd be in a good mood while they were there: that would help him relax.

18

Scandal

One August afternoon Jasmine came into the Arcadia in a rush to persuade Annie to go with her to Yorkshire and accompany her to Sir Bernard Fellows's funeral in the churchyard at Thrawn, the village in Yorkshire from which the Fellowses had originated and where many of them had been buried ever since. Sir Bernard's sister, Elizabeth, still lived at Thrawn Hall, once a farmhouse but extended in the eighteenth century as the family fortunes improved.

On this hot afternoon Annie and Vanessa were as usual doing the two hours' intensive preparation necessary before a reputable restaurant, however small, opens in the evening. Vanessa was on vegetables and fruit, Annie on the rest. As Vanessa was swiftly coring twenty-one peppers and Annie putting the white from the last of a dozen eggs into the mixer Jasmine arrived and pressed the brass bellpush outside. Annie dropped the eggshell in the rubbish box, wiped her fingers and went to the door.

Jasmine, dressed in pink, came in quickly and sat down. She looked up at her sister, still standing in an overall. Jasmine appealed, 'I know you're busy. Nigel's father's being buried the day after tomorrow. Please come with me. I can't face it on my own.'

'Jasmine. You won't *be* on your own—'

'No, but I really need a friend. Thrawn Hall's so gloomy and everyone's under such strain. Nobody knows what's happening. Nigel's terribly upset. And poor Mary! And Nigel's sister Claudia is coming and everyone's annoyed with her because she's challenging the will. It's ghastly, Annie. Please come.'

'I can't come to Yorkshire with you, Jas. I can't leave Vanessa to organise the snack bar and the restaurant by herself.' She went back to the kitchen, turned on the mixer and took a sharp knife from the holder above one of the counters. She got a whole salmon from the fridge and began to slice it into steaks. 'I'm sorry, but you can see what it's like.'

Jasmine followed and stood in the kitchen doorway talking to her. 'Oh – all right,' she said reluctantly. 'It's not your business, I suppose. At least once poor Bernard's buried it'll be over. But,' she added more resentfully, 'I could have done with support, and actually it *is* your business. One of Samco's subsidiaries is Savernake Developments. It's controlled largely or completely by the family. Nigel said, ages ago, if they pulled off this Savernake Village complex you wouldn't regret starting the Arcadia. You'd get loads more customers with money to spend.'

'You didn't tell me that,' Annie said.

'I couldn't. He told me not to. They were just getting the project organised.'

'On the sly,' Vanessa said.

'That's what business is like,' Jasmine told her.

'So's bank raids,' Vanessa said sourly. She began to behead and core large tomatoes, while Annie poured sauce from a jug over the salmon steaks and put the poacher in the fridge.

'I thought you had a cook,' said Jasmine.

'We had to get rid of her. Couldn't afford her.'

'It's a relief, in a way,' Vanessa added. 'She was very snooty.'

Annie opened the freezer and began counting and checking items on a list. 'I'd help,' said Jasmine, 'but I'm so tired. Poor Nigel can't sleep since his father died. I'm trying to keep Mary company as much as possible. It's made Sim's disappearance seem worse. I believe she thinks he must be dead, or he'd have turned up when he heard about his father.'

'Perhaps he's somewhere where he wouldn't have heard,' suggested Annie, amending a list. She looked at Jasmine sharply. 'There's more, isn't there?'

'Yes. There's Claudia coming from New York. She's already been on the phone, saying it's illegal for Sim to get so much and Nigel the rest. She says she's going to court to challenge the will. Mary's trying to persuade her not to. She dreads the fuss, but Claudia says it's 1990 now and wealthy families shouldn't go on giving everything to the eldest son, the rest to the other boys, and just a pittance to the daughters. She says she doesn't expect to marry a rich man who'll keep her for the rest of her life, so she wants fair shares. Of course, Mary says it means breaking up all the big estates if this starts happening.'

Annie was pulling out frozen food containers and stacking them on the counter. She said, 'I thought the place was entailed. The court couldn't overturn that, could they? OK on chocolate mousse, Vanessa.'

Vanessa, chopping determinedly, just nodded.

Jasmine said, 'Maybe the entail couldn't be disturbed, but there's the rest.'

Vanessa stopped for a moment. 'There's more?' she enquired.

'There's tracts of Yorkshire for a start. And elsewhere,' Jasmine told her guardedly.

'It makes you think,' Vanessa said, stuffing peppers and tomatoes.

'If people knew,' said Jasmine, dropping her guard a little, 'there'd be a revolution.'

'I doubt it,' Annie said. She added, 'You can't blame Claudia for wanting a fair slice of the cake.'

'By the way,' Jasmine said, 'Nigel's very upset about you putting that reporter on to us—'

'I didn't,' Annie said. 'He only rang for information about Sir Bernard. It's his job,' she said. 'His editor asked him to find out. You know the *Kenton Post*'s very interested in the Savernake project. Ben simply—'

Vanessa paused with the spoon in her hand. 'You've spoken to him?' she said indignantly. 'Ben?'

Annie pushed past Jasmine, went to the computer next to the till and began to tap in entries. 'What's this about Colindale, anyway?' she asked.

Jasmine said, 'That's the point, Annie. How did he know? You must have told him. Nigel's very upset—'

'I'm tired of hearing about Nigel's being upset,' snapped Annie. 'Yes, I'm fed up, Jas. Shut up about inheritances and that egomaniacal family you married into! Ben was at your party.' She turned to speak to Vanessa, now standing in the kitchen doorway, still holding her spoon. 'I'm sorry, Vanessa. Perhaps I should have told you Ben was there but I thought I'd spare your feelings. As a matter of fact, he was drunk and saying how much he missed you—' Vanessa looked more and more incredulous. She opened her mouth to speak but Annie swept on. 'Anyway, Jas, Nigel invited Ben to that party through a PRO. Ben was standing behind me when you went back to Bedford Square after you heard the news. That's where he heard you say Colindale. What's it about?'

Jasmine hesitated. 'I can't tell you, Annie. It's not very pleasant. And nor are you.' She sniffed. 'I should have thought you could have been kinder at a time of family bereavement. I should have thought you'd have wanted to come to the funeral with me.'

'Well, I can't, because unlike you I've got a living to earn,' retorted Annie. 'So you can take your entails and Colindales elsewhere.'

'Well, goodbye, then, Annie,' said Jasmine in a wounded voice, and walked stiffly out of the restaurant.

'Oh, God,' said Annie angrily. 'I should have been nicer but what does she expect?'

It was Vanessa's turn to reproach Annie. 'Why didn't you tell me you'd seen Ben? What makes you think I *want* my feelings spared? Come on, Annie. Give me all the details.'

'I will. While you get on with your popular *boeuf en croûte*.'

While Annie recounted the story of the party in the kitchen at the Arcadia, Jasmine, in a taxi she'd luckily found in Foxwell High Street, felt her rage evaporating and a familiar sense of anxiety returning. Again she went over the circumstances of Sir Bernard's death. Unpleasant, she had called them, but they were more than unpleasant. They were mysterious and slightly sinister.

Sir Bernard Fellows had been found lying on a pavement in a side street in a north London suburb, recently dead. He was discovered by a local man walking his dog who called an ambulance. His undisturbed wallet proved his identity immediately but although all the signs indicated that he had died of a heart attack, there were small stab wounds in his chest and arms. The wounds were clean and his clothing was neither bloody nor cut.

To the startled doctor who made a superficial examination, it looked as if this prosperous-seeming man had been stabbed repeatedly but ineffectually, either before or after his death from a heart attack. If he'd been alive at the time of the attack he'd washed his wounds and changed his clothes before his death. If he was dead when the attack was made there would have been no blood, but his clothes would have been cut, so somehow he had been re-dressed. Unless, speculated the doctor, the man had been naked at the time of death, in which case some other person must have dressed the body. He still wore an expensive watch and his wallet contained £120, so no attempt had been made to rob him.

Jasmine and Nigel arrived at Bedford Square late that night very shaken, horrified by the phone call from the police and still only half believing the news. 'Could it be some kind of cruel hoax?' Jasmine had hazarded on the journey, knowing that the powerful are often hated. She had to open the door with Nigel's keys, for his hands were shaking.

Charles Head met them in the darkened hall, already in a dark suit and tie. 'Nigel,' he said, coming towards him. 'I'm sorry. So very sorry.'

Jasmine put her arm round Nigel. Tremors were running through his body. 'The lights – why hasn't anybody turned on the lights?' he demanded.

Charles Head quickly put the lights on. The large hall and great staircase sweeping upwards in a curve were suddenly illuminated. Jasmine saw the party as very small figures in all that space. She, Nigel, Charles Head and the housekeeper, Mrs Craven, coming forward grave-faced to offer condolences, seemed minute and unimportant.

'The police are upstairs,' Head told Nigel. 'So is Hugh Brown. I got in touch with him as soon as Mrs Craven told me.' He glanced at Mrs Craven, standing a little further off.

'That was a bit premature, wasn't it, Charles?' Nigel asked, irritation in his voice, though Jasmine, still with her arm round his waist, could feel him trembling. He started for the stairs. Charles Head took his other arm to hold him back. Nigel moved on, prepared to pull them with him. 'Let's get this over with,' he muttered.

Head turned to face him at the foot of the stairs. 'Look,' he said in a low voice. 'I don't know how to put this. Your housekeeper's a very intelligent woman – you probably owe her a debt. When the police initially rang here she got the impression that all was not well—'

'What!' demanded Nigel.

Jasmine murmured, 'Listen to him, Nigel.'

'How did he die?' asked Nigel. 'What happened?'

Charles spoke to Nigel. 'Your father was found dead in a part of London he never went to and had no reason to go to—'

'For God's sake, Charles—'

'The police won't give me, Brown or Nigel any information,' Head told him softly. 'But they told Mrs Craven that all the indications were that he'd had a heart attack. And then they asked her straight out over the phone whether he had any enemies.' Nigel gazed at him. Charles Head went on quickly, 'I don't know what that means but I imagine they were trying to get an answer out of her before she had a chance to think.'

Jasmine said quietly, 'I think we'd better go straight up and see them, Nigel.'

Charles Head went first. He said, 'I left a message for Campbell Straker. He's at a dinner. He'll ring as soon as he gets in.' He paused and added, 'In case any medical information is required.'

Nigel stopped, holding the banister. It was Jasmine who replied, 'Thanks, Charles, for all you've done.'

Two policemen, one an inspector, were sitting uncomfortably by the marble fireplace in the big drawing room on the first floor. Sir Hugh Brown, the lawyer, faced them.

It was a room for receptions, so large that it was seldom used by the family who had a smaller sitting room elsewhere in the house. In spite of its curtains, pictures and the flowers in vases it still gave the impression of being part of a public building, not a private home. To Jasmine it seemed chilly, although the evening had been warm. She and Nigel sat side by side, near the solicitor. Charles Head pulled a chair away from the big table by the windows and brought it over. The police inspector offered his condolences to Nigel and Jasmine, but the story he told, closely attended to by Sir Hugh, who occasionally cut in asking questions in his clear voice, was not in the least consoling.

The policemen waiting at the hospital until the doctor had finished his examination already knew that they had on their hands the body of an important man, a baronet and chairman of a multi-million-pound conglomerate. The news that Sir Bernard had apparently been attacked before his death drew their complete attention. And, of course, there would have to be an inquest.

Nigel, frozen with horror, coughed, found his voice and agreed. 'Of course there must. And a full investigation. We must find out who did this.' Jasmine noted that as her husband spoke Hugh Brown stiffened in his chair. He attempted to persuade the police that an inquest would be unnecessary. The hospital doctor who had seen Sir Bernard when he was brought in had given the opinion that the stab wounds on his body could not have killed him. The police inspector told the solicitor that Sir Bernard had been attacked, the attack had probably contributed towards his death. It was their duty to try to find the perpetrator. Sir Hugh tried further arguments but at that moment Sir Bernard's doctor rang. He had not seen his patient for several months. An inquest was therefore inevitable.

The inquest proved only what the hospital doctor had suspected, that the stab wounds had not been serious enough to cause death. They had been inflicted before Sir Bernard died of a coronary attack, which must have killed him almost instantly.

Forensic investigation suggested that he or another person had washed the blood from his body, using soap. As there were no fibres in the wounds he must have been naked from the waist up when the attacker stabbed him, with a small knife, possibly a penknife, a weapon no one with any serious intent to kill would use. Charles Head put much effort into news management of the inquest results. Speculation died down.

Meanwhile, no one in the short suburban street where the body had been found seemed to be able to help with information. Some had been out that evening; many more, on a hot night, had been in their back gardens until it was time to go to bed. Sir Bernard's Rolls-Royce was still in the garage at Bedford Square, but his Rover was discovered parked in a street near Hampstead Heath. No one there remembered seeing it before; no one in Colindale recognised it.

The investigation was reasonably thorough, but Nigel, who had initially wanted to find out what had happened and see the perpetrator punished, was urged not to push for more work by the police. He quickly saw the possibility of more undesirable publicity for his family and the company. There was no point in doing anything which would attract more attention. In addition, he himself began to veer away from wanting details of the death of his father. The answer might be disturbing. In his mind's eye he saw those washed, gaping, penknife stabs in his father's flesh, and winced.

The situation as it stood was serious enough already. Sir Bernard's untimely death had prevented him from putting everything in Nigel's name as he had proposed. A third of the companies making up Samco were, in one way or another, stalled as far as major decisions were concerned. No one could vote Sir Bernard's shares, or execute business in the companies where he had been sole controller until his will was probated or a temporary legal arrangement had been made.

It had not taken long for nervous shareholders to take in this fact that it could not be business as usual at Samco. Shares in companies Sir Bernard had controlled completely, or as a major shareholder, dropped fast and showed no signs of reaching a plateau. Nigel sought to gain rapid executive powers over the affected companies but the law of the land, often flexible where money is concerned, is rigid when it comes to matters of death and inheritance. The board of Samco met and conferred and decided to decide nothing immediately. Either Sim had to be found to take possession of his inheritance, or Nigel would have to seek executive powers within the company. This would take time and those powers were bound to be severely limited.

All the Fellows family could do was step up the search for Sim and appoint trustees to govern the affairs of the company. Sir Hugh Brown, the family's and the company's solicitor, had to be appointed as trustee, but trustees are cautious, appointed not as entrepreneurs but guardians. Nigel, the other trustee, knew his hands would be tightly tied by Sir Hugh's carefulness. Sir Hugh made this plain. 'I must stress to you that neither of us is the owner of anything previously belonging to Sir Bernard. We are only custodians, responsible to the law for our actions. In the event of anything going wrong in terms of losses, bad contracts and so forth, we can be held accountable by the estate. As a trustee, and a lawyer to boot, I see it as my responsibility to keep us both out of trouble. By trouble,' he added, seeing how unwelcome this statement was to Nigel, 'I mean a possible lawsuit by the estate. You will see this as improbable. Let me assure you it can and does happen.'

'That's all very well,' said Nigel, 'but business involves risks.'

'The demand is that any risks you take should be justifiable.'

'What does that mean in practice?'

'That if anything went wrong you could defend the decision in court.'

Nigel said nothing but his face betrayed dismay, even anger.

'I'm sorry,' said Sir Hugh.

At his club that evening Sir Hugh met Sir Bernard's doctor. The two large men sat in leather armchairs in a quiet corner under a portrait of George V, discussing events in the Fellows family. 'Bad business,' said Campbell Straker.

Sir Hugh knew that if Sir Bernard had transferred his assets to Nigel earlier the present complications would not have arisen. Keen to avoid any suggestion that he himself had been lacking in forethought he asked, 'Campbell, Bernard saw you regularly. Did you have any idea he was suffering from a heart condition?'

Campbell Straker shook his head. 'He had a complete check-up in March. Nothing wrong with him at all. He had the body of a man ten years younger. I know some doctors will urge their patients to get a top-to-toe check every month. Every six months has always seemed enough to me where a relatively young, healthy man like Bernard's concerned. The check-ups themselves can be mildly stressful, especially to powerful men like Bernard. They're not used to thoughts of mortality. They often take it hard.'

'Used to having it all their own way?' suggested Sir Hugh.

'Terrifyingly, sometimes,' said Campbell Straker, who had been reared as a strict Protestant. 'Bernard's sort are healthy men, usually, and not introverted. So there's little standing in their way to blight them but that one fact of life none of us, eventually, can ignore.'

'So you had no idea . . . ?'

'Not just I,' Campbell Straker pointed out. 'He had thorough tests. But something crept up on him.'

'And then somebody crept up on him, it would seem,' Sir Hugh added. Campbell Straker said nothing. 'Come on, Campbell. You must know something,' urged the solicitor. 'What was it – gambling, rent boys—?'

'In Colindale?' queried Campbell Straker. 'If so, it must have changed a lot since I was last there.'

'It didn't necessarily happen in Colindale,' Sir Hugh said. He appealed, 'Campbell?'

'If I knew anything,' Campbell Straker said firmly, 'it would not be ethical to disclose it. I hardly need to tell you that,' he added more jovially, calling, 'Waiter,' and snapping his fingers.

'It isn't just common curiosity, Campbell,' Sir Hugh said, as the other man ordered another two whiskies, a single for himself. 'I'm the family solicitor, and a trustee of the company, for my sins. This matter's apparently over and done with. But your experience in your own field will have shown you how often matters like this don't disappear completely, just lie dormant for a bit then crop up again. I'd like to know what I'm dealing with.'

Campbell Straker sighed. He paused as the waiter returned with the drinks. He said, 'I don't know what happened. I can guess but that's hardly good enough. I'm afraid you'll have to be content not to know. For the time being I should think you've got enough on your plate with the search for Bernard's son. Any results?'

'All the British embassies have already been contacted with no result. Now we've got one detective flying all over the world, and another sunning himself in the Caribbean where Sim was last seen. I'm in touch with various dubious characters, some working for themselves, some for HMG—'

'Tried the Sally Army?' Campbell Straker suggested unexpectedly. 'They get some amazing results worldwide. Doesn't cost so much, either. He could be sleeping under a bridge. You can be just as cut off sleeping rough in London or Edinburgh as you can be in the middle of the Amazon jungle.'

Sir Hugh reflected that nearly everyone he met these days had a theory about where Sim Fellows was to be found, or where he might have died. He said wearily, 'We're combing the gaols of the Far East and the doss houses of the East End. I've had a man in Colindale for a week, trying to find a connection.'

'Perhaps an unfortunate one.'

'Very unfortunate, if it existed. I don't think it does. But – no stone's to be left unturned . . .'

'A sorry business,' Campbell Straker said.

Sir Hugh nodded.

To the funeral at Thrawn came twenty of the Fellowses' family and close friends. A memorial service in London for Sir Bernard was planned for the autumn.

It rained on the day of the funeral, which was held at St Michael's, Thrawn. Three men had been hired to get rid of the press and stood discreetly among the gravestones.

Sir Bernard's only sister stood rigidly by the grave with David Elliott, the man she had lived with since her husband, a Catholic, had refused her a divorce in the fifties. Her son, Adam, was on her other side.

She felt little grief for the loss of a brother with whom she had never got on. Jennifer Fellows, Bernard and Elizabeth's stepmother, had flown in from Lugano, and had been wheeled to the graveside by her maid. Their real mother, Baroness Susan Fellows, now eighty-two and a member of the House of Lords, was ignoring her supplanter and the son of the second marriage, a fifty-year-old executive at the World Bank. In this atmosphere of family tension, loaded with memories of old quarrels, divorces and disinheritings,

Sir Bernard's funeral service took place. No one present could forget the still unanswered question about how Sir Bernard had come to die as he had.

In Thrawn churchyard eight generations of solid and prosperous Fellowses lay. The others, younger sons, ne'er-do-wells, lay all over the world, from Ballarat to Bruges, forgotten, their bodies marked, if they were marked at all, by overgrown, crumbling stones. But here at Thrawn lay Thomas Fellows, founder of the family, farmer turned shipowner, slave- and cotton-trader, and his two wives, Dorcas and Dorothy, and many of their offspring. The rise of the family had been favoured in its early days by a pure water supply in the locality, although later the mortality rate rose due to the fouling of the water by the Fellows weaving sheds. But by that time the strong branch of the family had moved on, to Liverpool and to London.

As the first clods of earth fell on to the coffin, Jennifer Fellows sobbed loudly. Lady Mary stood silent, Nigel's arm supporting her. Almost everyone at the graveside had a thought of Sir Bernard's eldest son, Simon, still missing. How could he be alive, Jasmine wondered, and not be here now, at his father's funeral? She wondered if the tears in Nigel's eyes were for his father or for his brother. Then she turned her attention to grave Claudia Fellows, in a smart black dress, accompanied by Al Dominick, a dark man who had flown in with her from New York. In a brisk wind, which tossed the trees outside the graveyard about; in a profound country silence, broken only by birdsong, the wind and the sound of the earth as it fell on the coffin, it was particularly horrible to imagine Sim Fellows's death somewhere else, far from home with foreign voices round him.

There seemed to be too many people in the small parlour at Thrawn Hall, which connected with an equally small dining room by open double doors. Both rooms were sparsely furnished. There were some poor oil paintings by a local artist on the walls. In one corner stood a stopped grandfather clock. Pushed into another was a large television. The windows beyond looked on to a field with an old horse in it. Elizabeth Fitzpatrick was notoriously mean and the funeral lunch, laid out in the parlour on tables ranged against the panelled walls, was meagre, as everyone had known it would be. There was plenty to drink however – David Elliott, a cheerful, thirsty man, had seen to that. The combination of poor food and too much to drink did not help the atmosphere. It might have been improved by the presence of a child, or the knowledge that a Fellows child, too young to attend, was tucked at home somewhere.

Tactlessly, Bernard's stepbrother referred to the absence of grandchildren in a jocular remark to Al Dominick which even more unfortunately was overheard by Lady Mary. Claudia's boyfriend, holding a plate of salad, responded, 'Right. Well – Claudia and I have no plans. How about you?' It was Bernard's stepbrother's turn to wince. He was homosexual. The sad exchange made everyone who heard it feel uncomfortable, especially Jasmine, and also called to mind Claudia's possible challenge over the will. David Elliott brought this issue out into the open, saying, 'Well, then, Claúdia. What's all this about a lawsuit? Some kind of feminist gesture?'

Claudia gave him a hard stare from her beautiful eyes. She was a tall, strong woman with dark hair piled impeccably on her head, secured by a tortoiseshell comb. She had very long, fine legs in black stockings.

'Is this quite the time—?' Lady Mary's sister said clearly in her penetrating voice.

'I don't think so,' Nigel said. 'We'll discuss all this later.'

'Sorry, sorry,' said David Elliott, and began to refill glasses, urging the guests to try the cheese. 'Local, you know. Almost all this,' he pointed to the sideboard and tables, 'comes from our own farm. You must try the blackberry and apple pie. Lady Mary, a little more wine? Or would you like coffee?'

'Would you like to go and rest, Mary?' Jasmine asked her. 'You look all in. Let me take you upstairs.'

Lady Mary nodded and Jasmine supported her up to her bedroom where she sat on the edge of the bed.

'Can you get Nigel to make arrangements for me to go back to Durham House tonight? I don't feel like spending tonight in a strange bed. It's very rude to poor Elizabeth . . .'

'Of course. I'll explain,' said Jasmine. And waited, for she felt Lady Mary had something else to say. But she, after a pause, leaned back on her pillow in the big wooden bed and closed her eyes.

'I'll organise the return to Durham House and I'll wake you in an hour, if you're asleep,' Jasmine said and went out quietly.

Downstairs, grief for Sir Bernard and the contemplation of human mortality inevitable at funerals was being translated into lethargy and discontent. Most were sitting on the unwelcoming furniture when Jasmine entered.

'Well,' said Elizabeth Fitzpatrick in a harsh tone, on hearing Lady Mary's plan to go back to Hampshire that day, 'of course. If that's what she wants – she must do what she wants.'

David Elliott winked at Jasmine. 'Escaping from Hardship Hall,' he muttered.

Elizabeth Fitzpatrick heard the remark and shot him a cold look. 'Draughty as it is,' she said, 'I'm lucky to have salvaged even this from my meagre patrimony.' At Claudia Fellows's approach Elliott took his drink to the far window and began to talk to Sir Bernard's stepbrother. When Sir Bernard's father died he'd inherited almost everything, and his stepbrother a substantial sum. There'd been nothing for Elizabeth, who'd already had her dowry. She'd made a terrible fuss and her brothers had clubbed together and given her Thrawn Hall for her lifetime and a small income.

'Well, *you* can hardly blame me,' Claudia said to her aunt. 'You can't deny it's unjust.'

'I'm the last person in the world who would,' said her aunt. 'More power to your elbow.' She looked at Jasmine. 'Sorry, Jasmine, but there it is.'

'I don't care,' said Jasmine.

'You're middle class, of course,' Elizabeth said to her. Jasmine was not sure how to respond. 'I've read somewhere that the British imposed a law on the Irish making it compulsory for an inheritance to be split up equally among the children,' Elizabeth said. 'Over the years this ensured that their landowners stayed weak and powerless because the estates were so small.'

'So – you're not really on my side,' Claudia accused.

'My dear. It doesn't matter whose side I'm on. I have no power to alter anything now,' Elizabeth said craftily. 'I'm only telling you what I read.'

'I'll just look in on Mary,' announced Lady Margaret.

'So depressing for those girls, isn't it?' Elizabeth said after she'd left the room. 'I mean, look at *their* family. Four girls, and then finally the boy. They know most of them wouldn't have been born if their parents had got a boy first time!'

'I was the youngest,' Claudia burst out.

'Yes. So. Lucky for you. Well, Jasmine, you'll have to do your bit now, I suppose.'

Jasmine couldn't answer. She went off to find Nigel who was

standing alone in front of the house. 'I suppose Mother will be planning to move now,' he said.

'I can't see why she has to.'

'It is usual,' Nigel told her.

'Nigel,' she protested. 'I don't want to take over. You know that. It's not as if I've been waiting all these years to get my hands on the key to the still room.'

'I imagine she'll want to go,' Nigel said shortly. 'Are we almost ready to leave?'

'So soon? It looks bad. Anyway, let's leave Mary to rest a little longer. Margaret just went up.'

Jasmine went through the front door and found Claudia putting on her cardigan. 'It's freezing in this house,' said Claudia. 'It always has been. I can remember staying here as a child. Nanny always used to pack a whole suitcase of extra woollies for everybody. Christ, I wish I knew what had happened to Sim. Haven't they any idea?'

'I don't think so,' Jasmine said.

'I'd kill him if he turned up,' Claudia said vehemently. 'And, Jasmine, what happened to Dad? There's something they're not talking about—'

'Shh,' Jasmine warned as Lady Mary and her sister came along the landing above.

They went back to Hampshire in two cars, Nigel, his mother and Lady Margaret in the bigger one, Jasmine, Claudia and Al Dominick in the other.

'You travel in style here,' Al remarked, stretching out. 'Two limos between six. That's great.'

'Not usually,' said Jasmine.

'What about Aunt Elizabeth – bitch of the year, isn't she?' remarked Claudia. 'Thank God we got out.'

'It looked very rude,' Jasmine said.

'She wasn't too polite herself. Face like a fiddle the whole time, no attempt at hospitality. Can you imagine what a night in that place would be like? Who was staying?'

'Only your step-grandmother, overnight. She's getting a flight back to Geneva tomorrow.'

'She and Elizabeth are well matched. They can have a good bitch together about everybody. And what the hell's been going on here? Sim's gone, nobody knows what's happened to him, and, Jasmine, I've got to know – before we left New York Al heard an odd story from a man at CBS about Father being stabbed. Everybody seemed to be keeping quiet about it at the funeral, so I couldn't say anything, but what's been happening?'

Jasmine looked helpless. 'Come on,' urged Claudia, lighting a cigarette.

Al protested, 'Claudia, you promised—'

'Al — I've just been to a funeral. And this is England,' Claudia told him. 'Come on, Jasmine, don't spare my feelings. I haven't got any. I hated my father, quite frankly. He was a horrible man. That's why Sim left. Bernard was a bastard. He constantly had other women and Mother tolerated it because that's how she was trained. The only interest he had in any of us was because we were continuing the family name, and that left me out in the cold because I wasn't going to continue it properly. Sim had brains — he saw it too clearly. He had to leave. No criticism of Nigel, of course, but Nigel's different. If Sim's dead, Bernard drove him to it, just by being Bernard, that's how I see it. Sim's worth twice my father, and God knows where he is, or if . . .' She began to cry. Al put his arm round her. The car sped noiselessly on. 'Just thank your stars,' sniffed Claudia, 'you were brought up at Froggett's. Your parents might be a bit cracked, but your father's not a raving megalomaniac like Bernard was.'

'You don't think your mother should move out if she doesn't want to, do you?' Jasmine asked.

'What do you think?' Claudia responded. 'In Britain, Al, when her husband dies his widow is supposed to move out of the family home to make way for her daughter-in-law.'

Al was astonished. 'Jesus Christ. You mean, like an eviction? You Brits certainly know how women ought to be treated.'

'You'll have to stop her, Jasmine,' Claudia declared. 'Otherwise she'll do it whether she wants to or not. You'd better get Nigel to speak to her.'

Jasmine hoped she could. She feared there were signs of Nigel stepping into his father's big boots, perhaps because he thought he ought to.

As if guessing her thoughts Claudia said, 'I hope Nigel doesn't feel he's got to play Hitler.' She began to wail, 'I wish Sim would come back.'

'You in love with your brother, Claudia?' Al asked. 'I never guessed, but it looks like it.'

'Everybody loved Sim,' Claudia said. 'You couldn't help it.'

Jasmine leaned back on the comfortable upholstery and closed her eyes. It had been a long day, and it wasn't over yet. She'd missed a period and if she was pregnant she didn't know if it was her husband's child or Gerald Rafferty's. She began to count back, for the umpteenth time.

19

Some Reconciliations

Just after Jasmine left the restaurant in a temper, Vanessa's mother and sister Cherry came in, with her seven-year-old twins, James and Mark, both in immaculate miniature Arsenal kits and baseball caps with their names on them. James carried the football, James had the rattle. Blond and square-faced, they were singing, "Ere we go, 'ere we go, 'ere we go.' The women were carrying plastic bags. 'We went to the snack bar to find you, but it was full of women with banners,' reported Vanessa's mother. 'Look what one of their kids did. Look at my tights. The mothers don't seem to have any control these days.'

James was trying to put a chair on a table.

'Leave that alone, James,' Vanessa said.

'I'm Mark,' he replied.

'Well, Mark. You'll scratch the table.'

Cherry, tired, in a floral cotton suit, told him, 'James. Pack it in.'

'Little monsters,' said Vanessa's mother fondly. 'Any chance of a cup of tea, Ness? Look what we got for Cherry for Sandra's wedding.' She pulled a dress from one of the plastic bags and held it up in the kitchen doorway. Looking over it she said to Annie, 'Lovely, isn't it? She'll look so nice, with her hair. I think I saw your sister getting into a taxi in the High Street. Lovely girl, isn't she? And the clothes – well, I suppose she has to, in her position. On second thoughts, cancel the tea. We'll have something stronger. My feet are killing me.'

'Can I have a Coke, Auntie? Can I?' the twins were asking.

'What are those women doing in your snack bar?' complained Cherry.

209

'It may be another demonstration at the Town Hall,' replied Vanessa.

'Tsk,' said Cherry.

The twins were drifting towards the door. 'You're not going out there to play,' Cherry said in alarm. 'In a market? There's all sorts out there. I think you're brave to work here,' she told Vanessa.

'We've got a minder,' Vanessa said. 'White wine?'

'Yes,' said Cherry patting her hips. 'Don't need any more on here. Ian's starting to complain.'

'Mum?' enquired Vanessa.

Anita looked round. 'Well, in these surroundings,' she said, 'I think I'll go for a Bloody Mary.'

From the kitchen Annie, keeping out of the way, heard the chink of bottles.

'All right,' Cherry said impatiently to the boys, 'go next door and ask Melanie if she'll give you a Coke. No playing in the market, though. It's going down,' she told Vanessa. 'It's that recreation centre, attracts the wrong type. Well,' she added, 'you'll see something new next September.' From another bag she pulled out two school caps. 'The twins are going to Valley Lodge. Ian said, it's no good, they're not staying at that local primary. It's nothing but finger painting, sex education and Hindu Christmases, he said. Let's get them somewhere where they give them the three Rs and a bit of manners.'

'The language they've picked up in that playground,' Anita added. 'I wonder you don't put Alec down for somewhere in good time. All these schools have got a waiting list.'

'Yes,' said Vanessa. 'But it costs.'

'This place must be making a mint,' said Anita.

'Not so's you'd notice,' Vanessa told her.

A big black woman led one of the twins into the Arcadia. The other followed. 'I told him off for fingering the fruit on my stall and he kicked me,' she reported, looking round. 'Who's this boy's mother?'

'You let go of my son,' Cherry said loudly.

'Gladly,' the woman said. 'But will you tell him in future to keep his hands off my stall?'

'Well, I've only got your side, haven't I?' said Cherry.

'I don't want an argument. I've got to get back,' and the woman marched out.

'I told you to keep out of the street,' Cherry said when

210

she'd gone. 'Why don't you two ever do what you're told?'

'Angels with dirty faces,' Anita added, tousling the hair of one of them.

'Not so much of the dirty, Mum,' Cherry said. 'Oh, well, better be off, I suppose, get the monsters' teas. Then there's Ian – I never thought I'd end up waiting hand and foot on three men.'

Anita spotted Annie in the kitchen. 'Why don't you come out of there, Cinderella?' she called in a forgiving mood.

'We have to open at six and there's a lot to do,' Annie called back.

'It's hard for women on their own,' Cherry declared. 'Anyone in your life at present, Annie?' she said in the direction of the kitchen.

'No,' called Annie. 'Not really.'

'Dear, dear,' Cherry deplored.

It was at that moment that Ben Gathercole came through the door. He looked extremely pale, very nervous and carried a bunch of red roses. Annie came from the kitchen, looked at Vanessa and thought she might faint. Anita and Cherry stiffened with interest. Anita stuffed her feet into her discarded shoes.

'Hallo, stranger,' Cherry said. Ben looked at her blankly. 'Cherry. Vanessa's sister. Don't you remember – Portugal.'

There was the sound of a dispute outside the restaurant. James and Mark came in protesting. 'He knocked over a chair and that girl Melanie said we had to go out.'

'Sauce,' said Anita. 'Who does she think she is, giving orders?'

'You two are pests,' Cherry said mechanically, still scrutinising Ben.

Annie was the first to pull herself together. 'Hallo, Ben. Would you like a cup of tea?'

Ben said, 'I'm on my way to the Town Hall. I just brought these round. Here you are, Vanessa.' Thrusting the roses into her hands, he turned and left.

Edward came in and said, 'Anythink you want doing, Annie?' He glanced at the group, Vanessa, holding the flowers, Cherry and Anita.

'You could dust the lights,' Annie said absently.

One of the twins had locked the other out of the restaurant. The shut-out boy began to hammer on the door. 'Let me in, dimbo.'

'He'll break that glass,' Anita said.

But Cherry was on her feet, 'I've had enough,' she declared. She seized the inside twin fiercely by the shoulder of his Arsenal

211

top, opened the door and walloped the outside twin. 'You two stand there, don't move, we're leaving.' She raced back, collected her bags and said, 'Mum, I've got to get them home.'

'They want locking up, that pair,' observed Anita, picking up her bags and standing up. 'Lovely flowers,' she observed to the stunned Vanessa. 'Maybe there's a light at the end of the tunnel. What does she look like, this wife?'

'Mum!' called Cherry urgently from the door.

'School teacher, isn't she?' Anita said. 'Come on, Mark, behave yourself. Say goodbye nicely to your auntie.'

After they'd gone Vanessa fell into a chair, still clutching the roses, saying weakly, 'What does he mean by this?'

Annie couldn't help laughing. She slopped Edward's tea in the saucer.

'What does he mean?' Vanessa was saying. 'Is he trying to come back? I won't have him. He can't have two women. Annie,' she appealed, 'he can't have two women.'

Edward drank his tea and went off for the ladder.

'Sit there quietly for a moment,' Annie advised. She went back into the kitchen and started peeling a mound of prawns from the refrigerator. 'He doesn't want two women,' she called out. 'Only one – you.'

Vanessa got up mechanically. 'I told Melanie I'd take over in the snack bar. She's going to get Alec and Joanne from the play centre.' She went off like a zombie.

Edward moved the stepladder to allow her to pass, studying her face. 'She all right?' he asked Annie through the kitchen doorway.

'It's love,' Annie told him.

Andy Campbell came in unexpectedly, looking as menacing as usual. He stopped dead, demanding of Annie, 'Why is my man up there, dusting lights?'

'Because it's boring, man, hanging round here all day,' said Edward boldly. 'You try, you do it, too.'

'I don't think so,' Andy Campbell commented.

'He might as well be dusting as terrorising,' Annie said, wiping her hands and going to the till. 'You're early this week.'

'You should try to be a little polite,' said Andy Campbell.

'It doesn't matter, because we'll soon be out of business,' Annie retorted. Sam Abbott hadn't rung to see if the Arcadia was for sale.

212

She was wondering if he'd withdrawn his offer. She handed over the envelope containing £300.

'You could be a nice-looking woman if you did something about yourself and spoke more nicely to people,' Campbell said, eyeing her proprietorially. With this he took the envelope and went out.

'Right,' Edward agreed.

'I suppose then he'd offer to put me on the streets and take a percentage of that,' Annie said bitterly.

'No trouble, Annie,' warned Edward.

Annie sighed and went back into the kitchen as unhappy as she always was when Campbell came round to collect his fee. The phone rang. She picked it up. 'The Arcadia restaurant,' she said. She heard someone breathing, then, 'Annie? It's Tom. Please speak to me. I want to meet you. Will you?' When there was no answer, Tom went on, 'Please, Annie, I miss you. At least we could be friends – and I want to explain—'

'It's because you didn't explain years ago, Tom, that this happened,' Annie told him. 'I don't want to see you.'

'You were so young. How could I tell you—'

'You didn't tell me then. You didn't tell me a fortnight ago. None of it matters now, Tom. Just go away and leave me alone—'

'I'm coming over.'

'Please don't. Where are you?'

'Rutherford Street. Melanie let me in.' He put the phone down.

'Somebody bothering you?' enquired Edward. 'Do you want me to deal with him?'

'No,' said Annie despondently, slamming the peeled prawns into the refrigerator. She phoned Rutherford Street. Melanie answered. 'Tell him I can't stop to talk to him,' said Annie. 'Tell him not to come here.'

The Arcadia was so busy that night that there was even a queue outside the door. They ran out of duck. Edward had to deal with a fight on the pavement, and eject a drunken client whose partner had left him after the first course. Exhausted, Annie and Vanessa tottered home through the dark hot streets. Edward sympathetically went with them because they were too tired to avoid any trouble they might meet. Then he went to a party. Vanessa paid her babysitter, washed up a sinkful of dishes and went to bed.

Melanie and her boyfriend were still up when Annie came

in, her back and legs aching painfully, her face stiff with smiling. Annie was not pleased to see Jack. She hadn't realised for weeks that the Jackie Melanie constantly went with to a disco or a film was this quick shrimp of a London boy. She'd thought that he was a girl, and Melanie had done nothing to correct the impression. This Jackie's influence had got Melanie into a tight white skirt, white high heels and dangling earrings. Annie hadn't liked the development and had been even less delighted when she came home one evening and caught the supposed Jacqueline drinking Coke and watching a video on the couch wearing only jeans and a back-to-front baseball cap on his blond, spiky hair.

'Jackie, you'd better go home,' she said. 'I thought we agreed, eleven o'clock.'

'Tom's asleep in the spare room,' Melanie reported.

Annie sighed. 'Jack . . . ' she prompted.

He caught the tone of a tired and irritable adult, and left.

Annie went to bed and out like a light. She hardly noticed Tom getting into bed with her, just moaned, and pushed him away. In the morning there was a note on the dressing table. 'Darling A, I have an early meeting with my bank manager. I'll come straight back.'

Downstairs Annie found Jack asleep on the sofa. Unable to get into his house, he claimed tiredly, he'd had to come back. He looked too pathetic and skinny to be told off. Annie persuaded Melanie to take Alec and Joanne by boat to Hampton Court together with Jack. 'Come down to the snack bar,' Annie cried as she left. 'I'll give you a picnic.'

Madame Katarina was waiting outside George's with her suitcase. 'Sausage, bacon, mushroom, tomato, toast and a cup of tea,' she called as Annie banged about the kitchen, trying to catch up. 'I've got an emergency consultation at nine. I came from Brighton early. There's no food in my flat.'

Annie lit the grill, put on the frying pan and called back, 'Madame Katarina, this can't be doing your arteries any good!'

'Annie,' came the reply, 'I starved from when I was twelve, I was hungry from when I was fifteen. My arteries can take care of themselves. How are your troubles?'

Annie thought of Tom's betrayal and attempted return, if that was what it was. She thought of Abbott's offer, evidently withdrawn, presumably because of the uncertainty over the Savernake Village plan, the debt on the restaurant. 'My troubles are increasing,' she said.

Turning the sausages, she wondered what happened to love, money and revenge. All there was was debt, fatigue and responsibility.

She handed Madame Katarina her loaded plate.

'Melanie's sister's on her way,' the clairvoyant said confidently.

'What? The sister they can't find?'

Madame Katarina nodded.

'Good,' Annie said politely, too busy to discuss Madame Katarina's premonition.

She checked the sandwich list for that day, fairly certain Melanie had forgotten to do what she'd asked and confirm with their clients how many of their staff were on holiday. If the food was returned there'd be arguments about the bill. A van driver pulled up on the pavement and began to carry in fish for the Arcadia's freezer. Stallholders protested. The phone rang. Annie wondered how she was going to get through the morning until Vanessa arrived.

20

Trouble at Durham House

'Don't be a bloody fool.' Harry Paine, Samco's new deputy chairman, was discussing the company's future with Nigel by the lake at Durham House. His attention was distracted. 'Jesus Christ. That swan looks sick.'

'They've got a disease,' muttered Nigel. 'One died last week.'

'Perhaps you should call the vet,' suggested Paine. 'Look, what I'm telling you is that it doesn't matter if you can't go on with this Savernake business for the time being, anyway. It's small beer and, God knows, you've got plenty of other things to sort out. Why are you so worried about Ikeda's withdrawing? Don't invest any more money. Put it all on ice. Abandon the idea, for Christ's sake. If you try to push through a vote to spend another ten million of Samco's money on what's essentially a small building project, I've already warned you, I'll oppose you.'

Nigel looked at the tall thin man, with his lean, composed face, and disliked him. He said, 'You might not see the point but others on the board do. Here's the Savernake Village. We put in ten million now. In a year's time we get that back, and ten to twenty million in profit. I call that a good deal for Samco. But it has to be financed now. We've already put a lot of money into developing the idea. If there's a delay – well, we may never get Kenton Council, the Department of the Environment and all the other interested odds and sods on our side all at one and the same time. It's now or never. And you haven't produced one argument why Samco shouldn't invest. The money's standing idle—'

'Temporarily,' interrupted Paine. 'It can be made to work. It will be. But not, as far as I'm concerned, on the Savernake Village project.'

There was a silence. Peaceful dusk was descending over the cornfields, over the far-off rolling hills where sheep clustered in little white groups, over hedges and clumps of trees. The sun was low behind Pennyfeather Hill, three miles away. Paine felt bad about arguing with Nigel so soon after Sir Bernard's death. Nigel seemed to need the tranquillity his home and land should be offering him. But Nigel had forced the argument on him. Paine believed that Samco's participation in the Savernake project was large enough. While the project was being backed by Kataro Ikeda's bank and Samco in more or less equal proportions, he had been content. But after Sir Bernard's death, the Japanese bank had withdrawn. Now Nigel wanted Samco to back the Savernake Village project alone, something Paine thought too risky. If it went wrong Samco would be solely liable and Paine was a man who would not, on principle, have made himself solely liable for his own arrival home at night. He knew the project was Nigel's pet, but that, in his opinion, did not justify his obtaining backing from the parent company up to any sum he cared to name. What troubled him was that some of the board, enticed by the potential profits, would go for it. What angered him was being forced to refuse support to a man who had just buried his father, who couldn't find out what had happened to his brother and was even being persecuted by claims from his sister, whose challenge, Paine considered, was thoroughly selfish and inconsiderate at such a time. He was far from certain that Nigel Fellows should be making decisions so soon after a bereavement.

Now he laid his hand on Nigel's arm, drew it away and said in as kindly a tone as he could manage, 'I seriously advise you not to press this. I must be quite frank. I think you're still shaky after your father's death, understandably enough. Ikeda's coming here, cool as a cucumber, smiling and being polite, and then dropping his bombshell over the port, certainly did nothing for anyone's peace of mind. I understand your feelings, Nigel. Ikeda's backed out when things look difficult – your father's death, all this legal business – and we both know that's exactly when people do back out. But, and I have to stress this, we mustn't let anger with him cloud our judgement and over-invest in Savernake to compensate. We mustn't push forward when sound judgement dictates otherwise. I wonder, Nigel, if you're not being a little over-emotional here. God knows, you've reason to be—'

217

'I am *not* over-emotional,' Nigel told him in a cold, furious voice. 'Frankly, Harry, I think you're being an old woman about this – "Oh dear, what about my savings?" This is business. Business is about risks.'

Paine sighed. 'What more can I say? I'll have to oppose you, Nigel. Come on, we've been here long enough. We'd better get back.'

'Oh, yes. I've got to chuck some more hospitality at Mr and Mrs Ikeda, ask them if they'd like another drink, hope all's well in their room – I'd like to poison the little rat.'

Paine was impatient. 'Don't let it show, Nigel. Take it and smile. You know the rules.'

Nigel did not answer but set off across the lawn towards the lighted windows of the house, too fast for Paine to keep up. He decided not to try, and strolled back taking his time, planning, without too much hope, ways of preventing Nigel from using his influence with the board to get them to invest Samco's money in the Savernake Village project. He might also ring Max Craig – in fact, he decided, he certainly would.

Paine reached the drawing room to find Jasmine urging Lady Mary to go to bed now that Nigel had returned. The two women had been left to entertain the Ikedas alone when Nigel and Harry Paine went out.

Lady Mary, unusually enough for her, had tried to stand firm, refusing to accept the business meeting which seemed to have been forced on them. 'It's too soon, Nigel,' she'd said. 'And he and his wife won't expect to stay here, in the circumstances. I'm sure Mr Ikeda would happily meet you in London.' But Nigel had refused to withdraw his invitation, now he'd offered it. This had angered Lady Mary's sister, who went off suddenly to visit her daughter forty miles away.

Claudia and her American boyfriend were also staying. Al had tackled Jasmine that morning as she tried to sort out the placings for dinner. 'I hope you won't be angry if I tell you something. Nigel's very distressed. He needs to slow down. He needs to grieve.'

'Ah. I know that,' Jasmine replied. 'His mother knows it. But how to persuade him, that's the question?'

'Claudia asked me to speak to you.'

'Claudia could help by not being on the phone to her solicitor all the time. It's agitating for Nigel. She doesn't have to do it here, does she?'

'I don't think that's the real problem.'

'But it does exacerbate things.'

'I tried,' he said, leaving the room.

Claudia came next and sat down at the long dining-room table. She read the scribbled label in front of her. 'Mrs Kataro Ikeda.'

'I'm trying to imagine where everyone should sit,' Jasmine said. 'I can't ask too much help from Mary.'

Claudia was annoyed. 'I suppose you realise Al Dominick is a doctor, medically qualified and a psychotherapist. You were rude to him. About me,' she added.

'I'm sorry,' said Jasmine. 'I'm upset. I'll apologise. But if he's a psychotherapist he ought to know I'm upset. About Bernard's death, and Sim being nowhere, and Nigel making all these efforts to keep going. What's the point of someone coming and telling me he's mad? He's doing what he thinks is right. It's all right for you. You didn't even like Bernard.'

'No one's saying Nigel's mad,' Claudia told her.

'He's trying to cope when he's barely able to do it. It's all very well to say slow down, grieve, try to understand what's happened. Bernard died in the middle of everything . . .'

'OK. I understand, Jasmine.'

'All I can do is try to make things all right. I'm trying,' Jasmine said despondently.

'Tell the cook cold soup, salmon and raspberries,' Claudia said. 'Mother hasn't always been the hostess with the mostest. When she got desperate in the summer in the old days she always used to say, cold soup, salmon and raspberries. I forget what it was in the winter. Come on, let's go and pick the raspberries. Al can help.'

'He's dodging me,' Al Dominick said neutrally, as the three picked along the raspberry canes in the sunshine. 'I don't believe he knows I'm a doctor, but he smells the threat.'

The Ikedas went to bed shortly after Lady Mary. Suddenly, in the hall, Jasmine heard Nigel shouting at Paine, 'If you think ringing that charlatan is going to help, then go ahead, but don't do it from my house.'

She felt too tired to go to him. She was now sure she was expecting a baby. She hadn't told Nigel and the child might not even be his. She felt completely bewildered.

In bed that night, Nigel told Jasmine about Ikeda's withdrawal of his bank's money from the Savernake Village project and his row with Harry Paine, who was going to oppose him at the board meeting. He'd said he'd caught Paine ringing Max Craig, though he didn't tell her he'd been given advice by Craig weeks earlier and ignored his warnings. Jasmine, tired, feeling queasy, decided now was not the moment to reveal her pregnancy. She said, 'But wouldn't it be better to put the plan on ice for a little while? There's so much else for you to attend to.'

'It's a perfectly simple proposition,' Nigel said sharply. 'And, as it happens, Samco will back the project. I'm just upset about Paine's opposition. I'm wondering if he isn't making some kind of bid.'

'Bid for what?'

'Power,' Nigel said simply. 'That's what it's all about. With Dad gone, he may have an eye to the chairmanship.'

Nigel turned away from her. Jasmine sat up, poured herself some water and said to his back, 'You're over-working, Nigel. I wish we could take just a short time off. Even a long weekend.'

'I'm doing this for all of you,' Nigel said shortly. 'The family.'

Hearing this, Jasmine felt even more reluctant to mention her pregnancy. Since the thought of his duties as head of the family was unbalancing him, how much worse would he get if he thought about an heir? She fell asleep, worried.

But if Nigel or Jasmine had known what had taken place at George's Café in Foxwell that afternoon there would have been no sleep for either of them.

21

The Arrival of Twins

Annie stood behind the counter, her mind partly on the chip fryer, the rest on Tom Pointon standing in front of her. It was very hot. Arnold sat in his corner, over a cup of tea, looking discontented. Two workmen were eating an early lunch.

'OK, Tom,' said Annie. 'Let's go to the Duke of Westminster for lunch when Vanessa turns up to relieve me. But I'll have to be quick because I've got to go straight to the Arcadia afterwards. There's eleven bookings for tonight. That means we'll probably be full all evening.'

Melanie came in with a message. 'Vanessa rang from the doctor's. She said I can take over for half an hour. Joanne was sick this morning and there was a big queue in the surgery. She's been waiting for over two hours.'

Annie went into the kitchen and turned down the fryer. Melanie put on an overall and went behind the counter. Tom waited. A delivery man came in and ordered sausage and chips.

'Sausage and chips,' called Melanie.

A young black woman in a pink tracksuit eased a double buggy containing two pale brown one-year-old children through the door. The babies wore shorts, little trainers and T-shirts each inscribed with a name. One of them had gold earrings. The woman bumped the buggy and a large plastic zipper bag through the tables. 'Is Annie Vane here?' she asked Melanie.

'In the back,' Melanie replied. Annie came out. She had taken off her overall and was wiping her hands. The woman scrutinised her quickly. 'I'm Arlette Jones,' she said. 'I'm leaving these children with you.' She took her hands off the handles of the buggy.

221

'What – why?' Annie asked in amazement.

'Your sister's Jasmine Fellows – right?'

'Yes,' Annie agreed.

The young woman was firm, ready to get angry. 'Well, this is her niece and nephew,' she stated, 'Joseph and Miranda. Me and my mum have been looking after them for nine long weary months and now we're going to Portugal. Somebody's got to look after these kids and it should be you.'

'This is ridiculous,' Tom said.

'Who are you to talk?' Arlette said challengingly. She looked at Annie and went on, 'I'm sorry, but we've had enough – what with the nursery closing and having to go two miles, and then they get the measles and my mum has to take time off to look after them—'

'This is a mistake—' Annie said.

'I'll gladly collect them in two weeks' time. But my mum needs a break. So do I.'

Melanie said loudly, 'This lady is not these children's auntie. She can't look after them. It's got nothing to do with her.'

'I don't believe this,' said Arlette. 'How can you do this?'

The delivery man said loudly, 'I'm sorry, but I'm parked on a yellow line. Can I please have my meal that I ordered?'

Perhaps because he was black Arlette turned to him. 'Can you believe it? Two weeks and they won't do it. What is it? The colour they are? What do you think?'

'Look here,' said Tom.

'I'm not looking here at all. I'm leaving these children here and that's it . . .'

The delivery man waiting for his order said steadily, 'Girl – I don't think these people know who these children are. Do you think you made a mistake?'

'Sim Fellows,' said the young woman, putting her face right up to Annie's, 'is the father of these children. Their mother's my sister Josie. Now, you take care of these children. I'm leaving.' And she did. There was a profound silence. Annie came round from behind the counter. 'My God,' she said. 'Supposing it's true?'

But Melanie had disappeared and was running after the young woman. She caught sight of her as she crossed the hot crowded street. Melanie dodged through hooting traffic, caught up with Arlette and grabbed her arm. 'Who're you? What do you want?' the young woman demanded furiously.

'Where's their father?' Melanie cried urgently. 'They're all looking for him.'

'So am I,' the young woman said. 'Two postcards in nine months. I'd like to catch him.'

'Where's your sister?'

'Same story,' the woman said. 'You let go of my arm now or I'll make you.'

'Did they get married?' Melanie asked.

The girl looked at her with rage and contempt. 'Church of the Angels, Bridgetown, Barbados. We didn't get invited. We saw the photos. And the christening. Does that help you? Now let me go.'

A big hand took hold of Melanie's shoulder. 'Oh,' Melanie cried in pain. Turning, she shouted in alarm, 'Dad!'

'I need a word with you, my girl,' said Pickering grimly.

'Dad,' wailed Melanie. She had let go of Arlette, who slipped away.

'I've been trying to get hold of you,' he said.

'I'm always in the same place,' responded Melanie.

'Don't get cheeky with me.'

'I'm not cheeky.' She looked round for Arlette, but it was too late. She was gone.

Pickering spoke into Melanie's ear, 'Your mother's going to ring you – she wants you home. I don't want any arguments. I want you to get back home and help her. Colum and John are getting out of hand in the long holiday. Someone's got to keep an eye on them.'

'Did she say so?'

He paused. 'That's what she wants. Now if you don't get there I'm going to report you've run away. Go of your own free will, or get taken back by the police, that's your choice. I'll be round tomorrow to take you to the station. Twelve o'clock. You be there.'

In the café Vanessa, unaware of what had just occurred, asked, 'Who left these behind?' while Annie bent over the buggy trying to console the howling twins.

Customers were waiting. The phone was ringing.

In desperation Annie and Vanessa picked up the twins and marched them round the café, talking to them, trying to calm them down. Customers were now leaving, all except Arnold, who sat and studied the confusion.

Melanie decided to ring home. It was a relief to hear her

mother's familiar voice. 'Melanie, love,' she said, 'I know you don't want to come, but your dad's blackmailing me. He's offering me £100 a week if you come, and a divorce if you don't. It's unfair, I know that, and I'm sorry, but I think you've got to come.'

Melanie felt very sad. Her life in London over the last eight months had been too good to be true. At the back of her mind she had always known that her father would put a stop to it. She gazed blindly at Annie and Vanessa, walking about with the bawling twins. Tom took the girl from Annie.

'Don't blame me, Vanessa,' Annie was shouting over the twins' heads. 'They came out of the blue. If you want to ring Kenton Social Services, ring them. But don't you think I should ring Jasmine first? In case they're really Sim's children?'

Tom sat the little girl on his non-existent hip and said loudly, 'Would you like a sweetie?' whereupon she stopped crying and looked at him.

'Get a packet of sweets, Melanie,' Tom said, seeing Melanie standing vaguely at the back of the café. He sat down and unzipped the bag Arlette had left. 'Look,' he said, and pulled out a fluffy yellow duck which was lying on the pile of clothes inside. Vanessa, holding the boy twin, sat down opposite Tom. Melanie gave each child a Smartie, and found a toy car in the bag. Suddenly there was silence. Annie turned the notice on the door to 'Closed' and Melanie began to cry.

'What's the matter?' asked Tom.

Melanie unburdened herself, stopped crying and started thinking. 'I've got a funny feeling about it. As if there's something going on.'

'He works for Geoff, you know,' said Vanessa. 'He may be doing it to be spiteful. For one thing, Melanie, you're a vital part of the operation.'

Annie said, 'Can't we just get some time? Why don't you ring your mother and tell her you'll come next week—'

'He's coming for me tomorrow.'

'Well, if your mother says next week that's what it'll be. I'll talk to him.'

'*I'll* talk to him,' said Tom unexpectedly. 'I'd like to try and find out what he's up to.'

Melanie went back to the phone.

In the meanwhile the quietened twins were playing on the table-top with the duck, toy car, two spoons and a sugar shaker. Mercifully, they seemed content.

'If they're really Sim's children,' Tom said, 'Lady Mary's the best person to look after them. Anyway, she must be told. They all must. They're the best indication that Sim's still about.'

Melanie came back. 'Mum's given me a week,' she announced.

'That gives us a chance to work something out,' Vanessa said, relieved.

'I caught that woman who brought them,' continued Melanie. 'She said her sister married their dad in Barbados.'

'What?' Annie cried. 'Where is he now?'

'She didn't know. She was angry about it. She said she'd had two postcards but I don't know where from. I thought she was going to hit me.'

'Where's she gone now?'

'She dashed off when my dad caught hold of me.'

'How can we find out where she is?' Annie said.

'Sounds as if she's on her way to Portugal,' Vanessa said. 'There is one person who might help us, and that's Ben. I'll ring him.' Still holding the little boy she phoned the *Kenton Post*. Upset, the little boy began to cry and his sister joined in. 'Ask him to contact me urgently,' Vanessa said above the noise.

'I do think we should ring Lady Mary,' said Tom.

'Not now,' Annie said emphatically. 'We don't want to raise her hopes. Second,' and she pointed at the crying boy, 'This situation is more complicated than we think. If Sim's dead, this is the missing heir. We need to think carefully.'

'Good God, he is, isn't he?' Tom said, startled.

'If this is true, you've got nothing to cry about,' said Vanessa sternly to the boy.

'All he wants at the moment is his parents or his auntie and gran,' Melanie said.

Annie wondered, 'Perhaps I should just tell Jasmine about them.'

'I can't think at all, with all this noise,' Tom said. Vanessa gave him a shrewd glare. Somehow, she guessed, under cover of the confusion, he would creep back into Annie's affections.

'And we're all tired,' Annie added. 'And there's Melanie. We must think about it calmly.'

They agreed that this was so.

'It's got to be against the law. Poor little things. What was that girl thinking of, leaving them here?' Vanessa said.

'She felt like a holiday. You can understand it,' Annie said, against the noise.

'They're black,' said Vanessa hesitantly. 'Will the Fellowses mind, if it's true?'

'They're not that black,' Melanie said.

'If it's true they'll find a specialist to turn them white – privately,' Tom said. 'And if it's true, I'll kill Sim,' he went on, clutching Miranda, who was now sobbing quietly. 'Why did he leave them? And what was their mother playing at? Where the fuck is she?'

They sat while the twins cried despondently and fell miserably asleep in their bewildered hosts' arms in the snack bar. No one quite knew what to do.

22

The Savernake Vote

Ben had not gone to the *Kenton Post* that morning, for that was the day he'd told his wife it was over. Frances had been on holiday since her school broke up at the end of July. 'Do you expect to be making arrangements for any kind of a holiday?' she enquired over their late breakfast. 'If we don't go soon my break will be over. The term'll start and I'll have had no holiday at all.'

'It's this Savernake story,' he told her. 'I've got to keep following it. I've got as good as a commission from the *Observer* to do a two-page feature, anatomy of a property deal, involving council property going into private hands, that sort of thing. I can't go anywhere now.'

Frances, up, dressed, lightly made up, and after three weeks at home spent attempting to mend the marriage, spoke out loud the thought she'd had so often while cleaning, putting flowers in vases, cooking the careful meals Ben so often didn't turn up to eat. She said, 'You've had your holiday, of course. You got to Portugal, didn't you?' And in Portugal Ben had met Vanessa. Ben looked at his plate. A silence fell during which his son, Martin, stopped eating and stared at his parents from his highchair.

Frances waited. Ben said, 'I know you're angry, Frances. I can feel it all the time.'

'I don't know what else you'd expect me to be in the circumstances,' she replied, regretting having spoken. She added quickly, 'All right. Forget the holiday. I can see you're busy. Anyway, Martin is going to Gerrards Cross to stay with my parents for a fortnight. I thought it would be a chance for us to get away together. But if you can't, you can't.'

'You could go down . . .'

But this was not what Frances wanted, not what she and her mother had planned. 'A second honeymoon,' her mother had prescribed, 'free of the child.' She now thought a second honeymoon at home was the best she could do. Rapidly deciding to get theatre tickets, book at least a weekend at a country hotel for herself and Ben, she said, 'No. Martin can go. I'll stay.' But this was not what Ben wanted. He wanted to spend no time alone with Frances. Only the presence of Martin cut the tension he felt at home and made staying seem worthwhile. 'Perhaps we can get a weekend away,' Frances continued, as it seemed to him, remorselessly. 'And at least you'll get some peace when you get home, while you're so busy.'

'Peace is the last thing I'll get.' Ben spoke as people do when they must, his eyes on the table. Frances stared at him across the checked cloth, flowered plates and cups, wedding presents. Another woman might have said, 'Oh, so you get no peace here? You're still thinking of her, aren't you?' might have called him a bastard, sobbed or dashed out of the room. But Frances knew if she said or did anything at all he would respond with words she didn't want to hear. She sat perfectly still. He looked up and met her eyes. 'It's not working, is it Frances?'

'What do you mean?'

'Look at me. I was drunk last night – and the night before. You must realise I go to the pub instead of coming home. You know how often you replace the vodka at Sainsbury's. I'm fucked up, Frances, and you don't say anything. We don't talk about it, do we?'

'I don't want to talk about it, Ben,' she said. 'It's always words with you, isn't it? I'm not a talker, I'm a doer.'

'I know.'

'I had a lot to put up with from you, Ben, one way or another – your job, irregular hours, too many phone calls, low pay, you're at home in the day, you get wound up about things that have nothing to do with us, stories you're on. I asked you to get another job . . .'

'I know all that,' he said. 'What you're not saying is that you got thoroughly fed up with me. I wasn't meeting your expectations, your family hoped you'd do better for yourself than marrying a local reporter and you began to see it like that too. You had to go back to work after Martin was born – so you kicked me out. That's right, isn't it, Frances?'

'I just wanted time to think.'

'You asked me to go,' he persisted.

'Oh, do we have to go on like this in front of the child?' she exclaimed.

'He's not listening,' said Ben.

'How can you tell what a child's listening to? They hear more than you think.'

Ben fell silent. He didn't want to hurt his child. He didn't want to hurt Frances. 'It's not working,' he repeated.

'You won't let it. Why can't you just relax—'

'I've tried. I just feel like a zombie.'

'Feel, feel, that's all you do. What *you* feel. What do you think I feel? Do you ever stop to think about that?'

'I've tried. But you don't tell me.'

'You're sentimental, Ben. Marriage isn't meant to be a bed of roses. All couples have their sticky patches—'

'You think this is just a sticky patch?'

'Yes, that's what I do think. I love you. I'm trying to make this marriage work. It's one-sided.'

'You say you love me?'

'Of course.'

'I'm putting him in the living room,' Ben said, pulling Martin from his highchair. 'I'll leave the door open.'

'Why are you going on like this now?' Frances said in a high voice.

'I won't then. I'll go to work. I'm late, anyway. But I don't want Martin to go to Gerrards Cross.'

'He needs some fresh air,' she said. 'Why shouldn't he go to my parents?'

'Because I don't want him to,' he said roughly.

She bit her lip, knowing all this was about his not wanting to be alone with her, and said, 'All right. I'll ring up and say it's off.' She added, 'I don't know how I'm going to explain the change of plan.'

Ben opened the front door. 'I'll be late tonight. It's the Savernake vote.'

She said despairingly, 'You won't be in. You stop Martin going to my parents, and you won't be here to see him.'

'Frances,' he said. 'You won't talk. You learned not to as a child. Don't talk, don't above all ask any questions. That way you won't have to hear any answers.'

'Please don't stand on the doorstep saying these things,' she pleaded.

'I'll come in then,' Ben said, coming back into the hall, putting down his briefcase. 'It isn't working—'

'Please shut the front door,' she said quickly.

'There are too many people in this,' he said, shutting the door, then leaning against it. 'There's us. There's your mother and father, and then there are the neighbours. For years I've felt as if I was on trial in front of a vast jury. You, your family, the neighbours, the editor of the *Kenton Post*, the whole bloody lot of you. Then the jury went out, they brought in a guilty verdict: Ben Gathercole, unsatisfactory husband and poor wage-earner; sentence: kick him out. Suddenly there's an appeal, and for some reason the old verdict's overturned. Why? Because I met somebody else. Don't deny it, that was what happened. Suddenly it's "Come back, Gathercole". So I come back, but now I don't have to feel so guilty about being a wash-out. I'm allowed to feel guilty about Vanessa, instead. I just don't get it. I just don't.' He sat down on the hall floor beside his briefcase with his head in his hands. Martin ran up the hall and put his arms round him. 'Fell down,' he said. 'Never mind, Daddy.' Ben sobbed.

Frances walked into the kitchen and stared out at the garden, thinking it needed a good hosing, but there was a ban on hosepipes. She stood by the window, heard her husband go upstairs. She knew he was packing a case. She stared down the garden. She hoped he was taking what he wanted because the minute he was out of the house she'd get the locks changed. Then she'd go to her parents with Martin. She'd never speak to him again. She'd make sure he never saw Martin again, either.

By the time Ben got to the office at lunchtime he was drained. There were messages from Les Dowell, South East Television and Vanessa. He ignored the first two and went straight to the snack bar. He felt guilty. He'd ended his marriage. Vanessa was the superficial, if not the root, cause. He felt guilty about his son – he could try to get custody, but what judge would agree that, just because a mother was going to bring up her child in the same emotional desert she herself had been reared in, the boy should be handed over to the father, worse than that, a father who was a journalist while the mother was a primary school teacher? He didn't stand a chance.

The confusion at George's at least gave him something else to think about, though his brain was muddy.

Vanessa went straight up to him and asked, 'What's the matter?'

'Everything,' he muttered. 'Will you take me back, Van?'

'All right,' she said in a low voice, 'but don't you never do that, leave me, again.'

'Think I would?' he answered. Then, looking round carefully, he asked, 'So what's the trouble?'

Tom was changing Miranda's nappy. Joseph was asleep in the buggy. Annie was wiping smears from the table. Yet another customer came to the door, looked at the 'Closed' notice and mouthed an enquiry. Melanie had gone next door to the Arcadia to wash the lettuces and make chocolate mousse and spaghetti sauce. At that moment Joanne arrived, holding Alec's hand.

'What are you two doing?' gasped Vanessa.

'The minder hit Alec,' reported Joanne looking guilty. 'So when she went to the toilet we came here by ourselves.

'Oh, my God! I'll murder that woman! You've crossed three roads to get here.'

'A copper held up the traffic,' Joanne said. 'Why are you closed? You've got babies in here. You're always saying you can't have children in here.'

'It's getting like a crèche,' Tom said. 'Look, Ben, can you help?'

Tom outlined the situation concerning the twins and said, 'I don't think anyone wants to decide what to do about them until we've contacted the Joneses to see what's going on.'

Ben rang a friendly policeman who owed him a favour. The policeman searched the computer for the Joneses. Ben relayed the facts aloud as he was given them – 'Miss Arlette, Miss Josephine and Mrs Elaine Jones, no Mr Jones on the premises, no Simon Fellows. It's twenty-one Rodwell House, on the Savernake Estate. Arlette works at the post office. Mrs Jones works at a bakery. Nothing on Josephine. Any kids there? You wouldn't know, unless they've done anything, even on that estate one-year-olds are usually innocent. One more thing,' he asked, 'how do you find out if anyone got married in Barbados? Thanks, mate. I owe you one.'

He put the phone down and said, 'We've got to ring Barbados if we want to check the marriage story.'

'Let's do it,' Annie said.

'What's the time there?'

Annie put her head outside the door. 'What's the time in Barbados?' she asked Roland on the cassette stall. He looked at his watch. 'Middle of the morning,' he called back.

Annie came in. 'I'll start phoning,' she said. 'I'll phone the vicar of that church. Ben, can you get down to the Savernake Estate and check around?'

'I'm going there to get a story about how people voted anyway, what they think. I'll give you a ring when I find out. Don't give this story to anyone else,' he added.

'All right, Ben,' Annie said.

'Coming, Van?' he asked.

'We've got to get on with the suppers,' Vanessa said. 'We've got bookings galore. We're right behind. We're going to have to run from now to when we open. Someone's going to have to look after the kids—'

'I'll take them back to Rutherford Street,' Tom volunteered. Ben and Tom left together with all four children.

'He's good with kids,' Vanessa said doubtfully as the door closed behind them. 'Really fond of them. Seems a pity he won't have any of his own. Or . . .' she looked even more doubtfully at Annie.

Annie ignored the implied question, saying briskly, 'All we can do is sneak out of here, lock up, have a quiet cup of tea at the Arcadia, and then start rushing. Melanie can do the menus now her writing's improved. I'll ring Barbados between bouts of cooking.'

'Right,' Vanessa said, getting to her feet.

Although they managed, the diners were pleased, the bills were big and the till rang gaily, Annie and Vanessa did not enjoy the evening and Melanie was so depressed by the thought of her father's arrival next day that Vanessa said she should stay in the kitchen because her face was upsetting the customers. There was no time to talk, only to provide money for Melanie to go to the cinema with a friend. 'Not a disco,' Annie warned.

'No,' declared Melanie untruthfully.

Annie went to get a bottle of Bollinger from the larder and shook her head in disbelief at the patent lie. Then she heard voices at the entrance and felt Vanessa stiffen like a dog. She was standing with a big metal spoon over a saucepan, plate in one hand, sauce dripping from the holes in the spoon, 'That's Geoff,' she hissed.

Annie took the champagne to the party in the corner and saw, standing near the door, Geoff Doyle, Sam Abbott and a short blonde girl in a tight dress with pearl combs in an elaborately tousled blonde hair-do. 'What do you want?' she asked them.

'One of those,' Geoff Doyle said, pointing to the champagne. 'We're celebrating.'

'Couldn't you go somewhere else?' Annie asked.

'No, no way,' Geoff said expansively. 'We want to be here. With all of you. Enjoying ourselves.' The blonde girl looked at him possessively. Abbott looked uncomfortable. Edward, always knowing, put his head in, and gave an enquiring look. Geoff Doyle retaliated by looking angry.

'Sit down,' Annie said quickly. 'I'll get you a menu.' She went to tell Vanessa what was happening. On the whole she thought it might be better to put up with the party, since Geoff looked belligerent. But if Vanessa wanted the party to leave Edward would have to eject them, even if it meant a row in the restaurant.

However, when Annie went into the kitchen Vanessa had already seen the party. 'Take their order,' she said grimly. 'We'll take their money.'

'Is the girl Cindy?'

Vanessa nodded. 'Champagne on the house,' she said. 'Act generous – let them worry I'm putting something in the food.'

'You're not going to . . . ?'

Vanessa shook her head. Annie handed round the menus and began to uncork the champagne. 'It's on the house,' she said.

'On the house?' Sam Abbott said doubtfully.

'Yes,' Annie said. She poured the champagne, smiled, said, 'I'll come back for your order,' and departed, confident that the party was, as Vanessa had predicted, a little worried by all this generosity.

'Well, to success,' she heard Geoff Doyle say as she left the table.

'The voters of the Savernake Estate,' said Abbott, lifting his glass.

Vanessa had been listening. 'This means they've won the vote,' she declared. 'I suppose Abbott's fixed Geoff a nice little contract so he can keep Cindy in silk knickers.' She took two plates of profiteroles to a couple in the corner of the restaurant, ignoring the table in the middle.

'We're going to be rich, rich, rich, aren't we, Geoff?' said Cindy in a clear, childish voice.

Vanessa put down the plates, spoke pleasantly to the customer who had spoken to her, and returned to the kitchen with dignity. 'Rich, rich, rich,' she mimicked to Annie in an undertone.

Annie, closing the dishwasher, said, 'You're all right, aren't you, Vanessa?'

'I'm not frightened of Geoff Doyle any more,' Vanessa said.

233

'I know what he is, and it's no good. He's a bully. I just realised when he came in. I don't have to live with him any more. He doesn't pay my bills. And if he misbehaves Edward can deal with him.' She added, 'And do you know what? I think he's celebrating too soon. I can feel it in my bones. Anyway, Joanne, Alec and me are well rid of him and all his works.'

Annie went back to the table to take their order.

'About time,' said Cindy. 'I'm starving.'

Annie, pad in hand, stood waiting.

'Well, darling, what's it to be?' said Geoff.

While Cindy thought, Geoff lifted his head from the menu and said, 'The vote going our way is a nice bit of news for Mr Vane, too.'

Annie had to pretend she knew of Julian's involvement with Savernake Developments. She didn't succeed. She said, 'Then I hope he'll be able to repay the money he owes me,' and wished she hadn't spoken.

'I wouldn't count on it if I was you. That's a very expensive lady he's got in tow,' Geoff said. 'Let's see – I'll take the duck pâté, so will the lady – Sam?'

It was plain that Abbott was now feeling uncomfortable. He was not naturally spiteful, and, with Savernake Village going ahead he might want to renew his offer for the Arcadia. He said hastily, 'I'll have the same. And a bottle of wine.'

Geoff suggested one, Cindy another, Annie let them flounder. 'Shall I just take your order to the kitchen and come back?' she asked. 'Give you a moment to decide.'

'Can't tell the difference between port and whisky, Geoff Doyle,' observed Vanessa. 'It's all put on. Mind you, whatever you bring, he'll send it back.'

They called them SIBs, send-it-backs, men who compulsively returned the wine saying it was the wrong year, or corked, or too cold, too warm or not cold or warm enough.

Geoff sent the wine back, twice, and told Abbott a dubious joke while Annie waited for the order for their main course. Hearing this, Vanessa made a point of taking their order for dessert, something in her neutral gaze preventing the curvaceous Cindy from ordering any and Geoff Doyle from looking at her at all. Nevertheless, they laughed a lot and toasted each other merrily. Cindy mentioned Portugal and the Bahamas loudly and talked about a new car, a Mercedes. Geoff suggested brandies, but Abbott had had enough. When he'd finished eating he announced that he was going home. Geoff and Cindy seeming unprepared to sit alone at the Arcadia, the party broke up.

'Is service included?' Geoff asked Annie as he let fall from a leather pouch a long roll of credit cards, as if asking her to admire a card trick.

'No,' Annie told him, bending respectfully to hand him the bill.

'Well, what's it worth then?' Geoff asked Cindy.

Cindy pouted. 'I don't know.'

'Entirely up to you, sir,' Annie said.

In the kitchen the phone rang. It was the vicar of Bridgetown confirming the marriage of Simon Fellows and Josephine Jones a year and a half before, and the christening of twins a few months later. Annie thanked the vicar and apologised to Geoff and Cindy for keeping them waiting when she returned. Looking at Geoff she wondered, as she took his credit card, whether the discovery of Sim's heir would make a difference to the Savernake Village project. What if it led to the discovery of Sim? Sim would be able to cancel the project if he wanted to. Could it be, she wondered, that Vanessa's instinct was right, that Geoff Doyle's celebration was premature, that he – and Julian, for that matter – might be in for a disappointment?

Her parting smile alarmed Cindy. 'I'm sure they put something in the food,' she whispered when they were outside.

'Nonsense,' said her father. 'They wouldn't risk it.'

'Well, I didn't like her face when we left,' Cindy persisted.

'Shut up, Cindy,' Geoff said, leading the way to the car. He hadn't had as much joy out of the evening as he'd hoped for, and though he didn't believe he'd been poisoned, or even given an overdose of laxative at the Arcadia, he felt indigestion coming on.

Vanessa and Annie shook hands briefly as they swept up. 'He didn't enjoy it as much as he thought he would,' Vanessa said, grinning.

A knock on the door after the last customer had left and they had carefully locked up was Ben's.

'What a day,' groaned Vanessa wiping down the kitchen counter.

'Still, Geoff looked sick when he left,' Edward volunteered from the doorway. 'D'you put something in his food, then?'

Ben nursed a brandy. 'I can't see any problems for him or anyone else associated with the project,' he said gloomily. 'Joe Banks got that vote through pretty cleverly. First they stop the owners of flats and houses on the estate from voting at all. Then they hold the ballot in mid-August, when the biggest number of people – tenants entitled to vote – are on holiday, and, since anyone who doesn't vote against the project is counted as having voted for it, there you are. About two hundred people own their houses or flats, so they aren't eligible to vote. Another two hundred are away for one reason or another – holidays, doing seasonal work away from home – and people who never vote for anything didn't vote this time either. And that's how the Savernake Estate's gone to the developers. Only about fifteen per cent of the people actually voted to accept the bid. All the rest voted against or didn't vote at all. It's incredible, but it happened. It's the law.'

'Can't be,' Annie said, horrified.

'It is. There'll be an appeal to the Department of the Environment, but as they've already overruled the council, taking no notice of the adverse report and insisting on the vote, how much chance does the appeal stand? The people on the estate are going to have to go.'

'So if Sim's dead his child Joseph is part-owner of Savernake Developments, which means he's evicting his own aunt and grand-mother,' Annie said as she swept the floor.

Ben nodded and ran on obsessively, 'Les Dowell's mad now. He's going to start trouble, marches, representations. The whole council's furious. What are the residents on the other estates going to think about this? Did you know almost a third of Kenton's on council property. There could be real trouble.'

Vanessa, putting glasses back on to shelves, said, 'What do you mean – riots?'

'Could be.'

'Oh, Christ,' Vanessa said. 'Well, that's the end of the Arcadia. No one would come here again.'

'Well, it hasn't happened yet,' said Annie.

When Annie got in she found Tom asleep in an armchair. He woke and said, tiredly, 'I've put them on a mattress in your room. They're asleep at last. They're very healthy, active children and they keep each other awake. I feel more sympathy now with that woman, Arlette, and her mother. I don't know how they managed. No wonder she was frantic.'

'The Savernake Estate's voted to sell itself off,' Annie reported. 'But the vote was rigged.'

'Nigel will be laughing,' Tom said.

'I don't know,' said Annie. 'The vicar rang from Barbados. It

236

looks very much as if the twins are Sim's legal children. It's been an odd evening.' She described Geoff Doyle's visit to the restaurant.

'My God,' said Tom. 'But it's been eventful here in its own way, I can tell you.' He yawned. 'We've got to try and find Arlette, but whatever happens, let me tell you, the twins'll have to go to Durham House. They're nice children, very happy, very energetic – but they need full-time care.'

'What if they reject them at Durham House?' Annie asked.

'Don't even think about it,' Tom told her. 'Look – like it or not, Annie, I'm going to have to sleep with you tonight. You won't want to be alone if they start waking up.'

They went upstairs. 'Don't forget Pickering's coming tomorrow,' Annie warned.

'I'll deal with him,' Tom said tiredly.

'I don't know about sleeping with you,' she yawned as they went into the bedroom. Studying the twins, on their mattress in red and blue pyjamas, she changed her mind. They looked alert and active, even in their sleep. 'All right,' she said.

'I thought you'd see it like that,' he told her. In bed he muttered, 'About John Woodford – he was upset, well, in fact, he was crying. He only wanted – just once,' he said, 'I had no choice. Can you understand?' He looked at her, but Annie was asleep.

23

A Country Fête

Two huge red-and-white-striped tents stood on the lawn at Durham House, one for teas, the other for the flower and vegetable show. A smaller tent housed a fortune teller and there were booths for clay pigeon shooting, a coconut shy, a merry-go-round for small children, a candy floss stall, a hamburger stand, cake and homemade jam and bring-and-buy stalls. The sun shone. Jasmine, wearing a pink and white cotton dress and a straw hat, stood beside the organiser on a small platform with bunting tacked round the bottom. Having nervously thanked everyone, in a small voice, for coming, warned the mothers of small children not to let them go near the lake and hoped everyone would enjoy themselves and spend freely for such a good cause Jasmine declared the fête open. Nigel, at the front of the small crowd, cried, 'Hear, Hear,' and led the thin clapping.

Jasmine and Nigel wandered off to buy a cake and a bottle of wine from old Mrs James – aged eighty-three and still running the annual fête cake stall – and walk about a bit before returning to hide in the house. Jasmine stopped to talk to Mrs James, then to Nigel, 'Can you believe it? Mrs James has a vine in her greenhouse from which she regularly gets enough grapes for three bottles of wine a year.'

'I say,' Nigel said. 'Why don't we buy one?'

'I keeps those for myself,' said the old woman firmly. 'You can choose between elderberry, gooseberry and plum.'

There were shrieks from the children on the merry-go-round, the hum of voices from the tables outside the tea-tent, the crack of the rifle range, the thud of the coconut shy.

Inside the big tent, where flowers and vegetables, cakes and preserves, labelled with the producers' names, lay on trestles, local experts cast brooding eyes over roses, cauliflowers, sponges, quinces and jars of jam. The tent was hot, and smelt of vegetation.

Jasmine fled from the humid marquee and bumped into Al Dominick and Claudia Fellows.

'There used to be a band,' remarked Claudia.

'That was a long time ago,' Jasmine replied.

The local MP, Arthur Fairclough, came up. His wife, in a flowered hat, said to Jasmine, 'So sad about Sir Bernard.'

She responded, 'Thank you for your kind letter.'

Music of the thirties, the tango, 'Tea for two', 'Summer time', came from amplifiers mounted on the back of a truck. A small boy with a balloon bumped into her. Jasmine felt detached, as if she really wasn't there. Mrs Fairclough said, 'I do hope you'll come to dinner with us before the House goes back into session. After that I never know where Arthur's going to be, or when.'

Sam Anstruther was at the rifle range, holding a rifle and demonstrating to Al how to compensate for the pull of the tricky barrel and still hit the target. 'I can't see what I'd do with a giant panda if I won it,' Al was saying. 'Have you got any use for a giant panda? Well,' he said looking round, slightly depressed, 'this is certainly typical.'

'I'll tell you why I'm here,' Anstruther confided to his compatriot. 'I'm here because I cannot in any way get hold of Mr and Mrs Browning, the parents of Jasmine Fellows. Now, they have—'

'I know. I heard about the suitcase—'

'What use can it be to them?' Anstruther appealed. 'Lodged at the rear of a damp closet, probably being eaten by mice? The papers in that case could make a contribution to scholarship, but they won't let anyone see them. They're hanging in there – can you explain that to me?' He shook his head. 'It does not make sense.'

'Guess not,' Al said. 'Well, maybe it makes sense to them.'

'Maybe,' Sam Anstruther said.

'Do you know they're definitely coming?' Al asked.

'Jasmine said they were but who knows?' replied Sam Anstruther.

Al Dominick shook his head. 'Better you than me, friend,' he said sympathetically.

Inside the house Lady Mary sat on an old chair in her sun-filled room, hearing the music and the sound of voices. Her thin hands in her lap, she thought about Sir Bernard. When her sister brought her in a cup of tea, she said, 'I didn't like Bernard.'

Lady Margaret put her finger to her lips and said 'Shh, darling. Of course you didn't. Many of us didn't. But you mustn't go about saying so.'

'I'm not going about, Margaret,' her sister said. 'I'm here, with you.'

'Oh, that's all right,' Margaret said. 'I thought you'd gone potty for a moment. Would you like some cake?'

'Is it old Mrs James's?'

'No. Mrs Bleasdale's,' replied Margaret.

'In that case, I think I will,' said Lady Mary. 'Such a relief not to have to open that fête and buy one of those boring cakes.'

Lady Margaret again laid her finger to her lips and said, 'Shh, Mary. You mustn't start saying these things. People might start calling you eccentric, or say it's shock, but others will just call you mad. You don't want that, do you? Of course, it's time to begin to think what you *do* want.'

'I shall have to come to terms with my memory of Bernard first,' Lady Mary announced clearly.

'Well, quite,' her sister said.

'And someone had better find out what's happened to Sim,' Mary said.

'They're doing all they can.'

'You don't need to talk to me in that soothing voice, Moggins, not any more,' Lady Mary said. 'I clearly see Sim has not been found, that Bernard died in ambiguous circumstances and Nigel is on the verge of a breakdown. None of this is very satisfactory, to put it mildly. In idle moments I wonder exactly how and where I went wrong . . .'

'Mary,' interrupted her sister reproachfully. 'You mustn't—'

'In idle moments, I said,' Lady Mary continued staunchly. 'But here we are with the family in a bad spin no one seems capable of correcting, and somehow it has to be stopped.'

'But how?' asked her sister.

The amplifiers which had been playing 'Temptation' cut off and a voice began to announce the results of the fruit and vegetable show. At the side of Durham House Juliet Browning in a cotton dress, sandals and an old straw hat, came through the kitchen door and spoke to an irritable Mrs Bleasdale who was handing a bucket of water for the tea urn to the lady from the WI.

'She's not to be disturbed,' the housekeeper said crossly.

'I've got to see Lady Mary, Mrs Bleasdale,' Juliet said firmly. 'It's very important.'

'You can deal with Lady Margaret then,' said Mrs Bleasdale, turning her back.

Juliet went through the cool corridor connecting the kitchen to the rest of the house and up the beautiful curved sweep of stairs to the first landing. Beside a portrait of an old man in a long Tudor robe, holding a book, she knocked loudly on a thick door and opened it slowly. 'Mary,' she called. 'It's Juliet. I'm sorry to disturb you.'

'Please come in,' said Lady Mary. 'I've been telling Margaret I feel ready to be disturbed now. Or disturbing. Do sit down.'

Juliet sat and took Lady Mary's hand. 'There's some rather strange news for you,' she said. 'Not bad news, though.'

'I hope not,' said Lady Margaret levelly. She remained standing and did not offer to leave.

'It's hard to know where to start,' began Juliet. She drew a deep breath. 'Annie and her friend Vanessa and Tom Pointon arrived this morning with two small children, twins, a boy and a girl of about one. They'd been dumped on them at their café by a young woman who said she was their aunt. She said she and her mother had been looking after them but now they wanted to go on holiday. They'd be back to claim them later. Then she disappeared.' Juliet took a deep breath. 'Look, Mary – Annie's found out where they live, and even what travel agents they used, but they can't get any more details. In the meantime they have the twins and it looks very much as if what the girl told them about these children is true.' She paused. 'It may shock you,' she said.

Lady Mary said, 'Go on.'

'She said they were the children of her sister and Sim,' Juliet said, studying Lady Mary's face. 'Sim and the twins' mother, Josephine, were married in Barbados over a year ago. Before she disappeared, the woman said that she didn't know where the children's parents were. She hadn't seen them for nine months.'

'My God!' said Lady Margaret.

Lady Mary's response was simple, 'Are you sure they're Sim's children?'

Juliet said, 'They've checked the church in Barbados. There was a wedding, also a christening.' She added, 'The mother is black, born in London.'

'My God!' Lady Margaret said again.

'Annie simply didn't know what to do,' Juliet told Lady Mary. 'We all agreed that whether the story's true or not we couldn't keep it from you any longer.'

'It's some hope, at last,' Lady Mary said in a low voice. She closed her eyes. 'It may mean he isn't dead . . . Where are the children?' she said, suddenly alert.

'At Froggett's,' Juliet said. 'They brought them down in the van.'

'Does Nigel know?' asked Lady Mary.

Juliet looked at her cautiously. She shook her head. 'I thought I'd tell you first.'

'I'll phone Jessop,' said Lady Margaret, referring to her husband.

'I'd like to see them,' Lady Mary said. 'We must find this young woman, the aunt. She may have some clue about where Sim and his wife went.'

'I'll phone Jessop,' Lady Margaret announced again and went to the telephone. Lady Mary got to her feet, went over to the dressing table and combed her hair. She said, 'Margaret – you know best but I don't think Jessop is a good idea.' Her sister took no notice. Then Lady Mary took Juliet's arm and they left the room. Together they crossed the grass, and negotiated a path through the crowds of villagers. 'First prize, sponge cake, Mrs Bleasdale of Durham House,' came the voice over the tannoy, 'second prize, Mrs J. Corn, Bassett's Farm.' Sam Anstruther made a lunge at Juliet, who only shook her head. 'Perhaps tomorrow,' she said. Anstruther withdrew, shaking his head in disbelief. Arm in arm Juliet and Lady Mary walked past the lake, down the path, went through the gate and up the hill to Froggett's.

Les Dowell was shouting above the voices at a packed meeting in the Savernake Community Hall. 'Friends,' he cried, holding up his arms, 'Friends – let's keep calm. We can get this vote overturned. We can get a new vote—'

'Rubbish,' shouted protesting voices.

'Your advice is not helpful,' cried Mohammed Nasruddin.

'Get up there, Mr Nas,' called a voice.

Mr Nasruddin marched forward and stood on the platform. 'I'm sure I speak for many of us,' he said. The noise began to abate. He went on, 'I'm sure I speak for many of us, when I say, with all respect to Mr Dowell, that we may not be able to fight this any longer. Yesterday tenants received notification from the Town Hall that their applications for new tenancies elsewhere must be in by 1 September. Failure to comply would mean being given low priority on the list. We all know what that means. Late arrivals will get the worst housing possible. They add that all rent arrears will be voided, and that Savernake Developments has raised its relocation offer to households to two thousand five hundred pounds. You ask us to strike, refuse to apply for new tenancies, refuse to move. And we are saying we don't believe in this new vote. We don't believe we'll win and if we stand out against the council and the developers we and our families will be crushed. We came here to see what you had to tell us and, Mr Dowell, with all respect, you have told us nothing new—'

There were sounds of approval. Most of the audience sat glum, listening. Nasruddin went back to his seat. A big, solid man in a T-shirt and jeans stood up. 'They've got us,' he said. 'All right, it's a clever conspiracy, no one's denying that, but you've got to know when you're beaten. You,' he said, pointing a finger at Dowell, 'are trying to persuade us to fight back, but it's not your home and your family on the line. Be honest now, admit it. OK, we can ask for a new vote. We can go to the Town Hall. But don't come here and tell us not to fill those forms in because it's us and not you who'll wind up on bad estates – noisy, broken nights, no repairs, women with prams getting mugged for the housekeeping—'

Les Dowell said, 'Look. All I'm doing is saying we'll fight them, if you stand firm—' but already people were leaving.

Betsey Jones stood up shouting, 'You've got to *try*,' but she wasn't heard. Those who weren't departing to catch up on the housework, go for a drink at the pub or give the children their tea stood in small knots, talking amongst themselves. Betsey Jones looked at Les Dowell. She was furious, 'This is a victory for Joe Banks,' she said angrily. 'And as for the Right Honourable Willie Carlyle MP—'

'Like I said, there's a drink in this one for him, somewhere,' Dowell remarked bitterly. 'Well, I'm not finished yet.'

'We've got to keep trying,' she replied. She knew Les Dowell's disappointment. The people had not risen; as a career fomentor of social discord and revolution he had failed. Then the two elected councillors of the Borough of Kenton got into Betsey Jones's dusty Renault and drove away.

In Rodwell House Mrs Walters got her letter from the council from behind the clock on the mantelpiece and she stared at it. 'Two thousand five hundred pounds in exchange for a lifetime,' she said to plump Mrs Wainwright.

'It's disgusting,' said her friend from the chintz-covered armchair. 'But what can you do? Maybe they'll get this new vote, but even if they do I reckon this estate's doomed. There's too many powerful people involved.'

'That's what I think,' Mrs Walters said. She looked small and frail, Mrs Wainwright thought. She was too old, now, to take the shock of moving so abruptly and under pressure, too.

'Don't suppose we'll be seeing so much of each other in future,' Mrs Walters remarked, still facing the mantelpiece.

'We'll keep in touch,' said Mrs Wainwright to her back, but they both knew that once they were no longer neighbours the bonds of a long friendship would quickly dissolve.

On a mattress at the foot of Juliet's and Howard's four-poster lay the twins side by side. They both wore red dungarees. Dark-haired Joseph, who, awake, had sharp blue eyes, lay on his side, thumb in his mouth. Miranda slept on her back. A friend of Vanessa's had redone her pale brown hair in little plaits all over her head. Lady Mary stood for some time in the darkened room, looking down at the babies who might be her own grandchildren, noting the long skull characteristic of many members of her own family, including two of her own three children, Sim and Claudia. Then she left the room and went downstairs. Her face was expressionless as she sat down, saying nothing.

'I suppose the process known as DNA finger-printing could establish definitely if the children are really Sim's?' said Howard.

Lady Mary nodded. She said calmly, 'I believe so. We'll do that. But I think myself the children *are* Sim's.' She paused. 'Will you be wanting to keep them with you, Juliet, or shall I take them?'

'Well, as you have more room, and I'm trying to finish the last painting for my new exhibition . . .' Juliet's reluctance was clear. 'Maybe only until the aunt comes back . . .'

'Quite,' said Lady Mary. 'Good, that's settled then.'

The sound of the back door opening broke the silence that had fallen on the group round the kitchen table. Nigel came in, Jasmine close behind him.

'What's going on?' he asked. 'Margaret tells me some children purporting to be Sim's are here. Jessop's galloping south. She's summoned the solicitor – Hugh Brown will be here by dinnertime.

What on earth's happening?' Large and demanding in his pale suit, Nigel stood in the long kitchen at Froggett's, the setting for years of plain living and artistic endeavour, looking as if he had landed accidentally and unwillingly in a slum. He gave the impression his lungs needed all the oxygen in the room and that he was prepared to breathe it.

Worn out with coping with the twins, who had woken twice the night before and been sick in the van on the journey, Annie realised she was not prepared to be bullied by Nigel Fellows. She quickly outlined the story of the twins' arrival. Nigel became more irritable as the story went on.

'Why weren't we told all this earlier?' he demanded.

'It's only just happened,' said his mother. 'You weren't about at the time and my impulse was to come straight here and see them.'

'I gather they're black,' Nigel said.

'Not particularly,' responded Lady Mary. 'I think you've jumped to the conclusion that they're impostors. But if it's a plot, it's a remarkably clumsy one. In any case, Howard points out that genetic fingerprinting could establish whether or not they're Sim's children. Nigel, I think this might be a way of finding Sim.'

'If they *are* Sim's,' he said.

'I think they very well might be.'

'Mother!' Nigel exclaimed.

Jasmine looked at Annie, despair in her eyes. Annie returned the glance and remembered Jasmine's childless state and her stupid plan to remedy it.

'Perhaps we should be discussing this at home,' said Jasmine.

Belligerently, Nigel said, 'Well, I think I should see them first.'

'I suppose it's about time they got up for tea,' murmured Juliet. 'Jasmine, come and help me.'

Over the sleeping twins Juliet asked, 'Jasmine – are you pregnant?'

'I think so,' Jasmine said. 'But I don't know whose it is.'

Juliet closed her eyes. 'I suppose it doesn't really matter,' she said faintly. They both jumped as Nigel came into the room looking like thunder. He glared down at the sleeping twins who woke up and began to cry. Juliet and Jasmine picked up the children and, with Nigel following, went downstairs.

Tom held out his hands and took the little boy from Juliet. 'Jasmine and I will change their nappies in the kitchen,' he said easily. 'You'd better sort out what's to happen next.'

They stripped the children who escaped and toddled about, cheered by having nothing on. Tom said, 'Honestly, Jas, the look on Nigel's face as you left the room made me think of the little princes in the Tower. What's come over him?'

'Claudia's boyfriend says he's got to mourn his father properly,' reported Jasmine. 'It's a strain on all of us. He's obsessed with this Savernake business – half the board's against him. He thinks he can cope but he can't. And all this just makes him think about Sim. He's mourning him, too, I think, but he won't admit it. Is there any chance of finding him? Are these children really his? This is killing Nigel, you know. You should have heard him, coming over . . .'

'Glad I didn't,' muttered Tom. 'Of course these nippers, especially the boy, really muck up an already complicated situation as far as Bernard's will's concerned.' He gave Jasmine a sharp look. 'You look awful.'

'I love Nigel,' Jasmine said simply.

'I know,' Tom said.

They captured the twins as Nigel reappeared.

'It's all settled,' he said. 'They're coming with us. Soon as they're ready.' He left the room.

Tom stared at Jasmine. She said, 'Don't be silly, Tom, if you're thinking what I think you're thinking. I expect Lady Mary'll telephone Lady Margaret's daughter to borrow their nanny.'

'I hope she's got weapons training,' muttered Tom.

'Don't be stupid,' said Jasmine as they pushed the children into shorts and T-shirts.

'They've called in the family solicitor,' mused Tom. 'And Jessop. That proves it's serious. There's going to be trouble, Jas.'

'Please don't,' pleaded Jasmine. 'I can't bear it. Those poor little babies. I don't suppose their aunt realised what a maelstrom she was plunging them into when she disappeared. She must be found. If only Sim were here.'

24

Savernake Blues

The imposing office of the leader of Kenton Council overlooks, from one set of windows, the four lanes of traffic going up and down Foxwell High Street and from the other, the road south-east and the Edwardian central library. Joe Banks, seated in his leather chair, was having a word with Willie Carlyle, MP for Kenton South. Banks was aware that Carlyle had been offered a consultancy with a subsidiary of Samco for not opposing too vigorously the sale of the Savernake Estate and Carlyle knew he knew.

Carlyle, a small, pale man of fifty, once a teacher, glanced apologetically at Banks. 'There's a lot of pressure on me to take up the matter of this revote with the Department of the Environment. It's pretty worrying. I'd like a briefing from you on it.'

Banks thought. He hadn't known until then that Carlyle's opposite number, the Conservative MP for Kenton North, was pushing for a revote. If they got it and then the vote went to the tenants, Carlyle, a Labour MP, would be in the absurd position of having given less support to them than his Conservative rival. And although Carlyle's reselection depended largely on Joe Banks, it was just possible that if there was enough resentment by others in the local party about his failure to support the Savernake tenants, a campaign to get him deselected might begin. And if that happened they'd both be in trouble, Banks reflected. In fact, he might have to dump Carlyle . . .

Carlyle was saying uneasily, 'I'm with you all the way in believing the borough desperately needs the cash from the sale of Savernake, but with a Conservative supporting the tenants, even though they're not in his part of the borough my position's getting very difficult.'

'Yes, Willie, I know,' said Banks, his eye catching a furious argument between two policemen outside a parked police van and a gesticulating man with long Rasta locks tied in a bunch at the back of his head. 'Tricky for you!'

'Mind you,' he added. 'I don't think you've got a thing to worry about. I have reason to believe there's no way the Department of the Environment is going to allow a revote just because the original vote took place while people were on holiday. Insufficient grounds, that's what they'll say.'

'Well then,' said Carlyle. 'In that case, I can support the tenants, can't I?'

Banks looked shocked. 'I wouldn't go so far as that—'

'You're telling me the appeal will be overturned anyway—'

'That doesn't mean you can rush in—'

'Look here, Banks,' Carlyle said. 'I don't like the sound of this. It isn't going well, is it?'

'I didn't tell you I knew every detail of how it would all happen,' Banks said defensively. 'But I've been right so far, broadly speaking,' he appealed. 'I mean, for goodness sake, they're already moving off the estate, taking the money and going.'

'Good. Glad to hear it,' Willie Carlyle said, but his tone was unenthusiastic. He stood up and held out his hand. 'Well, keep going, Joe. Best of luck.'

Joe Banks shook the hand, but once Carlyle had gone he muttered, 'Bastard.' He suspected Willie Carlyle, a man good at looking after himself, was preparing to renege. It was a bad sign.

Hot though it was in Banks's office, if he opened a window the noise of the traffic would fill it. He'd hardly be able to hear his own phone ring. It rang. The editor of the London *Post* group was on the line. Banks said cordially, 'Ken – what a surprise! What can I do for you?'

'I wondered if you had any comment on this plan at the Savernake Estate for the residents to barricade themselves in when the bulldozers arrive,' Ken Lambert asked.

'I should say this is premature. We're still waiting to see if we appeal to the DoE on a revote,' Banks told him, sweating and concealing his anger. 'I think you're jumping the gun, Ken.'

'That's not my point,' Ken Lambert said. 'Obviously, if the residents of the estate go ahead with banners out of windows, the police called in and so forth, from our point of view we'll have a big story on our hands.'

'I see that,' Banks said. 'But I think you'd be wise to wait and see how this really turns out.'

'So – a comment?' asked Ken.

Banks could barely keep his temper under control. 'Not at this time.'

'Fair enough,' Lambert said. 'Well, take care, Joe . . .'

'And you. Glad to comment at the proper time, of course.'

'Bye for now, then.' Lambert hung up. In his own office, he turned to Ben Gathercole and winked. 'No comment – but he's worried. I don't think he knew about this.'

At the Town Hall Joe Banks leaned back in his chair, fuming. The *Kenton Post* was opposing the Samco plan to buy the estate. There'd been a leader last week deploring the sale of a public park, no matter how great the financial needs of the borough. The selling of the family silver had been mentioned. Savernake Park, the article had declared, was Savernake's family silver – a funny way, Banks thought, to describe eight acres of rusty swings, strewn Coke and lager cans, condoms, crisp packets (some used by glue-sniffing teenagers) and benchloads of alcoholics and homeless people. And the *Post* had dragged in the environment, the ozone layer and the Amazon rain forests. What was worse, Banks mused furiously, this planned tenants' revolt had Les Dowell's name all over it, and his sidekick's, that feminist Betsey Jones. They'd be describing it as a manifestation of grass roots democracy. Grass roots codswallop, Banks muttered aloud.

He rang Sam Abbott in the planning office. He was out. Banks swore. He rang the housing department and was told thirty tenants had opted for other flats and would be moving out. The man who gave him this information was polite but not friendly.

'Have you any information about a plan by some of the tenants to barricade themselves in and resist the bulldozers?' Banks asked him.

The man was interested. 'Is that a fact?' he asked.

'A rumour,' Banks said. 'Probably nothing to it.'

'Probably not,' said the man he was speaking to, but he sounded pleased. Banks silently put his name on the mental blacklist of enemies he kept in his head, a list headed by Les Dowell. Then he rang his contact, Gerald Rafferty, at the Department of the Environment.

That same morning Julian Vane was making a late breakfast for himself and his lover at Tamsin's small house in Islington. He looked from the kitchen window at the flowers in pots on the paved area at the back of the house. He pushed down the plunger in the cafetière and put it on a tray. There were brioches he'd just bought from the French bakery on the corner. As Tamsin did not have to get to the advertising agency for which she worked until two, this morning was like a Sunday, or better, because their Sunday mornings so often involved jumping up and dashing off in the car to visit friends, or jumping up and clearing up because friends were visiting them.

In her chintzy bedroom, where even now Tamsin's old teddy, Uncle Ned, sat on a corner shelf under a vase of dried flowers and grasses, Tamsin lay in bed. Julian put the tray into her hands, stripped off jeans and T-shirt and hopped in beside her in his boxer shorts.

Tamsin poured. 'Though it's never quite the same as breakfast in France,' remarked Julian taking his green cup and saucer. 'Why not? It's one of the great unsolved mysteries.'

'I suppose everything else smells of home,' Tamsin said. 'Listen, Julian, they're really nagging me about holidays. I've got to take some soon. Gilly's hinting I'm trying to look as if I don't want a holiday, just to impress—'

'You know I'm just hanging on for the final go-ahead on the Savernake project.'

'But you can't make any difference,' she said. 'Wouldn't it be better just to go away and relax? You could keep in touch by phone.'

'That's what people always say until they're stuck somewhere with a strike at the telephone exchange or tricky atmospheric conditions. I'm sorry, Tamsin, but I'm slightly anxious about this Savernake affair. We've invested a lot of time and money in it. Ten people worked night and day to get to this point, three are still sitting in an expensive office, drawing their pay, waiting for the starter's gun. I know it's hard on you, but you yourself said if we went before it was all tied up we weren't likely to have a very good time. I was very grateful you saw it like that.'

She smoothed his soft hair as he sat beside her against the padded, corn-coloured bedhead. He slid down a little and looked up at her, the lines on his face relaxing. 'It doesn't matter.' Tamsin smiled. 'Of course we'll wait. Think how wonderful it'll be when everything's signed and we can go away peacefully.'

'Mm,' he muttered.

'If only Bernard Fellows hadn't died,' she sighed. 'He could have kept that Tokyo bank man sweet. Half the uncertainties come from his death.' She paused. 'I do wish the Fellowses would come to dinner.'

Nigel and Jasmine had turned down an invitation on the grounds that the family bereavement was too recent and had avoided fixing a later date to meet. Julian thought privately that Tamsin was ambitious to entertain them more for social than business reasons, but in this he was mistaken. Tamsin did want to entertain the rich and successful, but her sharp nose told her there was something to find out. When it emerged a little later that after Sir Bernard's death Savernake's Japanese backer had withdrawn, and that the board of Samco was sharply divided about increasing its investment in the project, she hastened to remind Julian of the instinct which had led her to want to get Nigel Fellows on her sofa, brandy in hand, for a gentle probing chat. She tactfully did not point out that her uncle had backed Julian's company, expanded chiefly to handle the huge Savernake plan, or that less backing would have been necessary if Julian's wife Annie had not been sitting, still undivorced, in the unsold house at Rutherford Street.

Julian, leaning into her contentedly, could not see Tamsin's hard and thoughtful eyes staring in the direction of the battered Uncle Ned on his special shelf.

A so-called friend at the agency had, as someone always will, drawn her attention to the restaurant column of *Harper's & Queen*, where the Arcadia was described by the food columnist as having a surprisingly excellent cuisine, considering its location in one of London's more *louche* areas. The restaurant was presided over, the writer had suggested archly, by two beauties, one with a PhD in history.

Tamsin had disguised her irritation about the progress of the Arcadia and made sure *Harper's* didn't appear in the house, but the article disquieted her. Julian's account of Annie as mousy, high-minded, studious, and, above all, as otherworldly as Mother Teresa, had satisfied her at first. Now she'd learned to know Julian better, she knew him for a gifted somewhat lazy man, disinclined to trouble and worry. He'd been later to feel any concern about developments in the Savernake project than she had. Annie's and Vanessa's restaurant was evidently thriving and Tamsin began to wonder if Annie's efforts in Julian's firm had not been a lot more useful than he'd ever suggested. It crossed her mind, also, that she, Tamsin, had found herself giving Julian a lot of help, raising money for him, keeping up his spirits, warning him of trouble ahead. She was starting to feel creeping doubts. Julian was talented, she told herself, as she buttered him another piece of brioche and playfully fed it to him. But as his smiling mouth opened, like a child's, her heart sank a little within her. It wasn't only the Savernake Village project she hoped would work out.

On an Algarve beach Geoff Doyle, bikini-clad Cindy lying beside him, counted the minutes until lunchtime when he could go back to the hotel and take the phone call from Sam Abbott he dearly hoped would come. Cindy was a strict holidaymaker, sun, sea and sex were what she'd come for; sun, sea and sex were what she intended to get, and if she didn't get the first two, Geoff didn't get much of the latter, or, if he did, it was not very enjoyable. The eight days of their holiday so far had been punctuated by Cindy's little moans of 'Geoff. Try to relax. That's what we're here for,' 'Geoff – don't start making phone calls now,' 'Geoff – I'm here, remember.' As a result, his nerves weren't improving. He phoned Sam Abbott every day, reluctantly allowed to do so at convenient moments by Cindy, but he couldn't always get through, or Sam couldn't get back to him. Sam, too, had heard about the withdrawal of the Tokyo bank and Samco's reluctance to invest further. In addition he was close to sources in Kenton and what he'd heard about the local protest movements was disturbing. Yesterday Geoff had asked Sam to get from Joe Banks an account of progress, or lack of it, and a view of the future, and it was this call he eagerly awaited. He lay staring at the cloudless blue sky and listening to the buzz of the other holidaymakers, resting under sunshades or, like Cindy, oiled and fully extended under the hot sun. 'Pre-lunch drink?' he enquired.

'Ugh? Oh, Geoff, I was asleep,' she said in reproach.

'Sorry, Cindy,' he said. 'Didn't realise. Still, how about a little aperitivo?'

'You're always rushing back to that hotel,' she said. 'Don't tell me – Dad's due to phone up.'

'Maybe,' he said. 'Well, I'm going back.'

'You can't leave me here,' she said.

'No harm will come,' he assured her, though as he spoke he reconsidered his move since everywhere they went every male over twelve and under seventy was aware of Cindy's blonde beauty.

Aware of his hesitation, she replied, 'Oh, all right, you go. I'll come later,' and stretched out luxuriously.

Geoff wandered up the beach, turning once to see if Cindy was now surrounded by tall tanned men in bathing trunks, commenting on the weather and the beach, inviting her back to the villa but she wasn't. He went on, reached the hotel and waited for Sam Abbott to ring. He'd sensed that Abbott was nervous now and wondered what the price had been for his services via Kenton planning department on behalf of Savernake Developments. He'd used his position before, Geoff thought, otherwise where did the extension, the new car, the patio with built-in barbecue come from?

Geoff ordered a drink and sat down among the potted plants in the lounge. Abbott had told him the *Kenton Post* was writing editorials against the scheme. 'Puts you and your ex-wife on opposite sides of the camp, I suppose,' he'd said. 'You should have a word with her, Geoff. After all, you've still got some rights.'

'Too right,' Geoff had responded stoutly, but he was far from confident that he any longer had influence over Vanessa. He'd learned of the write-up about the Arcadia in *Harper's & Queen* from Cindy who'd read it in her private dentist's waiting room. Although Geoff put the Arcadia's success down to the other woman involved, the snooty bitch Annie, seeing Vanessa's name in print, and described as a beauty, stirred in him some involuntary respect. Geoff hadn't given much thought to Vanessa's future when he walked out. He'd vaguely assumed that she would get Alec into a nursery and go back to work as an audio typist – tough, but that was life – and that somehow, whether he ever decided to return or not, for a time she'd go on sitting there, waiting. She'd never have much money. He'd be able to keep her in line.

Now she had her name in a magazine and a boyfriend who was a newspaper reporter and a stirrer. What's more she still had Joanne and Alec. Meanwhile, here he sat in a hotel he couldn't afford with Cindy moaning half the time and her dad in the pub, probably, not bothering to phone. Geoff Doyle was not a happy man; he ordered a second drink, a large one, and waited.

Two days later, the police raided the Savernake Estate; and two days after that they did it again. The result of the raids was the uncovering of a flat in Savernake House full of stolen washing machines, several residents who were not the legal tenants, a three-year-old child who had been locked in a wardrobe overnight as a punishment and a teenager with half a pound of marijuana on the ground floor of Rodwell House. It was not, in police terms, a good result for a week-long surveillance of an inner city housing estate, followed by two early-morning raids involving twenty policemen. There were upholdable complaints made by three seemingly innocent families who had had doors perfunctorily knocked on, then rapidly kicked in by the police before dawn, one of them being old Mrs Walters. The general view in Kenton was that in order to justify these serious raids the police ought to have found a big drug-dealing operation or a nest of IRA bombers, not just a few stolen washing machines, a child in a wardrobe and a comparatively small amount of marijuana. Mrs Walters was on *South East News*, shaken but shrewdly maintaining what plenty of other people in Kenton thought, that the raid was connected with the appeal to the Department of the Environment to allow a second vote on the future of the estate; if Savernake could have been proved to be a nest of villains and degenerates then the incentive to clear it and get it into respectable hands would be greater.

Joe Banks caught the local news in his detached house in Leadham Common. His wife was away and his daughter, who had come over to clean up and cook a meal for him, found him with his head buried in his hands. 'What's the matter, Dad?' she said as she put his meal of steak, mushrooms, tomatoes and chips on the table. 'Come on, it'll get cold.'

Banks, reluctant to forfeit her goodwill, poured himself a whisky and took it to the table. His daughter sat down at the other end. 'You're drinking not eating,' she complained.

'Stupid idiots,' he mumbled. 'I told them. Don't let it be said I didn't tell them.'

'What?' she asked, a chip in her fingers.

'Nothing,' returned her father shortly.

The row about the abortive police raid on the Savernake Estate would soon blow over as such things did, but, as such things do, it would leave behind the familiar faint aroma of urban corruption, a compound of money, crime, unattributable orders from on high, unadmittable friendships, and favours given and received.

He'd already had Charles Head, general manager of the Savernake Village project, on the phone, reproaching him in a call Banks suspected was taped. Head blamed him for having originated the notion of a police raid during their first discussions of the project. It was true that at one point Banks had said, 'A good police raid will always shift a few tenants, the ones who oughtn't to be there, anyway, and the ones who won't be, once the law catches up with them. A raid like that usually turns up some villains – it's good PR.'

Later, some instinct had told him a police raid on Savernake would be a bad idea, but by that time the ambitious, striped-shirted Head was pressing him to act. 'Come on, Joe,' he'd said. 'You told me a police raid would have an effect.'

'I expect so,' Banks admitted. 'A raid's bound to flush out a few malefactors. But—'

'What's the harm then?' Head had demanded. 'Even getting a few tenants out would be a plus.'

Banks hesitated. 'It could turn against us.'

'Can you do it?' asked Head. His voice was firm. 'You said a word or two with the Chief Super and it was as good as done.'

'If,' Banks said heavily, 'he considers it wouldn't lead to more trouble.'

'What do you mean?'

'If it's seen as persecution, or being prompted by other considerations—' began Banks.

'Oh, come on, Joe,' reproached Head. 'If there are a load of villains on the housing estate and the coppers arrest a few and put them where they ought to be, and we can put pressure on the situation and get them out for good and all, what's the harm? Society loses a few villains, we get hold of a few flats.'

Against his better judgement, Banks agreed to have a word with the Chief Superintendent. Now he regretted it.

He cut a mushroom on his plate into halves, then quarters. He ate one of the quarters. He'd spoken to the Superintendent, a fellow mason: the two raids had taken place. They'd gained two, possibly three flats. But the press had somehow been keener on Mrs Walters as an elderly widow who'd had her door kicked in before dawn than they'd been about the child discovered in the wardrobe, much as their attention had been drawn to it by the police PRO. Joe's instinct told him that this reluctance by the popular press to focus on the depravity of Savernake residents was a straw in the wind; an indication that times were changing, sympathies altering. Of course the Department of the Environment would deny the appeal for a new vote. Their decision would finally put the estate and the park into the hands of Savernake Developments, bringing seven million much-needed pounds to Kenton's public purse, but this consideration did not cheer Banks as much as it should. Everything was going according to plan, but he still felt uneasy . . . And if it all went wrong he'd lose credibility, might never lead the council again.

At the other end of the table his daughter had finished her meal and said sharply, 'Dad. If you're not going to eat that I'm taking it home for the dog. Now, do you want some apple pie?'

'I'll just have a cup of tea, thanks,' said Joe absent-mindedly.

'We vowed we'd get love, money and revenge,' Vanessa said. She and Ben, Annie and Tom had taken Monday, usually quiet, off, leaving the restaurant in the hands of Abigail, now re-employed since the restaurant was becoming so much more successful. They'd gone out for an expensive West End meal, to check the competition and give Melanie a treat because she had to go home. They were now drinking Armagnac in the bar under potted palms,

'You've got the love,' Tom said boldly, kissing Annie's cheek. Annie gave him a stare, but said nothing.

'And the restaurant's making a profit,' Vanessa said. 'At least, it has for a few weeks. But revenge is thin on the ground. Now, if the Department of the Environment had allowed another vote by the Savernake tenants and the estate sale was blocked, then that would have put Geoff and Julian in trouble. But the Department's gone along with the sale, and Geoff and Julian are going to make a bomb out of it. Still, never mind revenge – who needs it?'

'It's the last cherry on the cake, sometimes,' Ben claimed. 'Come on – let's admit it. Who really feels upset when someone who wronged them falls flat on their face in the mud? It might not be the only thing in life, but it can be fun. There's a child in all of us, who enjoys the school bully turning up on crutches.'

'True,' said Tom.

'And then there's Melanie,' Annie said. 'She's got to go back home tomorrow.' All the faces at the table sobered, except Melanie's.

'I'm not going back,' she stated. They stared. 'I'm not,' she insisted.

Earlier, Melanie had been sitting in the corner beside the kitchen at the Arcadia, looking blankly at her grapefruit. There was only one other table occupied in the restaurant, where a couple were quarrelling in low voices. Edward had sneaked off. Abigail was sorting out the freezer in the kitchen and her partner smoking by the dustbins in the yard. David Pickering, driven off by Tom earlier in the week, had just rung Melanie and told her she had to get the four-twenty to York next day, or else.

'Or else what?' she'd asked.

'Or else the police'll take you back,' he'd told her. 'And after them, you'll have me to deal with. I'm in charge now, not your soft-headed mother – and she needs you at home.'

She still thought Geoff Doyle, his employer, had put him up to all this, as a gesture of spite against Vanessa, but there was nothing she could do. On impulse she jumped up, put her head round the door and spoke to Abigail's back. 'I'm just going out for five minutes.' Abigail didn't hear. Melanie ran past the snack bar and rang Madame Katarina's bell. 'It's Melanie!' she called into the grille on the doorpost. Upstairs she burst out, 'Please, Madame Katarina, tell me if I'm ever going to get back here. What's going to happen to me?'

Madame Katarina took pity on her and sat down at her small table with the fringed cloth. She asked Melanie to shuffle a pack of cards.

'Can't I have tarot?' Melanie pleaded.

'You're too young,' Madame Katarina said severely. Melanie leaned forward as the cards went down.

'Am I coming back?' she asked keenly.

Madame Katarina looked round the circle of playing cards. She studied them again, and shrugged.

'I'm not,' moaned Melanie. 'I'm not, am I?'

'You're not going,' said Madame Katarina.

'I'm on the train tomorrow!' cried Melanie.

'Not according to the cards. Very soon, someone is coming to you. Someone close.'

'I'm not going back?' Melanie asked, excitement mounting.

'No – I don't think so.'

Melanie stood up. 'Thanks, Madame Katarina – got to get back.'

She glared at the astonished faces in the restaurant, saying fiercely, 'I'm not going back! I'm not! Madame Katarina says I'm not!'

And, for a time at least, she didn't.

25

Poor Ruth

Madame Katarina was right. Melanie did not catch the four-twenty train to York because at nine the next morning, after Annie had gone to open the snack bar, Jenny Pickering rang up.

'Melanie, love,' her mother began tentatively.

Melanie began to whine. 'Mum – have I got—?'

Her mother's voice was serious. 'Melanie,' she said heavily. 'Melanie – pay attention. The police have been round. Ruth's been found. She's in St Thomas's Hospital, in London.'

'What's the matter with her?'

'Bad pneumonia. Double pneumonia. She's very ill. She's been sleeping rough.' Melanie knew her mother was suppressing panic. 'I don't know what's been happening to her. Melanie – now listen. Don't get on the train this afternoon. We're coming down this morning. We'll be in London by dinnertime. Does your friend Annie's invitation still stand – we'll need somewhere to stay?'

'Yes, Mum – yes,' said Melanie.

Her mother's voice went on. 'She's safe, thank God. Now – can you meet the train – the one ten, King's Cross. We'll go straight to the hospital. Can you get some little things – flowers and sweets and all that—'

'She's not going to die, is she, Mum?' burst out Melanie. There was a note in her mother's voice which frightened her. Her mother said, 'No – no. I don't think she'll die, Melanie.' Then there was a cry of 'Mum'. Melanie recognised her brother's voice, and Jenny Pickering said hastily, 'We're not packed properly and the cab's due soon. Bye love, see you. One ten. Don't forget.'

Melanie was left staring at the receiver in her hand. She put it back on the cradle, stared at the fireplace and gave a great sob. She ran upstairs, crying, put on her clothes and ran over the road. She rang Vanessa's bell wildly.

'What's the matter?' said Vanessa, opening the door in jeans and a T-shirt, a piece of toast in her hand. She took Melanie in her arms. 'I know it's awful. We aren't half going to miss you—'

Melanie was gasping out, 'Ruth. It's Ruth.'

'Ruth? – What – your sister?' exclaimed Vanessa, stepping back. 'Come in. What's happened?'

Joanne and Alec were now standing in the hall staring. 'Go and finish your breakfast, you two,' ordered Vanessa. 'Here, calm down, Melanie, and tell me.'

Melanie sat at the kitchen table and explained. 'Well,' said Vanessa, 'we'd better ring up the hospital and find out how she is. Then you'd better buzz off and get some flowers and fruit and orange juice and all that.' She got the phone and telephone book.

'Who's in hospital?' asked Joanne, coming in.

'My sister,' said Melanie.

'That why you're crying?'

'Shut up, Joanne,' Vanessa ordered, tapping out the number.

'I don't want to go and see the hospital,' said Alec, who had been to visit his grandfather in hospital a month earlier and been threatened by his grandmother that if he didn't behave they'd leave him behind when they went home.

Melanie spoke to the ward sister, who told her Ruth was a little better. Then there was a pause. The nurse came back to the phone. 'Sister wants to be sure your mother sees her when she comes in. It's important. Please tell her.'

Melanie put the phone down looking worried. 'What's going on?' she wondered.

Vanessa told her it was routine. 'Hop off and get the things she wants,' she advised. 'Got some money? Dinner at the Arcadia tonight. I'm on. I'll do something special. What do they like?'

'Roast turkey and all the trimmings,' Melanie said. She went to the door, turned, and said, 'You never believed Madame Katarina when she said I wasn't going, did you?'

'I never said I didn't,' Vanessa told her. 'That was the others. I'm the uneducated one – I don't have to act sceptical.'

'You're wise,' Melanie told her, and went out.

'Is Ruth the sister who ran away?' enquired Joanne, when Melanie had gone.

'That's right. Now she's ill in hospital. That's a lesson for you,' said her mother.

'I wish you hadn't run away like that,' Melanie told her sister. 'What made you do it? Now look at you.'

Ruth Pickering lay flat in a ward full of women, her round face very pale on the pillow. Melanie sat beside her. The two Pickering boys, Colum and John, sat at the other side of the bed in their best clothes, sobered by the journey and the visit to the hospital.

'You ran away,' Ruth whispered. 'So don't lecture me. You know what Dad's like.'

Melanie was worried by her sister's pallor and evident illness, but more by her eyes, big and brown like her own, but now somehow staring, ever-terrified like an actress in a horror film. Frightened, she asked the face on the pillow, 'What happened to you, Ruth? Was it something bad? Don't you want to talk about it?'

'I can't,' Ruth said, but Melanie didn't know whether it was really impossible for her to tell, or just the presence of Colum and John which prevented her.

'Whatever it was, it wasn't much fun,' Melanie said.

'It seems like an adventure at first, making a big decision and sticking to it, going somewhere big and trying to make it on your own,' Ruth said. She stopped.

'You tired? Do you want us to go away?' Melanie asked.

'No. Just hold my hand,' Ruth said. 'And don't keep on kicking the bed, Col.' Colum stopped. They all sat in silence. Colum's and John's eyes darted round the ward.

'There's Mum,' said John.

Mrs Pickering, at the other end of the ward, was standing with a doctor and the ward sister. The doctor hurried off and the ward sister beside her spoke to her rapidly. She was nodding. A small woman, with lines on her face and the same large dark eyes as Melanie and Ruth, and John also, Jenny Pickering was wearing her good grey suit and high-heeled shoes. She came over with the nurse. They both looked very serious, and Melanie and her brothers recognised instantly a look on their mother's face which meant something very bad was happening, like Grandfather's cancer operation and death or the morning she had told them Ruth was gone and no one knew where she was.

Melanie thought the nurse and doctor had told her mother Ruth was going to die, and burst into tears.

'What's the matter?' asked the sister, but she couldn't explain, not in front of Ruth and her brothers. 'So we'll be seeing you tomorrow morning, Mrs Pickering,' the sister said in a firm voice. Jenny Pickering nodded.

Then they parted from Ruth, who nodded weakly as they spoke to her, and left.

'I'll go back alone tonight to visit her,' announced Melanie's mother as they got into the lift. 'Blow your nose, Melanie. I don't know what's come over you. We've found Ruth. I should have thought you'd be smiling.'

'What did the doctor and nurse tell you?' Melanie asked.

'Not for your ears.'

'I'm her sister—'

'It isn't for you to know.'

In the lift Melanie sniffed and gasped out, 'She's going to die, isn't she?'

'Yes, that's right, Melanie,' her mother said, though with a little humour. 'She's going to die, just like we all are. But not now. She's getting better. I think we'll go to the Tower of London. It's not too far.' But as they made their way there, and walked round inside the great walls of the Tower Jenny Pickering seemed distracted and anxious. Her eyes studied the two ravens on a lawn without really seeing them.

'Can I come and see Ruth with you tonight?' Melanie asked, as they ate hamburgers in a McDonald's before going back to Rutherford Street.

'No,' her mother told her. 'Ruth and me have got to have a private word.' Melanie shrank. There was something very bad going on concerning her sister and she was scared.

Next morning Jenny went straight to Vanessa's house, after her third visit to Ruth. Vanessa had rung Geoff Doyle's office, pretending to be St Thomas's Hospital, and obtained David Pickering's address and phone number. This she gave to Jenny, and it was to Vanessa in Vanessa's kitchen that Jenny unburdened herself.

'They're not telling it all,' she said. 'But Ruth's got to have treatment from a therapist on account of what she's been through. They're saying she was picked up in a squat, very ill, and brought in by ambulance. She'd not been there long and before that she was somewhere else.' Jenny Pickering paused. 'Where that was, I don't know. I've asked her to tell me, but when I do she gets a strange look on her face and won't speak. I daren't press her. The nurses won't tell me. They say she said a lot when she was in a fever, but now she's clammed up. They say it would be wrong to insist – well, I can tell that for myself – but, oh Vanessa, I'm that worried. What can have been happening to her? It's been over eighteen months she's been away from home—'

'If she's been living rough,' suggested Vanessa, 'well, I don't know . . .'

'I know what it must mean,' Jenny said bravely. Her round face looked old for a woman in her thirties. 'How does a young girl live when she's got no job, no money and no home? Men, of course. It has to be. And she's had a good haircut, I can see that.' She shook her head. 'I told them at the hospital – she may have been living rough for a bit, but it's not been long. That life leaves a mark on you and, ill as she is, the signs aren't there. Do you know what I mean? I asked them if she'd been on drugs. They couldn't say definitely, but they didn't think so. Where's she been? What's been happening to her?'

'You might have to be prepared not to know – ever,' Vanessa told her.

'I know,' said Jenny. 'I can bear that, if I have to. But you see, she's not right. She's nowhere near the Ruth I used to know. She's different. She's very quiet. She's like somebody who's had a terrible shock. It's not just the illness.' There was a silence. She said, slowly, 'The hospital wants to see my husband.'

Vanessa said, a little too quickly, 'Of course I don't know, Mrs Pickering. But for the time being, I'd just say I couldn't find him. Mrs Pickering,' she appealed, excusing herself for having made the implicit criticism, 'we know what he's like.'

Jenny Pickering sighed and shook her head sadly. Her face looked even more drawn. 'He was a different man when he had a steady job,' she said.

Vanessa didn't argue. 'It's no good for a man, not having a proper job,' she replied. She changed the subject, saying, 'To think Melanie was on the verge of coming back home and now you're down here instead. Did she tell you about Madame Katarina?'

'I wanted to ask you,' said Jenny, sitting there, tired, in a blue and white cotton suit. 'Do you think she might give me a consultation? How much does she charge?'

Vanessa regarded Jenny Pickering, ten years older than herself

262

and so troubled, and replied carefully, 'She might be able to. But she has lots of appointments.' She thought to herself that she had an inkling, as did Jenny, of the kind of thing that must have happened to Ruth. She knew how hard it would be for the girl to get over the experiences she must have had. If she ever could get over them. She wondered if Madame Katarina would agree to tell Jenny's fortune. It seemed to her that the Pickerings might have no luck at all.

Annie was handing out white cardboard boxes stamped 'George's Café' to two boys and a girl, recruited from Melanie's class at school to do deliveries. 'Go straight there. I've heard you're often late. Don't get chatting. These people want fresh food on time. It's all organised – you're the weak link in the chain—' She broke off, and shouted, 'Arlette!' Arlette Jones, in a pink dress, advanced towards her. Between relief and anger Annie exclaimed, 'Thank God – we've been searching all over the place for you—' The delivery team crept off, glad to miss the rest of the lecture, and it was Arlette's turn to be alarmed.

'What's happened?' she said sharply. 'Are the twins all right?'

'Yes,' Annie told her. 'They're in the country with their grandmother. She wants them to stay. But they're hunting for Sim. Where is he?'

'Don't worry about Sim,' Arlette said forcefully. 'I knew it'd be all like this as soon as the posh side of his family got hold of the twins. It'd be all for them and nothing to do with us. My mother wants the twins back now and so do I. So if there's going to be any trouble . . .'

Annie went to the microwave and got out two pies. She put them on a plate and took them over to a customer. Over her shoulder she asked, 'Do you mean you're afraid you won't get them back?'

'We'll get them back,' Arlette told her. 'Depends how difficult it's going to be. So they went to the grandmother?'

'It seemed the best idea. She's very attached to them.'

'They belong to us. They're meant to be with us. That's why Sim and Josie left them with us. I only brought them to you so we could have a break.'

'But, Arlette, where *are* Sim and Josie? Sim's father died three weeks ago. The family's been trying to get hold of him—'

'They've been trying for years,' Arlette said. 'He doesn't want to be found.'

This was news to Annie. 'Why not?' she asked.

Arlette shrugged. 'That's his business,' she said. 'I only want the children back.'

'If they found Sim he could tell the family that he and their mother want them to stay with you. But where the hell is he, Arlette?'

'If I knew,' she said angrily, 'I'd go after him myself. I love those kids, but we've had them too long. They were babies when we got them, now they're all over the place.'

'I know that,' Annie said with feeling. 'But, Arlette – they're desperate. He's inherited a lot of money and land and no one knows what to do. Give them a ring and they'll invite you down—'

'No way I'm going to some heritage home like a beggar!'

'All they want is some clue about where Sim is.'

'Colombia – they were going there.'

'What for?'

'It wasn't for a holiday,' Arlette said. 'There's a war there, poor people and I don't know what.' She added, 'He'll give it away, the lot.'

'What? His inheritance?'

Arlette nodded and thought better of saying more. 'Give me the number of that stately home. I'll phone for the kids. If I get any nonsense I'll go round my brother's. He works for a solicitor.'

Arlette vanished into the crowd and Annie phoned Durham House.

'Arlette's back,' she announced to Jasmine. 'She's phoning Lady Mary.'

'Oh, thank God,' breathed Jasmine. 'That must mean they can find Sim soon. It's getting awful – they took a blood test from the twins this morning. And Nigel and Lady Mary. They're going to try to match up the cells to prove the children are Sim's. The atmosphere's horrible here. Julian's coming down to discuss the final plans about the Savernake project, nudged in, probably at that awful Tamsin's instigation. Now I'm putting them up – sorry, Annie. Can I come up and stay with you? I really can't stand it any longer. And there's someone I have to talk to.'

'Oh, Jas,' Annie groaned. 'What are you up to?'

'No business of thine,' asserted Jasmine.

'There's no room. All the Pickerings are staying.'

'Pickerings? Oh – Melanie's family. Any room at Vanessa's? Would she?'

'Jas, what's wrong with your little house in Kensington?'

264

'I don't want to be alone. Nigel's gone crackers, and there's something else, as you suspect—'

'Well, I expect Vanessa can squeeze you in. Bring some food with you. She's not a millionaire.'

'Annie,' came Jasmine's annoyed voice, 'I'm aware of that. I'm perfectly willing to help in any way I can.'

'Sorry. You've lived in luxury a long time—' Annie heard Nigel saying something in an angry voice.

'Got to go,' said Jasmine quickly. 'So the twins' aunt is phoning?'

At this, Nigel's voice rose. Annie put the phone down, very gently. She thought sadly of the little twins, unwittingly now part of a dynasty and subject to all the vagaries and dangers of the position. She wondered where Sim was, why he'd gone to Colombia, why Arlette thought he was going to give his inheritance away if he got it. Also, she knew there was something Arlette wasn't saying.

Next door at the Arcadia, Jenny Pickering helped Vanessa with the preparations for dinner. Melanie, with Jackie, had taken the boys to a film so it was not until she returned to Annie's house to wait for the boys and get ready to visit Ruth that Mrs Pickering got the call from a sister at St Thomas's. The nurse's voice was deliberately calm. She told Jenny that she'd been trying to contact her all afternoon. Ruth had insisted on having the telephone brought to her bedside that morning. Later, a police inspector had arrived asking to talk to a Miss Pickering. The hospital had refused to allow him to speak to her until one of her parents had been consulted but even now a constable was sitting outside the ward, by the lift, waiting. Jenny Pickering asked the sister what she thought was happening.

'She told me,' came the woman's voice, quite calmly, 'that she'd confessed to murder.'

Jenny was first terrified, then she exclaimed, 'That's ridiculous. I can't believe it. Ruth's hysterical.'

The sister answered only, 'Well, I think you should get here as soon as possible, Mrs Pickering.' And Jenny Pickering, still refusing to believe that her fifteen-year-old daughter could have taken a life but feeling sure now that whatever secrets Ruth had been guarding were due to come out, picked up her bag, phoned a minicab, left a note for her children and went outside the house to wait. When she sat down in the cab she noticed her legs were shaking.

26

Some Mysteries Revealed

'I told them she was upset and about to begin therapy,' the sister reported to Jenny Pickering when she arrived at the hospital. 'They won't accept it. I can only assume when she phoned she said something which interested them.'

'You don't have to let them question her,' said the woman in a blue linen suit standing beside the nurse. 'She's under age and in medical care. It's your decision.' She began to tell Jenny her rights, over-emphatically, as if she were not capable of understanding. Jenny became confused. She glanced from one to the other, then down the ward towards where she saw Ruth in bed, sitting up in a yellow cardigan, wearing the headphones Melanie had sacrificed to her. The sister advised, 'Go and talk to your daughter.'

Jenny Pickering nodded and walked towards Ruth, afraid of what she might see in the girl's eyes. When Ruth took off the headphones, put down the book she was reading and smiled, though wanly, Jenny was reassured. This was more like the daughter she used to know.

'Hallo, Mum,' Ruth said.

Jenny sat down. 'Perhaps you can explain to me what you've done,' she said, sounding more annoyed than anxious, or grieving, as parents can in such situations.

'I had to tell them, Mum,' Ruth said to her. 'It's on my mind. I haven't had any peace since I did it. Oh, Mum,' she said, leaning towards her mother and bursting into tears.

Jenny Pickering held her, but stared quite fiercely over her head as she wept. Finally she pushed her off and took her by the shoulders. She said, 'Look, we've no time for all that. What's been happening? What have you done? There's a policeman waiting outside. What have you told them?'

Ruth stared at her, tears still running down her face.

'What have you told them, Ruth? We must know,' urged her mother.

'Don't get Dad,' Ruth said in alarm, thinking Jenny Pickering's 'we' meant herself and Ruth's father. She stared at her mother in horror.

'No worry about that. I can't find him,' declared Jenny, deciding on the spot to take Vanessa's advice and pretend she did not know where David Pickering was. She looked at Ruth and remembered her big girl, at home with the others. In a pitying, domestic way as if she were talking to a child over-distressed about some petty guilt, like pushing her brother off a bicycle, or breaking an ornament, she said, 'Oh Ruth. You're a silly girl. Pull yourself together now and tell me what it's all about. I don't believe for one minute you killed anybody. You'll have to tell me what happened. I've got to decide what to do.'

Ruth stared at her, looked at the sheet on the bed.

'Come on,' urged Jenny. 'You've got to get it out some time. You know that.'

As Ruth began to speak, the ward sister and the woman in the blue suit looked down the ward, carefully watching both mother and daughter. The ward sister turned to the police constable behind her and said, 'You'll have to go back and sit down. The girl's speaking to her mother.'

The woman in the blue suit added, 'I'm afraid that's the case. There's no question of your being able to talk to her now.' The policeman retreated back to the lift, radioed a superior, then sat down again to wait.

During the next half-hour Ruth Pickering told her mother a story which, very often, Jenny felt she could hardly bear to hear although she knew she must.

'I was in this house – well, it must have been near London, because that's where I was when they caught me and said I could come and live in this hostel but when I got there, it wasn't – wasn't a hostel and they never let us out except with Mrs Hedges and Mr Johnson,' Ruth began in her clear voice, so like her mother's. 'She was always there, Mrs Hedges, in case we ran away. There were six of us and we had, like, little cubicles, the bedrooms were split up like that. We got ten pounds a week spending money, but we couldn't ever go out alone to spend it. It was very clean. There were two bathrooms. A nurse used to come and inspect us. And a hairdresser, for our hair. I could have run away. I could. Somehow. I could have killed myself. But I didn't. Sometimes what was happening didn't matter. I made it like a dream, when I could.

'Mrs Hedges would give us a treat, like the pictures, or we'd all go to Richmond Park. And these men would come in, two or three times a week. And then, one night . . . one of them was there and it came over me I hated him, and I hated what he was just going to do, so I ran at him with this knife I'd bought on the sly, when we were out. I didn't know what I was going to do with it when I'd got it but I'd just pretended to get lost and bought it quickly and put it in my pocket and then caught up with the others, that was what I did, and then there I was, late at night, and I thought, I ought to be going to bed somewhere, watch the telly, go to bed, get up in the morning and go to school or work, or something, just like other people do, and I looked at his red face with its horrible stupid expression, and that big body coming towards me and I just thought – no. No. So I reached behind me into the little white dressing-table drawer, that was the idea you see, little white nightie, little white dressing-table, little white bedspread just like a young child might have, and I thought, I'm going to kill you. So I did. I stabbed him and stabbed him and he fell down and made a choking noise. I don't care that I did it. He deserved it. I grabbed my clothes from the bathroom and shoes, and ran downstairs. The front door was locked, of course, so I ran in the dining room and I broke the window and got out, before they knew what had happened, and I just ran and ran.

'There weren't many people about, and the ones that were there didn't seem to notice. I went round the back of somebody's garage and put my clothes on. Then I just walked on and on not knowing where I was going, looking behind me all the time. Later on I met a couple of boys on some steps somewhere, and they didn't have anywhere to go either. We found a place you could sleep and we hung about the streets, getting what we could. I don't remember much about it. I was too afraid of the police and getting caught.

'But since I've been here I've been thinking. I don't care. I want them to go to that house and let the others out. They ought to be punished, them men, and Mrs Hedges and Mr Johnson, they ought to, didn't they, Mum? They're only young, Bob was only eleven. He'd run away from a children's home and she kept on telling him if they caught him he'd be put in prison. She was taking a lot of money for keeping us all there. We hardly had any in case we ran away. That's wrong, isn't it? She should be punished. That's right, isn't it, Mum?' She had been staring ahead of her as she spoke, as the scenes had gone through her head. Now she looked at Jenny and saw that tears were running down her face.

'Don't cry, Mum,' came Ruth's now composed small voice.

'Oh, my God. My God – what've I done?' wept Jenny.

'You haven't done anything, Mum,' said Ruth bewildered.

Jenny Pickering brought her head up. 'No, I haven't,' she said bitterly. 'Not enough, anyway. I've been a fool.' She sniffed, brought a tissue out of her handbag and blew her nose. 'Don't worry, pet. Don't worry. They'll catch them and punish them. I'll take care of you from now on.'

Not long after the blue-suited doctor came up on her long legs. She said, 'Mrs Pickering. Could you spare me a word now?'

'I don't think I can leave her,' said Jenny Pickering. She paused. 'But Ruth's right. She has to talk to that policeman.'

The raid on the house in Hall Avenue was not a success. It was plain from the first that the house was empty. Ruth, stiff and terrified in the police car her mother beside her, muttered, 'They've gone away,' as the police walked at speed up the drive of the detached house, while others scrambled over the fence separating the back of the house from the front. To Jenny it also seemed that the house was empty. She sat gazing at the anonymous front – a green front door, and windows, painted green, curtains hanging tidily beside fresh net curtains – and tried, for Ruth's sake, to stay calm.

Number 63 Hall Avenue had been a child brothel containing three boys and three girls, the youngest eleven, the eldest a girl of fifteen, all of them, according to Ruth, runaways of one kind or another, picked up from mainline stations and public places in London. Three of them, Corinne, Peter and Susie, were London children and already prostitutes. Paul was a fugitive from a children's home in Northampton, Celia from a remand home for girls on the south coast. It seemed to those who heard the story that Celia had been mentally subnormal, Paul just bewildered into numb stupidity. But now they, and Mrs Hedges and Mr Johnson, their exploiters, had all disappeared. Inside, said the policewoman later to Mrs Pickering, the house was clean and well furnished, with a neat lounge, three-piece suite, large television set and a clock on the mantelpiece. The dining room had a long table with eight chairs ranged round. The fridge in the kitchen had been cleared. Pots and pans hung on hooks. The electric stove was clean. Upstairs were four bedrooms, one double and three divided into two, with single beds and small wardrobes and dressing-tables, but there was nothing in cupboards or drawers, the beds had been stripped, pillows, duvets and bedcovers lay on them neatly. The carpets had been hoovered. The pane Ruth had said she had broken had been replaced. The place was bright and ordinary, with the appearance of a well-run bed-and-breakfast hotel, from the lightly flowered wallpapers to the medium-quality fawn carpet and the pot plant placed outside on the patio to give it a chance of life after the departure of the occupants.

One policeman, sent to look over the garden, stood in the sunshine on the lawn, which was tidy but long from not having been recently cut. He said to another, 'Do you think the kid's been having her mother on? You know, it's all a story to explain where she's been and what she's been doing?'

'She must have got the name and address right,' said the other. 'Anyway. There's something wrong in there. I can feel it.'

Later, when the neighbours were interviewed, it turned out that they didn't mix with the residents at number 63, but then, they barely mixed with each other. Mrs Hedges had moved in three years before, claiming to be the house mother of a small local authority hostel for young people with problems, designed to shelter them and reaccustom them to normal family life. The neighbours, relieved the place was quiet and well conducted, had accepted the story. From either side of the house neighbours would have found it difficult to see who came and went, but a woman opposite said she had been surprised at the number of good cars usually, though not always, containing only men, which drove up at night. Mrs Hedges, stopping one day to ask if the engines and opening and closing of car doors were disturbing her in the evenings, had explained that while some of the visitors were friends or relations of the young residents others were council inspectors, experts conducting research and psychiatrists and therapists supporting the young people. The woman said that at first she'd been slightly suspicious but knew nothing about what such experts might be, or what they did. She told the police officer, 'The children looked happy and well cared-for. They were orderly and they wore quiet clothing. They seemed to get on well with Mrs Hedges and her husband. And she seemed such a nice woman. I still can't believe it.'

But she paused then, in her front room, her library book on a table beside her, and added, 'Actually I can believe it. That's the awful thing. But there was nothing you could put your finger on. Not really.'

The police spoke to the milkman, who had delivered eight pints a day, the postman, who told them that the young people never had any letters, and the clergyman at the Methodist church on the corner. When he heard the story he looked grave. He told the police inspector that people in his corner of London were not neighbourly or, to put it more charitably, they saw not probing into each other's business, not interfering or making unwanted visits to each other's houses as the most neighbourly thing they could do. This sad affair, he said, proved just how wrong that idea was. Anyone who actually entered that house might have sensed something was amiss.

As it was, the police were not very welcome when they rang bells in the vicinity to make enquiries about 63 Hall Avenue. It had hardly been more than a month since they'd been round asking questions about a man found dead in a nearby street.

It seemed Mrs Hedges and Johnson had escaped the law. The police inspector who came back to the hospital with Jenny Pickering and Ruth said, 'We'll get her in the end, but probably not before she's gone somewhere else and started up again.'

'Where?'

'Anywhere,' he told her, 'where the neighbours keep to themselves, near a town where there are kids on the loose and men who want them and can pay. I'm sorry, Mrs Pickering. As I say, she'll be caught sooner or later if that's any consolation.'

Jenny Pickering sighed. 'My main concern's my daughter. I'm sorry – I don't care about you catching them. I don't even care about the others, I ought to – but I don't.'

'Talk to the staff here,' he advised. 'Take their advice. They've seen it all. Is your husband available?'

Jenny admitted that he was.

'Well, that's a good thing,' he told her.

Jenny Pickering didn't think so. She was exhausted, her feelings were confused. She blamed herself that things had gone so terribly wrong for Ruth. She was her mother. She was to blame. She should have prevented her from leaving home, and, if not, have found her when she had. But another part of her felt that, had it not been for Ruth's father's behaviour, Ruth would never have run

271

away. Yet, when he heard the story, he would blame her for what had occurred and she knew that she would believe him. The thought of this additional burden was unbearable. *Could* she bear it? She felt she couldn't but knew, for Ruth's sake, she would have to.

Dr Smith told her Ruth would soon be well enough to leave hospital. She could, she said, refer her to a hospital near home, where Ruth would receive help to get over what had happened to her. But Jenny Pickering knew she trusted Dr Smith and needed her support herself. And Melanie was happy in London. Would it not, she wondered, be better to stay? But her husband would insist they went north. Finally, on the day before Ruth was due to leave hospital, she rang David Pickering.

He listened to the story of what had happened to Ruth one evening at Rutherford Street, while Melanie and the boys hid at Vanessa's. He expressed no sympathy, only impatience. 'Silly little bitch,' he remarked.

'Haven't you got any blame for the villains who took advantage of her?'

'If a girl of fourteen runs away from home to London what the hell else can she or anybody expect? She's damn lucky she didn't kill that man, otherwise she'd be in real trouble. As it is, you take her home and look after her properly this time.'

'Dave—' his wife appealed.

'What's done cannot be undone,' he said. 'Now I've got a good job down here. I'm sending money. Ruth's found, Melanie's going home with you before the same thing happens to her and we're out of the wood, so let's stay out, for Christ's sake. I know what that kid's been through, and it hurts me. Why not? I'm her father, aren't I? But like I say, it's done. We can do nothing about it. And the less said, to anybody else, the better. I don't want you going blabbing round what's happened to her,' he warned, 'and if I find you have I'll have something to say, I tell you that. We'll keep this little lot to ourselves – you can tell Ruth to keep her mouth shut, too. That's what I'm saying. We've paid the rent arrears back home, we're getting straight. There's this new job on a big site starting next month and it'll last six months at least. So with what I send home and your own bit coming in, we'll be all right. And what we don't want is a lot of gossip and scandal about our Ruth.'

'So I'm to go back?' his wife asked.

'Go back? Of course you'll go back,' he declared. 'There's nothing for you here. My God, look what's happened to Ruth. Go back up north and try to bring the kids up decently—'

'But I'd like her to stay with Dr Smith—'

'If she's got to have a doctor, let him be one back up home. And you can keep that lot quiet too. We don't want folk thinking our Ruth's gone barmy – you'd better say she's getting treatment for something else, a leg injury or something. Physiotherapy,' he said. 'That's the thing.' He paused. 'I hope you're listening, Jenny.'

'Yes. I'm listening,' she said in a neutral tone.

'Really listening,' he said, somewhat grimly.

'I am listening,' she told him. He glanced at her sharply. There was a sullen note in her voice he did not like.

And so, a few days later, Jenny, Ruth, Colum and John and Melanie left from King's Cross. Vanessa was sniffing. Annie looked shocked. Melanie tried not to cry.

'Do well, Melanie,' Vanessa said.

'We can try and get you into a sixth-form college in London,' Annie told her. 'But you'll have to do well in your GCSEs.'

Melanie nodded. She was bewildered now, at leaving, and because there was a secret concerning Ruth which no one had told her, and because Ruth was so tired and so strange. At the barrier, when David Pickering was away buying sweets for the journey, Vanessa said, 'There'll be a document arriving in a week or two, Mels. Keep it carefully. It's your share of George's and the Arcadia. We're giving you five per cent, that means you own a bit of both the businesses. Not much to get excited about at present, seeing the bank still owns half the Arcadia, and there's the VAT, protection money, etc.'

'That's very generous,' said Mrs Pickering in surprise.

'We couldn't have done it without her,' Annie said. 'But we'd prefer this to be our secret. Melanie can't do much until she's eighteen, anyway. But it means if we sell up she'll be entitled to her share.'

'But,' Vanessa said bluntly, 'we'd just as soon Mr Pickering didn't get to hear about this. A woman, even if she's a girl like Melanie, needs a little bit behind her, tucked away where nobody knows, hers and hers alone. Let's face it, once a man knows a woman's got something he automatically assumes it belongs to him . . .' She looked at Jenny, who nodded. 'It's no blame to him,' Vanessa continued tactfully. 'That's the way it is. Anyway, let's keep this between us, eh?'

Jenny looked Vanessa in the eye and said softly, so that the others wouldn't hear, 'Could be Dave may not be living with us much longer.' Vanessa stared at her quizzically. 'Who knows?' Jenny added.

'Who indeed?' Vanessa responded as Pickering returned. He gave her a dirty look.

As they went through the barrier Annie called, 'Come back soon, Melanie.'

Melanie turned on the platform and put her thumbs up. 'I'll be back,' she mouthed, then walked on with the others. She turned round again. 'Give my love to Jackie,' she shouted boldly. Jack was on holiday, like Melanie's friend Viv, so neither knew Melanie was going home.

'So long, then, Mr Pickering,' Vanessa said loudly and she and Annie quickly left him alone in the busy station concourse. 'What a father,' she said to Annie as they walked to the Underground. 'Jenny Pickering'd be well shot of him.'

'I wonder how much he contributed to what happened to Ruth,' commented Annie as they went into the Underground station. 'All that bullying, the fact Jenny couldn't stand up to him . . .'

'And the groping,' Vanessa added grimly.

'Yes,' said Annie. They stood silent as the train came in.

On the train, Vanessa said after a pause, 'She can come back.'

'She's done better than Ruth,' Annie said. 'What's going to happen to her?'

'I'd kill that Mrs Hedges with my bare hands if I found her,' Vanessa declared savagely.

'She could get caught and punished,' Annie said. 'And Johnson. But the men who went to that house and used those children will never be found. And where are the rest of Mrs Hedges' little charges?'

Vanessa shook her head. 'It's the worst thing – that's got to be the worst thing anyone can do. And when you think about it, you realise how much of it must be going on. You don't think about it, do you? You can't. You'd go mad.'

'Mm,' said Annie.

'Look at that man opposite,' Vanessa said bitterly in an undertone, not looking at a middle-aged man in a suit, opening his briefcase. 'You begin to wonder about everybody. Who's to say he isn't one of them, slips home, has his tea, tells his wife he's off to the Dog and Duck for a pint and, next thing, there he is driving to some place like that one. They must look like everybody else, those men. Like you say, the chances are Mrs Hedges and Johnson will never be found. The other kids they had have scattered and there's no one to rescue *them*.'

The man with the briefcase shifted uneasily under Annie's eyes. Even as they left the train Vanessa looked behind her, as if to catch some betraying gesture from him which would show him for what he was, a child molester, rapist and pederast. Then she went to the Arcadia, as it was her night on there. Annie took over the snack bar from Madame Katarina, who had offered to help, and later locked up and went home.

A savoury smell reached her as she opened the door. Jasmine came from the kitchen, a glass of wine in her hand, saying, 'I've made a macaroni cheese – I thought it'd make a change from your monotonous diet of oysters and champagne. Tom rang up and said he'd be arriving later. But I see signs of hasty packing. Does that mean the Pickerings have gone? If so, can I stay here? Vanessa can do without me, I suppose.'

'Yes,' said Annie rather sadly. 'I was thinking how quiet it would be without Melanie.'

'Has she gone home? What happened?' Jasmine asked. So Annie told her, as she went about the kitchen, making a salad, getting out knives and forks. As she concluded she turned to Jasmine saying, 'Isn't that an awful story?' then took in Jasmine's white face and cried out her name in alarm as her sister bolted out of the room, one hand over her mouth, and dashed upstairs.

Annie waited a bit, then went up after her. She stood outside the lavatory door, listening to the sound of Jasmine's violent retching. 'Jas – are you all right?' she called.

Jasmine came out, pale and sweating. 'I'm OK,' she said numbly. 'Have you got any brandy?'

'If you're sure it's what you need—'

'It's what I need all right,' Jasmine said.

'Are you ill?' Annie asked.

Jasmine shook her head and sipped the brandy Annie poured her. Then she said gloomily, 'I'm pregnant, Annie.'

'Congratulations!' exclaimed Annie. 'That's marvellous, Jas.' She hesitated studying her sister's grim face. 'But—'

'No – I don't know whose it is,' Jasmine said. 'It was worrying me so that was why I came. Now,' she added, 'that doesn't seem to matter so much.' Annie wanted to ask why not, but something in Jasmine's manner discouraged her.

She turned on the television to watch the news. Over the voice of a man talking with assurance about an opinion poll she asked, 'You're having the baby, Jasmine?'

'Christ – I don't know. I shouldn't be here. But where else? I can't even go home to Mother, because Mother's only half a mile away from the matrimonial home.' She added, 'The family's trying to hang on to the twins now. They're definitely Sim's so the Fellowses think they own them. They can't help themselves. They think they're entitled to them. I was hoping the baby was Nigel's but – well, I have to ask myself if I want to bring another little Fellows into the world. And it's not only that,' muttered Jasmine after a pause.

Annie's anxiety increased. Was Jasmine breaking down under the strain?

Tom let himself in, finding the two sisters silent in front of a television game show neither could have been watching. He kissed Annie, then Jasmine, muttering, 'You look awful. Have you told her—?'

Jasmine looked up at him and she was crying. 'I'd like to talk to you, Tom.'

'Yes – sure – of course,' Tom replied.

There was a silence and Annie asked, 'Without me, you mean?'

Jasmine said, 'You know I—' and Tom said at the same time, 'I think so, Annie—'

Annie shrugged, annoyed, and said, 'All right. I'll go – er – I might as well go to the Arcadia.'

'No,' said Tom. 'You stay. We'll go. All right, Jas?'

Jasmine nodded doubtfully. 'Will there be many people there?'

Tom looked at Annie. Annie shrugged. 'Ring up and ask,' and sat resentfully in her chair as Tom questioned Vanessa about the state of affairs at the restaurant. 'We can have a booth,' he told Jasmine. To Annie he said, 'It's serious,' and Jasmine added, soberly, 'It is, Annie, really,' and Annie was left behind, feeling like a child from whom secrets are kept and yet again wondering how it was that Jasmine and Tom were, and always had been, so close – closer than she and Jasmine were although they were sisters.

It was only half an hour later, when she stood up to turn off the dried-up macaroni cheese that she began seriously to wonder what on earth was upsetting Jasmine so much. It couldn't be, could it, that Tom was among the possible contenders for the title of father to Jasmine's child? Jasmine had asked. Tom said he'd refused. But – supposing he hadn't? He'd hardly been candid with her about his past, had he? No, Annie thought angrily, he hadn't. Another mess, she thought, picking up some of Colum's comics and throwing them in the wastepaper basket. Another mess. As she sat down to read she became suddenly nostalgic for the quietness of the library where she'd once delved into the hard and often shameful lives of the Victorian poor.

In the Arcadia Jasmine said in a nervous voice, 'I didn't want to tell her. I was so shocked. I still don't know if I want to tell anybody—'

'Jasmine – just tell me,' said Tom steadily, trying to calm her down. 'Then I'll tell you what I think. It can't be that bad.' He paused and said uncertainly, 'Is it?'

Jasmine gave a short laugh, like a cough. 'Oh no?' she said. 'You'd be surprised.'

'So – surprise me,' Tom requested.

Vanessa came up with a menu.

'Hi, Vanessa,' said Tom.

Vanessa, looking at Jasmine, said, 'I'll leave you two alone. Call me when you need me.'

Tom said, 'Thanks, Van. You're a brick.'

Vanessa pulled a face, then went back to the kitchen. There was a large party of ten, on the other side of the restaurant from Jasmine and Tom. As it was early, none of the other tables was taken.

'OK, so . . . ' prompted Tom.

Jasmine steadied. 'You've heard what happened to Ruth?'

'Melanie's sister? I heard she was in hospital with pneumonia.'

'Oh, God. You mean you don't know about the house she was kept in. Annie didn't tell you?'

'No,' Tom replied. 'House? What house?' An idea dawned on him. 'You don't mean that kind of house?'

Jasmine slumped, seeming unable to speak.

Then Vanessa plumped down in the seat next to her and chin on hand regarded Tom. She said, 'I've been snooping. I know all about it. They're looking for the man and woman who kept Ruth in a child brothel.'

'How did she get there – someone picked her off the street?' asked Tom. Vanessa nodded. Tom groaned, 'Oh God. Bloody hell. How long was she there?'

'She's not sure. About a year. Then she escaped – after she'd attacked a man with a knife and thought she'd killed him.'

Tom's mouth dropped open. He looked at Vanessa, then Jasmine, then back again.

'Jasmine,' he said soberly. 'Do you think the man she attacked was Bernard Fellows? Where did it happen – where was the house, Vanessa?'

'Colindale,' she told him. 'I'd better get on, Tom.'

'Thank you, Vanessa,' Tom said. He looked at Jasmine and asked, 'Do you really think Ruth Pickering attacked your father-in-law? Do you think he was the sort of man to be a client in a child brothel?'

'You heard about his wounds?'

'There was an inquest, wasn't there? Not too much came out. There was some intelligent news management. But, yes, I heard. So did a lot of people. I gather it hasn't helped business much.'

'Tom – you know a lot of people,' pleaded Jasmine. 'Can you believe Bernard would have gone to a place like that?'

'Easily,' Tom replied with assurance. He added, 'You do hear these things, you know. There's a great big underworld out there, seething away, all the time. It's like old Annie's famous paper she wrote at Oxford, "Threpp Street 1888". It hasn't changed. When she was so chuffed about it I told her she should go back to Threpp Street, or whatever it was called now, and do a sequel called "Threpp Street 1990". She just gave me a hard stare and said she wasn't a sociologist.' Tom was talking to give Jasmine time to think. He now concluded, 'It's over. There's nothing you can do, Jasmine. Except live with it.'

'I want to help the girl,' she replied simply.

'Yes,' he said patiently. 'So what are you going to do? Put up a stained-glass window to her at the parish church? Or send a cheque and a letter and start the biggest lawsuit of the century? Anything you do involving that man Pickering can only lead to trouble. And there isn't even any proof.' He leaned forward. 'What Ruth Pickering needs is to get over what's happened, if she ever can. You can't help her. The damage is done. It doesn't matter now if Sir Bernard was involved. Dozens of others were. Don't start thinking about that girl as if she were just another adjunct to the famous Fellows family – you're learning the Fellows egotism, and it doesn't suit you, Jas. Ruth Pickering's the one with real problems and her family has got to help her work it out and whether Bernard Fellows or someone else got jabbed with a penknife doesn't matter to them, much. It's the year she spent in that place that matters, not that one episode. And also,' he went on firmly, 'it's your decision, Jas, but stop and think if exposing all this won't do more harm than good. There's Lady Mary – Nigel—'

'I'm carrying Sir Bernard's grandchild,' Jasmine said.

'Possibly,' Tom pointed out. 'Or someone else's.'

'Well, how do you think I feel?' said Jasmine.

'God, Jas,' Tom said in a low voice. 'If every dirty old man's grandchild was born with a big red splodge on its bum few of us would be without one. You don't know what men are like. Guys like John Woodford get all the criticism, dirty jokes are made about them while these heterosexual old beasts walk about with their heads held high—'

But Jasmine, not listening, went on, 'You see, Tom, Nigel's gone mad. He's so upset. He's been so disturbed since his father died, like another person, and now there's this – I can't stand it, Tom. I really can't. How could Bernard?'

Tom said gently, 'That's not your problem. You can find out how Ruth's managing through Melanie. Then, perfectly normally, you can help, in the ordinary way. Pay for a shrink, or something, if necessary, but I doubt if it will be – she'll get help on the National Health. Probably better than you could pay for. The rest's up to her, her mother – and Melanie, whose own short girlhood now ends in a big way once she hears this story. Bernard's been a bastard. All right – Bernard's wrecked a family, but not his. Bernard's got away with it. Bernard's gone, respected by all, with full pomp and ceremony into the family plot. It's over. You've got to forget it.'

He looked at her, hard. 'You're having a baby, never mind who's the grandfather or if he was an evil man. It's not genetic. Do you want some food?'

She shook her head.

'Well, I do. If we're not going to order dinner I'd like to go back and have a sandwich. I think you're going to have to tell Annie the whole story but that'll be your little luxury. After that, your lips are sealed.' He stood up, 'Come on, Jas. Tell Annie, have a cup of cocoa, then bed, that's what you need.'

'It's not too late for an abortion,' she said.

He subsided into his seat. 'That was a matter I didn't like to raise.'

She sighed. 'I'm thinking about it.'

'It might wreck your marriage.'

'I know.'

He put his hand to his brow, stared at the table, and said, in a low voice, 'Oh, Jasmine. Not again.'

'I know,' she said.

Annie, unable to sit still at home any longer, now came into the Arcadia in a rush. She stood by them staring at the two sad faces, turned startled in her direction. She felt a childish sense of exclusion and said loudly, 'What's going on?'

Vanessa, carrying a tray of liqueurs to the large table on the other side of the restaurant, glanced at her. A woman at that table was also staring.

Annie looked at the empty table in front of Jasmine and Tom and said, accusingly, 'You haven't eaten a thing.' She paused and went on, 'Come on, Jasmine – Tom. He's one of the lucky fathers of your child, isn't he? What are you doing, taking up subscriptions?' Her voice, though fairly low, carried towards the far table, silencing the diners, in front of whom Vanessa was placing the glasses.

'Have you got any port?' a man tactfully enquired, but the others couldn't resist listening. Vanessa filled their glasses as swiftly and calmly as possible and, ignoring a whimper for more coffee, moved efficiently across to Jasmine's and Tom's table where Annie stood, her body rigid with pent-up energy.

She put her hand on Annie' shoulder and said, 'Annie – not here.'

Annie shook off her hand. Vanessa persisted, 'Annie – I haven't heard every word, but it's about Ruth.'

Tom nodded, 'Yes, Annie.'

Annie subsided. 'Why are you talking about Ruth?'

'We shouldn't discuss it here,' he said.

'Why not?' she asked, sitting down. Vanessa went back to the table to ask who wanted coffee, but the possibility of a scene involving a man, two women and the paternity of a child had spoiled the mood. As the three at the table opposite the party now continued their conversation in mutters, the frustration of knowing they would never find out the end of the story was enough to break up the final part of the dinner. The guests settled up and left. Vanessa began to clear the table. Tom got up and helped himself to a whisky from the bar. He put down two pounds.

'No need, Tom,' Vanessa said.

'Just ruined the evening of a large party,' he replied.

'They're the sort who'll enjoy a little episode to talk about afterwards,' she replied. He sat down at the table she was clearing.

He waved at a chair, saying, 'Can I get you a drink?'

Vanessa in reply got herself a clean glass and poured the last glass from a bottle of wine on the table. She took a sip, observing, 'Not bad, and it's free. Am I allowed to hear what's going on?'

Tom hesitated. 'It's not a pretty story,' he said. 'And can you keep a secret from Ben? It really shouldn't go much further.' Vanessa paused and thought. 'He couldn't print it anyway,' Tom told her. 'Samco would crucify the paper.'

They told Annie and Vanessa the story. She finished her glass of wine and told them, 'I expect you're right that Ruth doesn't need to hear any more, not now, anyway. But,' she added wisely, 'of course if they catch Mrs Hedges or Johnson, it'll all come out.'

It was a week later that Melvin Johnson, Mrs Hedges' twenty-four-year-old handyman and lover, twelve years younger than his partner, had a row with her in Northampton, caused partly by fear and the discomforts of life on the run. During the argument he demanded a share of her savings so that they could split up. He wanted to go abroad. She refused to give him the money. He then went to London and attempted to blackmail a National Theatre director who had been a frequent customer at the Hall Avenue brothel. The director, throwing him out of his flat was seen by a passing patrol car shoving Johnson down a flight of steps outside his front door. As the car passed the police saw through their rear mirror that Johnson had fallen and failed to get up. They stopped at the end of the street, turned and sped back. From inside his house the theatre director saw, with horror, two policemen bending over Johnson's prone body. Later he attempted to maintain that the fight had been an ordinary argument with a friend but Johnson, barely hurt by the fall, had lost his nerve. He was full of rage about Mrs Hedges cheating him, as he saw it, and about the assault by the theatre director. He was afraid that Mrs Hedges would get caught and lay most of the blame on him. He confirmed that if he co-operated with the police and revealed Mrs Hedges's whereabouts he would get a lighter sentence and also shrewdly suspected what turned out to be the case – that even while he was in custody before the trial some of Mrs Hedges's clients would manage to get in touch with him and make it worth his while to keep their names out of it.

Johnson cut his losses and made a full statement to the police. He told them where Mrs Hedges was to be found. Although absolutely no one – not Lady Mary Fellows, or Nigel or the entire board of Samco or the Pickerings, least of all Ruth Pickering herself – wanted the scandal of Bernard Fellows's death to resurface, the police, putting together evidence for the trial, revived Ruth Pickering's statement about her detention in Colindale and her assault of a man there. They asked her if she would give evidence at the trial of Mrs Hedges and Johnson. The other young people from the house had scattered and her story was therefore vital to get a firm conviction. She was told that she would not be asked to give the names of clients at the brothel, even if she knew them, and that there was no need for the matter of the stabbing to be mentioned in court. All that was required was that Mrs Hedges and Johnson should be convicted of keeping a brothel and corrupting under-age children. Ruth, bravely, agreed to give evidence.

In theory Sir Bernard Fellows's name need not have been mentioned at the trial but word leaked out. *Private Eye* wrote about it; the City talked about it and the news spread even to Latin America – to Colombia where Samco had forestry interests. This was where, high up in the hills, one Englishman in a Samco lorry with an armed guard met another driving a Land-Rover full of blankets and bags of food, with a machine gun on his lap. There, Simon Fellows heard for the first time of the scandal concerning his father. One of the chief positive results of the arrest of Mrs Hedges and Melvin Johnson was that it brought Sim Fellows and his wife back to Britain.

27

Carnival!

Arlette Jones spotted Sim first. She'd taken the day off from struggling and worrying all week – she had been obliged to organise a formal letter through the solicitor who employed her brother asking Lady Mary for the twins to be returned to them. In addition, she and her mother, realising the Savernake Estate, to all intents and purposes, had been sold off to developers, had been forced to examine their resources to see whether they could raise a mortgage for a home of their own. It meant cashing in Arlette's mother's life insurance and squeezing their incomes of all they would yield but, as they both agreed, it was not simply that alternative accommodation offered them by the council might be very poor but that if it came to a legal battle with the Fellows family for the twins they would need, in court, to demonstrate that they had nice living conditions. Mrs Jones had said grimly, 'They've got millions and a mansion. All we got is the best we can do and Sim's word he wanted the twins to stay with us.'

So on the Bank Holiday Monday Arlette and her boyfriend decided to put their cares behind them and go to the Notting Hill Carnival to have a good time.

At three that afternoon Arlette and Wayne were in Ladbroke Grove dancing behind a big float in a crowd of gyrating people dressed in gauzy outfits, waving big coloured wings, like butterflies, until, out of puff, they dropped out and went to sit on the steps of a house to wait for the next float to come by. The streets were ringing with music coming from all points. Crowds wandered past, eating, drinking, calling out to each other.

'Quiet this year,' observed a woman sitting on the step above Arlette.

'No trouble,' agreed Arlette absently. She couldn't get her mind off Lady Mary Fellows's polite refusal, for that was what it amounted to, to return the twins forthwith. 'They're enjoying themselves *so* much. Do let's agree to leave them here in the country for longer. I'd love you and your mother to visit them one weekend. An old man living here has some collie pups and they're both in love with them . . .' However disarmingly put it still added up to losing the twins to the Fellows family, thought Arlette. In one minute they'd have a puppy of their own, ponies to ride. It was obvious already that a nanny in a uniform was caring for them. 'Like the royal family,' Mrs Jones had said. 'And they send them away to school when they're still small. Of course,' she added, 'they get the best of everything.'

'Josie'd go mad,' Arlette sighed.

'Then she shouldn't have left them in the first place,' her mother stated conclusively. 'And no word from her – what are we supposed to think? That she'd die for her children?' She sighed. 'Well, we got no chance if we're living in a tower block on that terrible Speedwell Estate. The judge wouldn't hesitate – he'd give them to the other family straight away. After all,' she added conclusively, 'he one of them, not one of we.'

'I'd like to catch that pair, Sim and Josie,' Arlette said. 'I'd let them know what I think.'

Sitting on the hot and dirty step in the sunshine she watched, without much interest, another float approach, smaller than most of the others. It was a lorry with the tailboard down, a small sound system and a few musicians on the back. Because the music from the bigger, heavier float going round a corner was louder, the sound from the small lorry was almost inaudible. However, as it came closer to Arlette and Wayne they began to hear the treble of a pipe played by one of the musicians, a guitar and the rhythm of a high drum, like wood on hollow wood. In all, the sound was more Latin American than Caribbean and on the side of the lorry there was a hand-painted sign in blue and red, reading 'Colombian Liberation Aid'.

As the lorry drew level with Arlette, she saw, standing on the back, a familiar figure. She leapt to her feet and yelled, 'Josie! Josie!' The black girl, in an embroidered peasant skirt and blouse, started and looked round. Arlette was now in the street, running up to the lorry, Wayne beside her.

'Arlette!' cried Josie, looking down. Now Arlette spotted a tall, very thin man in a T-shirt and loose khaki trousers bent over a couple of small drums. Arlette, in tight skirt and stilettos, got hold of the back of the slowly moving lorry and tried to clamber aboard. Wayne gave her a push. She landed on the platform of the lorry on her knees and struggled up. Wayne scrambled on too.

A knot of policemen on the corner began to take an interest as Arlette got her sister by the shoulders and began to yell into her face. The musicians stopped playing. Finally the thin man looked up and raised his drumsticks, only to have Arlette, still yelling, seize one and start hitting him. People in windows, on balconies and roofs began to concentrate their stares on the Colombian Liberation Aid lorry. There was a mild cheer as Arlette drove the thin white man, a startled look on his face, his arms raised against a hail of drumstick blows raining down on his head and face, against the side of the lorry. Wayne, meantime, stood nervously at the back, not wanting any trouble with the police. One of the other musicians banged on the cab of the lorry, calling out in Spanish, and the lorry stopped half-way round the corner. All that could be heard was the distant sound of music from another float, further up the road, and the quack quack of police speaking into their radios. Arlette felt Josie pulling her away from the thin man. 'You bastard, Sim,' she shouted. 'What do you mean, leaving the children with us and disappearing like that? Now they're stuck at your mum's and we can't get them back. And I find you drumming, *out of time*, on a lorry—' Wayne joined Josie in grappling with her.

'Arlette,' Wayne was saying, mildly but loudly. 'Arlette – you leave him alone,' Josie was crying.

A policeman clambered on to the lorry. A bigger crowd was collecting rapidly, including large, calm black men with wary eyes. Sim's T-shirt was raised to his nose, which was bleeding heavily. The policeman, a constable from Surrey, not liking his position stranded alone on the back of a float surrounded by black people, tried to assert his authority. 'What's going on? You can't stop this vehicle here. Madam,' he said to Arlette, 'if you continue to assault this man I'll have to arrest you. Would anybody like to explain what's happening?'

It was Wayne, still holding Arlette back, who found the appropriate words to defuse the situation. 'It's domestic,' he said. 'This man's her brother-in-law.'

A police inspector called up from the pavement, 'You'll have to sort your family problems out somewhere else. This lorry's got to be moved on.'

Looking straight at Sim's blood-stained T-shirt, Arlette said, 'I should think you ought to be visiting your children, not playing on a truck.'

Wayne muttered to Josie, 'His family got all sorts of problems. What's he doing here – and you?'

'I don't want to arrest anyone,' the inspector continued. 'This is supposed to be an enjoyable occasion for all – ' There was a subdued, ironical cheer ' – but if you can't resolve the situation you'll all have to get off and let the float proceed without you.'

The Colombian musicians, who had been talking between themselves, spoke now to Josie. A boy of ten took the drumsticks discreetly from Arlette. The music began again softly.

'Arrest them,' Arlette ordered the police inspector. 'Arrest them now – no way are they escaping again.'

A man in a tropical suit addressed the inspector. Sim's voice, muffled by the T-shirt he still had bunched to his nose, said, 'I've tried to ring my mother. No one came to the phone.'

'Off,' the inspector said firmly.

As the four scrambled down from the lorry and on to the pavement it started up and moved round the corner.

'Names,' demanded the inspector.

Arlette dug into her bag and produced a packet of tissues which she handed to Sim. 'Simon Fellows,' she stated, nodding at him.

'Your name?'

'Arlette Jones.'

'Address?'

She gave it.

'Yours,' said the inspector to Wayne.

'Wayne Corrington.'

'Address?'

Wayne gave his address.

'Sir?' the inspector said, looking at Sim.

'Simon Fellows.'

'Address?'

'Colle Verde, San Miguel, Colombia,' Simon said.

The inspector stared at him hard.

'His address in this country is Durham House, Belshaw, Hampshire,' Josie said strongmindedly. 'He's a baronet. I'm his wife, Lady Fellows.' The young black woman dressed like a South

286

American peasant and the large, white man in police inspector's uniform stared at each other long and hard.

'This is her sister,' supplied Wayne, to break the deadlock, his arm round Arlette's shoulders.

'All right,' said the inspector as two police cars sped towards them, scattering people all over the road and pulling up sharply near by. 'If I can take it this is a family dispute you can sort out peaceably between yourselves we'll leave it at that. Can you assure me there won't be any more trouble?'

'Yes,' Josie said. 'There won't be any more trouble.'

Wayne was putting sharp pressure on Arlette's arm to restrain her from speech or action and as Josie spoke he tightened his grip threateningly. As soon as the police went off he let her go. The focus of public attention switched, another float came along surrounded by dancers and the group became simply a number of anonymous people arguing on the pavement. Arlette grasped her sister's shoulder and spoke into her ear. The music was deafening. 'We're going back to Kenton right now. Mum wants to see you. She's been worried to death, poor woman. Not like me. I knew you were alive.' She turned to Sim and threatened, 'You're not even going to the gents.'

'Oh, God, Arlette,' said Sim. His nose-bleed had slackened and he dropped the T-shirt over his chest. It lay bloodily against his prominent ribs as though he had taken a ferocious beating. 'We only arrived yesterday,' he said. 'I tried to ring—'

'It's true,' Josie added angrily. 'How are Miranda and Joseph?'

'Fine, no thanks to you. But Sim's mother's got them and she's not giving them back.'

'What's this story about Father being murdered or attacked by a girl?' asked Sim. 'I can't get it straight – what happened?'

'You've got no feelings, only for those Colombians,' Arlette declared vigorously. 'You leave your children, you don't turn up for your father's funeral. Your mother thinks you must be dead—'

'You don't know, Arlette,' Josie said. 'You don't know anything. Why don't you shut up till you hear?'

'We can't stand here on the pavement, with him all covered in blood,' said Wayne. 'We need a cab, if one will take us. A nice day out,' he added.

Swapping stories and arguing, they plodded up to Notting Hill Gate. Wayne and Arlette made Sim and Josie stand apart from them until a taxi stopped. Then they all got in quickly. The cab driver was cautious, not liking the bloodstains or the kind of people he was being asked to carry all the way across the Thames to Kenton. There was an argument.

'Might as well go to Bedford Square,' said Sim. 'I know a way in if there's nobody there.'

There was no one there. Sim squeezed through a hole at the back of the house which led into a cellar and let them in, through the front door. While he went off to wash, the others sat down in the huge chandeliered drawing room. However, a vigilant passer-by seeing a bloodstained white man in old clothes opening the door to three young black people, called the police. Sim, coming out of the bathroom in a shirt of Nigel's which was too big for him, found it hard to prove his identity. Thus, the first news Lady Mary had that her son was alive came from a policeman on the phone asking her to describe him. Even then, Sim had to roll up his trouser leg to show the policeman an old scar on his thigh.

When the police had left Arlette made a cup of tea in the palatial kitchen. Sim rolled a joint and passed it to Wayne.

'You were lucky they never searched you on that float,' Wayne remarked.

The phone rang. 'Certainly, Ma, I'm very sorry. Don't send the car. We'll get the train. Nige, look, I'm really sorry—' Nigel Fellows's voice, welcoming at first, was getting angry. 'OK, we'll sort it all out,' Sim said calmly. 'A day or two with lawyers. No, I haven't made any decisions. Yes, I know it's been intolerable – we can get a train down, I'll let you know. Yes, today, for certain. Untwist your knickers, Nigel. All will be well.' Sim put the phone down. 'What a fuss,' he remarked coolly.

'Easy to accuse people of fussing when you've walked out of all your responsibilities,' Arlette said bitterly, taking the phone and dialling. 'I found Sim and Josie, Ma,' she reported. 'On a float at the carnival.' There was a torrent from the other end. She put the phone down. 'Poor woman. She's crying,' she reported. 'You two, you been disgusting.'

Vanessa and Annie, relaxing at the end of the evening over glasses of wine from a bottle abandoned by a family party when the topic of Aunt Margaret's will was raised, were startled by the chimes of midnight. The clock on the spire of Kenton Town Hall stuck at ten to three for the past six years, due to spending cuts, had been mended three weeks earlier to restore the morale of Foxwell residents. More or less inaudible during the day, the chimes did a good job, once the heavy traffic had ceased, of waking people up at night and in the early morning. It had been a successful Bank Holiday for the Arcadia. Once the chimes had ceased Vanessa, her feet on a chair, lifted her glass to Annie. 'Another day over – cheers to us. This place is a success – we're having to turn them away – who'd have believed it?'

Annie looked across affectionately at Vanessa's pretty, healthy face so unlike that of the peaky, pale waif with the grizzling child she had first met in the dentist's surgery on that cold day in December. 'We've worked for it, Vanessa . . .'

'Worried for it . . .'

'You've had to miss your children for it . . . '

Vanessa grinned. 'You found yourself in that Threpp Street you wrote the article about. Come on, Annie,' she urged. 'Admit it – you thought all that Victorian slum stuff was over – well, it's not exactly the same but things haven't changed as much as you thought they had on that happy day we took over George's when you were young and innocent.'

'Tom says occasionally there's a hard look in my eyes,' Annie admitted. 'But at least people don't keep on telling me these days I don't live in the real world.'

Vanessa looked at Annie and thought that she'd bloomed. She and Tom were in love again, which accounted for a lot of it, of course. She didn't say this to Annie, for she and Tom were still pretending to themselves and each other that they were only together by accident and for convenience.

Vanessa closed her eyes and sighed happily. 'Do you think this can go on? Things being all right? The businesses making money, children all right? And Ben? It seems too good to be true.'

'Yes,' agreed Annie. 'Somehow it does.'

'Perhaps you won't want to go on being a restauranteur for much longer,' Vanessa said doubtfully. 'You might want to go back to the history—'

'I don't know any more than you do,' Annie said. 'You might marry Ben and he might get a job somewhere else in the country. But it's so far, so good—'

'Think how lucky we've been,' murmured Vanessa.

In this reconciled mood they left the Arcadia and walked quietly back through Foxwell High Street. They were asleep before the big town hall clock struck one.

28

The Temple of Mammon

Sam Anstruther of Watney Aspell, New York, dealers in rare books and manuscripts, had intruded through the back door of Froggett's on a fine afternoon in early September and caught Juliet Browning making plum jam. This time she could not invent an excuse and escape him because the jam had reached the stage where, if left to cook for even a few more minutes, it would turn into a toffee-like mass.

'Mr Anstruther,' she was saying, stirring the large preserving pan with a ladle. 'I can't discuss it now.'

'I have a letter of authorisation from the literary executors of your aunt's estate,' Anstruther repeated. 'I have to tell you now I have a legal right to examine the contents of the suitcase containing Christian Cunningham's effects.'

'Who does it really belong to?' Juliet dropped some jam on a saucer and examined it closely. 'Wonderful colour,' she said, 'streaked, with a visible texture, if you can say that.'

'To your aunt's estate.' Anstruther sighed inwardly.

Juliet glanced at the American as he stood on the flagstones of her kitchen, tall, pale and tidily dressed in a shirt, sports jacket and green trousers. She looked back at the pan and stirred again.

'I question that,' she said. 'The case was left with Howard. He recalls reminding Dorian Jefferson about it later. He says Jefferson asked him to look after it. You must admit the case could belong to his estate, or Christian Cunningham's, or to us.'

'There are fine points involved,' agreed Anstruther. 'But in simple practice you are Christian Cunningham's niece and, as I recall, you gladly handed over various letters and writings of hers to the custodians of her estate at her death.'

'A couple of letters about a vase she thought was hers – her letters to me were few and far between. I'm sorry, Mr Anstruther. I don't intend to hand over the case.'

'I shall have to inform the executors—'

'Inform anyone you like,' Juliet said briskly. She took jam pots from the table, put them on the draining board and began, carefully, to ladle in the jam.

Howard Browning, a book in his hand, came in to the kitchen from the inhospitable parlour. He glanced at Sam Anstruther and sat down.

Juliet said, 'Annie and Vanessa are coming down tomorrow with Alec and Joanne – and Vanessa's boyfriend.'

'Oh, God,' said Howard. 'I could do without that.'

'I really think you should go and stay with Nell—'

'I refuse to go all the way to Wales at this stage.'

Sam Anstruther said, 'Mr Browning. I wonder if you realise I have a letter of authorisation from the literary executors of the Christian Cunningham estate.'

'Yes, we had a copy. Juliet may not have mentioned it. But I'm writing a novel, almost finished, centred round that suitcase.'

'Then you know the contents,' Anstruther said.

'Certainly not,' Howard said in alarm. 'I've invented the contents. I'm thinking seriously, Juliet – I'll have to finish the book by tomorrow.'

'Does that mean you'll be up all night again?' Juliet asked.

'Looks like it,' he observed gloomily and left the room. Juliet, rapidly filling the remaining five jam jars, said, 'That's the point, you see. I couldn't really tell you. Howard's been hesitating over his next book for years. Suddenly he began to think he wanted to write a novel concerning the Cunninghams – that set – and ourselves to some extent – about art and the lives of people who produce it and the history of the times. That unopened case became a talismanic object as he wrote – a kind of symbol of the novel. I hope I'm making some kind of sense.'

'I believe I'm a person who can understand matters of that nature,' Sam Anstruther said with some dignity.

'Of course you are,' said Juliet quickly. 'I hope you understand now why we couldn't yield it up.'

'He's almost finished, Mrs Browning,' Anstruther reminded her.

'Well, yes,' Juliet agreed. 'But the trouble with you is that you don't really care what a living writer is doing now. Only what a famous dead one did years ago. You'd rather have Christian Cunningham's old holey stockings, or an unpaid bill or a scribbled note from Dorian Jefferson to some woman saying he couldn't see her tonight, than see a real book by a real live author finished—'

Anstruther broke in, saying emphatically, 'Mrs Browning, I am not – I would not, ever, insist on the case being handed over in such circumstances. Of course your husband must finish his book. I would never have been so pressing if you'd told me the facts.'

'Good. I'm glad we understand each other,' Juliet said briskly. 'By the way,' she added, 'I'd get out of Durham House pretty quick if I were you. I expect you've heard Sim and his wife are coming.'

'I'm leaving this evening,' Anstruther told her. 'I felt it would be inappropriate to stay. Mrs Browning, have I your word that when this book's finished you'll allow me to examine the contents of the suitcase?'

Juliet replaced the ladle and took the pan to the sink. She ran hot water into it then led Anstruther to the door. She walked him across the lawn in the sunshine, talking as they went. 'Of course you can have the damn thing. But I'm going to sell it to you. Howard and I are getting older, and we may need the money for our old age. I know Rupert wants to sell it on behalf of the estate, but that's so he can get some of the money himself. Also he likes to be in a position of power over his great-aunt's work.'

'You'll have to prove it's yours to sell,' Anstruther said.

'I won't have to,' she said. 'I've taken advice, and there's a strong case for Dorian Jefferson's children, not that the profits would do them any good. Not one of them has done a stroke of work in their lives. They take it for granted they live off the fruits of their father's short, drunken life. I find it tragic.'

They paused, looking down the slope to the river, the lake, to Durham House itself on their right, glowing in the autumnal sun.

'You seem,' Anstruther said drily, 'to be fairly confident that the case contains material which could be sold. Not old stockings.'

Juliet Browning winked at him. 'There are loose pages, dated and part of a diary. Would you believe Christian Cunningham had an affair with Margot Asquith? There's an interesting set of notes for a novel. There's a poem to her by Jefferson, comparing her with a gaunt goat and a black and white drawing of two somewhat hieratic

292

figures, arced, hands touching, presumably bought by Jefferson or Christian Cunningham or, I suppose, in the case of Jefferson, stolen – in my opinion the drawing may be by Aubrey Beardsley. Now, questions of ownership are difficult – does the poem belong to Christian Cunningham or Jefferson, for example? Did the sketch belong to either of them or is there still some owner wondering what happened to it?'

Anstruther was moved. He stopped dead under a loaded apple tree and gazed at her. After a pause, he asked, 'Can you guarantee I'll be first in on this?'

Juliet Browning nodded. 'You certainly deserve it,' she said.

Anstruther exhaled. 'It's been a humiliating experience,' he stated. 'In fact I'll go so far as to say most of the time I've felt like shit.'

'Been treated like it too,' Juliet said. 'Sorry.'

'Well,' he held out his hand. 'I'll call you on Monday, around twelve o'clock.'

'I'll be there.'

A car drew up at Durham House from which figures could be seen emerging.

'I think it's time I left,' said Anstruther. 'Goodbye, Mrs Browning. It's been a pleasure. Hope the jam turns out well.'

'I'll save a pot for you.' Juliet smiled.

Anstruther loped off down the slope then turned. 'Mrs Browning – about your husband's manuscript, it could prove a valuable part of the archive.'

Juliet nodded. 'I know.'

The American raised his hand in greeting and quickly strode away.

In the hall at Durham House, Anstruther was very much aware of voices, raised in dispute, coming from the half-open door of the drawing room. He quickly gathered up his luggage and made his polite but brief farewells to Lady Mary, got into his small hired car and set off for the road. At one point he had to pull over as a Bentley passed him on its way up to the house.

At the bottom of the drive, Al Dominick leant against one of the pillars, smoking. Anstruther slowed down and called out, 'Hi, can I take you anywhere?'

'Why not?' answered Al and got in, dropping his cigarette and stepping on it.

'Anywhere, or just somewhere?' Anstruther asked.

293

'How about the next pub you're passing?' Al said.

'Suits me,' said Anstruther and restarted the car.

'You look like the cat that just got the canary,' Al said. 'Did you get to peek in Mrs Browning's suitcase?'

'No, but I have a deal. Some time next week I get to look at it.'

'Really?' Al asked with some scepticism.

'Yeah,' said Anstruther as he drew up at the village pub. 'Really.'

They sat on a bench overlooking the village green and a great chestnut tree in front of the old church.

'Isn't it great?' Al said. 'It's like an art form in its way. Some people have temples, great paintings. The British have these houses, gardens, cottages, village greens.'

'You're escaping one of these pieces of art momentarily, I guess,' Anstruther said. 'It's certainly been a little tense at Durham House.'

Al regarded him steadily, 'Come on, Sam, you're in love with the house and the aristocrats who live there, but you've got to agree with me, and I'm a doctor, they're all mad in there. They're suffering from a condition we psychiatrists describe as having too much money.'

'All families go through times of crisis.' Anstruther sounded defensive.

'Sure,' Al agreed. 'But here there wouldn't be a crisis if it weren't for the money, the land, the shares—'

'Are you giving it as your medical opinion that money makes people insane?' Anstruther asked.

'Yep,' Al said crisply.

'So we have Freud on the unconscious, Jung on archetypes and Al Dominick on bank balances?'

'You said it.'

The two men sat in silence, though not much in sympathy. Anstruther envied Al his access through Claudia to the centre of a way of life, it was true, he admired, even coveted. It annoyed him, however, that Al thought he was an American dedicated to European snobberies, a man repudiating his origins.

Al said, 'Maybe you think I'm a toad to be saying all this about my hosts. But I'll be honest. I really don't want to be here. I came over to be with Claudia because her father died. And now I find it wasn't just the simple matter of a bereavement. It all goes on and on and I don't consider this is any way to spend a vacation. Originally, we were going to the funeral, then Claudia would spend some time with her mother, and then we'd go to France and Italy. On the plane coming over we even discussed asking Lady Mary to come with us, if it would help. Nothing so simple was possible. Claudia's sueing the estate for her rights and I believe she should do that. Lady Mary is keeping something back, I know that. Nigel's disturbed, Jasmine also has something on her mind, now the son's returned, the men of business are arriving in big black limos – I keep wondering – did I see this film already?'

Anstruther laughed in spite of himself. He surprised Al by doing a good imitation of Marlon Brando as the Godfather and added, slightly jealously, 'Have you thought of leaving?'

Al shrugged. 'It's a temptation, but Claudia couldn't handle it on her own.'

'Well,' Anstruther said, standing up. 'I have to be going. Can I take you back first?'

Al shook his head. 'I'll take a look round the church. Look at the tombstones in the graveyard, get a sense of perspective, take the annual bus back, or hook a ride.'

Anstruther nodded. 'Well, goodbye, Al – and good luck.'

'So long, soldier,' Al said.

When Sam drove off he was still sitting on the rustic bench, staring across the village green.

'Don't try to do that yourself, Mary. It's too much for you.' Lady Mary Fellows, observed by her sister, was tugging at a sycamore sapling which had grown up by the kitchen-garden wall. As she spoke, Lady Mary staggered back, nearly losing her balance, the uprooted sapling in both hands. She looked behind her in dismay.

'There you are. You've broken a tomato plant,' said Lady Margaret.

'Damn,' Lady Mary responded, picking a few ripe tomatoes from the damaged plant. 'Perhaps I should pick the green ones – oh, what's the point, really? I suppose with Sim back I'll be leaving the house. It's no moment to start making chutney.'

Lady Margaret sighed. 'Thank goodness Jessop's already here.'

Lady Mary said nothing. She dreaded her sister's domineering and, if the truth were told, not very intelligent husband. Handing Lady Margaret a few tomatoes and picking the remainder, she straightened up and said, 'I think I'd better get back and ask about tea.'

As they walked towards the kitchen Lady Margaret murmured, 'So wonderful about Sim.'

Lady Mary smiled. 'Isn't it? I feel as if a great cloud I've been living under for years has suddenly rolled away. I'd forgotten what it was like to wake up happy.'

Lady Margaret knew that the return of her eldest son was more than ample consolation for the loss of Sir Bernard. 'But what a crowd it's caused.'

Lady Mary didn't point out that her brother-in-law Jessop was one more. She said mildly, 'I did suggest to Nigel that the discussions might be better held in London. I wonder where Mrs Bleasdale's got to? I'll start getting the tea myself.'

Lady Margaret had opened the door into the passageway. Now she said, 'My God, Mary. They're quarrelling – I can hear them.'

'I imagine they are,' remarked her sister calmly.

In the drawing room Sim was shouting, 'I suppose I can do what I like with my own money, Nigel.'

Nigel replied, 'No, Sim. Not really. It's been taken care of for generations, for generations to come. And you've no right to deprive your own children or anyone else's because of a personal decision. As it happens, Jasmine's told me this morning we're having a child.'

Congratulations were murmured. Nigel himself was delighted, almost bursting with excitement, pride and relief. His happiness was only subdued by his failure to understand Jasmine's attitude. He'd been urging her for some days to return from London, saying she ought to be at Durham House during the family discussions, though not saying that he needed her moral support in what, according to the family solicitor, Sir Hugh Brown, looked likely to be a very sticky family encounter.

'Sim's new wife, I'm sure, would appreciate your being there,' he'd said. 'And it'll look a bit odd if you're not at home to greet the prodigal brother.'

Jasmine's instinct was to stay away from the conference, which she was sure would upset her and, she suspected, might put Nigel in a bad light in her eyes. She also felt she wanted time to think about her pregnancy. She stayed on at Annie's but actually, being in the torpid first months of pregnancy, thought nothing and decided nothing, just wanting to be left alone in peace. Finally she could think of no more excuses and, recognising Nigel's need of her, came down to Durham House.

On the morning of Sim's arrival, Nigel surprised Jasmine in the bathroom, her back turned, wrestling her way into a light cotton skirt. Forgetting what he meant to say he stared, suddenly aware that his slender wife had put on quite a lot of weight around the middle.

'Jasmine?' he said on a mild, interrogative note.

She rounded on him. 'Oh, God, Nigel. Do you need to sneak up on people?'

'I only opened the bathroom door,' he said pacifically. 'Your skirt doesn't fit.'

'I know,' she responded, looking at the bathroom floor.

'Well – what is it? You've been sick a lot, too.'

He was becoming surer by the moment that she had a secret, a little secret in fact.

'Come on, Jas,' he said in an encouraging tone, 'Are you or aren't you?'

'Yes. I think so,' she said. Then sulkily, 'Well, I might as well put on something loose and flowing.' She moved into the bedroom. Nigel followed.

'Jas! This is great news! Why didn't you tell me?'

'Shut up, Nigel,' she said as he moved to embrace her. She pushed him with her elbow.

'I don't understand—'

Jasmine put on a dress and looked at herself in the wardrobe mirror. She patted her stomach. 'Oh, well, that's that, I suppose. Goodbye, stomach, hallo, huge bulge.' Then, to Nigel's surprise, she went out of the room. He found her downstairs at the breakfast table, talking to his mother.

'Good news, Nigel,' Lady Mary said. 'But Jasmine says she doesn't want to talk about it at present. I hope you'll consider her feelings.'

'Whims already,' he remarked discontentedly. 'All right,' he sighed. 'Where's *The Times*?' He got up to fetch the newspaper. 'Perhaps I should just jump out of the window and run into the lake. I'm only the father, after all.'

'Oh, shut *up*, Nigel,' Jasmine said, and took herself off.

Nigel was so pleased to have heard himself say, 'I'm only the father,' that he hardly minded his wife's hostile and erratic behaviour. 'I suppose she'll stop running away from me when she actually has the child. Or will the doctor have to chase her round a field? I suppose this is normal?' he asked his mother.

Lady Mary's only comment was, 'Well, I am blessed. Up to a week ago I had no grandchildren. Next year I'll have acquired three. It's splendid.'

'A pity Dad couldn't have lived,' said Nigel.

Lady Mary looked towards the dining-room door and wondered, 'Where's Mrs Bleasdale? She's taking her time.'

Nigel, now sitting in the drawing room arguing with his brother, still wondered why Jasmine had broken to him the news that she was pregnant with their first child and, he hoped, heir in such a peculiar way.

Sir Hugh Brown, summoned to Durham House for the discussions, sat near the window next to Charles Head. He looked out across the lawn and down to the lake. The composed landscape glowed in the sunshine. For two hundred years, tree by tree, it had been cared for, planted, pruned, ever since John Flowerdew, future father-in-law of the thrusting Yorkshire shipowner, had decided one day to get the sheep out of the field in front of the house. First he would make a pleasant outlook and then he would bend his efforts to marrying his daughter to a wealthy man, quickly, with no fuss about the man's antecedents. This he had done. Since then the Fellowses had lived at Durham House. Thank God it's entailed, thought Sir Hugh, fervently.

Charles Head was in a sweat. Nigel's man, he'd been making his way nicely until the arrival of those black twins and now, worse, their father, which had really put the cat among the pigeons. Head was having serious thoughts about his own future now, especially as his particular baby, the beautiful Savernake Village, was threatened. The village that was to have been, in some senses, his monument. He'd planned to use it to prove his worth to the world for at least ten years and now, thanks to the arrival of this batty baronet, negligent, a communist, a man who, Head thought bitterly, had done nothing but be born into the right family, it looked as if the village might never happen.

Head glanced across at Claudia, at ease by the huge fireplace, patting the dog. She caught his glance and winked at him mockingly. He said to himself that Lady Mary must be deeply embarrassed at having produced a mad heir and a feminist daughter, not to mention the fact of baby Joseph, the future ninth baronet, being a darkie. But Lady Mary seemed unmoved, so supremely well bred, Head supposed, that no one would ever be able to guess how upset she really was. Lady Margaret's husband, Jessop, summoned from the Highlands of Scotland where he preferred to be, was consuming his own whisky, made in his own distillery on his own estate and keeping quiet. He knew more about this situation than anyone thought and he suspected a great deal more than that.

Jessop's aim was simply to use his knowledge and suspicions to limit the damage. There were a lot of skeletons in a lot of cupboards in this room, he thought, and it was now a case of keeping as many of them locked away as possible, or scandal, bad feeling and family break-up were on the cards.

Jasmine lay on a chaise longue opposite the fireplace, her feet naughtily on the upholstery, her intention to pretend to be asleep or nearly asleep. She was cornered now. She'd have to have the baby and hope it was Nigel's or, if it wasn't, that no one would find out – especially Nigel. The alternative was to tell him the child might not be his, which would lead to divorce. She sat up a bit and spotted the nurse leading Joseph and Miranda down the lawn. Children were nice, reflected Jasmine. On the other hand, if that particular pair had turned up earlier, there might have been less unspoken pressure on her from Nigel to produce an heir. Now she was stuck on a sofa, her hormones making her feel fed up, while Nigel battled for the unborn child. At least Sim's arrival had made her husband a little less barmy than he'd been since his father died. She'd told no one about Ruth Pickering's involvement in Sir Bernard's death. There was no reason why, even at the trial of Mrs Hedges, it should come out. But it might, because things did. She saw Josie Fellows in shorts dashing down the lawn towards her children and turned her gaze on Nigel who was facing the room now, demanding, 'What *are* you planning, Sim? We need answers, and we need them soon.'

Sim leant back in the chair by the fireplace, his long legs stuck out. Reaching into his trouser pocket he produced a cheap notebook, and said, 'I've got my ideas written down, Nigel. Are you listening?'

'Sit down, Nige,' Claudia appealed. 'You're getting on people's nerves.'

'Maybe we should start with you,' Nigel said aggressively. 'With all this, don't you think you could call off the lawyers? If you're not satisfied with what you've got, we can come to an arrangement.'

'No, Nigel,' came Claudia's voice, on a nursery note of protest. 'No. It's not fair. In any other family in the world, practically, Dad's assets would be split between the three of us. It's only in this kind of family the top boy gets almost everything, second boy the rest, and girls practically nothing. And look what confusion we've been in because of it. It won't do, Nigel. It's not fair. I'm not having my affairs pushed under the carpet and I'm not going to be paid off like a blackmailer. I'm not a blackmailer. I'm a disinherited person, and I'm going to get my inheritance. When some judge here, whose chief priority, like yours and everybody else's, is to keep the land together at all costs tells me to get lost, I'm going from here to the European Courts.'

'I'm on Claudia's side,' said Sim.

'This practice, however old-fashioned, possibly even unjust-seeming it might be has maintained stability in England for hundreds of years.' Sir Hugh spoke with authority. 'And however much you want to help Claudia, Simon, you'll be helping her at the expense of your own son.'

'Then I have to help my son at the expense of his twin sister,' suggested Sim. 'In fact I'm here to disinherit everybody, aren't I? Claudia, Nigel, Nigel's coming child – and I can pass this legacy on to my son, so that when he grows up he can disinherit his sister and any other brothers and sisters he might have.'

'The alternative,' said Sir Hugh, 'is that over the generations the land is continually divided and redivided until it turns into so many potato patches, bled away, sold off, used up. Can you really face beginning that process?'

'That's being melodramatic, Sir Hugh,' said Claudia. 'The entail ensures that Sim's son and his son's son will own this house and the hundreds of acres round it. Not to mention the rest—'

Nigel interrupted. 'We've really got to talk about the most active part of the business. The land's all very well. You don't need to tell me you'll be turning Durham House into a hostel for the homeless or something, Sim. I already know that. I think it's disgusting, but there we are. The fact is that Dad had a majority shareholding in Samco. He willed a third of those shares to you and two thirds to me, my proportion being greater in recognition of the fact that you inevitably inherited the entailed land and property, and a larger proportion of unentailed land—'

'And I got Badger's Farm, near Bromley,' cried Claudia ecstatically. 'What a lucky little girl!'

'Give us a break, Claudia,' Nigel said rudely.

'I just want you to reflect that whatever you and Sim do, I'm likely to turn up and undo it, when I've won my case.'

'*If*,' Nigel told her.

'I don't think there's much if about it, Nigel,' Sim said.

Nigel glanced at Hugh Brown for reassurance but Sir Hugh failed to meet his eye.

'Can we stick to the point – the running of an extremely serious business, already spiralling down because of all this uncertainty?' said Nigel.

'But it *is* the point,' both Sim and Claudia said together. 'Claudia's case, as I suppose we'll all start calling it, will be in five or six years' time,' added Sim.

Nigel turned to Sir Hugh. 'There's a strong possibility that if Claudia takes a case to the European Courts they'll declare in her favour,' said the solicitor. 'But that decision is many years off, as we all know.'

'Anything mine, not entailed, I'm splitting in three, between you, me and Nigel,' Sim said to Claudia.

'Good. I accept,' Nigel said with vigour.

'That's very nice of you, Sim,' Claudia said. 'I'd no idea—'

'I should have mentioned it before,' said Sim courteously.

Sir Hugh was depressed but not surprised by this news. When Sim revealed he wasn't giving eighteen per cent of Samco to the Third World he and Charles Head brightened up a little, recognising that Nigel, better off by a third of his brother's shares, which, added to his own share of Sir Bernard's holding, gave him forty-four per cent, now had only to get direct control of, or voting rights to, another seven per cent of the shares to achieve a majority shareholding in the company, valued these days at £200,000,000. He glanced expressionlessly at Sir Hugh, who returned the look. So far, so good. Almost safe, at least until Claudia got a judgement.

'I'm taping all this,' said Claudia.

Sim laughed. 'So is Hugh,' he hazarded. 'Anyway, that's the principle – I'll split what's mine with Claudia and Nigel. What I do with my own share is, of course, my business. Properly, every penny ought to go to others, but I suppose the Fellowses are genetically disposed to looking after their own families and I suppose I'm one of them.' It was plain the idea did not please him.

'Charity begins at home, Sir,' carolled Nigel.

'I know what begins at home, Nige,' his brother said grimly. Jessop, seated on an upright chair by a long mirror near the door, glass in hand, stiffened. Jasmine, lying like a log on the ottoman, heard the note in Sim's voice through her pregnant haze, and remembered what she was trying to forget.

Sir Hugh stood up. 'Well, I think we've all got a fairly good idea what Sim intends. I'll be going back to London to begin the work on the details. There'll be plenty of consulting, Sim, then signatures and so forth. You won't disappear again too soon, will you?'

Simon Fellows shook his head. 'I ought to say, here and now, thank you, Nigel. I owe you a big debt for keeping Samco running as you have and especially for handling all the business of Dad's death—' The whole room flinched at Sim's icy, neutral tone. 'But,' he went on, 'before we finish there's just one relatively minor Samco project I'd like stopped. It's this Savernake Village project which affects Josie's mother and her sister. I think it's quite wrong to buy up people's homes and take away a public park so that a lot of wealthy people can live there.'

'It's too late, Sim. The diggers are in, now,' claimed Nigel.

'But half the people are still there,' remonstrated Sim.

'Yes, but most are on their way.'

'What about the ones that aren't?'

'We'll have to see.'

'Let me get this straight,' Sim said. 'You're commencing to dig up the park, and presumably knock down any property now vacant, while there are still people living there?'

'Standard practice,' Nigel said. 'I'm sorry, but there it is. Everything's in place. People are depending on the work. Our terms to the tenants on the estate have been more than fair—'

'Oh, God,' said Sim. 'Well, you'll have to stop it.'

'Our investment in that site has been enormous,' Nigel said violently. 'And it's half your fault, Sim. If you'd turned up when Dad died and not left things looking so iffy at Samco, a major backer would probably not have withdrawn. And if he'd stayed in, many others wouldn't have withdrawn as well. And we at Samco wouldn't have had to make good the withdrawal of their investment, so Samco wouldn't be up the spout for a straight ten million or more, which, if lost now, will smack the dividends down, kick our quotation on the stock exchange where it hurts – have you got it, Sim? You, running round the bush with an Armalite in one hand and a bowl of rice pudding for the villagers in the other, when you heard on the sodding World Service Dad was dead, about one day after his death – which you did, some people in this room might be surprised to hear – and when you still didn't bother to get in touch – it's you who're responsible for Samco's heavy investment in the Savernake Village.' Nigel finished his remarks on a high note of righteous indignation. He was not going to tell his brother that Samco's caution about

302

investing in the project was so great that he himself had guaranteed six million of the investment – money he'd have difficulty in finding if the scheme collapsed. He banked on Sim's not checking and was relieved to see his brother's crestfallen expression. He concluded triumphantly, 'So, if you're going to devote your Samco dividends to poulticing the deep wounds left by Samco wherever it goes – a thousand new jobs due to start up in Liverpool next year, for example, where Lacon Pharmaceuticals is just opening up a new works, and other effects of ruthless capitalism—'

'And political pressures in Peru and Chile,' muttered Sim, 'lending money to death squads—'

'Death squads? What death squads?' Nigel said impatiently. 'Don't talk rubbish, Sim. You know nothing. You've taken care not to. I've been at a desk with my sleeves rolled up until ten or eleven at night for months at a time while you were hanging around the beach in Barbados, or Rambo-ing through the jungle in the cause of justice and truth, so don't come and tell me my business—'

Don't risk the shares, Charles Head breathed silently.

Why must he be so hot-tempered? thought Jasmine weakly from her couch. He damages himself. He's like a big bad baby breaking all his toys in a temper, then crying when he sees what he's done.

'If you want to help, Sim,' Nigel went on, 'well then – just donate some of that good old Samco money I've worked so hard for to the suffering inner city council tenants of Savernake and let the project go ahead. Give the money to them – it's what you said you wanted to do—'

If Sim rises to that bait, Head thought, he'll do us all a favour. Lay enough cash on the scroungers and they'll soon pack their bags and leave. Nice holiday in the Caribbean and don't bother to come back, he thought vindictively.

'OK,' said Sim, keen to conclude all the business. 'I suppose you're right.'

'No other way,' said Nigel.

Sir Hugh and Charles Head looked at each other. Nigel had taken a considerable risk in challenging his brother, risking making him angry enough to demand the shut-down of the Savernake Village project, but it seemed to have paid off. Good old Nigel, thought Head. Nigel's loan was safe and his own career still flourishing.

'Well, then,' said Nigel easily. 'All's well that ends well.'

* * *

Sim set off to find Josie who was talking to his mother by the lake. They turned towards him as he approached.

'Lunch is ready,' he said. 'Don't worry – I didn't say anything.'

'I'm so glad,' said Lady Mary.

'It was very stupid of me not to have assured you earlier I wouldn't.'

'I wouldn't have minded that much,' said Lady Mary. 'It's only for Nigel's sake. Is everything resolved now?'

'Yes – a few fireworks, but you can come in now.'

'Jessop was going to knock you down if you said anything,' Lady Margaret said.

'What happened about Savernake?' asked Josie.

Sim looked puzzled. 'I don't think I did very well.'

They walked on up to the house, Josie and Sim ahead of Lady Mary who paused outside the dining-room windows for a moment, looking into the sun-filled room. She watched the well-dressed men and women helping themselves from the buffet, observed the good china and the old family silver lying on a long linen cloth. It was odd to think that very soon, by Christmas at the latest, that room and all the other rooms in the house would be the territory of homeless families from big cities. She'd bargained harmlessly with Sim to save some of the silver, cutlery, china, furniture, offering her own help in administering the house in exchange. He was quite pleased. She could help and, secretly, try to preserve the house from accident and dilapidation. She herself would live in a small house not far off. But, however hard she tried, the inside of the house would get battered, with so many people in it. Children would play in the garden, help with the herbs and vegetables, and perhaps do more harm than good. Partitions would have to go up in the rooms – there would be scuffs and scrapes. She wasn't sure if it was right or wrong, but the uncertainty did not worry her. She watched him, smiling, opening a bottle of wine, offering a sniff to his little daughter who sat on Josie's lap, Josie reproaching him. Sim had been her strangest child, led by conscience from an amazingly early age and even now, she thought, partly expiating his father's crimes, especially the one against the young girl he'd found in Barbados on his visit almost a year earlier. Though Sim must guess, as she did, Lady Mary thought, that there'd been many other girls and many other crimes. Of course, Sim hadn't told her of his discovery of a girl of fourteen hidden away in a building among the thick trees of the estate, far from the main house. But she'd found out for herself when she'd asked Sir Hugh to discover any unfulfilled obligations left by her husband in Barbados after his sudden death. The solicitor had tried to spare her the unpleasant information but as she persisted, asking about the house and servants, attempting to find out about anyone who might be owed money, need assistance or require reward for long service, the truth had come out. Sir Hugh had described the girl as a maid of two years' standing, but she'd unwittingly asked all the wrong questions, such as the girl's age and duties. The answers had been inept and, finally, embarrassed, pointing in only one direction. And of course she'd known for years, without admitting it to herself, where her husband's inclinations had been taking him. She had not spoken directly to the solicitor about the girl, but it must have been plain to him from the instructions she gave that she knew what had been happening.

And now, thought Lady Mary, here was Sim making amends for the girl, and the others she supposed there must have been and, more than that, probably for his father's whole life. Was it right? If it was right, was this the proper way to make the correction? Right or wrong? It was no use – she didn't know.

The story of Ruth, Mrs Hedges's brothel, her assault on Sir Bernard, causing his death – all that was to come out later. Then, Lady Mary would see more point in Sim's giving up all he could of his inheritance. Just for now she calmly watched her family and guests moving about the graceful room, talking to each other. She straightened herself just a little and walked in.

29

The Temple of Fortune

It was the end of the summer holidays and Vanessa and Annie took Alec and Joanne to a Disney film. Melanie, who had popped down to London to examine her very new investment, was with them. After the film came the search for the burger and the special ice-cream and before they knew it they found themselves strolling in the afternoon sunshine across the bridge back to their own side of the Thames. To reach home they walked past Savernake Park where quite a crowd was watching its destruction. As they stopped to look the sun went in and the air became instantly chillier. Alec insisted on looking over the strengthened parapet the builders had erected all round the building site. They had grubbed up the park and gone deep down into the earth as they prepared to lay the foundations for the new Savernake Village.

Opposite, between the tall blocks of Savernake House and Rodwell House, hung a big, hand-painted banner, 'Hands Off Savernake. Leave It For The People Of Kenton'. Les Dowell's protests had received some support and some media coverage but the explanations of the Department of the Environment representative and Joe Banks had been smooth, plausible and above all successful. Joe Banks had not wanted to go on television or be in any other way prominently connected with the sale of the estate, but his masters at the development company had been stronger than he was.

'Get on with it, Joe,' Charles Head had told him crudely. 'Technically, it's over. One last push and you've done your job. A few words, then the seven million's yours. Each syllable's worth ten thousand at least.'

'It's all wrong,' said a woman beside Annie. 'All wrong. They say they can do good with the money, but however much it is, how long's that going to last?'

'Then there's no money and no park,' said an old man. 'All for flaming yuppies. I'd shoot them. I would,' he said, looking fiercely at Vanessa, as if she might disagree.

'It's depressing,' said Vanessa. 'I don't want to look at it. Alec and Joanne,' she appealed. 'Let's go home.'

But the children were fascinated by the three giant earth movers. Great scoops of earth were being pulled and dropped to one side. At the top of the great heap of scooped earth lay the metal skeleton of a climbing frame on its side. Below them the great teeth of a digger bit again, like a cannibal, into the tired London clay, dry and seemingly infertile, overtrodden for thousands of years by tens of thousands of feet.

'It's dreadful,' Annie said.

'Dreadful,' echoed a voice behind her. Annie turned to see a familiar plump, wrinkled face.

'Madame Katarina – having a walk, or did you come specially to see all this?'

'My new partner, Mr Craig, and I are taking a stroll,' said the clairvoyant. She made introductions.

'You said I wasn't going back,' said Melanie.

'You didn't – immediately,' said Madame Katarina.

'They say the spirits don't lie,' Melanie said. 'But they don't tell the whole truth, do they?'

Max Craig laughed. 'I'm sorry to say, you're right. Hey?' His sharp eyes caught sight of something lying in the pit below them.

Annie peered. 'Whatever's that?'

'It's like an eye, and a nose,' Joanne said. The big-toothed scoop was descending again. The crowd was mesmerised. 'It's big – it's like a big object,' Vanessa said.

The scoop hit a large lump which seemed to have the shape of a vast nose and above it, the size of a dinner plate, what might have been an eye. As it struck there was a metallic clang. Annie keenly picked up the difference in tone between the earth and the object embedded in it.

'Bronze!' she exclaimed and began to gesture at the man in the cab of the excavator. He waved back cheekily, mouthing what looked like an invitation.

'One of Geoff's men there,' Vanessa said. 'He makes a point of hiring the obscene ones.' She began to wave and shout. Max Craig waved his umbrella, then pointed it at the mysterious metal nose. Swivelling the scoop of the excavator the driver seized a mound of earth from one side, swung it over and dropped it on the spot from which the clang had come.

'Oh, he's burying it again,' cried Joanne in disappointment. 'I wanted to see what it was. Where's Annie?'

Alec pointed. Annie was over on the other side of the park, having run round by the road. She was emerging through the gap between the two towers and now, standing behind the protective barrier on that side of the site, was looking round. She spotted the row of Portakabins to her left, pitched just outside the windows of the flats on the ground floor of Savernake House. The big gaping hole which had once been part of Savernake Park, was in front of them.

'What's she doing?' wondered Vanessa.

'She's trying to get them to stop digging. She must think there's something important down there – an archaeological site,' Madame Katarina said.

Max Craig, clairvoyant to many financiers, said cynically, 'If so, she's got a fight on her hands. Property companies hate potential archaeological sites and busybodies trying to halt their work. Some insurers will insure against it, though the premiums are high, but in places like this I doubt if any firm would provide cover. Dig down anywhere in this sort of area of London and you'll find something of historical interest.'

'Ah – yes,' Madame Katarina said dreamily, remembering something, a prediction she had once made. To Annie.

'There's your dad,' cried Vanessa excitedly to the children. Geoff Doyle now stood on the edge of the pit he had dug, while Annie pointed towards the digger, which dumped another scoop of earth exactly where she was pointing. Now she tugged at Geoff's jacket, speaking to him urgently. He looked down at her, talking angrily. 'Why's Annie pulling him?' demanded Alec.

'I think she's trying to show him where that nose was,' Joanne interpreted. 'But he doesn't want to look.'

Yet another scoop of earth landed on the spot where the nose and eye had been uncovered.

'That man's had his orders,' Max Craig remarked drily.

'Barbarians,' said Madame Katarina.

'If there's anything there,' he observed, 'they're not above coming back late at night, setting charges, putting a nightwatchman on it and blowing it up early in the morning.'

Annie could be seen shouting at Geoff Doyle, then, with some final expression of disgust, she turned and ran. She was red-faced and breathless when she got back. 'He won't do a thing,' she gasped indignantly. 'I think it's a Roman temple. What can I do? I'd better ring the company.'

'I doubt if that'll work,' Craig told her. 'The best way is to get straight on to the Department of the Environment – and the British Museum. But, you see, they'll be ahead of you. They'll use explosives if they have to.'

'How can they do something so criminal?' she exclaimed.

'Easily,' he told her. 'Let me explain. Nigel, your brother-in-law, has a heavy stake in this—'

'I'm going to get a cab,' Annie said emphatically. 'I'm going straight to the British Museum—'

There was a clap of thunder. She ignored it. 'I'll find the appropriate curator and drag him over here—' Another clap of thunder and a big flash of lightning interrupted her and stopped the excavator. As heavy rain began to fall they saw the man in the cab climbing down.

Suddenly it was pouring. Vanessa pulled the children's anorak hoods over their heads and said, 'We've got to get home.'

Max Craig held his umbrella over Madame Katarina and the children. Joanne was shivering. He turned to the soaking-wet Annie and said, 'This is your chance. If it keeps up it'll give you time.'

Even now, two inches of water had materialised in the pits between the heavy mounds of earth. Annie grinned, turned her face up into the deluge, and said, 'Thank you.'

There was another clap of thunder, a sheet of lightning. 'Too close,' breathed Vanessa.

'It answered,' said Max Craig. He pushed the umbrella handle into her hand and leapt into the road, stopping a taxi. They all clambered in except Annie, who plodded off, drenched, in the other direction, heading for the British Museum.

It rained for several days. By that time Annie's efforts and insistence had ensured that work on the site was stopped.

It turned out that the middle of Savernake Park, a field during the Middle Ages, a squalid group of shacks since the seventeenth century, a private park since 1800 and a council estate since 1955 had been, during the years just before AD 100, the site of a temple set up by a certain Roman legion, soldiers of the Emperor Domitian. This temple was dedicated to the relatively obscure goddess Fortuna. It was her vast nose and huge eye that the digger had uncovered. The statue of the goddess proved to be of bronze, twenty feet tall with eyes like plates, nose like a small canoe, hair twisting and waving like big green pythons round her head. The Roman legion over whose temple she had presided appeared to have been a motley collection of Visigoths, Vandals, Angles, Saxons, Egyptians, Spaniards and Africans who followed many gods and cults. Perhaps, since they worshipped a huge pantheon of gods and goddesses – they had dog-faced gods and bull-gods, fountain-gods and mountain-gods, jackal-gods and elk-gods, three-breasted mother goddesses, murder-gods and suicide-gods and a whole rag, tag and bobtail collection of cults, mysteries, superstitions and fearful animistic rites – the goddess Fortuna was the only Roman deity all the legionaries could manage to get along with, since at all times men have known themselves to be subject to chance and fortune. Evidence from the site proved that Fortuna's temple had been a popular place to worship and make sacrifices during the second century AD.

In the following year the excavated temple, which covered two acres of the eight-acre park dominated by the mighty bronze-green statue of Fortuna, was opened by the Prince of Wales. Joe Banks, still, after a mighty struggle, leader of Kenton Council, was photographed swapping a joke with the Princess of Wales, who also gave Mrs Roxanne Fuller, the Mayor, a great big hug. Les Dowell had previously introduced a motion in the council to have the site opened by an ordinary member of the public, preferably Mrs Walters, still living happily at Rodwell House – but he was out-voted.

There was a flurry of financial reorganisation following the discovery of the temple and the cancellation of the Savernake Village project. Redesigning the village round the temple would have been quite uneconomic. Also, as Charles Head disgustedly told Joe Banks, 'You'd have all the *hoi polloi* marching about, staring at the residents.'

'Oh, well,' declared Joe Banks. 'The council'll just have to build a restaurant, sell concessions and so forth. It'll bring in some revenue to help the borough.' He paused. 'It's a proposition – are you interested?'

He was standing in Head's office. Head rose from his desk

menacingly. 'Get out,' he threatened. Joe Banks left instantly.

The affair practically ruined Geoff Doyle and wrecked Nigel Fellows's chances of getting a majority shareholding in Samco (though he felt compensated by the delight of the birth of his daughter that year). It put Julian Vane's company into bankruptcy, whereupon Tamsin left Julian. Geoff Doyle had an even worse time romantically – Cindy married him and gave him a hard life thereafter. He began to pine for Vanessa but Cindy's father, deprived by the collapse of the time-share in Portugal and new car which would have been reward for his work on behalf of Savernake Developments, only encouraged his daughter to persecute her husband more.

It was Tom who discovered that from the roof of Annie's house in Rutherford Street you could actually see Fortuna's large head, turned towards Foxwell High Street. 'To think that the goddess Fortuna presides over Kenton,' remarked Vanessa, standing on the roof beside him. 'Frankly, to look at the state of the place, you'd never believe it.'

'Ah,' said Annie. 'But she's been toppled for nearly two thousand years. Now she's upright again.'

'So are we,' said Vanessa Gathercole. 'And, what's more, we got love—'

'We got money—' said Annie, for the restaurant had been out of debt since the week before.

'And, in a way, you got revenge,' said Tom Pointon. 'Shall we get off this roof, now?'